ENTANGLED MOON

ENTANGLED MOON

A Novel

E. C. FREY

SHE WRITES PRESS

Published 2018
Printed in the United States of America
ISBN: 978-1-63152-389-2 paperback
978-1-63152-390-8 ebook

Library of Congress Control Number: 2018930868

For information, address:
She Writes Press
1563 Solano Ave #546
Berkeley, CA 94707

She Writes Press is a division of SparkPoint Studio, LLC.

For Phil, Megan, and Patrick,
mes raisons d'etre

And in loving memory of
Ralph and Ricky

1 The Apartment

He had been following the bird's husband all day. He wanted evidence. A foot in the door. A chance to say to her all the things he had been rehearsing in his head for years.

In the end, he had known where her husband was going. He had waited for him outside his mistress's apartment, where he had found a well-concealed and well-used hole in the bushes that bordered the parking lot's chain link fence. He imagined the bird's husband had left work without a care—imagined how his tousled hair and carefree whistle would have proclaimed it to the world. And now her husband had arrived.

He smiled to himself. He felt like he was back in a time when his life had meant something; a sense of renewal fluttered at the fringes of his heart.

Taking three steps at a time, the bird's husband climbed the stained and crumbling concrete steps to the second-floor apartment in the rundown complex. It was the kind of day when the thinnest of cottons sticks like sweat-shredded tissue. A row of drooping flower heads hung from a sagging flowerbox at the apartment's window.

He pulled his clammy shirt from his chest, and then his boxers from his thighs, which clung defiantly to the seat of his pants. He had killed most of the day waiting, and now the time was at hand. All he had to do was stay there until her husband emerged and he would take a series of pictures. He could imagine every little moment   each one framed, each one a moment of betrayal. How would she react? He could not give up now, no matter how tired and uncomfortable he was.

Retrieving a tiny camera from his pocket, he checked its settings. Next, he pulled a well-used, crumpled bag from his waistband and checked its contents. Needle, spoon, lighter, tiny white rock. His hands shook, but he touched each item reverently.

He leaned back, closed his eyes, and sat tight as the minutes turned into an hour.

He almost missed the bird's husband leaving. He opened his eyes in time to see him coming down the stairs, but his opportunity to snap pictures died before he could turn on the camera.

He rubbed his eyes. A haze had seeped in, was lending an orange hue to his surroundings. The halo from the outside apartment light lent a pall to the impending night and a low rumble in the distance promised a break from the day's heat.

Unfurling his aching joints, he rose to follow, but his mark was younger and quicker than he was—the bird's husband vanished before he could get out of his observation spot.

He was still standing there when a black car with tinted windows pulled quietly into the empty space. Sleek and expensive, the engine cut noiselessly. He moved to sit, but tin cans and bottles clanked and he froze mid-movement, lest he was found out. He watched as two men emerged from the car. One, in an elegant trench coat that fell crisply to his shins, led, glancing around him as he took the battered steps to the woman's apartment. The other, sheathed in black leather, followed, his head bent with purpose.

* * *

Tanya paced, her steps following the same worn pattern in the carpet the string of previous occupants had left. Her loins still throbbed and her heart raced; she tingled with the love she felt for her man. Her man had promised he would leave his wife. He would take care of her and the baby—their baby. She gathered her arms around herself, caressed her belly, imagining its hardness, and smiled. Everything was falling into place.

He had a good job, but she still needed hers back. She needed to bide her time until he could disentangle himself from his loveless marriage. Until then, she needed to work. But how could she convince her boss to let her back in? She would not grovel. No! It was unbelievable the way he had treated her. She wasn't trash he could just kick to the curb. She had worked hard to get to her position and all she had wanted was a promotion. Instead, he had come up with some bullshit excuse to fire her for lack of performance, and that stupid witch in human resources had signed off on it.

She knew where the bitch lived. She could go and show her some old-fashioned revenge from the 'hood. She gnawed on her lip. Only she couldn't—not really. That had never really been her life. That was a life from which she had run. She had to get her job back. She couldn't go back to that life. She had worked hard to get out of her New Haven neighborhood, far from the snickers, far from her fear and want. Even though she was trapped here for now, she couldn't go down from here. Her man would save her. She just had to hang on for a little while.

Her boss would relent. He would have to. After all, she knew everything, and that knowledge was worth a lot. He was a lousy lover and a lousy boss and an even lousier human being. She could start with exposing him for sexual harassment. A hint of what she was capable of, in case he didn't take her seriously. And she could save her trump card, the dirty truth about the company's dealings overseas—*his* dirty dealings. So many people dead, and even more dying still. He knew it too. He was a bastard willing to sacrifice everything—and for what? For his selfish pride? So the stockholders and board would laud him for their short-term gains? They didn't have to know about the dead. Out of sight, out of mind. But she had copies of everything.

She could expose them all to the world. All she wanted was her job back, and the promotion she deserved. She wanted a life like the one her coworkers who went home to something more than peeling bathtubs, worn carpets, and barred windows had. Damn it! She wasn't asking for anything she didn't deserve.

The soft knocking at the door interrupted her thoughts. She crept to the peephole. Maybe he couldn't leave her after all. She smiled and her heart skipped a beat. She would make sure he never left again. She would make him throw caution to the wind. Make him dump his two-bit, whiny mouse of a wife to the gutter. Her heart softened. But she would love the woman's daughter like her own, and they would have more. After all, the little girl was half of him, and she would cherish whatever there was of him in this world.

She lifted the peephole cover.

The prism morphed the two men outside into an unpleasant blob, but she recognized one of them: it was her boss.

Her joy seized into ice. She was not in the mood for his sick sex games. No doubt this was his way of turning the tables and letting her know he was still in control. If it got her the things she wanted, though, then it was all the same. She would still be in control anyway. She held the cards and he knew it. She had seen it on his face when she threatened to expose their affair to his boss.

She pulled her robe around her and quickly removed any evidence that someone else had been there. Quietly, she put the dirty wineglasses into a cabinet—she would have to wash them later—but the sleeve of her robe caught the cabinet knob and ripped as she moved. A tiny thread clung to the metal.

"Shit."

He knocked again. She sensed the impatience this time. She opened the door and both men waltzed in and brushed her aside. The stranger grabbed the door from her and shut it. He put a leather-sheathed finger to his lips.

"What are you doing here?" she asked. "It's a little late and I need to be in early tomorrow. I have someone I have to talk to."

"We need to discuss our little . . . disagreement."

"What's there to discuss? I deserve my job back, *with* a promotion."

She thought she saw a smile, but that only increased her sense of rising hysteria. She clenched her teeth; it did nothing to calm her.

The stranger moved to the window, peered out the threadbare curtains, and pulled them shut. She wondered if they knew no one would pay them any mind anyway. Her neighbors were notorious for "not hearing or seeing anything," even when it occurred under their nose. But wasn't she just as guilty?

"That's a little bold. I'm not sleeping with you both tonight." She hated the catch in her voice. He would think her weak. Men like him could always smell fear.

"Of course not," her boss said. "You've already done that . . . sleeping with that imbecile from Origin Sourcing Corp. Tell me. What do you see in him? Georgetown doesn't have a thing on Harvard." He snickered. "Of course, it has plenty on Southern Connecticut, doesn't it, sweetheart? It must have taken a lot for you to crawl out of that slum you called home."

He caught her slap mid-air, then squeezed her arm until the tears dimmed her vision. "You *will* give me all the information you stole from the office." Each enunciated word sliced like a knife.

Tanya shook her head.

"Don't shake your head. I know you have it. Angela caught you making copies." He pulled her closer. "Hand it over now and there's a chance you'll get out of this," he spat. "You might not have your job, but you'll have something worth even more."

Tanya pulled back. "I don't know what you're talking about. I suggested I might go to your boss and the board and tell them you've been sleeping with me. It's only a case of sexual harassment. I don't know about anything else."

He grabbed her again. "Bitch!" His spittle landed on her cheek and burned. "Do you think you can deceive me? Soon I'll be CEO, and no whore from the gutter is going to stop me."

He pushed her into the arms of the stranger. Tanya's robe opened to reveal her nakedness.

"I don't care what you do with her," he said. "Just make it quick. I have no use for her anymore. She's used goods and too much of a liability."

Turning his back to her, he rummaged for the contraband file. She tried to close her robe, but the stranger grabbed her hand and slipped his leather fingers into her easily, finding the lingering evidence of her lover. She squirmed. He pulled his fingers out and rolled his wet leather fingertips together. Fire rose and prickled at her face.

Her boss straightened and looked. She knew he would have to watch. Like he always did. He sneered. "What did I tell you? Fuck her at your own risk."

The stranger pushed her over the sofa and, pulling a rubber from his pocket, rolled it on with the quickness of habit. He ripped the robe from her, covered her mouth, and penetrated her backside. He tore at her with each thrust. His cruelty was too much to bear.

Her boss watched as he continued to search. He found her briefcase leaning behind the old credenza she had found at a garage sale. It was her first piece of furniture; she had bought it with her first paycheck. She remembered it had been a beautiful day—a day full of promise. She tried to go there, but it felt distant and apart from her. Like maybe there had never been anything but humiliation, and she had been a fool to believe otherwise.

And then he found it. He pulled the file from her briefcase, sifted through the tidy pile, and smacked it against the palm of his hand. She should've done a better job of hiding it. But she had never imagined this as a possibility. She should've known better. She felt her leverage slipping from her.

She squeezed her eyes shut, but tears slipped through anyway. The disappointment and hurt fused into one, and she thought her heart might break and she would die.

Her boss nodded to the stranger, who slipped out before he was done—except that he wasn't. He threw her up against the wall and penetrated her from the front. The brutality of it made her cry out. He slapped her and thrust harder. He stayed that way, a grotesque grimace smeared across his face. She felt the blood flow between her legs. Ruined. She was ruined. Her baby destroyed. She watched as her boss's crotch bulged, but he didn't move to take part. He nodded again to the stranger, who finished his task.

The stranger smiled as he hiked up his pants. He retrieved a pistol from his pocket. Wrapping his black leather–sheathed hand around hers, he forced her index finger into the trigger hole.

"What, what're you doing?" If only she could stop the thumping in her ears. She couldn't hear. She couldn't anticipate what would happen next so she couldn't figure out a move to escape. The noise was maddening.

"You're going to kill yourself. Your lover came. You quarreled. He forced you to have sex. Then he left you for his wife. It was too much to bear."

"You're crazy. No one will believe it."

"They will when they read the note you leave behind." He raised the piece of paper. Her signature swirled at the bottom.

"I didn't sign that."

He laughed. "Angela has many gifts—and she's loyal."

She needed time. Time to grasp the situation. Time to make him see that this wasn't necessary. "I don't understand. I thought you cared about me. I care about you. I promise I won't say a word about anything to anyone." Tears streamed down her face. She hated the way he looked at her. Like it meant nothing. Like she meant nothing. Surely they had meant something to each other. Surely her life meant something. "Please. I love you."

But he only smiled and scanned her broken, naked body. His eyes shimmered. He had turned the tables on her. She tried to cover herself, like that was possible. There would never again be anything capable of hiding her shame.

She watched as he smoothed the suicide note on her dining room table and then nodded to her tormenter.

It was a slow nod.

She thought of her mother. All the hours she had worked to give her only child a ticket out of the 'hood. Mostly, she thought of the moments with her when she had just sat and plaited her hair, humming tunes of her own childhood, her hands caressing her every moment. Her hands were callused from work, but her touch was so gentle that it reminded Tanya of the underside of a cat's belly—like the one that would meow at her window until she opened it and let the cat sneak into her bed. She could still feel the softness as she rubbed her face along its exposed undercarriage. Her heart pounded, and she could swear she heard its purr silencing the sounds of chaos out on the streets.

She thought of her room in her old neighborhood and was surprised to realize that she could only remember it as a refuge now. They had always been safe in her room. Even now, she could smell the cotton of the well-worn quilts that her mama's mama had sewn by hand from cast-off pieces of fabric down in Georgia. She had once thought of her room as a prison, but it had only ever protected her from the carnage outside the window.

She heard the thunder grumble in the distance—a beautiful and exciting sound. It sounded clearer than it ever had. Sharp. Insistent. She had always loved storms. She would miss the electric air that held the promise of roiling clouds, wild lightning streaks, and rain— rain that would wash away all the heat and bestiality of the day. She smelled it. Water and green leaves and clean earth and clear skies. It was like the smell of basil and grass and lavender as one. She thought of the dogs that barked and drove the neighbors nuts but also nuzzled her hand as she walked home and sat expectantly, tails wagging, waiting for her to scratch and hug their guileless little bodies. Mostly, she thought about all the little things she had taken for granted. She hoped she had lived her life in a way that would have pleased her mama's God.

There had been a few transgressions lately. She had allowed herself to be uppity. Maybe that was why God had left her. She begged His forgiveness now. She asked that He comfort her mama. She would need it. She was her only child; it might be too much for her to bear. She had already suffered so many losses in her life.

Last, Tanya thought of her baby. A life barely imagined who would never see the beauty of the world.

She thought all these things in that brief moment. In some ways, she knew it was the most beautiful moment she would ever have.

She screamed, but the gunshot slammed through her temple and cut the sound cold.

* * *

He let her drop and neatly posed her hand next to her temple. He removed a hankie from his pocket and wiped the blood from his face, then methodically folded the cloth and slipped it into his pocket. He knew how to start early so there was no trace of his presence.

He took a quick look around, but there was no evidence that they had been there. Nothing was out of place. It felt oddly wrong. He retrieved a pair of folding scissors and a snack bag from his other pocket. Precisely and with a skill that could only come with habit, he snipped off a large tuft of her hair, carefully avoiding the scalp. It was the only clue he would leave, and he knew the police investigation would hinge on it. He smiled. His favorite targets were randomized to make the real ones, the ones for which he was paid, appear similar.

In fact, the real ones were just part of the job. As a little boy, he pulled the wings from butterflies and marveled at their helplessness—the way they flopped around until they finally succumbed. Easy. It was the same with his human victims—the way they begged for their lives, thrashing helplessly until they surrendered to the inevitable. There was more pleasure when money was not involved. It was the random targets that made him feel alive.

He stepped to the door, avoiding the blood splatter and brain matter.

Before exiting the apartment, he cocked his head and stared at her open eyes. He could still see the moment of surprise lingering in the hollowness of her death. It was like that flash in the moment when a light is turned on and then quickly extinguished. He often thought of taking a picture afterwards, but that would be reckless. The last thing he wanted was there to be definitive proof. No, it was far better to simply remember, to allow the imprint on his brain to sustain him. Besides, he had her hair. Once he had it safely hidden away, stored under dehumidified conditions, it would not fade or decay in his lifetime.

He shut the door quietly and joined his employer in the hall. Together, the two men descended the worn steps.

He watched as his companion stopped at the bushes, pulled his zipper down, closed his eyes, and stroked himself until his hardness wasted itself, then smiled and pissed long and hard into the thicket.

Thunder grumbled closer.

He laughed. "Shall I get you a cigarette?"

The other man smiled, and they both slid into the car and drove away.

* * *

He stirred in his hiding spot. The smell of hot piss mingled with the wetness of the air. Everywhere, the stench of urine and wet earth mixed until he thought he would throw up. He was getting soft. He wondered whether the bird's husband had anything to do with the gunshot that had brought out a sole neighbor, who quickly shut her door after opening it. The husband was long gone, but the men who left must have been hot on his heels to get to her apartment so soon afterwards.

He needed to get far away. No bushes could hide him when the police arrived.

He crouched and ran through the streets until he was clear.

A flash of light, followed by a crack of thunder, split the air.

He listened to the sirens in the distance. They were closing in.

He continued through the trees until his sides burned. Then he found a dark corner of the park and unsheathed his needle and syringe. Another flash of light and another crack stirred the air and he felt the hairs on his skin lift.

Deep darkness descended.

His hands trembled as he set up the old spoon, lit the lighter, and melted the rock. A strong storm was brewing, and he didn't want to be caught out in the open.

He thought of his bird. Heather. He would have to tell her the truth of the woman's death. Her husband had betrayed her, but that was his only sin. Someone else had pulled the trigger.

"Heather," he whispered to himself. He would have to find her. Yes. He would have to tell her.

He slid under a musty, ragged-edged picnic table and found soft ground. He let the liquid slide through his veins until it found his place of forgetting, and he let his head and eyes roll back. The storm would have its way.

He let go.

2 Heather

This house, my home, used to be my sanctuary. When I was tired or the world became too big, I could shut the door and something magical happened. The world became less big and I, surrounded by walls, could hear the tempo of my heart, my mind free from its own noise. But now this house no longer holds me. Instead it closes in on me, and I cannot hear myself. Relentless demands fill my ears until I cannot bear it anymore. It is as if all the past lives of captured flies haunt me, surround me, drown me in their swarm, the buzzing and whirring reducing me to nothingness. I am becoming nothing. I am stuck here waiting for the plumber. He, too, will reduce me to nothing.

My nails click impatiently on the counter. Click. Click. I clasp my hands together. Knuckles white with effort. But why should I stop? At least it reminds me I am still here. Or perhaps it is disembodied noise and I, gone, only hear the echo. I dig my nails into the palm of my hand. Blood seeks the surface and reddens the paleness.

I am still here.

"Where is that man?"

He was supposed to be here twelve minutes ago. Twelve minutes of torture. Twelve minutes from a rare lunch hour. Uselessness turned into nothingness. What was his name? Ralph. Ralph and Sons. The plumber. His name, not even highlighted in the yellow pages, proves I am disappearing. I am reduced to hiring no-name no-box plumbers.

The growling in my stomach echoes in my ears. I snap on yellow gloves and retrieve the bleach. Everything has its place. Even me.

The intensity of the smell, pungent and antiseptic, soothes and repulses me. Mother loved its virtues. *Mother!* Bleach washes away all manner of sin. It also necrotizes. But water never eradicates evil. Evil just sits there and stinks up the high heavens. Heaven being the place you could get to if only you could apply enough bleach to all your transgressions. A good scrub helps but all the sodium hypochlorite in the universe is not enough. There is not nor was there ever a cure for wickedness.

I never understood the point of getting on with it, except, I suppose, Mother didn't want to have to tell people why her daughter had disappeared. Or maybe she just needed an excuse to buy bleach.

I've been shrinking my whole life, but it wasn't until a night long ago that even I noticed. It was a night of promise that turned into a night of fire and rage. An end to trump the best of beginnings, but the end was only the beginning. I went home to be fully baptized in the horror. Baptized in the full contents of the undiluted bottle of bleach, all ninety-six fluid ounces, each an ounce of torture, the liquid flowing into my open cuts, burning and cauterizing the moment, sealing it deep inside my heart. Mother watched me as the faucet spewed water into the bathtub. My tomb. I tried not to squirm, not to breathe, to become invisible, but she knew better and pulled the plug on the next bottle. My defiance enraged her. Her fists tight, she pummeled my head, careless of the bruises others would see. She broke her own rules. It was in that moment that I learned to watch. *Like Mother.* Outside, the fire burned the hill. We both watched the amber glow lick and shudder at the shadows. It is in the watching that one shrinks into the darkness.

That was the first night I carved it into my screaming skin, *Death moon.* The red drips of blood seeped into and were caught by the dead and peeling skin left from the bleach bath.

Twenty minutes late. I empty the bottle and the kitchen sink glistens white in the high sunlight. I open the cabinet to toss the bottle, but the smells assault me and my eyes cloud. I retch, swimming in the heavy mixture of memories and trash smells. Rancid cereal milk, rotting banana skins, decaying fat trimmed from last night's steak, old potatoes from the dark pantry, tomatoes with wrinkled skins and oozing middles, all the detritus of domesticity. Life is ugly like that. The bleach gone and my handiwork ruined. I rinse the sink, but it is soiled beyond redemption. It isn't like water can save me from the stench. Darkness oozes into the hairline fractures of the porcelain and spreads like blood pumping through tiny spider veins. I cannot stop it. It threatens to travel the floor, the walls, the ceiling, until the house is covered in veins of filth.

I flip the garbage disposal switch and yank at the gloves, pulling each finger free from its rubber confines.

The whirring halts and the echo of its finale reverberates through the house.

Twenty-five minutes and I am still alone.

I have always done everything that was asked of me; I have never deviated from the course others have chosen for me. I've watched my own life. Here's Heather. And I have always waited the way I am waiting now—for someone else. This time, it's for some random plumber to come tell me what has to be done to fix my bathtub faucet. For this man I have never laid eyes on to come into my house and put his banged-up wrench to the faucet I spent hours poring over magazines and shopping home decorating stores to find so I could get the look just right, so I could be absolved of all criticism. Waiting. Disappearing.

I disappeared into the business program at my father's alma mater. In Georgetown, 3,000 miles away from my posse and 3,000 miles from my art. My life was mapped out for me before I walked, before I knew my name. At school, all that reminded me that I still existed, that meant something, that spoke my heart, was silenced. Each art brush wrapped in a salvaged piece of tissue paper, the old cardboard box the only protection from the assailing dust of decay.

It was in Georgetown that I married Brandon Collings. Handsome and self-assured, he was everything I wasn't. He could not free me from my watchfulness and he could not make me visible. I shrank instead. *Mother adored him.*

Twenty-seven minutes. I again snap on the gloves and empty the contents of an abrasive cleaner into the sink, the powder airlifting and assaulting my airways. I cough and my eyes burn, but I have to clean. I scrub and still the filth creeps. I need more bleach.

Twenty-nine minutes. I flip the garbage disposal on and off and listen as the whirring dies, but footsteps fill the void. My ears thrum with the noise of blood. *Go away.* How long have the footsteps been moving? Was someone watching me as I scrubbed with my back to the house?

The stairs creak.

The doorbell rings and the house stills. Dust swirls and settles where the sunshine streams through the window. The doorbell rings again.

The stairwell is empty, but someone has been there. You know when something has been there even when it no longer is.

I open the door before the bell can ring again. Ralph Smith and Sons Plumbing. Is it Ralph or a son?

"I've been waiting thirty minutes."

"Um-hmm." He sighs and hitches his tool belt. His eyes travel to my Playtex-covered hands and then to my suit.

I remove the gloves and throw them on the nearest chair—my most elegant chair in my most elegant foyer.

The plumber shrugs.

I am shrinking or my house is stretching.

"It's your dime, ma'am."

"Fine. It's this way."

The thickly carpeted stairs are silent as we ascend. The hairs on the back of my neck prickle. What made them creak a moment ago? Ralph or Son is behind me, but I still don't feel safe. It is the same feeling that has been following me all day.

The bedroom floor is even and quiet as we cross it. Still, someone or something has been in here. It is as if the air has rearranged itself.

Ralph or Son unscrews the faucet filter and fiddles with it. "Your water is high in minerals. Your filter is clogged. You need to rinse and clean it unless you want to put in a water softener."

"Do you install water softeners?"

"Yes, but it really is very easy to rinse the filter. You'll still need to even if you put in a softener."

"Right now, I prefer the softener. I simply don't have time to rinse the filter." I need to get out of here.

We need to go.

Quickly.

The man produces a rag from his pocket, shifts his weight, and wipes his hands. "All right. We'll need to figure out the type of softener."

Do I have a choice? All the noise he makes will keep whatever it is away. I calculate the time needed, more time away from the office, now the entire lunch hour. "Fine. I'd like you to do it now, please."

"It's not quite that easy. My wife can call you with your options and make an appointment."

"I can't do this another day. I've already taken up my entire lunch hour. Can't you just get one from your truck and do it, whatever it is you need to do? I wouldn't know one softener from another."

His brow wrinkles and his eyes contain a hint of disdain. It is ridiculous. I have a more important job than he. I know my place. Clearly, he doesn't know his. Or maybe he does and I don't.

"Ma'am, I don't keep softeners in my van," he says. "My wife can call you. I'm sorry."

"I see. Fine. Call me tonight."

He shifts his weight again and continues to wipe his hands slowly. "My wife will call you tomorrow—"

"I won't be here tomorrow. I work for a living."

He sighs. "Ma'am. She can call you at work."

"Oh." I write the number on a piece of paper. The cold is moving in. I shiver. It's time to go back to work. There is nothing that can be done here. Ralph or Son is unhelpful and would no doubt be equally so if my stalker were to emerge. I dig my nails into the palms of my hands, but I still feel the panic. Sour saliva spills across my tongue. I can't heave here. Not in front of this man.

The man shifts his weight again and looks around. "Can I use your table to write the invoice?"

"What? No. I need to get back to work. I would prefer it if you billed me or let me pay you when you come back with the softener."

"I don't do business that way. There's no guarantee you'll go with me to do the softener. I have to do my invoices at time of service. I'm sorry."

"I'm sorry too, but I have to get back to work." I need to get him outside. We have to get out of here.

I grab my purse and walk to the door.

He gives up and follows me. "All right. My wife will call you and we'll settle up later?"

"Yes. Thank you." I take one last look at the empty stairwell. It is bigger.

I pull the door shut but it squeaks open before I can lock it. There is movement upstairs and the distinct smell of smoke enters my nostrils. A haze creeps with it. I grab the door, slam it, lock it, and move a little too quickly. My heel catches a pebble and there's no chance to catch myself. I lie there like an idiot, sprawled on the asphalt in front of Ralph or Son. He moves to help me, but I quickly get up.

Something is watching me. My hose are torn. I have another pair at work.

"Are you all right?"

"Yes, thank you."

"Do you want me to help you back into the house?"

"What? No."

"But your hose are ripped."

"That's fine. I have more at work."

I hate the look on his face. If only it was acceptable to slap a stranger. Fiona can. She always could. I wrap my arms around myself, but it is more than just this man. It is whoever is watching me. It is as if I am naked, my bones rattling inside a bag of skin. I scratch my nails along the skin of my arms, but I can't feel anything even as furrows of red materialize.

"I'm fine. Really. I have to go."

It is time to get an alarm system. Everyone in Fairfield County has an alarm system. How else does one keep the riffraff at bay? One simply can't live on the Gold Coast of Connecticut without one.

The keys dig into the palm of my hand as I unlock the car door. Pain is merciful. I can feel. *I am still here.*

I raise my hand in farewell as I pass Ralph or Son. He too will soon be gone from the property. What will happen then? Will the house come alive with whatever or whoever is in it? I will know by nightfall. For all I care, it can burn down like all those houses from so long ago. The flames reminded me of monsters the way they jumped at will and growled and snarled like dragons.

I take one last look in the rearview mirror. There is no helping it. Some unseen force bids me. An upstairs curtain flutters as a shadow moves across the interior space. The windows are sealed. This I know. I would never leave a window open, even when the forecast says there's a zero percent chance of rain.

I ease up on the accelerator and look hard for something more solid than a shadow. I will it to show itself. I have the safety of distance. What is the point in resisting if you don't know what you are up against? Even with Mother, I at least knew. I could usually see her fists before they got me even if I couldn't move fast enough to avoid them.

The shadow halts and returns the stare.

The door to Ralph or Son's truck slams and startles me. Does he know someone is watching him too? Can he feel it? But no, he doesn't look, just slips behind the wheel.

I peer back at the house. The outline of something lingers, then turns and vanishes into the shadows.

It would be pointless to call the police. They would think I was crazy. I would have to wait while they investigated and then stick around to answer questions. Then they would twist everything around like they always do. They would accuse me of seeing things, or worse, they would accuse me of doing something—to myself, to my home. They would look accusingly at the nail lines along my arms or the scars on my hands or the hint of something etched in my skin peeking out from a hemline and they would whisper things to each other, shake their heads in acknowledgment, and snicker as they returned to their cars. They would pause long enough to write something in their little notepads. "Crazy woman spins lies again." And they would return me to Mother.

Things are always worse after talking to the police. No. I have to get back to work.

I don't really want to know what is in the house anyway. And it definitely doesn't want to present itself to anyone but me. Otherwise, it would have been there when Ralph or Son was clearing the faucet filter, when he was stooped over and his back was turned to the door. No. It is better not to be there.

Brandon, my knight in shining armor, can deal with it. He, too, has accused me of making things up. Let him see it.

I grab the steering wheel and floor the accelerator.

Better yet, I can take Shannon somewhere after daycare and we can arrive home well after Brandon. Just in case he decides to work late.

Shannon. My miracle. Her name alone softens the edges around my discomfort.

I pull into a parking space at company headquarters. I slide my identification badge through the reader and press through the turnstile. Nothing can get me here. There is too much concrete and there are too many witnesses. I would scream. They would have to hear me. They would have to acknowledge that I am visible. And there is security.

I wave to the guard. He barely glances and nods. But he would have to do more than grunt if I were attacked.

The elevator doors open and a mass of people spews out, but I stand my ground. I am tired of waves passing over me. They are nothing more than non-exempts anyway. They and the cafeteria are the first defense against the world.

My department is the entire tenth floor, far from the street. The Vice-President and the other officers are on the highest floor, the sixteenth floor, with a floor in between—a huge, cavernous, windowless affair anchored by a large desk. Prime real estate. A lone receptionist protects the higher floors from unauthorized invasion, from the lower floors and especially from others, those from the outside.

It is on the top floor that I will be giving a status report in three hours. Three hours to prepare for the top floor. Bob wants to know my progress on the Saxton matter. What about the OFCCP audit and all the other cases on my docket? Yes, he wants those too. But he didn't want them until I asked. Why? Saxton, the CFO, is important, but the other things have as much potential for exposure for the company as his situation. What makes Saxton stand out to the exclusion of all others? Brown-nosing, I suppose.

Something flutters in my stomach. I didn't have time to eat. That was a strategic mistake.

"Hi Heather. Back from lunch? You have several messages." My secretary, Sharon, hands me a fistful of messages. Everyone has been at work while I've been wasting my time.

By the time I return the last of the calls, the sun has moved from my office window. Rain clouds hover. It reminds me of the shadow. The cold has settled, and I tug the cashmere sweater hanging on the back of my office chair from its place and pull it around my shoulders.

The cold leaches the warmth from my bones.

Was there an intruder?

Reality is a murky affair. I've been called crazy so many times, but maybe it is everyone else who teeters along that line between sanity and madness. Maybe sanity is something constructed to keep people in line, force them to conform to an idea of acceptable behavior that is only really right for those who wield the power. After all, people in power get to do whatever they want. It doesn't really matter that there are rules everyone else has to play by. Those below the sixteenth floor own corporate rules books to remind them at all times. One sits on my desk. I even helped write it.

I am breaking my own rules now. I should be preparing for the status report, but I don't want to. It is better to dream about that which is good instead of prepare for that which has the possibility of being bad.

I bought new paintbrushes this past weekend. I miss my old paintbrushes, but I like the new ones. I had to buy them to do an art project with Shannon. A memo was placed in her cubby at daycare. Dragonflies, birds, and flowers danced around the edges of the directions. They were making spring creatures with construction paper, grommets, and string to create a puppet show for an Earth Day picnic. Parents were invited to the 4:00 p.m. show next Tuesday. At the bottom was a cutoff section requesting an RSVP stating how many would be able to attend and whether anyone would be able to provide refreshments or paper goods.

I lifted Shannon into the seat of the grocery cart that day and we discussed the project as we worked through the produce section. Funny how she understands me better than anyone else. By the time we rounded the corner and headed down her "fun" aisle of cards and toys, we had decided on making a purple and pink polka-dotted spring dragon. He would be a kind dragon who would sweep us through the heavens until he landed on an island clothed in sweet-smelling flowers.

I threw everything we needed, including snacks, into the grocery cart.

Shannon clapped her hands and giggled. "Mommy, what's our dwagon's name?"

"I don't know. What would you like to call him?"

"Sir Galahad and we'll cover him in daisies, polka dots, and forget-me-nots."

I smiled. "What do you know about Sir Galahad and forget-me-nots, funny girl?"

"Miss Cohen told us. He's cute like Daddy."

"Ah, the wondrous tales of Sir Galahad and King Arthur, who drew the sword from the floating stone," I said. "Our dragon will be of pure heart and gallant mind."

"Yep, and he'll give all of us flowers, because we share."

"Well, we'll have fun, and we can plant daisies in the fields and forget-me-nots along the banks of the fruit punch stream."

"Mommy, you're so silly. The daisies and forget-me-nots are on Sir Galahad."

"Well, maybe he rolled in them when he was playing on the island."

I grabbed five bleach containers and placed them into the cart. A row of gloves dangled alongside the shelved bottles. I unclipped a pair.

By the time I hooked Shannon into her car seat she had solved everything. "Sir Galahad is a polka dot dwagon who wolled in flowers so he could wear lotsa colors. Sir Galahad is pwetty just like you, Mommy."

Her joy was raw and honest. I hugged her.

I had tried to have children for years, had tried to give Brandon something for which he could be proud of me, but the doctors kept saying there had been too much damage. Damaged goods. All I could remember was the perpetual knot in my throat, like a noose tightening and shrinking against my dying body.

Then I was pregnant. It was a gift, a reprieve from disappointment and guilt. The doctors clucked. My advanced age and damage made it "unlikely" I could see it through. But nine months of anxiety later, I gave birth to a perfect baby.

Shannon made me visible again.

"Not nearly as pretty or as special as you." I whispered the thought into the air, alive with nothing and everything. For a moment, I was of the world and engaged with it. It could all be taken away so easily. It always was.

"What did you say, Mommy?"

My daughter's question reminded me which world I belonged to and I knocked the crown of my head against the car roof. Stars swam against the interior of my eyelids. *Shit.* My momentary dance with joy was exacting an unequally vast amount of pain. It always did.

"Oh, poor Mommy."

The light of the parking lot was too much to bear. The dance was over. Perhaps it was no more than a walking dream, a dragon of my imagination. I slid into the driver's seat and started the car.

"Mommy, Sir Galahad will fix it when we make him."

"Thank you, honey."

We spent the better part of that Saturday afternoon creating Sir Galahad. Shannon covered herself in string, glue, and glitter. I watched her with her tongue tucked between her lips. I didn't care about dishes or any of the other things that would make the coming workweek bearable. I didn't really care about anything but my beautiful little girl and her vision of a great dragon of sweeping power and beauty. My skin felt calm.

Brandon smiled as he watched us, but by dinnertime he had changed. "Don't you think that project is starting to look a little too sophisticated for Little Steps Day Care?"

Shannon sighed. "Daddy, he's not a pwoject. He's Sir Galahad and he's supposed to be special because he's a dwagon."

Brandon ruffled her hair. "I didn't mean he's not special, Shannon. He's just a little sophisticated."

"What's sophisticated, Daddy?"

"It's grown-up, Shannon."

"Oh, like Mommy."

Brandon's cell phone rang. He looked at the screen as he moved toward the door. "I expect some perspective on your part, Heather."

"Go answer your phone, Brandon." I stuck out my tongue as he left. He always took up too much space. Shannon sucked in her breath and looked at me, wide-eyed. "Shhhhhh," I said. We covered our mouths and giggled.

We ate snacks, and by bedtime we had made a dragon with multiple moving parts dressed in forget-me-nots, daisies, and polka dots. His head was a crown of expertly rendered tufts, his nostrils delicate but strong, his toes and nails defined, and his tail long and playful. Submitting him to my Fine Arts 101 class at Georgetown University would have been an easy A if I had been allowed to pursue such folly.

Shannon, clapping with joy, wanted to sleep with Sir Galahad. For those brief hours, a little girl and her magical dragon kept the demons away.

It never lasts. The shame is always there. I gaze out the window. Dotted with picnic tables, the patch of grass next to the parking lot remains barren of flight, birds or insects. Unnatural. The milder temperatures of April have initiated the sprouting of brush and tree. The branches and new leaves have fashioned together to form a perfect rendition of the daycare director's disdainful look the morning we delivered Sir Galahad.

"Mrs. Collings, I believe the instructions were quite clear. The spring creature was to be designed and crafted by the children. That means we expect work equal to that of a four-year-old. You were merely supposed to be an aide or a guide. Since you're older than the other mothers, I would've expected you to know better."

What did age have to do with it? Her pinched face made her look older than me. "Shannon designed and crafted Sir Galahad and we were both immersed in his creation," I said. "We had a wonderful time together. He's the result of us working together. Isn't that what you want? Isn't that what you've been saying to me? Spend more time with Shannon?"

The daycare director moved in closer, her voice lower. "I think perhaps you don't understand what I'm saying. This dragon is more your creation and will therefore stick out when compared to the other children's whose younger mothers followed the instructions. How will Shannon feel when she realizes how different her dragon is from all the butterflies and birds?" She straightened. "Come along, Shannon. I'll take you to your room. Your mother has to go to work."

I watched her back as she moved away. "A child should be able to shine," I called after her. "We shouldn't have to bend to everyone else's idea of what we should be our whole lives."

The director shook her head and, keeping her back to me, continued to walk down the hall.

Shannon turned, smiled, and waved.

The telephone buzzes. I am no longer watching my beautiful child. Alone again.

The coldness of the office reflects the darkening day.

The room spins and I grasp the desk.

I don't understand. How did he get here? I have not seen him in years, but I would recognize him anywhere. He has the same dark eyes. His hair, wild and unkempt, reeks of motor oil and decay. And fingernails that have shriveled with overuse, encrusted with the grime of a life unheeded and uncared for.

He sneers. I scream but no sound leaves my lips, my vocal chords freeze. He lunges and my papers fly from my desk.

In my scramble to free myself, my foot catches under the carousel of the chair. Propelled backwards, I hit the floor hard. I cannot move. There is no air. Quiet engulfs the room. If I only I could make my lungs work. In and out. My own exhale startles me.

God, help me.

I have to know.

I have to look.

I peer over the desk rim, but an empty chair and the remnants of the horror, a tornado of white paper strewn to the farthest reaches of the office, are all that remain. Where has he gone?

The telephone buzzes again. My hand approaches the air he occupied moments ago. I feel him. I know because I still remember after all these years. Sometimes you can't forget things. Especially those things you wish you could. "Yes."

"Are you all right?" Sharon asks.

"Yes. I dropped something, and when I went to retrieve it, my foot got caught in the wheels of my chair." I try to project my voice, but it trembles. Sometimes Sharon makes me feel like an idiot, too. "Did you send someone in earlier?"

"No. No one has been to your office. Are you sure you're all right?"

"Yes. I'm sure."

Is Sharon lying? She must have let him in. There is no other explanation. She's trying to drive me crazy, too.

"Do you need me?"

"No, I'm fine."

I lie.

I put the phone down.

3 Eve

Time is running out and I'm still pacing the floor like that's going to give me more space in my head to sort everything out. My apartment, small even by Manhattan standards, is murderously hot. The wood floor, old and well worn by the thousands of footsteps that have crossed it, reeks of fetid feet and shoe oil today. I tear off my camisole and hair and dust stick to my skin; I know there isn't a chance in hell I'll be able to get the camisole back on. The man in the apartment window across the street will get a good look when I pass by the bedroom window.

There is so much to accomplish before I leave for Africa. The things I have to get and to accomplish keep running into each other in a circular, chaotic fashion and I can't seem to nail anything down and I'm not accomplishing anything at all and time is still running out and it's running out even more than when I first realized there isn't enough damn time. Worse, Jerome has stopped pressuring me to stay and has become silent and unavailable. He has abandoned me in every way but physically.

And before I get to Africa, there is Charleston. That is the sticking point with Jerome. How can I make him understand? I meet my childhood posse every year. Besides, I never lied to him. Well, maybe I never leveled with him either. But he wouldn't have gotten it anyway. What was the point? It's not like I could've told him when we first started dating, and now it's just too damn late. The things that bind us as a sisterhood are not something I could have casually mentioned on a first date, or even a second date for that matter, and I'm not sure it's something I can mention even now. If ever. Not if I want him to stick around.

Either way, he knew we were moving toward this point. We both put our cards on the table when we first made the leap and moved in together. I would be meeting my best friends in Charleston on the way to my job in Africa. Understood. And mind you, he laid down a few cards of his own and I've honored them. Like giving him time with his crew, for one. It's not my fault he wants to change the rules.

I can't and I won't.

Especially now, with everything happening to Heather. Not after our last phone conversation. Heather has always been fragile. I knew she would need protecting the first time I saw her. She was the reason we banded together in the first place, and now she needs us. Someone is watching her. Stalking her. Her voice was frantic, her words disjointed. She couldn't tell me if it's a real person or a ghost. A ghost? A ghost showing up in her house. A ghost showing up at work. My girl, our girl, is losing it.

And then there is Africa. Africa looms, and there are not enough hours to do everything. How do I extricate myself from all these conflicting obligations without disappointing someone? Worse, I'm needed here. For the first time in my life after Sunny Hollow, I am rooted in a single place that does not include an escape plan.

I can't breathe. I open the window, but the air is still and close outside. Car horns and sirens battle the air and crash against concrete and glass fortresses. Someone yells. The smell of piss and trash melting on steaming tarmac blasts my nostrils. Naked but for my jeans, sweat trickles between my breasts. Someone whistles. Yeah, that ought to get everyone's jollies off. They are breasts, for crying out loud—just skin over a gland. Getting a hard on over a gland? Go suck a milk carton.

So, how the fuck can I go straight from Charleston to the Darfur-Chad border anyway? It's impossible. My clothes for Charleston would be ridiculous in the refugee camp and I can't send them to Jerome. We still can't agree on whether he'll keep my apartment or move elsewhere. We avoid the subject by sparring around it.

The phone is shrill and interrupts my thoughts. My worries ain't goin' anywhere anyhow anyway.

"Eve? Are you ready?" David's voice is soft and musical—a contrast to his passion for development issues, different from the man with whom I have shared so much of my life, including an intense love affair in the heat of the Congo. But that was a long time ago. Jerome doesn't know about David and I plan on keeping it that way. Jerome's mental pictures of the jungle seem to grow more menacing as the day of my departure nears, and they only add fuel to our already difficult relationship.

"Almost. How bad is it?"

The satellite connection crackles.

"Bad. We're not ready for so many refugees. There are around 25,000 already. Conditions are going downhill fast. We have to set up the emergency water system before the rainy season. Livestock are already dying. There's no place to dispose of them or the human waste."

If anyone can figure it out, it's David. A water engineer for our aid organization, he was contacted to help with the emergent crisis in Darfur. Still, it surprised me when I found out we would be in the same camp.

Or perhaps I wasn't. There was a certain inevitability to it.

I wrap the telephone cord around my finger, but it does little to root me to the safe, knowable space of my apartment. The memory of foul smells and corpses swelling in the breezeless heat twists a knot in my stomach. There is no greater injustice to the senses than a dead body surrendering to the excesses of a tropical sun. I put my hand to my mouth to catch my vomit, but it rests partway up and burns my throat. Well, that sucks.

"Great," I say. "I guess we're needed."

David chuckles nervously. "We're always needed."

I close my eyes and begin to tip. The burn in my chest grows. "Yeah. I'll see you in a couple of weeks."

"We were hoping you would come sooner."

I knew this couldn't be a social call. "I can't. I have several loose ends here. I have to tie them up."

"Loose ends? That sounds . . . complicated. A love interest? That's unlike you." David's voice holds an edge.

I won't play. It would only get his knickers in a twist. "Yes, but it's not the only loose end. I can't come yet."

"We're getting older. I guess I miss you. Us."

I close my eyes. Please don't do this. "That was a long time ago."

"Maybe. We were different people then. Younger. I've changed."

"So have I. I'm sorry, but I can't go back."

"Well, we'll see. Go take care of your loose ends. We'll be here. Be prepared. Rainy season's going to be a bitch. We have a limited supply of cholera kits. I'm hoping more will come. Soon."

"All right. David?"

"Yeah."

"Our relationship can't be anything but professional."

"I hear you. I just can't commit to not trying. See you soon."

The phone clicks before I have a chance to respond. He leaves my words dangling somewhere across the Atlantic Ocean.

David is an intimate part of Africa; his soul is fused to it. The way mine is.

I return to Africa because I need to be needed and I need to forget.

Africa. The mother continent is a web of life that reminds me I'm a fraction of what it is to live. Wild and untamed, it shimmies along a dangerous line between survival and annihilation. I'm not sure that

I don't skate that same boundary—that we don't all. It's just easier to know it in Africa.

The magnitude of the terrain diminishes my problems. I remember the year in the Congo. Africa is full of paradox. But then, maybe I am most at home there. My life has been one of paradox: a white girl living in a black girl's body, a black girl living a white girl's life, growing up the daughter of a product of the Jim Crow South, living in one of the wealthiest towns in America. Paradox doesn't confound me—it defines me.

It reminds me of the women of the Congo. Through their pain, their gracious smiles comforted me, and their children pulled at my own discordant feelings about motherhood. I had embarked on my career with a sense of loss, bitterness, and injustice, but they set me straight. Why should my life be easy? When I was a little girl, my parents told me I could be anything I wanted. They weren't being disingenuous. They believed their words. But then, why should my life have been any different than those who I served in the Congo—or anywhere else, for that matter? What made me think I was so damn special?

I pick up a picture of my family and caress the smoothness of the glass that protects the moment. My hand comes to rest at the center of the framed image. God, I would do anything to have that moment back, to be safe and surrounded by those who once made me believe the world was good and I was safe in the middle of it.

They believed things were changing and they wanted me to be a part of the metamorphosis. My tear smears the illusion.

If such a dream exists in the sub-Sahara, it is veiled by the needs of survival. It is the sense of lack and sharing it that first drew me into my love affair with David. It was the camaraderie of desperation, the proximity to suffering, that drew us together. But lack also destroyed us.

My hair clings to my temples. No matter how many times I pull it back, I can't seem to rein in the wildness of it. Nor can I slow the evolving sense that I no longer belong in Africa. I now belong here.

An American with American problems, I have to finish what I've begun, but I also need an answer from Jerome—a final good-bye, or an agreement to pick up where we're leaving off in a year. The latter would be nice, but I lost my attachment long ago to getting hard-and-fast answers from others. That has been the only salvation in my nomadic life. As for my friends, that is an appointment I will never break. It is a commitment bound in blood. We are as different as oil and vinegar, but shaken, our bond is unbreakable. We are what we have witnessed. We are what we have done. We are the silence we have kept.

I have to convince Jerome. I dial his number.

"Jerome Davis."

"Hi. We need to talk."

"There's nothing to talk about. It doesn't matter what I say, you're still leaving."

"Jerome, you knew who I was when we met. I've never played you."

"What's the difference? I at least thought there was a chance."

"There is a chance. I'm only gone one year. We both . . . just wait."

"Wait for what? You're calling all the shots. I need some space. I'm hangin' with my boys tonight. I'll catch you tomorrow."

I smooth my hair back from my face. "Why don't you spend the night with me so we can figure this out? It feels so . . . unresolved."

"Talk about what? You've already made up your mind. Nothing we say tonight is going to change anything unless you agree to stay and be in this relationship."

"I guess I hoped we could spend as much time together as possible."

"Yeah. I guess I hoped you'd be staying so we could spend time together, too, but look where all that hoping has got us."

"You know this is my life. You've known it all along."

"Look, you met someone, decided to commit to that person, and stayed. End of story. Change your story, man. Quit running away to Africa."

"I'm not running away. I'm an aid worker. It's what I do. If I don't do it then who will?"

"That's a fucking cop-out and you know it."

"This isn't going to get us anywhere, is it?"

"Nope. Like I said, I'm hangin' with my boys tonight."

My head throbs. "I'll see you tomorrow then?"

"Yeah. Tomorrow." The click is emphatic.

The sunlight glares through the window. Sweat drips from my scalp. Why not just leave as a free bird? That's how I've always done it and I've been fine. Why am I willing to leave for Africa with a boyfriend tucked away in New York? Why am I even willing to come back to New York? I've never called anywhere home again since leaving Sunny Hollow. Africa is the closest I've gotten to calling a place home, and it is far too large a continent for the name to have any true meaning. It is more an abstraction.

I dial the number I've known by heart all these years, no matter how far away or how long I've roamed.

"Hello."

"Mariah?" Even now after all these years and the miles in between, I am that little girl again.

"Eve? Are we catching up in Charleston or are you out so you can spend an extra week with Jerome?"

Jerome may be right. I am running away to Africa—but there's not a true place I can call home in America. My home has been taken from me. But my friends still root me to this world, to my past. Like there is still the hope of a place to rest.

I thought I could test the waters, see if I can bow out and give the week to Jerome, but I know I will be in Charleston. Mariah doesn't have to say anything. Not that she ever has. She has always spoken volumes without even parting her lips.

"No. I'd never miss it. One week more or less with Jerome is not going to make a difference. Is it?"

"I suppose not. Are you okay with that?"

"Yeah, I suppose. How 'bout you? Are you done with your assignment? What was it on? Water, right?" I watch as the dust swirls. "Mariah?"

"Yeah. Instead of gold, the hot commodity is water, and guess who gets to decide who has it and who doesn't?"

"Careful, Mariah. You're losing your objectivity."

"Yeah. I can't help it. The entire concept of water as a tradable good pisses me off. Those who can't afford it will die of thirst. Seriously. It's screwed up. Africa is already in trouble. I just finished the section on the Middle East. But . . ."

"You're going to get yourself in trouble again. Right?"

"Right. If not already."

"What do you mean? You know, one of these days, you won't be able to talk yourself out of it."

"Yeah, I know. Listen, I can't wait to see you."

"You didn't really answer my question. What do you mean?"

"It's nothing. Really. I'll see you soon. Okay?"

"All right. Listen. Did you find out about the guy who Heather thinks is stalking her?"

"No. I've tried to find out who lived in that house. I left a message with Jake Cruise, who used to live where Heather's street met that line of houses. After everything burned down, a lot of people never came back. But that house was rebuilt. There's no record of a man by his description living there then, but maybe Jake will know when he calls me back. I just don't know how the man could have survived all these years. I'm afraid Heather hasn't really seen him."

"You mean, you think Heather is crazy?" That isn't an idea I want to entertain, but our last conversation left me with the same question bouncing around in my head. We are sisters. They are all I have. I know when one is in trouble.

"Maybe there's an explanation. And then there's the matter of the fire."

"Yeah. Maybe. But they haven't figured out who started it and it wasn't much of a fire anyway. They were lucky the plumber was there and could get to a phone to call it in."

I flex my calf muscle. It aches. Massaging it does little to abate the rising spasm, and my chest still burns.

"Yes, but he's the reason they're blaming it on Heather. He said there was no one else there, but Heather claims there was."

"And you question her claim?"

"No. I don't know. I'm not sure *she* even knows. In the meantime, I'll keep trying to find out something about the guy. Hopefully I'll have something soon."

"I hope so, too. Be careful, Mariah."

"I will."

"I wish I was as certain."

"What do you mean?"

"I don't know." Pacing the floor unwinds my calf muscle. I need to run. "Maybe I'm just feeling unsettled about life right now. Things aren't working out . . . easily. Nothing seems to be going right."

"Don't worry. It'll work out."

"Okay. I'll see you in Charleston. Have a safe trip."

"*Manana.*"

"*Maka Manana.*" Our old language comforts me. It's our way of saying good-bye without ever meaning it.

Heather needs me now more than ever. Mariah did little to change my mind.

And worse, Mariah is hiding something.

And then there is Jerome.

I don't bother wiping away my tears. Why shouldn't the world know? I've kept my sorrows stashed away for far too long.

How can I break my commitment to my organization?

I've worked for them for years. It's my job.

It's who I am.

I've been an aid worker so long I can't remember any other life except the one I led before the unfathomable sorrow.

I have to find my sneakers.

How can I turn my back on my African family? Turn my back on their suffering? How can I, in the span of a month, make a choice that will forever change the course of my life?

I don my sports bra and top. I find my sneakers. It's fresh air I need. I pop an antacid. If I have a chance of finding answers, it will be out pounding the pavement. I head in the direction of Central Park. My walk turns into a run.

Running is the one thing that is as natural as breathing in and breathing out.

4 Mariah

We live in a spider's web. Eve's phone call reminds me of this. Under the distraction of research and deadlines, it is sometimes easy to forget.

I light sage. I perform the same ritual to remind me where I am from, to remember this land for something more than the flag that was planted and now flies above.

Hello relatives. *Mitakuye oyas'in.* I am born where thunder and the mystery of water meet, born when the lone wolf cried into the frost of the Hard Moon night, his voice of and defined by the wilderness. I am a truth walker. My mother is of the Thunder Clan of the Ho-Chunk. My father is of the *Shawala tiospaye* of the *Sincangu Oyate* Lakota, and his mother was *Mdewakanton* Dakota, descended from one who was saved from Abraham Lincoln's mass scaffold only to die a far more bitter and cruel death as a prisoner of war at Camp Kearney. Her homeland by *Mde Wakan,* Spirit Lake, is gone and her people are dispersed to many reservations, the ancestors' bones cast to the winds like her tribe.

Relationships are the blood of the people and were the first thing taken, the knowledge of its value realized on first expression of invasion and consummated in forced boarding schools. This knowledge my grandmother weeps into the soil where the debt of suffering upon this land lays like an open wound. But I am also white, descended from those men who did their duty to strip us of our culture and language for our land, and married white women when they were done with their Indian experiment in civilizing, when the last breath was extinguished from their first wives who walked on. I am consumer and consumed, cheater and cheated, invader and subsumed.

Remembering is important. Like I said, I have long been entangled by the spider's web. Our words are *wakan*, powerful and reflective of our thoughts, our intent in the world. I hunt the hidden clues, those things that are not said. I stand between the *wamakaskan*, the living beings of the earth, and those who would destroy them. The web is tightening. The trickster is out and about. He reminds me of the stakes. He reminds me to take myself less seriously, lest I forget, and sometimes he reminds me of home. I am still in exile.

Heather needs us. We keep the secret, the one inconsolable secret. The flame of the candle dips and weaves in the quiet of my apartment. My dogs slumber, but I know their eyes will open if I move. Their slumber is watchful. The round robin of phone calls between Fiona, Heather, Eve, and Espy has woven my unease into a tight cocoon of nerves. Poor Heather! The web is wrapped so tight her thoughts are muted within. Eve believes I can crack the mystery of Heather's visitor and the fire, but I cannot. My own world is unraveling. My stints in war-torn Sarajevo, Congo, Beirut, and too many others to recount no longer seem to hold a candle to the mess I am in. No shots have been fired, but I am terrified of the powers against which I have pitted myself. At least in war, you know the bullets are out there. You have a 50 percent shot at surviving. This is different. I don't even know who my adversaries are. Not really. I just feel the threat of their power. It is as if they are ghosts.

But I promised Eve. I dial Heather's number.

"Hello."

"Heather? How are you?"

My movement stirs the dogs.

"I'm fine, Mariah." Her sigh tells me something different.

"You sound . . . worried. Did the police find any evidence of forced entry?"

"No. They have found nothing. I wish we weren't meeting in Charleston this year."

"What do you mean? Your vote is the reason we're going to Charleston."

"I know, but I guess I just feel safer at home right now."

I tug a thread that has pulled itself from my fraying couch. "Safer? It seems like meeting us in Charleston might be safer for you. Letting things settle a little."

"I know. I guess I would feel safer with Brandon around. Although, truth be told, that's not entirely true. I'm not sure he wouldn't feed me to the lions."

His name twists inside of me. I've known a hundred men like him. All dressed up in a designer suit, but you can smell the predator a mile away—and Heather is his prey, the quarry upon whose vulnerability he feeds daily. But I cannot say this to her. She is already too frightened.

"That doesn't sound like you. What's changed?"

"Oh, nothing. It's just a feeling I have. Like he's watching me or something. Like he wants to . . . I don't know, Mariah. That day the plumber was there, I had the distinct feeling someone was in the house."

"I know. Your visitor?"

"Now I'm not so sure. It could've been Brandon. The window was open in the upstairs guest bedroom. I never open that window except to air it when guests are coming. I saw a shadow pass. I thought it was my imagination—or worse, my visitor. But when I think about it, the silhouette reminded me of Brandon's. And then the fire started in the trash can in his den. Like he was burning something he didn't want anyone to see. Especially me."

"Are you sure? Maybe you opened the window at some point and forgot to shut it."

"Maybe, but doubtful. And what about the fire? I just feel odd about the whole thing. Maybe he needed to get rid of something, the fire got away from him, and to avoid suspicion, he said he wasn't there and blamed the fire on me."

"I thought the plumber was there. Wouldn't he have seen Brandon leave? Did the police see any signs of him or of his having been there to start the fire?"

"Are you a prosecutor? No. No one saw him, and yes, his DNA and fingerprints were all over his office, as they should've been. I know I heard someone in the house. I know I saw something in the window, and I know I didn't start the fire. It *feels* like it was Brandon. Listen, it's not just him or this incident, really. Work's trouble, too. We're in the middle of layoffs again. They're bad. And I have a case on my hands that implicates my boss and his boss. I'm feeling a little bit like a sacrificial lamb, when I should be a tiger."

"Then don't be a lamb or a tiger. Be a horse and run like hell and kick some ass on your way out of the paddock."

Heather giggles. "You make me laugh."

Thank the gods I still have some humor left in me. Lately, I haven't seen the humor in much of anything. I cannot see myself for the trees. I have been away from the Rez for too long. My grandmothers want me home, but I am stubborn, and I risk losing myself because of it.

"Seriously, Heather. Maybe getting away to Charleston is exactly what you need. Get out of the paddock. Besides, I need the break too."

"You? Why?"

"Oh, nothing." It's a bad day when a self-proclaimed truth walker becomes a liar to her best friend. "I just need a break."

"You're not going back into a war zone. Are you?"

"No. Nothing like that." It's not really a lie. It's just not the whole truth. But explaining the current state of water rights is not something one can explain in a minute. In a world of manufactured scarcity, water must be there for the taking and made into a consumable good.

"Are you sure?"

"Yeah, Heather. I promise." Sometimes, on the most peaceful of days, I can still hear the bombs. The madness of war dogs me. "No more war for a while. It's all peace right now." My words are trite and taste like vinegar.

"All right. I'll see you in Charleston."

"All right. Heather? Just call me if anything happens. You know we'll all come if you need us."

"Yeah. *Maka Manana*."

Right! If Heather needs me, I'm only four and a half hours away with no traffic. A lot can happen in that time. I've experienced people sitting next to me one minute and evaporating in the next. It only takes the blink of an eye to obliterate the trace of a human. Shattered for the gods of war and the glory of civilization. Dismembered and dis-remembered.

The series of articles I've been working on are worse than war. At least in war, there's the camaraderie of shared experience, shared threat. And yes, there's even the intoxicating allure of meaning. Life becomes defined by those who would kill or be killed. It takes on sharper edges. There is clarity in imminent death. The world of water cartels and public relations and banks and governments and organizations, though—they beat you up with all the things they don't say. The meaning is always inferred, like a black hole. They are ghost words.

But these are not the things my boss wants to hear. He has always championed my coverage of war, but the line between right and wrong, good and bad, is never blurred in life and death. Those lines are a lot murkier now, and the stakes for their meaning are higher. I need to keep my job, but I need to tell the truth. He wants me to "knock off the Indian shit." I choose objectivity, but it is always difficult when you come from a world in which truth has been shape-shifted. I will always see the truth through the prism of a world defined by the reservation—one is either on or off. In white man's speak, being off the reservation means going rogue. There is no gray area. My boss expects me to pick a side and "get on with it." Even though it is safer on the reservation, I've always been off. Going rogue now is no more a risk than it has ever been. And now I'm just lying to myself. But what do I know? I am a mixed-blood. My blood quantum is murky and my heart is suspect to both sides. I live in a world in between. And it is always somewhere in that in-between land, that frontier of human imagination, that the things not said hide their relevance.

It was supposed to be an uncomplicated series on water. Something you could print in a glossy magazine and suburbanites could place on their coffee table as a point of discussion when the conversation grew thin. But how the hell does a truth walker sugarcoat water commodification? And now the deadline approaches. I am closer to that border. Who knows what will happen when all the shit I've uncovered hits the fan. Will this article even see the light of day? Is all this danger worth it if my articles ultimately find their home in a vault or the bottom of the trash?

I need to go home, but not yet.

My dogs follow me to the kitchen. A quart of milk and some random leftovers are a pathetic reminder of my relationship to food. After Sarajevo, I ate little for a week while those journalists who had survived with me ate their first meal out of the war zone like it was their last. The soggy, sagging doggie containers weep into the metal refrigerator grates. I extract them and lob them into the garbage, but my dogs remind me that their relationship to food is not nearly as complicated as mine, so I retrieve the wet containers from the trash. While they eat the remains, I slather peanut butter on bread and coat both slices with a thick sheen of honey.

I let the article go. It is now out in the universe and I will know soon enough what all that energy will bring me. It has been a long winter, and the dogs need to unfurl their legs as much as I do.

The unusually warm spring air has liberated the scent of cherry blossoms and dogwoods throughout DC, and my neighborhood is no exception. It mixes with those of the many ethnic restaurants on my street. The aroma of barbecued meat and yeasty baked bread fills the air, accompanied by cumin, cardamom, and vanilla. The scents are heady and I long for something more, something bigger in my life. The want is enough to drown me. Pedestrians stroll the streets and join in animated conversations at the many cafés that dot my neighborhood. I am an observer, a traveler through their space, a wanderer in between.

I order far too much food at my favorite take-out place. All the food in the world cannot fill me.

Back at home, the dogs dance and pirouette around my legs, their tails wagging and thumping against my skin. I fill a dish for myself and scrape the rest into their bowls. They finish quickly and join me on the couch. I flip through the channels and settle on a sitcom. The show requires no thought and yet my mind flips through its own channels, the noise constant and ever changing. I snuggle into my quilt. The dogs settle into the folds around my legs. They are warm against me, but my mind is a minefield. Shadow twitches, but it is not from puppy dreams. I stroke his tail—strands of hair are soft and compliant to my touch. He settles down.

*** *** ***

I drift far into the light that dances and plays across the plains and illuminates the manes of horses. I am a part of them, a part of the herd, but they spook. The power of their hooves splinters the earth, muscles pulse with the wind, manes and tails fly and dance freely.

I am at once horse and rider, separate and the same. So much free-dom leaves me breathless and I close my eyes to the warm sun. I am the red fire of that which dances in the sky.

It happens fast. Thrown to the ground, my breath knocks free of my body.

Flesh rips. The spirit of my voice shreds.

I open my eyes.

A cougar snarls and drips blood, my blood. I lie in stillness and watch myself dissolve.

The sun glares in synchronicity with the two wild orbs barely hidden behind the slits of the cat's eyes.

Death is imminent, but I am not sad.

Drums beat, a pounding, primordial rhythm. The cougar backs away and I rise in direct proportion to her retreat. I cradle my throat, but it is whole again.

I look for the cougar, but she watches and withers as I grow. Where she stood, a circle forms. Women of every size and color dance in two concentric, opposing circles. They keep time to the constant drum, and from their belts hang scalps still red and dripping.

The horses stand proudly at the fringes, watching and waiting, pawing at the earth.

As the dancers pass, one turns to look in my eyes. Two eyes, deep and red, look into me. The dancer smiles. Torn flesh snags in the crev-ices between her ragged teeth.

A single drop of blood oozes onto the ground within the heart of the circle. I reach for my throat and find my voice.

* * *

The sound of a scream and a phone ringing wakes me. The dogs stand at alert, their ears perked.

The clock reads 3:33 a.m.

The TV speaks in hushed tones and fills in the corners of the room with disembodied conversation.

The phone rings again.

"Hello?"

The voice is coarse and muffled. "Watch where you go, Miss Westerman. Stop what you're doing. Now. Before it's too late."

"What?"

"Listen carefully. We assume the next article will pertain to your last little . . . expedition into things you don't need to know. That could be very dangerous for you. This is a warning. There won't be another one."

Click.

"Wait? Who are you?"

But there is no answer.

What am I doing? It's not as if I haven't known. The sense of a force, a spirit of evil, has been following me. Ignoring the premonition is like lying to myself.

I press my palms to my blurry eyes. Focus. Who could the caller work for? It's way too late anyway. The article has already been faxed. Even if I wanted to squash the story, my boss has the last say. I'm sitting here in the small hours of the morning contemplating my next move, and something tells me I better make the decision fast because the future could get ugly.

No. I will not be scared away from this. I have already seen the worst that man has to offer. And I am a journalist. High stakes and danger come with the territory. It's what makes the truth so precious—precious like water. Seeking truth requires understanding its opposite.

I settle back onto the couch. Shadow and Luna rest their chins on my chest. They will follow me into my dream sleep. I do not want to go there, but soon my eyes are heavy. Too heavy to rise and check the locks on my door, I am a prisoner to my body even as my mind screams to wake.

5 Ten-Year Reunion —The Garden In Moonlight

Mariah leaned toward the mirror and swiped the mascara wand across her eyelashes. Brown eyes gleamed back. She sighed. Makeup was her concession to the event. She had anticipated this reunion for months, but now that the moment was here, her stomach gurgled. Old memories flooded back and moved like a tidal wave, threatening to smother her. She smoothed out her dark hair and donned the long, glittery dress she had bought for the occasion. Fiona wanted them all to be dressed in the latest styles, Hollywood glamour. Mariah blanched. Beverly Hills was already wearing off on her friend.

Mariah took one last look in the mirror. She wanted to be taken seriously. She could not imagine how that would happen in this ridiculous dress.

She met Esperanza and Eve in the lobby.

"I guess we're all Hollywood now."

Esperanza giggled. "Oh my God, Mariah. You look so beautiful. Someone's going to get laid tonight."

Eve laughed. "Doubt it. They'll be all hot and heavy and she'll kill them with a lecture on the necessary rights for the IRA hunger strikers before she descends into a long sermon on the ways in which the Irish penal laws were a lot like federal Indian law."

"Very funny, Eve. You make me sound like a joy kill."

"If the shoe fits, girl."

Esperanza laughed. "Stop. We love you. You bring joy wherever you go, Mariah."

Eve threw an arm around Mariah's shoulder before throwing the other around Esperanza's. "Keep telling her that and maybe we won't have to talk about Bobby Sands tonight."

Mariah shrugged off Eve's arm. "Knock it off, Eve. Even if I thought someone would want to hear about the IRA hunger strikes, it would go over everyone's head. They're too caught up in their own lives."

"Ooh, Mariah. Watch out. You're making one of those blanket statements."

"Regardless, I'll keep the conversation light tonight. Okay?"

"Okay. That's good for me, 'cause I want to party."

Esperanza smiled. "I wonder what the Rose Garden would look like today."

Mariah perked. "Probably changed. It was already changing. We should go tomorrow." A cloud passed over her face. "So long as we stay away from—"

"Yes," Eve said. "We will avoid it. Let's do it. Our activity schedule says there's swimming and a golf tournament. I'm not up for either. Rose Garden?"

"Definitely," Mariah said.

"Well, that's decided," Esperanza said. "Shall we go? The ballroom awaits us."

They approached the reception table.

"Oh my God, Mariah. You haven't changed one bit." The girl handed her a nametag.

Mariah was at a loss.

Eve came to her rescue. "Mariah, it's our old friend Tammy the Tank!" She bobbed her head at the girl.

"Lose the attitude, Eve. No one calls me the tank anymore. I'm skinnier than you."

"Yeah, you're skinny all right," Eve said. "You're a skinny-ass bitch."

Tammy stood up, leaned toward Eve, and pointed her finger at her face. "I can still beat you up. You're just a skinny-ass bitch yourself."

Eve smiled as she reached for her nametag. "I thought so. C'mon, Mariah. Espy. Go howl at the moon, Tammy. You never had me fooled." She retrieved Esperanza's tag and ushered her friends into the ballroom.

Disco balls hung from the ceiling and music pounded from speakers. The sound bounced off the walls.

Mariah scanned the room. Fiona waved frantically from a table near the middle. Mariah could see the rock on her finger even from a distance. "No down-and-outs here."

Eve surveyed the occupants. "Thank God, Mariah. We gotta get through tonight."

Esperanza clucked. "Listen to you two. The evening has barely begun and already I feel like I need to pound some margaritas."

"You're right, Espy." Eve shrugged. "Let's just have a good time. Even if it's just the five of us. Who needs the rest of the world?"

Mariah smiled. "Except it's not the five of us. Fiona and Heather brought their husbands."

"Why shouldn't we honor their choices in life, Mariah?" Esperanza said, shaking her head. "It can't always be just the five of us. There's always room for more. Besides, we're not exactly the life of the party when it's just us."

Eve's eyes widened. "Speak for yourself. I think I'm a lot of fun." She moved toward her married friends.

Fiona and Heather met them before they made it to the table and they all embraced.

Fiona danced back and forth. "I'm so excited to see you guys."

Mariah hugged Fiona. "I am too."

Mariah felt a hand brush her bare back. She turned. Luke Genovese's eyes gleamed. "You're on fire, Mariah. Smokin' hot."

Eve giggled.

Mariah turned and maneuvered to rid herself of his hand, which was gravitating lower. "Thanks Luke. You look good too. So, what have you been up to?"

"Not much. How 'bout you?"

"Oh, I'm a journalist. I covered the Irish hunger strikes, for example. Have you heard about Bobby Sands and the other nine who died?"

Eve explosively expelled a laugh.

"Uh, no, I haven't."

Mariah coyly batted her eyelashes. "Oh, I could give you a little lesson."

Esperanza and Eve laughed. Luke regarded them sheepishly. "No thanks, Mariah. You are beautiful but you've always been too damn . . . weird." Luke finished off his drink and moved away.

Mariah turned to her friends with a frown. "What's that supposed to mean?"

Eve chuckled. "Seriously, Mariah. It's Luke. What do you think he means? He means you're not an easy lay and he's on the prowl."

Fiona grabbed Mariah's arm. "C'mon, you guys. I want to introduce you to my husband."

Eve followed. "We already met him. We were at the wedding. Remember?"

"Yes, of course I remember. I wasn't that drunk."

"Uh-huh."

"Knock it off, Eve. I may have been tipsy, but I was mostly just happy. Happy to be marrying the man of my dreams, and happy that my best friends could share it with me. Don't rain on my parade."

Eve squeezed her arm. "Sorry. I don't mean to. I think I need a drink."

"There's my girl." Fiona swirled in her beautiful gown, her diamonds meshing with the lights from the disco balls and refracting around the room. "Gavin, would you mind getting a drink for Eve? Thank you, sweetheart." She turned to Eve. "What do you want?"

Eve smiled at Gavin. "Red wine. Thanks, Gavin. It's good to see you again."

Gavin returned the smile. "The feeling is mutual." He turned to Brandon. "Brandon? Shall we get these beautiful women some drinks? Esperanza?"

"Red wine too. *Gracias.*"

Gavin bowed his head slightly at Esperanza.

"Mariah?"

"I'll take a Blood and Sand. Thank you."

Gavin smiled. "Classic."

Fiona grabbed his elbow. "No. What the hell is that? She'll take a Screaming Orgasm, like me."

Gavin rolled his eyes. "She doesn't want that."

"Yes, she does."

"No."

Mariah interceded. "I'll take a glass of red wine, then." She wiped a line of sweat from her upper lip. The conversation made her uncomfortable, but Brandon's intense gaze made her even more so.

Gavin gave his wife a curt look, but continued. "Heather?"

Brandon stepped forward. "Don't worry. I know what she wants." He grazed Mariah's arm as he passed.

Fiona sidled up to the group. "Did you see Tammy? Wow. She's changed."

Mariah snickered. "Not really."

"What do you mean?"

"Eve pulled the old Tammy out of her skin."

Esperanza laughed.

Heather moved closer. "What do you mean?"

"I've got this one," Eve said. "She means she hasn't changed much at all. Oh, she might've shed a few pounds, but she hasn't shed any of that meanness. She's still a punk- ass bitch."

The memory of the day Tammy laid her fists on Heather and cemented their bonds of friendship lingered unspoken in the middle of the group.

* * *

Sunny Hollow stretched to one side and Sycamore to the other. Hunkered in a hollow at the border lay the public Rose Garden. They were not allowed in Sycamore, not even one foot—except the Rose Garden. The garden was acceptable, revered even, and tended to by women with blue hair who wore gloves and hats and carried purses on their arms. It was a land in between. Their turf, lower Sunny Hollow, a hamlet of craft bungalows and storybook-style houses, bordered Sycamore.

The girls' friendship started in the autumn.

One Saturday, Mariah's mother took her school shopping and Mariah campaigned for a pair of penny loafers. If she had to go to church, she needed acceptable shoes. If she was going back to school, she needed new shoes. Either way, shoes carried the weight of her world. They made her less different.

Her mother didn't budge.

Mariah kicked the toe of her scuffed shoe against the base of the checkout counter. "But Mom, no one wears saddle shoes anymore."

Her mother smoothed a strand of errant hair from her face. "We're not everyone. Christmas is coming soon. Maybe for Christmas."

"That's too late. I'll be dead by then."

Her mother chuckled. "You should be an actress. Such drama."

She scowled at her mother, whose eyes, the color of melted choco-late, patiently regarded her. Mariah played with a piece of thread that had freed itself from the weave of her sweater. "Why can't we buy them now?" She ground the sole of her offending shoe into the floor. "Oh, I forgot. We're Indian. It's not our way. Right?" She practically shouted the last words, and was immediately sorry for it.

Waiting for the change, her mother held her hand over the counter. "That has nothing to do with it."

Mariah leaned toward her gentle voice, then watched in dismay as the clerk drew back and dropped the money away from her mother's hand. Loose coins missed their mark, rolled across the countertop, and spilled across the floor, pinging independently as they swirled and came to rest on the dirty floor. Mariah hated the way her mother scrambled to retrieve each piece, her shirt stretched across her hunched back and the outline of her bra etched against the aging material. She glared at the clerk, who vigorously wiped his hands with a ragged cloth.

Mariah wore her old saddle shoes to the first day of Sunday school at Unified Sunny Hollow Church. She did not know why she even had to go to church. Her people were peyote people. They expressed suffering on the Sun Dance pole—on the same pole for which they were massacred—not the cross. On the drive to upper Sunny Hollow, she had imagined a thousand ways to hide the obsolete fashion pieces on her feet.

She knew the mean girl, Tammy Pfeiffer, sported a shiny dime tucked inside her new loafers. Life was unfair like that.

Mariah was ready. She would not let Tammy get the best of her today.

But Tammy only had eyes for the new girl.

The girl tried to make herself smaller, but everyone noticed her. A sprite amongst giants, she could have been a lost dragonfly borne in on soft breezes. Impossibly small for her age, she sank deep into her chair.

Mariah wondered how long it would take for Tammy the Tank to squash the pixie.

It did not matter that the teacher stood in the same room. Kids were kids, and adults rarely interfered with the natural order of things. Tiny and fragile in her white gossamer dress, the new girl contrasted sharply with the modern pastels that surrounded her. Her Peter Pan collar and inverted pin tucks swallowed her as she picked at the light material overlay. Elfin legs peeked from her hem, white patent leather Mary Janes and lace-fringed ankle socks swung lightly against the chair. The teacher turned to the blackboard and Tammy shook her fist and pointed at the tiny girl.

Several girls snickered.

Oblivious to the brewing trouble, the teacher called for a prayer and dismissed the class fifteen minutes before their parents' service ended.

Alone, twenty eleven-year-old girls from four different schools stared at each other. Soon, they would break into their matching school groups.

Tammy moved first.

She closed in on the girl, pulled her chair out, and knocked her down with a single smack.

The girl fell like a sack of flour dropping from the bottom shelf in Jim's Sunny Hollow Market.

Tammy straddled her and struck her with large, balled fists.

The little doll's face moved from side to side with each blow. Mariah wanted her to protect herself. Her eyes, vacant and resigned, stared through Mariah each time her head came around. Mariah knew that look. She had seen it before along the road that led across the boundary of the Rosebud Reservation, her father's homeland, and she had seen it amongst her mother's people, the Winnebago. It was better to fight for something, anything, than to die without trying.

Everyone knew Tammy was an overgrown bully from upper Sunny Hollow. Her fists were legendary. But this was different. The screams from some of the other girls egged her on. She moved her fists to the little girl's torso, her swings harder and more exaggerated, her face a mask of gleeful determination. The pixie lay like a rag doll, taking each hit like she expected it.

So many pairs of gleaming eyes fixed on the girl, too small to stand up and too small to matter. It reminded Mariah of a beloved doll that her brothers had carelessly broken. She had cuddled its armless body, but it was impossible to love away the grotesqueness of the act.

She shoved Tammy.

Tammy whirled.

Mariah moved, and Eve and Esperanza pushed their way to her side.

"Watch out!" one of the spectators yelled. "The Injun girl is going to scalp you. That's what they do. She's a dirty Injun."

Mariah ignored her, focused on Tammy, but Eve pushed the girl. "Shut up."

"You shut up." She pushed Eve back.

Tammy stood, whirled, and planted her fist in Mariah's mouth. Mariah fell hard, mouth throbbing, tears welling, but got back up. Tammy tried to hit her again. Mariah was ready. She ducked and shoved her hard. Arms whirling like a pinwheel, Tammy went down.

Mariah fell on her. Anger swelled inside her, flowed into her clenched fists. She hit Tammy over and over, her face and the previous day clerk's fused into one, the words "dirty Injun" swirling in her head.

The group of girls moved closer to Mariah and Tammy.

Tammy tried to lunge up at Mariah, missed, and fell back to the ground just as a beautiful, blond, blue-eyed girl standing at the periphery of the fight stepped in.

"Stop it! Everyone stop it! We're all going to get in trouble."

Mariah backed away from Tammy, who glowered at the blond girl from where she lay on the ground. The crowd quieted. Mariah had seen the girl before. Everyone wanted to sit next to her in Sunday school. She wondered why someone so popular would bother with her fight.

Tammy sat up and banged her fists on the ground. "What's your problem, Fiona? That girl deserves it. She gets treated special. And this, this girl hit me. I'm telling."

"Go ahead and tell. You hit her first. Besides, you're treated special too. Your mom and dad make sure of it. For once, stay on your butt or I'll tell everyone you started it. And who do you think they'll believe?"

Laughter echoed through the crowd. Across the courtyard, the doors to the church opened and the adults spilled out into the bright sunlight. The girls dispersed and ran across the lawn. Stained-glass crosses illuminated by shafts of light played along the grass border. Mariah watched as each girl pierced the shadow of the main cross, Christ's arms raised, surrounded by the outline of the lancet windows. When she was younger, she'd desperately wanted to hold Him up so His weight couldn't rip at His wounds. She would do it by herself if necessary. But the adults told her it was the way it was supposed to be. Even then, she hated the way people gave up. She angrily wiped away a tear. No matter what, she would never allow herself to suffer like that.

Tammy struggled to her feet and lightly shoved Fiona. "See you in school, Fiona." She did not look back at the group until she had rejoined her parents.

Fiona bent to help the little broken doll, who was still lying very still. "C'mon, Heather. You have to get up."

"Is she dead?" Mariah thought of her broken doll.

"I don't think so."

"We better call someone."

"You better not. She'll get into more trouble."

"Why?" Mariah asked.

"Because."

"How do you know?"

"Because she goes to my school. Her parents keep her away from here. They probably don't want the minister to know."

"Why?"

"Just because."

Heather got up and straightened her dress, blood dripping from her nose and lips in tiny rivulets like a dressmaker's straight pins. Skin peeked through tears in the fabric as she unsuccessfully tried to press the remnants together.

"Are you okay?" Fiona gently wrapped her arm around the girl's shoulder.

She nodded, her bruised lips turning up into a half smile. She tried to smooth a strand of hair behind her ear, but it fell again from its perch. She lifted her dress and the four remaining girls gasped. She was black and blue, but not all of the bruises were new—yellow marked the aging offenses. She quickly smoothed her dress. Her smile disappeared.

Mariah wanted to take her home and hide her under her bed. Her mom would let her. Her mom protected those who could not protect themselves. Mostly birds but sometimes dogs.

"I have to go now. Thank you," Heather said.

"Where're you going?"

"I just have to go. Thank you."

They unconsciously moved as a group to watch her run toward a couple standing with other parents. A woman bent to talk to her. The distance magnified her vulnerability. Mariah instinctively took a step. Eve grabbed her arm. They watched as the couple disengaged themselves from the crowd. The woman grasped Heather's arms and pulled her toward the parking lot, her feet stretched in motion as they attempted to reach the ground.

Mariah shifted uneasily. The silence held no comfort. She swallowed the knot in her throat. "Do you guys wanna come over to my house? I'm just hanging out."

Fiona's blond hair shimmered in the high autumnal sky. "Sure."

Eve and Esperanza followed.

That same day, Mariah, Eve, Esperanza, and their new friend, Fiona, watched people move into the house behind Mariah's. No one moved on a Sunday. Sunday was God's day.

Her mother's rescued dogs howled at the commotion until Mariah retrieved each one and silenced them with a treat. But she could feel their discomfort from her room, their paws relentlessly clicking as they scurried from window to window.

Mariah and her friends traced the movements of people in each room as moving boxes and covered furniture found new homes. It was late when the doors of the rented moving truck shut, the sound of its departure final. Quiet descended and cloaked the hill. Mariah heard each dog slump into rest, their sighs muted in the fading afternoon.

Fiona tapped the windowsill. "That's Heather's new house."

"How do you know?" Esperanza asked.

"Because I know her mother. She picks Heather up from school every day. She probably doesn't want anyone to know about the bruises, but we all know anyway."

Noise punctured the calm. Through the trees, they watched the little girl run across the yard. Her mother followed. The fence hid them, but it did not hide the sounds of leather on skin.

The dogs howled from the room below.

Mariah winced with every hit. They listened to the girl's whimpers long after the noises ceased, the woman had returned to the house, and the dogs' howls had stopped. They could not move.

"Why did she hit her?" Mariah asked.

Fiona shrugged. "Probably because she spoiled her dress."

"She didn't spoil her dress. Tammy spoiled her dress."

"It doesn't matter."

"Why do you suppose they moved here?"

"I don't know, but she's your neighbor now. It doesn't matter anyway. No one cares. No one cared at my school. They won't care at yours either. They never do." Fiona said.

"How do you know so much?"

"I've been watching it my whole life."

"Someone should kick her Mom's butt." Eve pumped her fist.

Esperanza frowned. "Someone needs to horse-stomp her butt."

"I know," Mariah said. "We could be a butt-kicking, horse-stompin', kick-ass club. We'll tell everyone. We'll fix it. They won't be able to ignore all of us."

Esperanza gasped and held her hand to her mouth. The girls broke into awkward giggles that quickly died.

They waited long into that afternoon, until they could no longer hear Heather's whimpers—until the only noise was that of dead leaves rustling along the weathered fence line. Heather still had not reappeared.

* * *

The memory of that day lingered like an unhealed wound.

Esperanza was the first to break the uncomfortable silence. "We're going to the Rose Garden tomorrow. Like old times."

Heather gasped. "Are you sure? We'll have to walk by my house—my mom might see me."

Fiona waved her hand. "Heather. Your mom barely leaves her easy chair. Of course you can pass your house. Besides, I'm not scared of her."

Heather backed away. "She might still see me," she whispered.

"So what if she does? We'll take care of her."

Mariah hugged Heather. "Heather. Your mom will never hurt you again. We're going to the Rose Garden, like old times. Those are good memories."

Fiona shivered. "Well, mostly."

Mariah huddled closer. The memory chilled her. "Every day but that day."

"Yes, that day," Heather murmured.

The men returned to them as they huddled together under a bright disco ball.

"What are you talking about?" Gavin handed Esperanza and Eve their drinks.

"Old times." Fiona perked up and caressed Gavin's hand as he handed her the drink.

Brandon passed a drink to Heather and turned to Mariah with a glass of wine. Mariah thanked him as she took it, but he did not let it go. Startled, she looked at him. He exuded something primal. Mariah had never experienced such rawness. She recoiled.

"Excuse me. I need to go to the restroom."

His eyes flickered briefly.

Fiona and Eve found her dabbing water from her face with a rigid paper towel.

Fiona slid onto the counter. "Mariah. You need to freshen your mascara. By the way, you look beautiful tonight."

Eve put a hand on Mariah's shoulder. "Get to the point, Fiona."

"Oh yeah. We should take a picnic to the Rose Garden. To our special place. Jim's does catering now. We can grab a basket, bypass Heather's street, and hit it that way."

"Bypass the street?"

"Yeah."

The tears started anew. Mariah dabbed at her eyes. Eve hugged her from the side as they stared into the mirror. "I'm so sorry, Mariah."

"What?"

"Honestly, Fiona. Sometimes you're clueless."

Mariah felt the heat of that long ago night burn her cheeks, watched in the mirror as they turned crimson in the harshness of the restroom lights. Bruce Springsteen's "Streets of Fire" piped through the music system and taunted her. She dabbed cool water on her face but the vision of that night felt so close.

Her mother and brothers had watched as her beloved father had climbed onto the roof to hose it down, but the fire had found him, screamed and launched its rage upon him and their home. He had grabbed his chest and died as he fell from the burning roof. Their home was consumed and their lives destroyed. She had not even been there to help, to witness, or to say good-bye. Her mom had hung on for three more years, living in a tight apartment on the lower end of Sunny Hollow, but in the end had been defeated and returned to her husband's reservation, where suffering was understood. Mariah could only rage against the vastness of that acceptance.

"I know," Fiona said. "Oh my God, Eve, of course I remember. I'm so sorry, Mariah. I'm a clueless klutz and an idiot. I'm sorry." She hugged Mariah and cried with her. "I didn't even ask how your mother is."

Mariah wiped the tears with her index finger. "She never got over losing Daddy or losing her brother in Vietnam. The Rez is full of brokenness. She fits right in."

"Nah, Mariah," Eve said. "It's not full of any more brokenness than anywhere else. Life breaks people."

Mariah smiled halfheartedly. There were shades of brokenness.

"Let's say we get another drink at that open bar," Eve said. "I'm ready to get shit-faced."

Fiona whooped. "Now that's my girl. Let's do it."

* * *

The night grew deep, the lights spun for hours, and the open bar and restroom remained the only break from their table. Classmates visited briefly, but the five friends never left each other.

"Maybe we should call it a night." Gavin tossed back the remains of his watered-down cocktail.

"Maybe we should get another one. This is too much fun." Fiona's words slurred together.

"Well, I'm heading upstairs."

"Okay, you do that. I'm staying right here." Fiona tapped her index finger to mark the spot.

"Brandon. Ladies. I'll see you in the morning. Are you playing golf tomorrow, Brandon?"

"Yes. I'll see you on the course. I'm not sure who they've signed us up with."

"Great. See you tomorrow." Gavin bowed slightly and left the ballroom.

Fiona snickered. "When the cat's away . . ."

"Well, the cat's not away." Esperanza kicked her under the table.

"Let's go to the Rose Garden tonight." Fiona leaned forward excitedly. "The night is still young. C'mon. The Garden under the moonlight. I want to see it. I want to remember. All of our dreams and passions were right there. Have we changed so much?"

"Of course we've changed," Eve said. "We barely survived that night, for one thing."

"Oh, I don't mean that. There was so much promise in the world. We were going to conquer the world. Remember? Maybe it's still there." Fiona twirled the white fabric napkin around her hand.

"It's not there, sweetheart. It's just not," Eve said. "If you could see the horrors I've seen, you would know that we were just kids living a fantasy. Don't get me wrong; kids don't need to know all that truth so early. But we know it now. It was never safe in the Rose Garden. That lesson should've been well learned that night, before we ever left Sunny Hollow."

Heather straightened. "It was always safer in the Rose Garden. Even when the world wasn't safe, it was my haven. It was a safe place away from home. I could breathe there." She sniffled. "I'd go there now, Fiona."

"Really?"

"Why not?"

Brandon rose. "Well, it sounds like you ladies are taking a midnight stroll. I'll see you in the morning."

Heather reached for his hand. He took hers and kissed it.

Fiona kicked Mariah under the table. They watched him leave. Fiona leaned over to Mariah to whisper, "He is a stone cold fox."

Mariah leaned back. "Ew, Fiona. He's a creep. I don't like him."

"Have you seen the way he looks at me?"

"No. But I saw how he's been looking at me, and he's probably been looking that way at everyone else, too."

"No. He's been looking at me."

"Fiona. That's Heather's husband. Don't be stupid."

"I would never, but it doesn't hurt to flirt."

"Flirting has gotten you into trouble before. I'm not with you every day of the year, but I have no doubt it's gotten you into trouble plenty of times I don't even know about."

"Na-uh. I'm careful."

"I doubt it. I'm telling you. Don't mess with him. Don't even flirt."

"Why not? It's harmless."

"It's not harmless. Besides, that would devastate Heather. We're everything to her. Imagine how she would feel if she saw you coming on to her husband. She would feel betrayed."

"Hey, what are you two talking about?" Esperanza asked.

"Oh, we were just talking about going to the Rose Garden. Weren't we, Mariah?"

"Uh-huh."

* * *

Eve and Mariah strolled in front, arm in arm. Heather, Esperanza, and Fiona walked behind kicking rocks, bending to smell the fragrance of the heirloom roses, and talking about old times. The fountains sparkled. The Garden felt smaller, but it was still enchanting. Mariah sighed. She pretended her father was waiting for her, checking the clock for her return, the lamplights muted in the darkened night. She could snuggle next him while he read and wait for him to tell a story—their people's stories. She could smell his body, the way it made her feel like home was the only place that mattered on earth. She would give anything to feel safe again. He had always tethered her to the world in which she lived. Mariah hiccupped a sob. Eve held her arm a little tighter.

Fiona came up behind them. "Wait, guys. I have to pee."

"What? The restrooms are closed."

"There's always the trees." Fiona giggled as she ran toward the backside of the restrooms.

Eve watched her. "That girl can piss like a racehorse."

Mariah looked up at the moonlight. She could swear she saw two topaz eyes watching her from the street above. Dropping Eve's arm, she moved toward them.

"Where are you going?" Esperanza asked.

"I see my owl."

Heather smiled. "Well, don't go far. We need to stay together."

"I won't."

Mariah walked toward the eyes. They moved. She called her dad's name. A hoot answered. She approached more quickly.

She was seized with a sense of loss. She could not bear to lose sight of him.

He had wings. She had legs. She heard the rustle of feathers and lost the topaz eyes. She grabbed the air. The orbs opened again a short distance away.

She moved to the north to intercept him. She hooted. He answered.

He rustled his plumage.

Mariah stopped. Paralyzed, she listened. She could not lose him again.

She hooted.

The orbs closed and opened. The head peered sideways.

Something rustled in the piney down undergrowth.

That's when she saw them.

Brandon and Fiona.

He had her in a full embrace, the kiss passionate.

Fiona kissed him back.

Mariah ran.

6 Esperanza

Sometimes, God gives you a warning. Sometimes, you don't know it until later. Later, when the dust settles and you realize there were signs. Little things, like an owl perched precariously close to your window or hearing first thing in the morning about a robbery at the convenience store you were at last night. Or a phone call bearing bad news. The event touches you, but you barely note that your face is prickling and your stomach is churning. The day continues. You prepare breakfast for your family. You use the same pans. The sun drifts through your window the same as it did yesterday and the day before. The dishes clink. You gather your loved ones and shuttle them to school. But these normal things are no longer so ordinary. Or perhaps they are. They morph into banality in the face of rising change. Something has shifted. The mirror of your life has begun to shatter and the pieces crunch under your feet. The next piece falls, and by day's end those pieces have been strewn under your feet and crushed into a million bits of glass dust and you cannot go back to that moment you first got the sign of a warning. You must stand and respect the danger. *El respeto.*

"He is dead. I thought you would want to know," my sister said. She had read it in the newspaper in Mexico, where she now lived.

The words followed me that morning. He was the great love of my life. I think of that cave where my heart was first opened and broken, and realize I have been unable to reconcile my life now to all the possibilities I had let go in my heartbreak. So much of what happened that year has been packed away into a carefully curated amnesia. How else does one survive? The light so long ago extinguished floods back into the interior and illuminates the stage of my memory like a tragic operetta.

I miss the first traffic light.

"Mom! What are you doing? You ran a red light. Geez." Carlos, my oldest, has no patience for me. I am on a tight leash these days.

"*Lo siento*. I am sorry."

I focus, but my mind returns to that memory, a floodgate to all the others. He is not dead there. The words of this morning are alien. My memory cannot be false. No. The image is real. As real as the deep reflecting pool at the bottom of the cenote—a sinkhole and portal to a magical underworld.

"Mom. What's up?" Carlos yells. "You just passed school."

"Mom. You have to turn around." Izzy, my dreamer and second born, softens the tone.

"*Lo siento. Lo siento.* I don't know where my mind is this morning."

"Well, it isn't where it's supposed to be." Carlos scowls into the rearview mirror.

"I'm sorry, buddy."

Shaking his head, he grabs his backpack and climbs from the car.

"It's all right, Mom. He'll get over it." Izzy's smile is conciliatory.

"Thanks, my angel. Have a good day."

"Thanks, Mom."

Izzy closes the door. I look at my youngest, Angelica, in the rearview mirror. She smiles. My little miracle child, born late in my life, reminds me of the power of love. It is love that gives meaning to all. It gives meaning when all is else is laid to waste. I have to remind myself of this. Sometimes, the gift of love seems to lose its force in the light of everyday life. It is easy to wish for more when everything seems to be always the same. Monotony screams for excitement, but I know the allure of more is an empty illusion. It is a chase for a promise that cannot deliver. The clear turquoise of the cenote is also the chilled black waters of an earthbound abyss.

I had only just survived a night alone in the woods during one of our crazy teenage schemes when my parents whisked me off to the Yucatan. They imagined they could break the hold my friends had over me, but I was not under a spell. We fit because we did not fit. Misfits, we found an understanding in our differences. In my family, we did not speak of being Cuban in a Chicano world any more than we did not speak of being mulatto in a Cuban world. As if Mexican Americans could understand a Cuban or a black could understand a mulatto. My blood was tainted and my pigment was wrong. Mariah was right. The world of the mixed blood is no man's land.

But I did not complain too much. The Yucatan was a balm to my chilled soul. I couldn't save Heather any more than the others could. Even then she lay in a coma in a sterile Sunny Hollow hospital, tended to by her abuser. My father did not want to hear about it, but Mimi was a kindred spirit and she comforted me.

"Why don't you go to the cenote or the ocean, my darling?" Mimi loved the enigmatic force of the clear, dark pools as much as the angry power of the seas. Yemaya, the deity of the sea, is the great universal mother. She is the embodiment of motherly love but she is also wrathful. There were always two sides to everything. I was always sure of my mother's love and I was sure of the line at which I could incur her anger. Life was like that. I had embarked on an adventure with my friends on a day I had imagined chasing clouds and rainbows, tiny wisps of cumulus cotton candy and cirrus tendrils soaring far in to the heavens. I was still an innocent. But clouds are the bearers of deeper meaning, vapors of shape-shifting water, tears tucked deep within the cumulonimbus that pile up into thunderheads to release fire and ice upon those below who do not have the good sense to seek cover.

Basking in the sun, swimming in the warm waters of the Caribbean, and exploring Mayan ruins had made me hungry for life. The restaurants and markets spewed the smells of Tikin Xic, white fish marinated in adobo de Achiote and bitter oranges wrapped in a banana leaf and the zest of sopa de lima, lime-marinated turkey dressed with sizzling tortilla strips. And always chocolate, the elixir of the gods made from the toasted fermented seeds of the cacao tree mixed with the heady scent of vanilla, made from an orchid only grown wild in Mexico and pollinated by the stingless bee that produces Mayan honey. The mix of scents of burning wood, citrus, corn, chocolate, vanilla, and spices flourished with the sights of bright colors of huipil and the dyes of exotic flora. The sun tanned me a brown I could not know even in California. I wanted to slough my garments and catch only those things sensory upon my skin. But still I hunted the cenote. The keeper of secrets hid. Finally, Gabriel took me.

It is impossible to think about my life without remembering that moment I saw him. Sometimes, there are times that just take your breath away. It is impossible in those moments to find words. Language, in all its power, fails. My skin tingled and fire burned in my thighs. I tried to hide it, but how does one extinguish an inferno? Transformation becomes an imperative. This I should have known, but Mariah is the prescient one and she was back in Sunny Hollow even now, packing for her trip to the reservation. It is one thing to be naked and it is another to be without those who help guide you through the maze of feelings.

The cenote and Gabriel were waiting. My father was easy, but mother knew. Maybe not specifics. I told them I was meeting some other Americans to go swimming. Gabriel waited on his moped at the outskirts of the village.

The cenote was hidden, a sacred pool of unearthly peace. It was not so much that I stepped back in time, although a part of me felt tied to something ancestral—it was more that I had stepped into an altered place, a shift in reality. The ancient stain of human sacrifice could not alter its essence, the wounds of suffering would find healing.

Gabriel dropped his clothes and leapt into the stillness of the clear turquoise water. I watched him with forbidden curiosity, like when you pass an accident and know you should look away but can't because there is some force far greater than you demanding that you know this thing and find some understanding.

Naked, he was like nothing I had ever seen. I leaned against a rock. My breath shallow, my hands shook as I peeled off my clothes.

The cenote was partially concealed by the land that had not collapsed and had formed a roof over the water, but the other half was fully accessible and light. Part mystery and part truth, it enticed me. Stalactites formed a forest. The afternoon sun filtered through the trees and created a ray in the ceiling that illuminated Gabriel as he swam. God was there. I remember crossing myself. Something that beautiful and truthful, something this close to God, had to be sacred, had to be right.

I shed my undergarments and ran over the lip of the cenote. The water was warm and refreshing. It cleared my head, but did little to soften the tingling in my body. Gabriel emerged from the shadows and swam toward me, his limbs brown and lithe under the cover of water. He entreated me, but I was warm and safe huddled against the ledge. I was not yet ready to enter the heart of the cenote, where nothing but open air and sunshine reigned. There was a boldness I did not have even though I wanted what terrified me.

He smiled as he reached me. His smile intoxicated me. He embraced me and I let him. His eyes were dark, and as mysterious as the beckoning cave. I was in dangerous territory and I could not pull away, could not find the strength to disentangle myself and lift myself from the pool in which I was losing myself. He touched his lips to mine, gently at first. The fire spread quickly and devoured restraint as it consumed me. The kiss was tender and passionate. We separated and swam toward the ledge hidden within the stalactites.

It was there, deep within, on the cool altar of fossilized coral and limestone, that I lost my virginity. In the passion of the moment he plunged into me over and over, pain and joy matched thrust by thrust. I wanted to scream, but the noise was unbidden in this sacred space. I dared not destroy it. My heart exploded in my ears before peace descended and the cool water dripped from the roof into the liquid womb.

Perched over me, skin on skin, soul in soul, Gabriel's eyes reflected an abiding emotion. Was it love? Or was it something else? I wanted to drown in it, claim it, but it tortured me, too. He straddled me and slid into the water. Disappeared. I found the solitude remarkable. Alone, I was separate from the world and more a part of it than I had ever been. By the time he resurfaced, I was a part of something greater, a feeling new and equally ancient. I had felt flashes of it when the roses glistened in the garden or when the butterflies danced in the summer air. Love was new and as eternal as the water that ran deep within the ground. I had only to enter its abyss.

I splashed into the water, plunged to the sandy bottom, and surfaced where Gabriel waited. We swam, but it did not take long before we were perched again on the ledge. I wanted to explore the contours of his body, the softness of his skin, the feel of someone outside of me but now a part of me. I did not want the day to end. The air clung to us and time could not penetrate the veil around us. By the time I returned to the hotel, the sun had set.

"Where have you been?" My mother's eyes were wild.

"Um, I was down the beach with those Americans I told you about." Shame and guilt began to kill the peace within me, but my love was safe.

"Don't lie to me. Your father went looking for you. He couldn't find you."

"Um, where did he look?"

"He went way down the beach."

I stood like a pigeon, willing my legs to hold me up, not betray me. I have always been a horrible liar. Even if I had been a good one, my mother would have known. She always knew. A hush had quieted the lobby and everyone's eyes were upon us—a mother and her errant daughter. Could they see through me? My legs ached and mosquito bites raised little welts. Tiny creatures buzzed around my ears and I swatted at their invisible force.

"I was there. I bet he just didn't go far enough."

"He went very far. He was very upset and very worried. You can't just wander off like you did back home."

"I know. I didn't. He just didn't see me for some reason." The worst part about being in love and lying is the sense of betraying the universe. My legs could not hold the weight of it all. "I'm sorry, Mimi. It won't happen again."

"Do not think for one minute that I do not understand what is happening to you, love, but your father has had enough. He is taking us back home."

"No. You can't."

"Your father has to go back to work soon anyway. He doesn't have unlimited vacation. He would like to enjoy some of what is left of it back home. In peace. You have caused him much anxiety. Your brother and sisters want to be with their friends. And perhaps you would like to be with yours?"

"But I don't want to go." It was impossible. I had just discovered the most special and wonderful person on earth. I would rather die than leave him. I needed to be with him forever. I would rather hurl myself from the highest cliff or dash in front of a speeding car than live without him. If I found him tonight, we could run away together and live in the jungle.

"Of course I want to see my friends. I'll be with them all next year.

I'm not ready to leave Mexico yet." It was as rational and unemotional as I could muster.

Mimi's eyes softened. Hers was an enduring and complex love I had always known and never completely understood. The paradox of my mother made me crazy. I wanted to run away from her, but I would never be able to survive disappointing her or my father. What was there to do? How could I endure this in silence? I was not Juliet and Mimi was not Lady Capulet. Poison was off the table.

"It is time to go home, Esperanza."

"No, I can't."

"*Lo siento. Te quiero.* I want only the best for you. You know this, *sí?*"

"Sí, Mimi."

"We are leaving in the morning."

"In the morning? But how?"

"Your father made all the arrangements."

She shifted into a haze behind my tears. They fell hard and fast. "There's something I need to do."

"It must be quick. Long good-byes make it more difficult to leave."

"But I need a little bit of time."

"You have a little bit of time. But you must come to dinner now. Your father has been waiting and he deserves an explanation. Afterwards, you may have a little bit of time."

The finality of it overwhelmed me.

I pushed my food around on my plate under my father's watchful eye. I would never be able to eat again. Surely it is impossible for the heart to withstand such breaking. Surely I would die of starvation.

Blessedly, Mimi held Father's attention and he did not ask too many questions of me. But I did not know how to find Gabriel and he would not be in to work until the next morning. A glimmer of hope rested in the thought that he might have a plan. And I would run with him, no matter what, if he asked. We could live off the land.

We could nourish each other. We could be our own world together. I would miss my parents, my brother and sisters, my friends, but I would do it all for him. He could sustain me through my loss and I could be a world to him. If only tomorrow came quickly.

"Esperanza?"

"Sí, Mimi."

"You may be excused. I can tell you're not hungry. You need to pack and say good-bye to the friends you have made here."

"*Gracias.*"

I headed to the front desk. "Do you know how to contact Gabriel?"

"He lives in the next town over. He will not be in until tomorrow morning."

"Do you have the address?"

"No. But he will be in tomorrow."

"Do you know what time?"

We were leaving at 8 a.m. It would be close.

"He comes in at 10 a.m."

"Oh." It was hopeless. There was no way our love could be hopeless, but the universe was not being kind at this moment.

Tears began anew. "Will you give him a note?"

"Sí."

"Do you have a pen and piece of paper?"

"Sí."

I could not begin to tell him how I felt, so instead I wrote a quick note that included my address. I begged him to write me. How does one save an all-consuming love with the stroke of a mere pen? I folded the note and handed it to the hotel employee. "*Gracias.*"

"You're welcome."

Back in my room, I shoved everything into my suitcase. Who cared about the stupid clothes? What was clothing but a lie? They could not hide my broken heart. I could not sleep. The sweat tormented, the mosquitoes did not relent, and the memories of his touch burned into my flesh like a branding iron. My legs throbbed. By the break of dawn, I was broken, but the world would never be the wiser. I still looked like Esperanza. But that was the thing about a broken heart—it was only broken for you. The world would never treat you differently, even though you were different.

But that had only been the beginning of the storm. The eye was the calm that hid the destroying energy of the backside. The worst of it had waited for my return to Sunny Hollow. It had waited for all of us.

I could not believe I was reliving it. Gabriel was gone. *Muerto.* Dead. And my heart was breaking all over again.

"Mommy, look out."

Just like that I was pulled back. It was just enough time to see my folly. *Please, God. Take me, but leave my beautiful Angelica unharmed. Please pray for us and stay here, Blessed Mother.* When the car hit I saw a flash of white, felt the bones in my chest crush, and heard the screams of my daughter. And then it went dark.

7 Fiona

I slip into my pink satin bathrobe and wrap it tight before cinching the sash. I do not mind the view in the mirror, but it might be time to get a new color. I descend gracefully and admire my reflection in the mirrored grand staircase. I am California nobility, after all. After all these years of marriage to Gavin, it is sometimes easy to forget that he is the plastic surgeon to the royalty of Los Angeles. He has tweaked the natural aging process from some of the most notable faces of Hollywood, including my own. It is up to me to enhance his image—it is necessary amongst the ever-watching glitterati. They wait for every fault and applaud the fall. This is a role to which I was born, even if I did not always appreciate it in my youth.

As a child, my beauty was an everyday emphasis. My mother dragged me to every beauty contest within a hundred miles, and sometimes even beyond. I won more crowns than I could find a shelf for, and Mom proclaimed my right to grace the cover of every fashion magazine, dismissing those who actually did as being plain and displeasing. I never minded. Mom and Dad gave me everything I asked for and it was a small price to make up for letting my little brother, Rory, die. Still, at times the pressure of keeping up my looks was more burden than blessing and it made me the center of every drama. And there was always drama. My sisters hated me. I never knew if their malice was the reason they blamed me for Rory's death or if they just flat-out thought I meant for him to die. After all, he was first in my parents' eyes. He was the namesake and there never was another. But my sisters hated me for being beautiful. It was not my fault they were born plain.

I find a stash of my vodka nips at the bottom of the stairs, tucked under a secret compartment behind a loose piece of carpeting. I empty them, then tuck each one into separate pockets.

"Mom, I need new shoes for the dance Friday night. I want to hit Rodeo after school." Samantha, my eldest, slides down the rest of the stair rail and lands at my feet.

I quickly wipe my mouth. "Sam, you're going to fall sometime and your surfing days will be over."

"What's the diff between hanging a wave and a stair rail? It's all in the moves." Sam flexes her arms to simulate balancing on a board.

"I see. Well, I have a luncheon today, but I'm free in the afternoon. Your sister and brother have to come with us. Abella needs to get ready for the party on Saturday. God help me."

"Geez, Mom. You're totally weirded out by the strangest things. What's the big deal about a party?"

"We're not discussing the issue."

"Why not? And anyway, Molly and Sean can come if they don't bother me and if they don't act like total dweeb losers! Besides, they're old enough to stay home alone."

"I can't guarantee your brother and sister will be angels any more than I can guarantee you'll be one. And they're not quite old enough. You'll just have to deal."

"*Mom*! That's so not cool!"

Sam heads to the kitchen. "Abella! Abella!" The door swings in and out, muffling their voices. I hate the way Sam leaves me standing in the middle of the foyer, discarded like a pair of old worn shoes. I know what she's going to say before she says it.

"Why can't you watch Molly and Sean this afternoon so Mom can take me shopping, *por favor*?"

"I can't," Abella says. "I have to go to the market. I have very much to do. This party means a lot to your parents."

"You mean my dad. Mom hates to do anything on a Saturday night except drink a few cocktails, call her girlfriends, and cry. It's not like any of us actually exist."

My nerves prickle and little stabs of heat flame in my cheeks as I cross the foyer to the kitchen. This child is testing me.

"That's enough, Sam. Don't bother Abella. You have plenty of shoes. You don't know how I feel. I do everything to protect you." The deep scar on my shoulder tingles. It is the one flaw Gavin can do nothing about, and it is the one thing that reminds me of the past.

"God, Mom. You act like the world is coming to a frickin' end. Dad can't figure you out. You're not protecting me from anything. You're scarring me."

"How dare you! How your dad and I deal with this is none of your business."

"I'm your daughter, Mom. Whose business is it if it's not mine? It affects our family, but you act like we're not even a part of your life. You just bury yourself in your own little world. You talk to your friends who you only see once a year, but you won't talk to the people you're with every day. Why don't you try talking to me, Mom?"

"You're too young to understand."

"I'm fifteen, Mom. Wake up and smell the coffee and get over yourself." She slides her Louis Vuitton book sack from the counter and heads for the door. Pushing through, the door swings in on her and knocks her back. "God! What is your problem?"

Molly looks stunned. "I'm sorry. I didn't know you were there."

"Yeah, I know you're sorry, loser."

Poor Molly. I smudge her hair—little comfort, I know, but I follow Sam anyway. I can't let her get away without settling this. Whatever this is. I do not even know my own daughter anymore.

"You can forget shopping this afternoon, Sam. I won't have you treating your sister this way."

"Whatever!"

"You can wear an old pair of Marc Jacobs, or Chanels, or Jimmy Choos, or whatever the hell else you have. Do you hear me? That's half the problem, you have too much!" Now I sound like my mother. Next I'll be looking for the little people who spirited my offspring away. I am suddenly aware that I am standing in the doorway, in my bathrobe, yelling at my wayward daughter. I tighten the loosening garment, but there is no reining in my daughter. Maybe she has been stolen away and a substitute put in her place. A changeling. I finger the little gold fairy around my neck, but it does not comfort me or give me any answers.

"And whose fault is that, Mother?" The last word leaves a sharp imprint on my fast-reddening cheeks. Sam clears the gate and heads toward school, the top of her golden head barely clearing the spires of the wrought iron fence.

I retreat behind the massive paneled front door. I lean my hot cheeks against the cool wood and the door warms where my cheek rests. Could something so dead gain life through one's touch? Mariah does not believe there is absolute death. But then Dad never did either. Come to think of it, neither do Espy or Eve.

"Are you all right, Mommy?" Molly's voice caresses my back.

"I'm fine." I wipe away a tear. "What shall we have for breakfast? Daddy is driving you to school and I'm driving Sean. How does that sound?"

"Awesome!"

* * *

With Sam out of the house for the remainder of the morning, I gather my composure. Liquid courage and Valium calm my raw nerves. I waited to have children until later in life. It was important to maintain my figure, but also I had never been sure if I would be up to the task of motherhood. It is a question that continues to bedevil me. Unlike Esperanza, I am screwing up the whole parenting thing. Even Heather is better at it than I am, and she is holding down a full-time job.

I follow Sean to the car. Somehow he has grown tall and lean. Perhaps he too is a substitute, but that would not make sense. Substitutes are always smaller and withering. Of course, I could not blame the universe for doing so. After all, it is small payment for allowing Rory to drown. Or for all the other things. I am a sinner extraordinaire. But Sean is mine. He is thriving. Will he too change and become disillusioned with me? Will he someday see me for whom I really am? "Poser" is the word he uses for such people.

I retrieve another pill from my purse and swallow it whole, without water. How many is that? I am supposed to be keeping count.

"Hey, buddy, do you think I get weepy a lot?"

"Yeah, a little. But that's okay, Mom, I guess getting sad over a secret isn't any worse than getting sad over a stupid reality show like Tommy's mom. Now, that's twisted, dawg." He purses his lips, shakes his head like a bobble doll, and plants his hands under his armpits. I am becoming used to this new body language and street talk from my youngest. As familiar as it seems, it never feels right.

"Please don't call me dawg, Sean. You're not from the 'hood."

"Yeah, but Eve is and she's righteous."

"Yes, she's righteous but she isn't from the 'hood either. She lived in the same town as I did. It was far too privileged to be confused with the 'hood."

"But she's poor now."

"Eve chooses to be poor because she chooses to help people." I have never known the cold reality of scarcity, and my own bitterness, apparent even to me, perplexes me. Maybe I have been listening to Eve and Mariah's prattling about all the ills of the world after all.

There could be hope for me yet. I snort and it surprises me. There is nothing regal or graceful about the sound.

Sean scrunches his nose and giggles. I reach over to ruffle his hair, but he dodges the gesture.

"Is she happy, Mom?"

"Eve is very happy, but even she gets sad like I do." The sun, harsh and demanding, streams through the palm trees and sparkle-dances along the hood of the car.

"Will she visit us again before she goes back to Africa?"

"I don't know, sweetheart. It's doubtful."

We pull up in line in front of Sean's immaculately groomed school. The bright flowers and perfectly pruned palm trees are a stark contrast to my emotions. All the beauty and perfection in the world cannot camouflage the corrupted soul. I find myself snorting again. I am losing it today.

Sean looks at me with questions playing in his eyes. "I wish she would, Mom."

"Yeah. Me too."

Sean shuts the door to the Bentley and, just like that, I am alone.

I shift the car into gear and head to the gym. Sleek modern furniture and fixtures glisten through the tall windows. I stare at my reflection through the automatic glass doors. My legs are well-toned and tan enough, I sport a perfect manicure and pedicure, my body is sleek, my hair is thick and still blond, and any imperfections that crop up over time, well, Gavin will tweak them before anyone is the wiser. No matter what, I will attend to the illusion.

I perform my workout and finish. Stopping at the bar to buy a protein smoothie, I pay, exchange some chit-chat and pleasantries with a couple of acquaintances, and hurry to the car. I have the whole routine down pat. My sandals click on the gleaming marble floor, but I can easily put something on the bottom of my shoes to address that problem.

I drive the distance from the gym to home without noting a single detail of the world around my Bentley cocoon. If I don't see them, they can't see me.

Abella has left to run errands, and I am alone within the ominous stillness of the great house. Then the trilling of the phone reverberates around the walls. I hurry to answer before it has a chance to ring again.

"Hello."

"Hi, Fiona."

I lift the crystal top from the decanter and pour a shot of vodka into the remnants of my protein smoothie. I'll be able to handle whatever is coming my way much better with that fortification. "Mariah? Thank God."

"Why do you say that? What's wrong?"

"Nothing. It just seems everything is a problem these days. Gavin wants a party on Saturday."

"Yeah. I know how much you hate Saturdays. I'm sorry, but you'll get through it. Listen, I'm not sure how the Charleston thing is going to go down. Heather is pretty upset. I think she might be cracking."

"God. That was so long ago. Why would she think he's come back? This just doesn't make any sense."

"I know. I won't go into detail, but Eve and I are worried. She knows what she saw. What she experienced. Either way, it was real to her. And I believe he's back. I feel it. We have to help her. We were all there."

"Us? What can we do?"

"We need to find out where he is."

"But you have all the research and journalistic skills, and you've always been able to get whatever information you need. And you always get yourself out of trouble. I remember when you were held at gunpoint in Beirut and you talked your way out of it. You're amazing."

"What are you saying?"

"It just makes more sense for *you* to find him. Besides, if Heather's cracking, I'm the last one to help."

"Why do you say that?"

"Because. I'm not much better." I cringe as the words leave my mouth, but they are out before I can do anything about it.

"Yes, you are. Listen, I was hoping you would look into where he could be right now. If he's in Connecticut. Eve is struggling with Jerome and I have a prickly situation going on at work. I haven't been able to get in touch with Espy yet and I just thought you and Gavin might have some contacts in Connecticut. I need your help, Fiona."

"What prickly situation at work?"

"Oh, it's nothing to worry about. I'm doing some exposés on some water issues and I seem to have pissed off some big—"

The phone clicks and I miss the last part of her sentence. "Mariah?"

"Yeah."

"That was weird. I missed the last part of what you said."

"It doesn't matter. It's not important. We'll sort it all out in Charleston. We need to find this guy . . . together. In the meantime, I need you to help."

"But I can't." Gavin wouldn't understand. He doesn't know anything about my past, not really—just bits and pieces. Not the sum total, and certainly not the heart of it.

I need another drink. God, my life is a mess. I stroke the fairy amulet but it only makes me feel worse. It is as if it is coming alive. I have angered it. Why else would I feel this way?

"Yes, you can. I need your help, Fiona. Heather needs your help. I have to go now, but please try. We're all Heather has. We're all she's ever had."

"What about Brandon?"

"I don't know. She thinks he's part of it."

"What?"

"I don't know and I can't get there right now, but I don't think he's going to help her. It's just us."

Hiding my head in my hands doesn't help. Brandon! The thought of him makes me cringe. The world is just outside my fingertips. A black, bottomless pit stretches before my covered eyes and tiny white lights spread from the middle to the very edges. I am sinking into the black hole, its existence inferred by the tiny stars circling at the center. "Okay. I'll do my best."

"Thank you. I'll see you when we get to Charleston."

"*Maka Manana.*" I hear the click of the receiver.

Fuck! It would be so much easier if my friends believed, like everyone else, that I am a selfish and uncaring bitch. I walk to the bar, retrieve a cocktail glass, pour in two ounces of vodka, and empty it. The liquid warms me and fills out, softening my fired-up nerve endings. This is the first time I have not wanted to see my friends. The trip is more an obligation than pleasure, and the thought saddens me. I do not want to face my life anymore. There is no happiness, just a lot of expectations. How will I get through the party Saturday night?

I pour two more ounces into my glass and turn back toward the foyer. A black shadow appears and vanishes towards the stairs.

"Who's there?"

Silence. I empty the glass and tiptoe toward the shadow. I peer around the corner, but the bright stairwell is empty. Rich bone and floral tapestry carpet laid over white marble winds its way to the upper floor, where closed doors hide all the untidiness of family life. Stranded on the round marble foyer table that is anchored to the middle of the expansive entrance hall lies my calendar. The pages are turned to Saturday. Saturday is the day our teenage world fell apart. And Saturday is the day my brother died. Funny, I had never noticed. They all occurred on the same exact date. The same date as this Saturday. A perfect trinity.

I collapse onto the edge of the first step. I'm fucked. Why can't everything just go away?

8 Heather

In a faraway land, in a dream world, a noise beckons me. I do not open my eyes. The light hovers at the frontier of my consciousness, but I am a leaden vessel in that river through the hinterlands. How can I leave? It is safe and warm here and no harm can come to me. This I know in my heart as much as my head. But the noise persists, wheedles and cajoles, and finally wins.

Brandon's alarm screams.

I grab it, stumble to the window, lift the screen, and spike it to the concrete patio below. The sound of shattering glass, hardware, and an alarm stricken mid-scream momentarily silences the birds, but the quiet is brief and the anticipated satisfaction is reduced in proportion to my rising horror. Brandon is going to annihilate me. I am toast.

I lower the screen and shut the window.

Why do I think that? He has never hurt me. Not physically, at least. I can never put words to this fear. Come on. It has to happen at some point, doesn't it? Lately he has been looking at me strangely. Like how? Like my mother. Like he wants to kill me. Maybe he will never hit me. He will just kill me and I will never see it coming. Like I said—toast.

I wash the sleep from my body but the shower is not comforting. It is unsettling, in fact, like all the thoughts that keep popping up inside my head. I dry off, put on my corporate outfit, and squirm into my high heels. The reflection in the mirror mocks me, the deep circles under my eyes remind me of Morticia. But no. Her eyes were . . . exotic. My eyes are small and heavy. There is nothing mysterious about me. I'm a walking zombie. I twitch like the walking dead for the mirror. At least I think it's funny. I think again of the screaming alarm and its death. That makes me smile, too. C'mon. Brandon will hardly kill me over a broken alarm clock. No. It has to be something bigger than that. I'm worth more than a clock. Only the invisible are totally worthless. Right?

I lift the hem of my skirt and admire my latest work. It has been years since I cut myself, since I inscribed myself, but lately I have craved the release. *Equivocate.* It took me a long time. The blood slowed me down—each drop evidentiary proof of my existence.

I meet Shannon on the landing halfway down the stairs.

"Mommy, can I have a popsicle?"

"No. Mommy will get you some cereal. You can have a popsicle tonight."

"I need it now, for Daddy, or he's gonna cry."

"Daddy's already gone to work. Where are your socks and shoes? Please get them."

"Why?"

"Because we need to get ready and it's just you and me. Daddy's gone."

"No, he's not." Shannon gives me that little defiant pretend-grown-up thing she has been doing lately.

"What do you mean? He is too. Now get your socks and shoes."

"I don't wanna go to daycare. I don't want you to go to work. I want you to stay."

"Don't you want to see your friends?"

Shannon purses her lips and shakes her head. I wish I could shake it like that. I would probably hurt myself. I try anyway. Shannon giggles. I pick her up and kiss her cheek. She smells like a field of wildflowers after a spring drizzle. I linger and she begins to squirm.

I put her down and she runs off laughing. I wish I had more time to give her, to fix something less mundane than cereal, to revel in the unplanned day, to build another dragon.

She reappears at the top of the stairs and peers down, socks dangling from her hands. Strands of delicate hair frame her face. Large, luminous blue eyes reflect back far more wisdom than her few short years. God made the children of all creatures angelic and beautiful to protect them from the brutality of their grown-up versions, but nothing can absolutely prevent the potential for violence. Morsels of evil bleed through. Experience always proves the point. I am her last defense against the world.

I hold out my arms. Shannon leaps without fear into my embrace. I carry her down the stairs.

The muted click of a closing door stops me in my tracks. The house is quiet. Brandon? Could he still be home? Was Shannon telling the truth? My heart pumps a mile a minute. No. He would have said something. Wouldn't he? Or could it have been someone else?

The kitchen smells of coffee. Maybe Brandon came back for something and left just as quickly to beat the traffic. It must be that. Shannon climbs into her chair while I pour her a bowl of her favorite cereal. She hums and does not seem to think anything is out of the ordinary. But then, what would a little girl know about the ordinary? My mind drifts to work.

I have to track down the particulars of an ex-employee who filed a claim of discrimination and sexual harassment. Of all the dreaded tasks of the day, this one is the most. The company officials involved are my boss, his boss, and the chief financial officer, all of whom could and probably will make my life unpleasant. Typical. It only takes one man to transgress and the rest to follow in the cover-up. I have seen it a dozen times. A woman, on the other hand, would connive on her own, without pulling everyone else into her sordid mess. But if I want to protect the company, I have to do my job no matter how many people I piss off and no matter how many times I am threatened with losing my job. Only I need my job. Hence the need for diplomacy.

I turn to open the refrigerator and stumble over Shannon.

"But I don't want milk on my cereal."

"Since when?"

"Since fowever."

"Well, you don't have to have milk on your cereal."

"Well, I changed my mind. I want milk."

"Okay then." I retrieve the carton.

I lift her into her chair and ruffle her hair.

"No, you can't touch my hair that way." Shannon shakes her head to remove my touch. "Daddy's going to make me a piggy tail after daycare."

"I can make you a piggy tail."

"No. Daddy makes better ones."

"How do you know?"

"Cuz I said so."

"Oh, I see. Well, I just love you so much."

"I love you too, Mommy."

Shannon spoons the cereal into her mouth. I wipe a lone pearl of translucent milk that slips from her tiny, upturned mouth. She is growing up. I wonder at all the things I have been doing to miss this moment of independence. I cannot remember specifics, but they had to have been of great import, right? Or were they just the minutiae of a life driven by work?

Work? It is the pull on the personal moments that other people catalogue in their journals, celebrate in their scrapbooking groups, recognize in their photo albums. Moments slip from history before I even notice their passing, ephemeral and impermanent threads of my life. There are no pictures to prove their existence. Striving and toiling are my proof of life, my validation to my dead parents and the greater world, that I am worthy. Without such affirmation, I would exist only invisibly. Perhaps there are no pictures because I truly am invisible.

I duck as a bowl bearing the remnants of cereal-scented milk spirals past my head. The white liquid splatters on the cabinets, the floor, and my suit. The sweet, pungent odor saturates my clothing. Damn it! Paying the consequences again for not paying attention. I will never learn.

Shannon wails and I wipe the tears from her eyes. "It's okay, sweetie. I'm sorry. Were you trying to get my attention?"

"Yeah."

"What did you want?"

"I don't want my cereal anymore."

"Okay. " I lift her and kiss her heated forehead. Shannon wipes under her eyes and trots off to retrieve her toys. I scrub the stain with the dishcloth but it only makes it worse. Maybe the smudge will disappear if it dries.

I scoop up Shannon and head to the car. I push the button to the garage door opener, turn the key in the ignition, adjust the rearview mirror, double-check Shannon in the mirror, slide the gear into reverse, and back out into the day.

* * *

I arrive at my office at 7:59 a.m. My energy is already gone. It is all downhill from here. I need coffee.

Voices from the coffee cubby are clearer as I approach.

"She's such a cold fish."

"I don't see what her husband sees in her. Have you seen him? They just don't belong together."

I enter the cubby. Two women eye me nervously before they drift back to their desks. Are they talking about me? They don't even know me. But I know them. They are the same type of people who can sit next to an abused child and, turning away, pretend the bruises are just a little funky coloring. The illusion of ignorance makes life more comfortable. And everyone wants to be comfortable. I grew up with people like that. I walk amongst them but they cannot make me disappear.

And I know how to live amongst them. I just do not know how to make them friends. Yet working within the corporate environment requires it. I am reminded of that at every performance review. I struggle to remain visible and relevant. There are times I want to give up, go home, and be Shannon's sole caregiver. But that cannot be. My career provides validation, but it also chases away the ghost of the monster inside. Could I be my mother, the taint of genetic evil waiting to be set loose? No, it is better to avoid the answer, safer for Shannon.

And it makes me more equal with Brandon. I cannot afford to be invisible in our marriage.

I pour a fresh cup of coffee. The aroma, strong and sensual, suffuses my senses and pulls me back to a time when I sat in the alcove of my parents' kitchen and listened to weekend banter, times when my mother's guard was down and she almost seemed happy. It evokes memories of those Sunday mornings when my father stirred up a frittata, his only dish, and "Moonlight Serenade" played in the background, the California sun gentle and coaxing. The muffled sound of tousled silverware in soapy dishwater added muted noise to birds chirping under the wisteria, its flowered vines hanging from the trellis guarding the kitchen door. The perfumed fragrance and the scent of protected earth mingled with the savory smell of eggs and spices. Those were the good memories. They sharpened the sting of disappointment. The difference made them more affecting. But then there were the other memories. And that is the divide. The wisteria trellis harbored black widow spiders.

"Heather, you wanted to see me?"

I swish and spill my coffee. I am covered. Again.

Sharon has found me.

"I'm so sorry, Heather. I didn't mean to startle you."

Twice in one day. Sharon is spotless, of course, and she does not have to go upstairs to the big guns. We are dissimilar. Sharon's clothes are a cotton and polyester blend, economical in appearance. They are a reflection of how she views her job. It's a job and nothing more. Her garments are taken straight from the dryer, shaken, and hung on salvaged dry cleaner hangers. I, on the other hand, make sure my clothes are professional and designed with the barest hint of avant-garde taste, just enough to exude independent thought. My hair, cut and styled regularly, appears uncontrived. I work hard for the look. My secretary is a direct reflection on me. It is like carrying a brown vinyl handbag while wearing a pair of black designer shoes. And yet here I stand with separate and competing coffee and milk stains. Somehow it just does not seem right.

"What is it?"

"You wanted to see me?"

"Yes, please come to my office."

Sharon follows. When we walk inside, I pull the door closed.

I straighten the desk blotter while I assemble my thoughts. "We're performing a confidential investigation. I'll need you to be discreet. If people ask you questions, you'll have to answer without actually telling them anything."

"I understand. But how bad is it?"

"It's bad. It involves corporate officers, including our boss, who is accused of knowing and not responding appropriately."

"What are the charges?"

"Sexual harassment and discrimination based on sex and race. I don't need to tell you how this could turn out for both of us. In some ways, we're in deeper trouble than they are."

"Do the charges appear credible? Should I be looking for another job?"

"That would be premature. I know very little about the complainant. I do, however, have verification from the Equal Employment Opportunity Commission that she has been able to establish a very solid prima facie case. I have to go forward with collecting evidence, but let's assume for now that she's just a disgruntled ex-employee. I don't want to jump to any conclusions. I assume it's nothing, but if it turns out to be something, I'll keep you posted." I glance at the door. "You'd better return to work. Someone will question why we're behind closed doors. There are way too many eyes and ears around, and everyone is still gun-shy from all the talk of layoffs. I don't want to be the cause of rumors."

Things just seem to be spiraling out of control; I cannot keep my mind pinned to the tasks at hand. I need to keep this time bomb under wraps for everyone's sake. The weight cripples me, and yet still my mind wanders like an exile. The Charleston trip is less than a week away, and life is more complicated than ever. There are rumors of more layoffs, a politically dangerous investigation to be resolved, an audit in the Dallas division that has turned nasty with a government bureaucrat who has to be reminded of his own rules and procedures, and none of that takes into account my family life. There is still the little pesky problem of Brandon and an unwanted visitor.

I check my briefcase but my scheduling system is not there. I left it at home. My mental list of things to do blurs like vanishing ink. The smell of drying coffee on cloth reminds me of the stakes. It is 10:00 a.m. and the day just keeps getting worse.

I can at least start on the investigation. I head toward record keeping.

"Hello, records." The disembodied voice on the other side is muffled, but clear enough to understand.

"Hi. It's Heather Collings from Human Resources. I need some info on a former employee."

"Come in." The door buzzes.

"Hi Judy," I say when I see the person behind the speaker. "I didn't recognize your voice. There's been someone else here the last couple of times."

"That was my assistant. Her position was eliminated in the last round of terminations. You're not here to tell me mine is being terminated next, are you?"

"No. I'm sorry. I need a file."

Judy smiled. "I'm just kidding. What file do you need?"

"The name is Tanya Garrison. She's been gone about two months."

"Okay. I'll be right back."

The row of overhead lighting illuminates rows and rows of filing cabinets. Within this room, within those cabinets, lies the personal information of all employees, past and present, neatly catalogued and filed within communal chambers. That is the other side of human resources—all the human traits of the company's inhabitants eventually reveal themselves as they play out the dramas within the employment relationship. But human behavior can never be reduced entirely to a statistic. Even perceivable patterns are little more than an illusion. The human spirit always rises above and transcends such attempts at correlation. But that is a dying thought in a dying time. Soon, the files will be gone, lost to the digital age. A person will be reduced to a few blips on a screen. The gatekeeper won't have to be human. Poor Judy. Our company is just enough behind the times that she still has a job, but her days are no doubt numbered.

Judy emerges with the file in hand. "I need you to sign it out." She grabs the pen from behind her ear and I mark the name and number of the file on the ledger.

In my office, I open file number 163878. It is full of the usual. Name, address, telephone, references, social security number, number of claimed dependents for withholding purposes. It will be hard work shaking the truth from this file. The parties involved will not help, they may even hinder. I will have to solve it or I will be expendable.

I have four hours to make headway before I meet with Bob Hewitt. Charleston is becoming a pipe dream. I do not know when I will be able to break the news to my dearest friends. I have never missed one of our yearly vacations, and until now I have been unwilling to be the one to set a precedent.

But this year is different. It is more than the sum total of everything I have to do. It is this complaint, and the investigation. Something is horribly wrong. I can feel it in my bones.

My boss, Bob Hewitt, is named in the charge as being put on notice and not responding. Why didn't he pass the issue on to me, like usual? I suspect it has something to do with the fact that the Claimant accused both his boss, John Sturbridge, Vice President of Human Resources and the CFO, Michael Saxton, both residents of the sixteenth floor of discrimination. She also accused Saxton of sexual harassment.

I wash aspirin and antacids down with bottled water. What does Mariah say about bottled water? I know I am not supposed to be drinking it. Something about privatization and power and greed and human rights. I am supposed to be bringing my own bottle in—but then I just have to fill it up from bottled water in the break lounge. Mariah is an idealist. I live in the real world. I work for a real-world company that pays my real-world paycheck with real-world money. And I work in the corporate headquarters of a company that owns a division devoted to water. Life gets so complicated.

The phone interrupts my thoughts.

"Heather Collings."

"Hello. This is Angela Martin. I'm Michael Saxton's secretary. You left a message for him, but he had to leave for a business trip. He wants me to help you. I'm assuming it is about some human resources matter."

My job is to keep this confidential even if Mr. Saxton is an unco-operative pinhead. If it leaks, he will be fine and I will be jobless. It is still a man's world. The conversation will be between two women concerning the actions of a man against a woman. Such matters barely morph with the times. I do not care who tries to tell me other-wise. The sixteenth floor is still dominated by men, and they move as a pack. It is the same in Brandon's company. They have each other's backs, and the women who manage to rise to the top have to play their game by their rules. Testosterone rules, baby, and if you do not get that you will be annihilated. I am always on the edge of destruction.

"Yes, it's about an HR matter, and I'm not at liberty to divulge it to anyone except Mr. Saxton. I'm sorry, but I must speak to him directly."

"I'm afraid that's not possible."

"Please tell him I need to speak with him privately as soon as pos-sible. It is of the utmost importance."

"He was adamant. I'm supposed to take care of this."

"I'm sorry."

"All right. I'll tell him."

The hang-up is final. I open a new bottle of antacids and pop three of the fruit-flavored tablets. Drawing my sweater around me, I lay my head on my crossed arms to wait for them to take effect. I will have to figure out what is going on from someone else. I was crazy to think that Michael Saxton would talk to me. I am just some invisible HR flunky. What was I thinking? Let the jerk figure it out himself—but I need to decide what I will say to Bob.

* * *

Fire burned and sirens screamed.

His face burned. Eyes locked, he would not let me go.

I tried to run in terror, but my feet would not move. Firemen yelled at each other as the hoses, uncoiled and pulled up the length of the stairs from the street below, sprayed the burning house with torrents of water—baptism by drowning. I watched the maelstrom, my eyes shimmering and clouded. Mariah's protective arm was thrown around my shoulder, but it could not protect me from this. No one could protect me.

Bleeding, naked, terrified, I stood with her and watched the world crumble to the ground. I let myself die in that fire.

It was my shell that was washed clean in bleach. It was my shell that returned the next day to school and listened to the voices that whispered around me. The whispers hushed as it walked by. They pointed at it, but what can a shell feel? Humpty-Dumpty could not be put back together again, why was I any different? He was white and I was dark. He was smooth and I was jagged. I moved through a twilight world and no one could see me if I could not see them. I was becoming invisible. Esperanza, Fiona, Eve, and Mariah watched me, but all the love in the world could not save me from the shadows. It settled down thickly in my shell, like ash drifts from an inferno. An inferno that I lit.

And his face, peering down at me with a mixture of madness and pain, haunted me until I understood and knew that same madness and pain. God could not find me in the moonless night, but then neither could the devil.

* * *

The phone wakes me. Shit! I am late.

"Yes."

"Heather. It's Sharon. Did you forget your meeting with Mr. Hewitt?"

"No. Sorry, Sharon. Thanks. I'm leaving now."

"Okay. Do you need anything?"

"No. I'm fine. Thank you."

I gather the files but they slip. I sweep the papers into a heap. I have no answers, only the chaotic jumble of information in my hands. It is worse than the stains on my clothes. Tiny bits of grimy dirt cling to the undersides of the disordered paper.

It's clear when I walk in that Bob has been waiting. I cringe a little.

"Heather, have a seat."

He stands between his desk and the credenza that lines the window of his corner office. Tidy gardens and a park with a running path for employees creates an expansive picture. His world is larger than mine. Despite the detached look on his face, he jingles the coins in his tailored pockets. He does not know that I know he does it on purpose to throw his audience off. He is like Brandon. Their pockets are always immaculately creased, each pleat a promise of the next. But Brandon would never let someone know he wished to throw him or her off. He holds his cards closer than Bob.

"How are you coming along on the Tanya Garrison investigation?"

"Well, I've interviewed most of the people in her department and I've retrieved her personnel file. There were some rumors, but there was no verification of them. Her file is even less helpful."

"Have you spoken to Michael Saxton yet?"

"I requested an interview with him, but his schedule is . . . uncompromising. He had his secretary call me instead."

"I don't think I need to remind you of his position and the need to be as discreet and professional as possible. A lot is hinging on a good outcome."

"No. There's no need to remind me. I find it just as important for her as it is for him, if not more. We all know how these matters work to the disfavor of the woman, especially when she is in a less important position. We also know how much the courts love to make examples out of the management of large corporations."

"I didn't mean to diminish her need for your discretion. John

Sturbridge has informed me that Michael Saxton is uncomfortable meeting with you without some assurance of your . . . care in this matter. He also wishes to be ensured of a satisfactory conclusion without too much damage."

"I've been doing this type of investigation for years, Bob. May I remind you, I'm also working on the scheduled OFCCP audit in Dallas? I'm sure you remember how poorly Dallas did in our last company-initiated audit. The federal government will be less favorable in their dealings."

"Yes, I know. You've handled worse. But Saxton has been responsible for turning this company around, and the CEO and Board of Directors think highly of him. I just want to make sure that in your quest for the truth, you factor in that reality. If anything should harm his reputation, whether real or perceived, it would ultimately affect his career and this company. I don't think I need to tell you how that will affect yours."

"Are you telling me to make this go his way?"

"I'm not telling you anything except he's been earmarked for the CEO position when Charlie Woodson retires. It wouldn't be wise to unduly implicate him in this or to follow your investigation in a manner that could compromise his situation. You can draw your own damn conclusions, Heather. You're my best investigator, but I'm warning you to tread lightly. There are a lot of land mines for you and this entire department. There are people who have a lot vested in Saxton's success."

"I've worked for this company for eleven years. I've performed my duties well enough to receive excellent reviews and promotions. Are you telling me that won't matter in this case?"

"Like I said, Heather, you're my best. Remember, I've given you the majority of those reviews and promotions."

"That's my point. At no time has anyone ever made reference to a person's position in the company as a reminder of how to perform any aspect of my job. In fact, it has always been made abundantly clear that doing things right is what ensures the company's reputation will never suffer undue outside scrutiny. The truth has always been the happy by-product. Why the sudden change?"

"There is no change, Heather. Perhaps the change is in you and how you perceive things. I haven't asked you to deviate from performing your duties any differently than you have ever done in the past. I'm reminding you not to screw it up. There is no hidden message, except that the consequences won't be pretty if you do. Don't fuck this up, because no one will be able to save your ass. Do you understand?"

Shifting in my seat does not make me comfortable, nor does it hide the stains on my suit. I feel so . . . naked. "Yes," I say, "I understand. I'm sorry if I jumped to conclusions. This case has me on edge. I'm also dealing with an OFCCP Compliance Officer on the Dallas audit who insists on operating outside the rules and procedures."

"This case has everyone on edge. I'm named in it, for Christ's sake. In the case of the audit—you've handled plenty of investigators who have tried to operate beyond the scope of their duties. I haven't known an auditor who hasn't tried to flex their muscles and seek a broader interpretation It's rare they bother themselves with the intent of the law. Do your best without going to their supervisor, but if that doesn't work, pull out the stops."

"Sounds like the territorial imperative at work."

The mood lightens. I smile as dismissively as I know how. It is no more than a crack, but I am willing to pull at its edges.

"Look, Heather, you know I don't make the rules. I just try to keep this department moving within the parameters of those rules, both written and not. Right now, we're operating in a firestorm." Bob jingles the coins in his pocket as he moves around the desk. "It's not just your case. There are a million reasons why others would want to see us fall."

"I understand." I am bleeding into the chair fabric. Soon, I will be a hide-bound seat.

Bob gives me one of his full grins. It is that revelation of male charisma that allows him to move successfully through the halls of the company.

"I don't make the rules and I don't have to like them. They are what they are. I try to keep this in mind at all times. You catch my drift?"

"Yup. Thanks for the lesson in reality, boss. I'll try to keep it in mind. But what happens if the information I collect doesn't look favorable to Saxton?"

"You're letting the cart get in front of the horse. We'll have to sort that out if the time comes, but I think you should also ask yourself what will happen if it doesn't look favorable for his accuser. You'll have to hit back hard. Remember, she has the full burden of proof and he has the presumption of innocence until proven otherwise, even in the court of public opinion—in this case, that of upper management."

"You're right."

"There's nothing wrong in asking the question. It's what you do with it that matters."

"Thanks. I'll keep you informed of my progress. By the way, did you remember I'm on vacation next week?"

"No, I didn't forget. You know what you have to do and how to accomplish it. I have faith you'll succeed in time."

"Thanks."

I hurry back to my office. This day just could not get any worse. What the hell was he telling me? Lie. Take the fall. What? My visibility reminds me that I can still be obliterated. "Woman is Annihilated at Work," reads the headline.

I dial Brandon's office. I cannot imagine how he can help me. I just need him to make me feel safe.

"Brandon Collings's office."

"Oh, Martha. How are you?"

"I'm fine Mrs. Collings. How are you?"

"Fine. Is Brandon there?"

"He's been out of the office since this morning. Can I take a message?"

"No, well, just tell him I called. Was he expecting to be out all day? I don't remember him saying anything."

"I'm not sure. He just said something had come up, to take his calls, and he would be back sometime in the afternoon."

"It's already late afternoon."

"Yes, it is."

"I'll see him at home. Thank you, Martha."

"You're welcome, Mrs. Collings. Have a nice day."

To hell with Brandon, to hell with Martha, and to hell with Michael Saxton! I am in a dangerous predicament. I think of roller coasters, see myself as a whirring vision in air.

I could take Shannon to an amusement park on Saturday. I should work, but I desperately need a diversion, and it would not hurt if Brandon noticed my absence. It is maddening. I want him to care and I want to care less. Things have changed so much in our marriage, and I don't even know when it happened. It slithered up on me. I know why I married Brandon, but his reason for marrying me is still a mystery. I thought I knew, but somewhere along the line that knowledge disappeared. My work and marriage have become a reflection of everything that is wrong.

I do not have the stomach to bust loose from my life. I would not know how even if I did. I face the window. The haze of the late afternoon hangs heavily over the vegetation. The sense of oppressive heat reaches through the pane of glass and wraps itself around me. Spring has skipped southern New England and summer has settled in as if it had never left. I am stuck here, where I am a sitting pigeon. The only ones who can teach me how to climb out of this life will be in Charleston, and that trip is not looking promising. I cannot even blame it on everything I have to do. I have been avoiding life with thoughts of roller coasters and imaginary dragons.

I need to feel alive again. It has been a long time. The truth, I am not sure I even know what the feeling should be like. After all, I have never been alive any more than I have ever been visible. I lift my skirt and trace the lines of my recent wound. Equivocate.

9　Eve

I hurry home. I pray Jerome will be there. Each chore has seemed an eternity, coming back to the apartment a sense of destiny. My decisions are fated to collide. My life can no longer shield me from the past. Worse, it seems to be casting obstacles at me from every direction. I have been chasing the righteous path for years. But now things are different. I have been running. Running as fast and as far without actually getting anywhere. I am still the teenage girl who believed the world could make sense. How do I explain this to Jerome so he understands?

Last night he stayed out with his friends. No doubt they reminded him that New York City is big, so why limit one's selection, especially when the woman in question plans on leaving your bed cold for 365 days. Their world consists of the five boroughs: the epicenter of the universe, a reflection of the greatest accomplishment of man, a vision of how the globe should be. And I know they reminded him that if I am not there, I am not part of his world. It's simple arithmetic. It would be nice to live that simply. Just awesome. All I care about is how Jerome feels separate from his male pride.

It was in the small space of my apartment, the noises of the city street muffled, that I slept and awoke through a nightmarish night. Every bad dream vomited the pain of my memories back into existence. I've marveled at my ability to compartmentalize my life in the past, but everything is jumbled together now. If there was a particular point in time I could point to as the beginning, it all started the year Martin Luther King, Jr. was assassinated. The Black Panther Party created a force field that spilled next door into Sunny Hollow. My beloved brother, Terrell, wore a black beret as a sign of solidarity. Within two months, he was drafted. I remember the day he received the letter.

"You have to report for a physical exam? To Local Board No. 50? What does that mean?"

Terrell grabbed the sheet from me. "Don't worry about it, Pipsqueak."

"Why not? They didn't even spell your name right. Maybe it's not really meant for you."

"It's my address. I have to go or I'll go to jail."

"What's the difference if you're in jail or fighting in some stupid war? You'll survive jail."

"People like me don't always survive jail."

I wrinkled my nose. Terrell reached out and pretended to capture it between his fingers.

I tossed his hand away. "There has to be a way to get out of this stupid thing." I looked at Mama and she looked at Terrell.

"There's deferment, but I'm afraid we don't fit into that social class." Mama wiped her eyes with a well-used handkerchief, the embroidered letters of her initials dangling at the exposed corner.

"Why not? I know what you mean, but you're white."

Terrell and Mama exchanged a glance.

They were driving me crazy. "Why not? I wouldn't go. You could say no one by that name lives here. You could buy time. Pretend you're stupid and only answer to the correct spelling. They think we're stupid anyway. Then you could pretend to be sick, to be handicapped, to be crazy."

Terrell chuckled. Shrugged, his voice betraying his resignation. "That would only buy time. The end would be the same. I have to go."

"No. We could go to Mexico. No one would stop us. I'll go with you. We could all go. Or we could go to Canada."

Terrell smiled a one-sided smile. "You have to stay here. You have to do something with your life. Make me proud. Make Mom and Dad proud."

"No, I don't."

"Yeah, Mom and Dad need you."

"No. No one needs me. I need you. I won't let you go."

"I need you, Pipsqueak."

"Then you wouldn't leave."

"I don't have a choice. I'll be back. I promise."

Promise? Terrell never broke his promises. Ever. He would be back.

On the precise day at the precise time indicated on the notice, he reported to his local board and passed his physical exam.

It would only be a matter of time before he finished boot camp and left for Vietnam. There was no comfort in his geographic proximity—that was semantics. He was gone. Everyone told me to feel grateful he was not yet in 'Nam. As long as he stayed on American soil, he was safe. Safe? What about when he did finally leave? Hungry for young and inexperienced blood, Vietnam chewed up and spit out boys like Terrell. At eighteen in the state of California, they were too young to possess vodka in public, but they were old enough to kill or be killed. As if the act of killing or dying were benign compared to that of consuming a shot of vodka. What? Like I was stupid? I could no longer stomach the lies and apathy around me. My teachers and guidance counselor clucked amongst themselves. For me, they had become part of the problem. The establishment seeped right down to the school level. For all I knew, it began there. Mariah was right. No one seemed to care and that suited me fine.

A week from summer vacation, I'd had enough. The heat had been rising throughout the day, and by the time social studies rolled around, the rooms in the old school building were like a furnace. My civics teacher turned the lights off and opened all the windows to cool things down, but the edge in the air hovered the way smoke in a burning building swims around the ceiling.

Mr. Curtiss started his lecture by staring straight into my eyes, then quickly averted them. Busing. The issue was busing and desegregation. Was he looking at me? Was he trying *not* to look at me, now? I was the only black girl in class—or was I, really? My mother was white. What did that make me?

I stood, pumped my fist in the Black Power salute, and left the room, slamming the door on the collective silence.

Mama retrieved me from the principal's office. My parents finally noticed my anger, but their sadness added to my distress. I retreated into my shell. I had done it for Terrell, but he was gone, no more than a ghost, his promise buried safely in my heart. And I waited.

Granite, known only to the Earth, is the most abundant rock underlying the continental crust. Continents twitch and move along a foundation long ago forged from fire and magma. Even under the extreme forces of erosion, its strength and soundness are legendary, its crack systems the only sign that even the strongest may yield. Terrell had been the strength, the granite, upon which all depended. But every rock has its breaking point.

As a child, I loved the game of rock-paper-scissors: the paper, ever so gently, without violence, simply shrouded the rock and obliterated any trace of its existence, a fine and translucent membrane coating the most solid of objects. It was a game I played with Terrell. But his strength could not endure the shrouding jungle. No stone could withstand the torment of clinging vine and rotting earth.

Now I have Jerome. I promised Jerome that this would be my last sojourn in Africa. Just like that, I reversed course. It only took a moment to re-chart my path toward an entwined life—a life I have avoided since my teenage years in Sunny Hollow. I vowed then that I would never again lose myself, never again be cast out into the world. If I was already alone, I could never again be *made* to be alone.

When Terrell went to Vietnam in 1968, he did not return, nor did his remains. The mystery of it nearly drove me mad like it did Mama. In 1975, while I was still in college, my sweet mama put a gun to her head. I rushed home from classes. She had chosen the messiest of exits.

I understood. Something should mark the passing. Mama had lain for years imagining the worst of it—body parts spread across an inhospitable jungle. No time to gather the bits and pieces as the Viet Cong moved in; no talisman to mark his passing from the world, the ultimate violence, the ultimate betrayal, her beloved only son corrupted by the dark forces of the interior jungle. I knew because I had built the same scene into my history, because at night dark creatures slithered through my dreams, and somewhere between the dream and the waking, the figures materialized in the shadows that danced and spun across the walls of my bedroom. My bedroom could never again serve as sanctuary in a world that had lost its inviolability.

I smiled and thanked the authorities for their concern. How could they understand? Mama had ceased to exist in 1968. She had become a ghost moving through the days as if they were something to be haunted by the ambivalent, the betwixt and between. She had only destroyed the shell—they had gutted her soul long ago. After all, what was a mother without her flesh and bone?

Daddy was broken differently. He stooped against the weight of his losses. He had believed in the possibility of a different world. He had taken up the cross of non-violent resistance, and his son had died for the sin of his beliefs. And now his wife lay shattered in a sterile box of death, her brain matter gone but its casing neatly pieced back together, as if nothing amiss had ever transpired to mar the integrity of the illusion. He told me he longed to rip the head apart and reveal to everyone the truth. You could not crack a shell and make it whole again. The bits of shells were just so damned complicated.

I begged Daddy to hold on for me. But he too let go. His broken heart could not be so easily repaired, not even for me. Within the year, I was alone. And I planned to stay that way. The darkness did not yield easily to the light.

So how did I end up here? All that resolve nurtured through the years, gone, with one impetuous promise, one moment of weakness buried within the folds of compromise. Can I possibly quit my wanderings? Africa is as close to home as I have. Here, the pace of striving makes me want to tear my skin from my bones. Terrell, my reason for recreating my life so many years ago, will be reduced to the memory of a history I have maintained as the present—his promise still intact. He is still my rock. Can I forsake him for another? And this will be my reality, my wanderlust a torment. One year and I will be done.

I just have to convince Jerome.

I have a year to convince myself.

Jerome walks through the door ten minutes after me.

"What's up?"

I can't gauge his mood. "Nothing much. I got a bunch of errands done. How was your night last night?"

"It was good. You know the guys were giving me the business. You know how it is."

"No. I don't. My friends tend to support me and don't bother with the *business*."

He scowls at me.

I am tired. I did not want to go in this direction. "I didn't mean it that way."

He scratches his head. "They made some decent points. Why should we stay together when you're choosing to leave? It's not like you're going to Paris or Bangkok, where they at least have semi-decent phone service. No, you go to some war-torn country in Africa and I have to sit and imagine you coming home in a body bag. You're asking me to hang on to a prayer."

At least there would be a body bag. But I can't say this to him. I promised myself I would check my sarcasm and cynicism at the door. "I'd never thought of it that way. I've always returned to Africa with no one left behind to worry about me."

"Maybe you should consider sticking with that plan."

"Maybe that's not what I want anymore. Maybe I don't want to leave for Africa without knowing you're here when I return."

"Then don't go at all."

"You know I can't do that. I've already committed."

"Yeah, I know. So what does that make me, your afterthought?"

"No. I just don't want to lose you." I wipe the creeping sweat from my forehead.

"Okay, tell you what, we'll compromise. You show me how much you're willing to sacrifice in exchange for what I'm willing to sacrifice: you give up seven days in Charleston and I'll consider waiting 365. Sounds like you're getting the bargain."

I could sacrifice just about anything except that sacred pact. I can't begin to explain this to Jerome. It would require me giving up a secret I am duty bound to keep. My honor depends upon it. Besides, how could he ever see me with the same eyes again once he knows?

"I can't do that, Jerome. I'll do anything else, but that commitment runs so deep, I would never jeopardize it."

"I thought so. You have some weird thing going on. You take a detour to some little town without an international airport before you fly out for a whole year. A whole year, Eve? You have to take your smart-ass clothes with you. That's just fucked up. You can't even spend your last week with me. You gotta spend your last moments with your girlfriends. What does that make me? It makes me a fool. It doesn't make any sense but you want me to buy into it."

"You wouldn't understand, Jerome. I just have to go. Please, don't do this to me. I'm willing to stay home after this year. I will. I'll give up Africa after this year. Just give us a chance."

"Shit, this makes no sense, Eve. You can't even make the promise without breaking a sweat. Look at you. Jesus, what the hell am I supposed to do for a year waiting for you?"

"I'll be back before you know it. A year goes quickly."

He shakes his head, walks to the window, and pulls the curtain back on the grayness of the moment. Drops of water cling to the window where tiny beads dance along the perimeter of the apartment.

His voice is barely audible. "You're playing me now."

"No, I swear I'm not. I won't leave again. I promise. You have to believe me. I will never leave again."

Jerome looses his grip on the curtain before turning. "You're not giving anything up. Why should I believe you'll even come back? That leaves me sitting here like a bitch-whipped fool."

"No. I promise. I've never promised anything to anyone. Except . . ."

Jerome slides his hands into his pockets. "Except Terrell and your dad." He sighs. "All right, but one year and you're done. We will never have this conversation again. It's done. I won't be a fool again."

"One year and I'm done." I bury my face in his chest. I could stay like this forever. How will I survive Africa without him? Suddenly, the land I'm headed to seems as grim and perilous as the darkness behind my eyelids, vast and deadly. It is a momentous shift in consciousness, a rift as large and cavernous as that which divides East Africa from the continent. I have never feared the trip to the camp the way I do now.

I miss Terrell. I saw things more clearly back then. In Terrell's view, the truth of the world divided into black and white. I have never been able to capture his simplicity. And now his body lays fully decayed in some faraway Vietnamese jungle halfway around the world. He is no more than dust. But he is here with me now. He has always been here in my heart, safe and made whole. The answer is stronger and clearer than ever before, pulled from the heart of the jungle.

Open your eyes.

Stay.

But I am not ready to listen yet. There is still something to do. There is still a wrong to be remedied.

10 Mariah

I wait. Wait for my coworker Daniel's call. Wait to make sense of everything. Wait to impart my bad news to Eve. As if everything can be divined, clarified, and fixed with just a little bit of waiting. Grandmother can hold out forever. Patience is an Indian virtue. Perhaps I have been away from my people too long. I am impatient. I finish packing. Daniel will not call for a while, but my questions multiply. Like me, he's been investigating Astride Amalgamated Corporation, but from different angles. He's investigating malfeasance issues. I'm researching its impact on water issues. The bedside clock reads noon here—it's midnight in Kuala Lumpur. It will be another six hours before he calls.

His voice in the message unnerved me. Why is he sending me a flash drive? What is he so paranoid about? He is the coolest and most unflappable person I know.

I can't put those questions to bed for another six hours. I can deal with my bad news and Eve now.

"Hello."

"Eve?"

"What's up? And don't tell me nothing. Spill it."

"Well, I'm waiting for a call from a colleague. He sounds terrified and he is the least likely person. Second, I can't find anything on the guy from down the street in Sunny Hollow. Jake Cruise remembered him—remembered when the guy arrived straight from 'Nam, remembered that his name was Paul. It's just he can't find anything on him. No record that he ever lived there. It's like he never existed."

"What do you mean he never existed? Everyone knew him. He was the lunatic who yelled at all of us kids at Halloween. Did you call Sunny Hollow? They must have a record. His house burned down. Shit. The whole damn neighborhood fought that fire that night."

The room spins. The heat of the night burns my face. It is as if I have never left that place. My dad's spirit is there. Burning in the flames.

"Mariah?"

"Of course I contacted Sunny Hollow police. Jake Cruise did too. I'm telling you, there's no record of him. That house he was living in belonged to a woman named Esther LeBlanc and she claimed she was there at the time. She remembers the fire."

"What? That doesn't make any sense."

"I know. I'm telling you. He doesn't exist. At least, not officially. He's never existed—not by the name we heard, anyway. There aren't any records unless they're classified, in which case I wouldn't be able to gain access, but I would at least be able to see that he *existed*. Also, I had a vision."

"What happened in the dream?"

"The vision."

"Okay, the vision."

"I was being stalked by something. When I investigated, a cougar slunk down my hallway. She grabbed my neck and tore it out. I wasn't sleeping. I was sitting at my computer."

"Yes, but clearly you had zoned out or dozed off or whatever you want to call it."

"I understand you think I was daydreaming. I wasn't and that's the point. It's an omen. Like something bad will happen. Something is stalking me. Dogging my steps. It's a warning, Eve. Grandmother would tell me to listen to my senses. My heart is telling me something bad is afoot. I am packed to leave tomorrow for a border town in Mexico to investigate the water use of a company my colleague is calling to tell me about. A malfeasance issue. He is sending a flash drive. That's highly unusual. And I'm about to expose things about that water use using—"

"Your voice. I get it. Maybe he just wants someone to know, to be on the lookout, and he's sending the drive because he's worried about losing all his work. It could be simple."

"Yeah, I know. But he sounded freaked out."

"I don't understand why you don't call home. Talk to your grandmother."

"She doesn't have a phone."

"I know that. But your brothers do. Call them."

I shake my head. I cannot share this part of my world with them. "I'm not ready to do that yet."

"All right. I get it. Are you going to Charleston from Mexico?"

"No. I'll only be there two days. It's just a factory, and I'm just looking at it as an example of virtual water. It uses thousands of gallons of water to produce chips for computers that are then sent to Kuala Lumpur. My piece deals with embedded water in consumed products. Not just computers. I'll come home and finish my piece before I go to Charleston. I don't have to touch any malfeasance issues. Daniel is doing all of that."

"All right. When does your flight get to Charleston?"

"Thursday at five. When do you arrive?"

"Thursday night at nine."

"You want to meet for a night cap?"

"I'll be in the lobby waiting for you."

"It's a date. See you then."

"Mariah. We were young. Maybe we're not remembering his name or the house correctly. There's no reason to believe he disappeared and is just reappearing. Rethink it."

"I will. But Jake remembers him too. We can't all be wrong."

"Well, something doesn't add up."

"Yeah, I know. See you in Charleston."

As soon as I hang up I begin to review my notes on AAC. The production of one chip for one computer generates 89 pounds of waste and uses 2,800 gallons of water. The dicing and polishing of wafers uses huge amounts of water with hydrofluoric acid. Testing is conducted using other acids and toxic chemicals. AAC pumps huge amounts of water from an aquifer under the area that doesn't have a large recharge zone. I need to find the containment ponds to find out how close they are to the water treatment facility. I can't imagine one company producing tons of toxic wastewater next to their water treatment facility. It's a symbiotic nightmare. The International Monetary Fund, as a condition for a loan, required Mexico to guarantee AAC a 50 percent margin. AAC moved in and raised prices fourfold. Those who could not afford it had their water turned off. Those who worked on the computer chip manufacturing side and, of course, needed to keep their factory jobs. On the sanitation side of the agreement, AAC made some changes. I don't know what those changes are, but I plan to find out. It is the same story elsewhere. The International Monetary Fund, The World Bank, and the United Nations wield the economic carrot and supply the stick where a country is uncooperative. Past pattern and practice. I need more than two days to wrap this story up. I lied to Eve. Unintentionally. It was not my plan to investigate AAC's malfeasance issues, but that's what I'm already prepared to do. I can't help myself.

I begin the list of questions to ask and people to see. The lack of sleep catches up to me and my eyes grow heavy. I jerk and wake, but the fatigue overwhelms me. I'm safe in here. Outside, the sky has darkened and rumbles are distant.

* * *

I roll in the sun-baked grass. Mustangs graze nearby and my dogs roll around next to me. It was a bitter winter in the city. The warmth is welcome.

I shade my eyes. A few stray clouds pass overhead, but they only provide a contrast to the brilliance of a High Plains sky, not that of D.C. There are no buildings to obstruct its beauty, no trees to obscure its immensity. I am home.

My contentment is complete. There are no deadlines. But the heavens roil now with black angry clouds. A shaft or two of light shines on the earth like a ray gun searching out its target, but even those glimmers disappear under the anger of the inner atmosphere. The wind kicks up and for miles there is nothing to see but bending grass.

The horses run as a herd toward the barn. The dogs nuzzle me and bark. They want me to get up. The air is rent with electric charge and the hairs on my body stand and pulse with the electromagnetic field. I am in big trouble if the electric storm moves through and catches me out in the middle of the prairie. There is no shelter for a good distance. My limbs are leaden and I move too slowly. In the distance, my brothers shepherd the horses to safety and the dogs sprint toward them.

A lone light shines and outlines the interior of the barn, a warm and comforting sanctuary. I motion to my brothers to wait. I am coming. They wave back as the dogs bolt through the doors. My brothers each take a door and close them from the inside.

I am alone.

The tornado bears down on me.

I run.

I don't want to die alone. I vault toward the barn, but I feel a sharp pain in both my shoulders, and then I'm lifted into the air. I look up at an immense body—a lone eagle whose cries pierce the roar of the storm. He carries me to safety.

The storm spends itself, the clouds roll back, and the sun shines as though the storm had never existed. Those things that had been caught in its grasp are unscathed and moving toward home.

From the middle of the debris, something moves toward me. Whoever it is, he is confused. I motion him away; the figure continues to move intently. I turn to find the eagle, but he is perched on a lone tree, preening his feathers.

I turn again toward the figure. He is hideous and angry. His naked body is covered in paint in a symbolic fashion that I don't recognize. He is not Lakota or Dakota or Ho-Chunk. He wields a club above his head and large bones are woven through his nose and ears.

I recognize them as human bones still dripping blood. I scream but I produce no sound. He laughs.

Tears stream down my cheeks. I must flee, but he is so close I smell his rotting flesh. I cover my throat before he lunges, and then hear the piercing cry of the eagle as he lifts me high into the air. I look toward earth as the evil creature shakes his bones and curses me.

* * *

The phone rings. I knock the receiver to the floor as I climb from my dream.

"Hello."

"Did I wake you?" Daniel's voice is lighthearted.

"No. Sorry. I was reviewing my notes for my trip tomorrow and I must have dozed. You sound better than the last time I spoke to you."

"I think things have settled down."

"How were they unsettled before? What had you on edge?"

"Oh, nothing. I thought someone was following me. The things I've uncovered are nasty. I guess that's what made me feel nervous."

"Are you sure everything's okay now?"

"Yeah. Everything's been fine. I even got in some sightseeing."

"Good for you. What is this about a flash drive?"

"I sent it. It has all my notes. Listen. AAC is involved in some serious shit. They're dumping toxic chemicals directly into the sewer in Mexico and they know what they've done to the aquifer. My informant just got back from there and he showed me the test results. The TCA levels are out the roof. They've buried the findings. The aquifer goes directly under Del Sierra in Texas and affects the city's water and thousands of wells. The containment evaporation ponds and wetlands are a sham. They are there for show. The real dumping is being done inside. On top of it, they have claimed that they're being diligent by processing certain extremely toxic chemicals in their municipal sewage treatment plant, which has industrial wastewater treatment capabilities. Not so. Unacceptable impurity concentrations are finding their way into the water system. They have sort of bypassed the biochemical and chemical oxidation stages. They provide no disinfection and they've foregone the polishing process. All in all, they're making a lot of money from dumping the by-products of their manufacturing processes straight into the local water source and they're saving buckets of money on forgoing most of the processes required to deliver safe municipal water."

"I thought this might be a short trip."

"Yeah, me too. And Mariah?"

"Yeah?"

"It's been raining. A lot."

"Yeah. I know."

"Half the people who work in the factory get their water from surface water. Their water was turned off when AAC took over and they couldn't pay the new, inflated prices. There's some rumor that a member of the staff just returned from an aid junket in Haiti and brought cholera home. Perfect conditions. Could be a hell of a trip for you."

"Shit. What do you want me to do with the flash drive? Who knows when we'll see each other?"

"It'd be safer if you dropped it off at work. My plane leaves—"

The sound of glass breaking, muffled voices, and chaos leaves me straining to hear.

"Daniel? Daniel?"

Quiet.

A voice gurgles. The sound of oxygen mixing with liquid respires through the phone lines.

"Daniel? Are you there? Talk to me!"

The breathing is strong and heavy. The gurgling becomes background noise and turns raspy before it stops.

"Daniel? Are you there? Please!"

Click.

11 Jorge Nunez

He needed to get home. His family needed him now more than ever, but he had to bring home the paycheck—now more than ever. His worry coiled like a knot in his stomach.

He watched the chemicals swirl down the drain. It occurred to him he had no idea where they ended up. It didn't matter, really. Management knew, and they paid his check. He had left Mixteca many years ago, sending his pay home to his wife and children in San Juan Pinas. But he had missed the green hills of the mists and, several years ago, had returned to his pueblo.

He only stayed a year. The land could not sustain his growing family and he found himself once again moving. Like ancient times, his people were always moving. And now he was on the border, working for an American company, cleaning up harsh chemicals under harsh conditions in a harsh land.

He was worried. His wife had given birth to a very sick baby two months ago, and she was weak from the physical effort and grief. He had planted a tiny garden. Their house, a mixture of reclaimed aluminum and boarding he had been able to piece together from abandoned and clearance materials, stood in a neighborhood of equally fragile houses hastily built by other desperate people on the outskirts of the factory town. His wife had smiled at the little garden that claimed a tiny strip of marginal land at the front of the house. Every day she gathered water from the trickling stream. She tended to her crops and prayed that they would survive to feed her malnourished family, but they continued to wilt in the damning sun of the arid land. Thus withered, they were now drowned in the onslaught of heavy rain. They were too much of a reminder of their dead baby.

Their dead baby. He wiped a tear from his cheek with the sleeve of his shirt.

"She has anencephaly," the doctor had said.

"*Por qué?*"

"Perhaps it runs in your family."

But there was no story of such a birth in their village.

"Will she live?"

"No."

"Will she suffer?"

"No. She has no brain and no way to feel herself dying."

She lived two more days. They watched her fade and then she was no more.

And now his wife and one of his sons were throwing up and had been complaining of cramps since last night.

Jorge wiped the sweat from his upper lip and stretched his back. It was a brief break from his troubles, but the monotony of his job made his mind return to his problems. He picked up another bucket of wastewater and carried it to the drain, but it sloshed as he doubled over with a pain that had been gnawing at him much of the day. The liquid burned and he quickly set the vessel down. He watched it as it formed blisters. He could not go to the factory doctor. Conditions were abnormally hot outside the clean room and he was not wearing his protective gear. He would be in trouble. It was bad enough he had already been spoken to about it earlier in the day. The heavy garments made him hot and uncomfortable and he needed to think clearly, to not allow the walls of his worries smother him.

* * *

When he left for the day, his hand throbbing and his bowels grumbling, he hurried away from the factory complex. Astride Amalgamated Corporation, AAC, straddled Mexican Federal Highway 2 in the remote thorn scrub west of Ciudad Frontera, a sprawling city of 200,000 that had sprouted from the arid lands of the Tamaulipan mezquital. On one side, a giant complex devoted to the manufacture of microchips destined to Kuala Lumpur for packaging before the final transit to meet up with the motherboard, and the other side, the vast network of water treatment basins and tanks full of sparkling water. The side devoted to microchips consumed gallons of water, and the other was devoted to supplying water to the town and the other industries assembling imported components into products for export. But Jorge did not have his normal energy to marvel at these wonders tonight. Tonight, he needed to get home.

He traveled through the makeshift streets along arroyos now filled with stagnating water from the recent rains. He shook his head as the smell of raw sewage assaulted him and threatened to empty his bowels. If only he could stop breathing until he made it home.

He was one of the lucky ones. His family still had running water. He slipped and skidded through the mud-thick neighborhoods and wondered how many of his neighbors had had their water stopped for failure of payment.

Water rates had risen quickly when AAC took over the water business, and many people could not afford water and food for their families. The unexpectedly heavy seasonal rains should have helped people who used old ways of capturing rain, but it had only seemed to make everything worse. Water spilled everywhere. Jorge rounded the corner and felt comfort at the sight of his house, but that relief was short-lived.

The house was dark.

At that moment, he vomited and his bowels let loose in a torrent of watery diarrhea. He collapsed into his own vomit and the swirling foulness of his neighborhood. No one came to pull him out of the excrement.

12 Fiona

The soiree should've been uneventful. It should've been no different from any other of Gavin's little social events. Except that this event occurred on a Saturday on the exact date as all the other wicked Saturdays of my fucking life. How else could it have turned out?

Gavin could never stand the idea of a secret that didn't include him. Something that was only mine. For the entirety of our lives, I have given him six days of every week, but he begrudges me the one. One out of seven. A whole 14 percent of my week that I keep for myself. Whooptidoo. No amount of dissembling can prevent that seam from pulling apart. Besides, how could I ever explain my role in either tragedy? They're mine. Not his. And telling him I'm responsible for two deaths might be too much for his patrician ass.

When I was ten, Mom and Dad left me to watch my siblings. I only took my eyes off them for five minutes. Peeing was my great sin. Thinking back on it, I should've just peed in the pool. Everyone does. Better yet. God could've made an exception and exempted me from a bladder and a vagina altogether. If I didn't have a bladder, Rory would still be alive. And the whole vagina thing might've made a lot of things easier.

I pour myself another stiff vodka. It flows and warms me. God it feels so damn good. There's just one little pesky problem. It always ends up in the bladder. Fuck my life.

Five years later, it was my fault again. It was all because of me, because I wanted to see Damon, be with Damon, feel all the feelings I felt every time I saw him. He made me feel alive. Made me feel desired. Made me feel forgiven. It was that damned pesky problem of the vagina that time.

I throw myself into my chaise lounge and giggle. My robe slips open and I slide my fingers into myself. After all, I am a woman of sin. Isn't that what they call it in nice little places where nice little people go to feel good about themselves?

But he wasn't worth it. Everyone else knew it. How could I have been so stupid? I risked everything for nothing—my sin, that of singular purpose, *my* purpose, without regard for consequence. Trouble was, he was a really good tease and a really good fuck. Which is probably why Jazmin would never let go.

And then there was the problem of Brandon. One too many vodkas and a shitload of guilt and . . . well . . . I kissed the asshole. Broke the code. I never could get the consequence and guilt thing down.

But that was in the past. I keep those days a secret. Growing up, my kids learned not to ask for or expect too much. Saturday was my day and I took every damn thing to forget it. So my children learned to make excuses. They helped keep the façade of a glamorous family intact. They wore the mask for the world, mindful of the secret to which not even they were privy. Sunday morning always came early, and when it did they helped Abella clean up the remains of Saturday night. Sunday was never much better than Saturday, but I was at least there. The children would quickly disperse to the far corners lest they disturb the quiet that cloaked the house and sealed it in muteness. The custom had only lately been challenged.

Why? I don't know. This state of affairs had suited Gavin fine. His parents had been enthusiastic champions of the philosophy that all children should be seen and not heard. His upbringing in the better neighborhoods of Boston and requisite sojourn at Harvard solidified his New England reserve. The openness and friendliness of Southern California did little to melt his restraint.

Lately, he's different. His job seems to be an increasing source of dissatisfaction. His problem isn't so different from mine. He's aging, but everyone around him seeks a cure to that process. He's aging amongst those who refuse to do so. In the early days, he had everything—a beautiful wife, an enviable job, a showcase home, healthy and bright children—and Beverly Hills validated his brilliance. But something has changed. The terrain has shifted. It has shifted into something monstrous.

And now I seem to be the shining example of everything he hates about his life. I played by the rules—which, by the way, were also his rules. It was the one code he and my parents agreed upon. If I just stayed beautiful enough then I would be worthy. How the fuck was I supposed to know there were some wrinkles that could not be smoothed away?

I need my energy to get through my days. The party he forced on me was a clear example of the irks-and-twains in my life, the bifurcation of the before and the after. I'm still spinning from his demands. Even when I pled my case, he remained unmoved. It should've been a warning, but I attributed it to his job. It wasn't the first time I've missed a vital cue. But then, living with guilt as my constant companion cloaks the social cues necessary to survive the shifting landscape.

I verified my elegance in my Oscar de la Renta dress and collection of diamonds. Diamonds he has given me throughout the course of our marriage, I might add. My hair, coiffed into a chignon, was swept up tastefully. The expanse of mirror along the wall of our two-story grand foyer and staircase didn't lie. Even I knew I was stunning. I made my way around the large formal living room, spending just enough time with each person to make him or her feel special without insulting the next person. I'm a master at charm. I always have been. The night sparkled with all the who's who of our glittering little world.

I close my eyes.

I found Gavin, but he was detached from the entire affair. Why in God's name was he putting me through this if it meant nothing to him? Surely, he could at least pretend he was interested. Or was this some game? I headed toward the young hired bartender.

"A cosmopolitan, please."

"Yes, Mrs. McDermott. Can I get you anything else?" His eyes shimmered with appreciation. I caressed his hand as I took the drink—to hell with Gavin. I was sinking. He was just a kid.

The moment of conquest was short-lived. Sam stood in the high arch separating the living room from the dining room. She motioned to me. I had given her instructions to stay upstairs with her younger sister and brother. I went over to her.

"What is it?"

"Mary Jean and Katie want me to go out."

"No. You know you're supposed to watch Molly and Sean. Besides, how would you get there anyway?"

"I can get there. I don't see why I have to watch the babies. Besides, they're old enough to be upstairs on their own. You and Dad are here."

"They're not babies, but they still need someone with them, especially Sean. Please be helpful. I don't ask much of you, so I'd appreciate it if you didn't fight me on this. Your Dad and I are busy entertaining."

"What d'you think they're gonna do, Mom, set the house on fire or ingest too many of Dad's Viagras? Besides, Abella's here."

"Abella's busy. And what do you mean by Viagra?"

"You're clueless Mom. Everyone in the world knows what Viagra is."

"Of course I know what Viagra is, but your dad doesn't take them. I don't know what trouble you're trying to stir up, but it's not going to work." My cheeks burned underneath my makeup.

"I'm not stirring up trouble. You're the one who's troubled."

"How dare you speak to me like that! Go to your room! You're not allowed out. You better get upstairs before I lose my temper. My parents would've smacked me if I'd spoken to them like that." I pointed to the stairs.

"First, Mom, Granddad and Grandma would've never touched their precious princess, so you can drop that fable. Second, Dad does too take Viagra. Third, the babies can look after themselves and, fourth, maybe you should throw a better temper tantrum than that, because you act like you're some constipated zombie freak. Look at me, look at me, my life is so bad and poor me."

"Who died and made you the great know-it-all?"

"You did, Mom. You've been acting like you're dead since I can remember."

"Go to your room, Sam. You're grounded. That was hurtful." I practically choked on the words and tears streamed down my face, along with a thick trail of black mascara.

Sam didn't budge and I moved through the door into the kitchen. Sam followed.

"Dad will unground me. He'll even agree with me."

"No he won't, Sam. Go upstairs."

"I'm going out, Mom. Do I need to go into the party and ask Dad right now? I know how much you hate public spectacles. I would hate to have that perfect reputation ruined."

Who was this child? The changeling was back. "Are you threatening me? Get upstairs. *NOW!* Or you won't like the consequences."

"Ooooh, Mom, I'm so scared. Dad already told me I could go out tonight if I wanted."

"When did he tell you that, Sam?"

"This morning. I just didn't have plans at that point, but now I do."

"I don't care. Go upstairs before you're grounded for the next week."

"You can't do that. I'm telling Dad."

"Yes I can and I am. Upstairs, Sam. Now!"

Abella swung through the kitchen doors and stopped herself short. She turned the same way from which she had come, but Sam caught her.

"Abella, didn't Dad say I could go out tonight? Mom won't let me."

"Yes, your dad did but your mom had already asked you to stay in." Abella headed for the bowels of the kitchen.

Sam followed her. "That's not fair, Abella. Dad said I could."

"Sam, my darling, I figured you knew you couldn't because your mother had already said so."

Sam turned to me. Betrayal evident in her eyes. Abella had never abandoned her before. *Ever!*

Now Sam knew how it felt.

She wiped at her angry tears. "I hate you. I hate your secret and I hate your lies. You're ruining my life. You've *been* ruining my life. We have to tiptoe around here every weekend while you drink your little cocktails and cry like some pathetic rag mop. Dude, you're like a bad disease. I can't wait until I get out of here." She ran through the kitchen crying. I couldn't believe the tirade, but even worse was the look on Abella's face as she stared in horror behind me. I turned and came face to face with five of my dinner guests.

Margret, the wife of one of the denizens of Beverly Hills society smiled. "Well, that's quite a spitfire for a daughter you have there." She turned on her heels and left. The other women smirked and followed.

12 Jorge Nunez

Jorge picked himself up from the mud and vomit. Normally, children played in the street and the smells of corn and chilies perfumed the hot and dusty air. Today, there were no smells of food to aggravate his already troubled stomach, but the stench of sewage from the recent downpours made him double over and heave. He clung to the side of a makeshift house and emptied the rest of his stomach.

The neighborhood was silent. There were no women carrying buckets from the river. No balls to dodge. Jorge felt the panic rise, but his body would not cooperate. He needed to get home, but he could not gain any ground against his illness.

Delirium threatened to overwhelm him. His hands shook and he brought them close to his dimmed eyes. Black and blue spider veins spread from the throbbing blisters he had received at work.

He vomited again.

His stomach spasmed and he fell to his knees.

He could not lie down here. He was so close—only a few steps from home. He called weakly to his wife. There was no answer.

He called out for help, but no one came. He fell back and vomited yellow liquid. How would he go to work tomorrow? A little thing like this could mean he lost his job. It could mean he could not feed his family.

He struggled to get up. Staggering to the front door, he collapsed into the house. He called out again. His wife. Where was his family?

Where was the laughter? There was only an odor of death. His death? He wept. He tried to push on.

He prayed to God then. If only the darkness of his nightmare would lift. He would wear the protective gear next time. He would help his neighbors more. He would be more thankful for every morsel of food with which they were blessed. He would be thankful for his job. He would go home. There were so many things he would do.

He vomited again but nothing came out, only a heaving that threatened to break his back.

He moved again through the nightmare and called to his children. They did not answer. It was too late for them to not be home. He called to his wife. She had not started dinner.

He called again.

He found the door to the bedroom. The knob refused to turn. He was too weak. He turned it again and it twisted in his palm.

He pushed through.

The room smelled of death, up close and personal, and he collapsed to the floor.

Opening his eyes, he stared into the shrunken, discolored face of his wife. Folded into her arms were his children.

Cholera had come to Ciudad Frontera.

14 Esperanza

It's June and the air is warm and scented. Winter is a long and introspective affair in New Hampshire. Summer visitors leave with the first snowflake and don't return until the ice recedes. We live too far from the ski slopes. I initially bristled at the idea of a New England life—it doesn't suit my temperament—but we couldn't turn down a post at Dartmouth College. So I packed up our house in Tampa Bay and headed north.

Tom worked, published, and networked until he became tenured. I adjusted by focusing on my family and spending at least one month a year in Puerto Rico with my retired parents. It's as close to Cuba as Mimi can get. Tom comes for a week, but then he returns to the mainland to focus on his research and writing. It's not his world. His family has long roots in California. Californios, they were granted lands from the abandoned missions that followed the El Camino Real Trail on the last coast.

Carlos and Izzy climb into the SUV and Angelica follows, her arm cast the same size as her body. The memory of the car crash remains. Sideswiped by someone playing with the radio, I was not faulted. It doesn't matter. I fault myself. I should've been paying attention. I should've seen it coming.

I agree with Heather and Mariah. Fate is dogging us.

"Izzy, buckle up." Izzy stares out the window, twirling her hair and humming a tune. *"Izzy!"*

"Yes, Mommy."

"Buckle up, *por favor*. Stop dreaming, my angel."

"Oh. See that cloud up there? Over to the left? It looks like an eagle. Mariah would say I'm having Eagle medicine today."

"How do you remember that?"

"She told me over the phone." Izzy's voice drifts.

I adjust the rearview mirror so I can see her. "What do you mean?"

"She called."

"When?"

"Yesterday."

"Yesterday? What did she say? What did she want? Why didn't you tell me? Izzy, get your head out of the clouds and focus. Did she leave a message?"

"No. She wanted to know how we are. How Angelica is. She said she would call you later. Mom, why can't we go to Charleston?"

"You know it's just us girls. When today?"

"I'm a girl."

"That's not what I mean, Izzy. We have a lot of catching up to do and not a lot of time. You know how you can't wait to see Katrina after you've been in Puerto Rico and you spend hours talking and catching up?"

"Yeah."

"Well, that's one month of catching up to do. I have twelve months of catching up to do."

"That's not the same. Katrina and I are best friends."

"What do you mean? Those are my best friends."

"I don't know, Mom. Katrina and I are pretty close. We've been through a lot. Like the time Melissa and her weirdo friends decided I couldn't play with them but Katrina could. Katrina left them. That's a real best friend."

"You're right, Izzy, that's a tough one to beat."

"You're such a dork, Izzy. It's not the same thing." Carlos rolls his eyes.

Izzy sticks her tongue out.

"That's not true, Carlos. Everything is relative. In Izzy's world, that's a big thing. If Katrina had gone with those girls, it would've been a monstrous betrayal. I'm older now. Perhaps, it takes more to betray me."

"That's lame, Mom. Betrayal is betrayal. Maybe you can argue degrees but it still hurts when someone does something to hurt you."

"Did something happen, Carlos?" Sometimes I have to remind myself he's fifteen. Fifteen is when my world turned upside down.

"Nothing happened. Why do you always think something happened?"

"I'm sorry, it's just you don't usually know this unless you have experienced it."

"That's not always true. Sometimes you just have to watch people and they screw up. You don't always have to be the person they're messing with."

"That's true."

"Don't worry, Mom. This has nothing to do with you or anyone in our family, if that's what you're thinking."

"Maybe I wasn't thinking anything."

"Yes you were. You're always thinking. You're always trying to figure out the hidden meaning, and what you think we could be up to, and what you could do to make it better, but sometimes what we say is exactly what we mean and nothing more. It doesn't always mean something else is going on. You can't fix everything, Mom."

"It's just it's hard to imagine you would naturally have such insight."

"Mariah says perception is nine-tenths of reality."

"Did you talk to Mariah too? Where was I?"

"You were at the grocery store. Dad took the call and we all talked to her."

No one told me.

"Don't worry, Mom. There's no great mystery or conspiracy. She called for you but you weren't there. She said she could talk to you about it later."

"Quit reading my mind, Carlos." It comes out sharper than I intend.

"I'm not reading your mind. It's just I can figure out what you're thinking."

"I'm sorry. I didn't mean to snap at you."

All three kids watch me now.

"Golden rainbow, Momma." Angelica claps her hands as we approach McDonald's.

"Angelica, Mommy doesn't like fast food," Izzy chides her.

"Why?" Angelica demands.

"It's bad for you," I say.

"Why?"

"Because it has lots of chemicals in it."

"Why?"

"Because it makes it easier."

"Why?"

I sigh. "Oh, I don't know Angelica. You're wearing me out."

"I wanna treat." Angelica claps her little hands again, the monstrous cast a stark white in motion.

"There's a cool treat you get with the kids' meal now, Mom. Can we go for Angelica?" Izzy looks pleadingly at me, a huge, goofy grin animating her face.

What harm could this once do? "Oh, all right."

Izzy and Angelica clap. Carlos remains unfazed.

"Is that okay with you, Carlos?"

"Yeah, sure, whatever."

* * *

I dial Mariah the minute I get the kids settled down with homework. The phone rings and her message machine answers.

"Mariah. I'm sorry I missed your call. I'm at home the rest of the evening. Call me. *Te quiero.*"

I need a cup of tea. The hot water kettle screams and I pour the steaming water over the tea bag. I retreat to the table in the garden, where the children can easily find me. The birds chatter, jump, and land on the newly sprouted tree limbs. Their energy reminds me of my teenage years in Sunny Hollow. We too had such vitality. Even in the midst of trying to save Heather, we believed anything was possible. I still remember watching Eve and Mariah marching to the principal's office, proud and determined.

It was the same time of year, June. It was steamy. Mr. Curtiss turned down the lights and used a film to demonstrate the misunderstandings inherent in civil disobedience. His point? The danger of the anti-war movement. Poor Mr. Curtiss. He tried too hard. He used the movie *Cheyenne Autumn* as a case in point. When it was over, he called on Mariah to explain its relevance. We knew his mistake, but it was fun to watch him make it.

Mariah tapped her desk. "I don't know what you mean."

"Well, you're Indian. You must have some thoughts on history."

"Well, which history are you talking about?"

"Indian history."

Eve and I giggled. Moron.

"You mean Cheyenne. I'm not Cheyenne. I'm Lakota and Winnebago. As to the history and so-called disobedience in the movie, the US government broke its promise. Isn't that a big surprise? The only thing that makes Cheyenne history similar to Lakota or Winnebago history is their relationship to each other and to the lying thieving government. So, 'civil disobedience' was caused by the government. Gee, there's another surprise. Why don't you make your point without dragging me into it? Or, was your point that the government begins all disobedience, so we should all carry on with the anti-war movement?"

Eve's eyes widened.

I was proud, but I knew Mariah was in trouble now.

"Get out of my classroom, you little brat. Get out now. Go straight to the principal's."

"Oooooh." The whole classroom pretended to be shocked, but everyone knew Mariah.

Eve turned around and stared each classmate down.

It didn't matter. It never did. Her parents never punished her.

After class, we rushed to the principal's office. Mariah's mother had arrived to pick her up. Her mother hugged her and spoke something in her language. I never knew what it was, but it made Mariah smile.

Three days later we retreated to the Rose Garden. Even that most special of places had lost its enchantment. The elderly women shushed us and the caretakers trailed our movements, prohibiting us from "loitering" on the benches or dipping our feet in the fountains. We moved aimlessly, but someone was always on our tail. The borders of the Rose Garden had retreated, hemmed in on four sides by streets and houses that watched our shrinking world. No longer vast and sacred, the Garden had become part of the establishment. And the system didn't want anyone who didn't fit into its well-ordered world. We were being chased from our childhood.

It was Fiona who came up with the plan to hang out in Tallon Park in the Berkeley Hills. Fiona rarely took note of current events, except when they affected her friends. She was more pulled by the effect her beauty had on the opposite sex. If she was not obsessing about Jazmin's boyfriend, Damon, she was mad about the students at UC Berkeley. So she hatched the plot to hitchhike in groups to the Park. The first time we tried it was successful. The second time was a disaster.

I hear the phone ring inside, and then Carlos walks out holding the portable phone. "It's Mariah, Mom."

"Thanks, honey." I take the phone and settle back into my seat. "Hi Mariah."

"Hi Espy. I can't wait to see you."

"Me too." I wait, but she's quiet. "Is that what you were calling about?"

"No. I'm in Mexico."

"Mexico? Why didn't you tell me?"

"It happened quickly. There's something going on here and I need to know what that organization is called that Tomas told me about. Do you know when he'll be home?"

"What organization? What's going on? It's almost time to meet in Charleston."

"Remember I told you I was doing a series of articles on water? Well, I'm in Mexico doing a piece on virtual water, but it's become more complicated. There's a company polluting the water and acting unethically in its water management contract. My colleague who was investigating it in Kuala Lumpur has gone missing. I can't contact him. He was in the middle of explaining everything to me, but he was cut off. I think he might've been . . . killed."

I sit up straight. "What? Mariah, you're always in the middle of things. One of these days you're going to have to accept that there is bad in this world that you can't fix."

"I know, but now is not that time."

"You're talking about Tribunal Latinoamericano del Agua. I'm assuming that's what you're talking about? LAWT. They're only a judicial tribunal that issues nonbinding decisions, but they hold a lot of clout in the court of public opinion. I'm not sure that will help a lot with a multinational company that knows what they're doing is wrong, but it might help kick them out of the water business at least in Mexico."

"That's it. I don't know what else to do. I've contacted World Health Organization because there's a cholera epidemic, but I need someone to bring this more fully to the world's attention. WHO is not here yet."

"Oh, *mierda*. But what about your articles? That will bring it to the spotlight."

"No. These articles aren't like that. They're just supposed to be informative."

"You mean you're doing something more than your work asks of you."

"Yeah but my coworker was too and now he might be dead."

"Are you going to make it to Charleston? I mean, were you exposed to the cholera?"

"No. I'm fine. I'll be there. I'll bring my work with me."

What else can I say? "Okay. Be safe, *chica*."

"Thanks. *Maka Manana*."

My tea is cold. My soul is colder. I need Mimi's rosary.

* * *

The night descends quickly despite the longer daylight hours. Dartmouth demands long hours these days—exams will begin next week and graduation will follow. Angelica and Izzy are in bed, but Carlos, who negotiated for a later bedtime some months ago, is in his room. The television and electronic games have to be off by the time the girls go to bed, but I relent on the computer issue. After all, I was a telephone junkie at his age.

There was a time when the five of us, the posse, lit up the phone lines. In truth, we still do. Cell phones have just made us mobile junkies. We are wandering conversants.

I stand at the dryer in the mudroom. Often, no one thinks to look for me here—either that or they're avoiding an obvious work zone.

The night is quiet. Tom will be home soon. The stars are brilliant against the inky darkness of the night sky. I fold the warm laundry and hug it up against my face. The fresh scent comingles with the comfort of my well-lit world. It's safe in here.

Out there, the cosmos crashes and reinvents itself in great cataclysmic events. Stars collide and black holes suck up neighbors. Creation and destruction—God is out there. The universe stretches and flexes, space-time warps in response to massive bodies, my body, curved space, and disturbances to the fabric of the universe travel at the speed of light, the light which never sleeps and never ceases its journey, the consummate wanderer. To surrender to those forces is to surrender altogether. They terrify me even as they thrill me. I am losing myself. I know, even as I pray to God, I will have to seek forgiveness for my part in that night before it is too late. I will have to be reconciled before I can fully redeem myself and return to Him. I need time, but the storm is fast approaching.

The shrill of the buzzer signals the end of the dryer cycle. I peer out into the night sky. This is the year. It is time. I feel it in my bones. Destiny calls.

15 Heather

My day-timer system rests open-faced on the bed. The boxes of days line up in rows, but the orderliness is an illusion. More like hopscotch. The meetings and events require things to be done days and weeks ahead. I've ordered the driver to pick me up at 6:00 a.m. sharp four days from now and deliver me to the airport. Three days from now, Eve, Mariah, Fiona, and Esperanza will already be there, rejoicing, while I'll still be here. Jealousy gnaws at my core, but it's my fault. I'll need the extra day to plow through the investigation and the audit.

I should've worked last weekend instead of going to the amusement park. I can't explain that decision as anything other than a deep-seated need to self-sabotage. I teeter along the line between being seen and disappearing. Brandon had made some excuse about working at the office and vanished for the remainder of the weekend. Shannon and I went on rides, made brownies, and drew butterflies all over her bedroom walls. Work was simmering on the back burner then, but it sizzles and pops now.

Charleston is four days away. My ass is grass. I haven't spoken to Michael Saxton yet. The Dallas audit is reaching a conclusion, but I doubt a good result will save me if the sexual harassment investigation goes south. One cannot equal out the other. Bob made that clear.

Some paperwork can be done in Charleston but most has to be done here. Taking work with me is forbidden, and I can't jeopardize this investigation. My job depends on it. In some twisted way, my life depends on it. Leafing through the papers doesn't ferret out the story.

My original notes didn't shed any light. I leaf through Tanya's personnel file again in the hopes of finding some odd and out-of-place piece of information that would shed some light, or at least give a clue to my next step.

The standard documents are in order. After college, Tanya had paid her dues in an entry-level position in the finance department of a mid-size company and worked her way up to a supervisory position. According to her application, she'd wanted a more challenging position with potential for advancement in a larger corporation. The position didn't require a graduate degree, but it was strongly recommended; Tanya did not have one, but she was hired one month from the date of her application as Manager of Accounts Receivable.

The events in between hiring and firing aren't good. Tanya's first performance review a year after hire came with a rating of Excellent and an 8 percent salary increase—something that would have required executive approval. The standard increase for that rating is 4 percent. Nothing in the review had been so exceptional as to warrant such an increase; however, all the required executive signatures were there.

A year later, Tanya received another rating of Excellent and a promotion to Manager of General Accounting. The change form reveals an 8 percent increase for her merit review and a 10 percent increase for the promotion. Again, the required signatures are in order. Seven months from that performance review and promotion, she went on disability for two months. She returned to work and was fired one week later. The cause for termination was insubordination, a cute catchall word to denote behavior requiring immediate termination and not a three-step warning process. Again, all the required signatures are there. The diagram is clear as day. Tanya Garrison was terminated for something quite different from insubordination, the

CFO was somehow involved, Bob Hewitt was privy to the information, and her disability leave is somehow pertinent.

The last piece of the puzzle knocks the wind from me. I remove my sweater and turn the thermostat down. I could turn the place into an igloo and I'd still be sweating.

My boss performed the investigation himself and recommended termination, and I was obviously chosen to review the findings and sign off on it. My signature, dark lines and circles, are all I can see. My skin screams and I etch the scribbles into my thigh with my fingernails.

I remember now. They called me into the office, where all three of them hovered over me. Vultures. I questioned their need for my approval when the Vice President, well experienced in such matters, was involved. Surely his recommendation carried more weight than mine? He accused me of being uncooperative and made a vague threat. I signed the damn investigation as if it were my own. Idiot. I imagined it would go away. Poof.

I dig my nails deeper into my skin and reach for the phone.

"Michael Saxton's office."

"This is Heather Collings. I need to speak to Michael Saxton."

"Mr. Saxton is out of the office."

"That appears to be a chronic state. I need to speak to him. It's urgent."

"Yes, well, he's unavailable."

"He's unavailable all the time. Does he ever take anyone's calls?"

"Of course he does."

"Well, why won't he take any of mine?"

"I told you before, he wants you to deal with me."

"Fine. It's all yours. Mr. Saxton is the subject of a sexual harassment, sexual discrimination, and race discrimination charge. The details of my investigation appear quite damning, i.e., he's fucked if this goes to trial. So what is your involvement in this little affair, Ms.

Martin? And how can you help me to help him?" I'm losing it. Either way, my job is on the line. "Ms. Martin? Are you there?"

"Yes. I'm sorry. I didn't realize."

"Yes, of course you didn't. I have asked the EEOC for more information. The prima facie case is right on, and the investigator has provided me with the full complaint, which is quite detailed. The Complainant alleges that she had an affair with Mr. Saxton, she got pregnant with his child, he accused her of infidelity with an executive at another company and claimed the other man was the true father of the child, and fired her as a consequence. The investigator has informed me that Ms. Garrison appears to have other personal documentation to back up her claim. I'm just wondering what Mr. Saxton has to say in response to those allegations."

"Ms. Collings, I assure you I knew nothing about this. I'll have Mr. Saxton call you. I don't think I can help you with this."

"No, of course not. Please have him call me. Immediately."

I do not believe for a second that Angela Martin knows nothing.

The investigator warned me there was another executive in another firm involved, but not named, in her suit. This complaint carries a high price tag. Tanya is accusing the two executives, who appear to know each other, of conspiring to ruin her ability to work. Compensatory damages, lost wages, and front wages are mounting, but Tanya is already demanding punitive damages. This one might go to trial. An attempt at settlement is inescapable. Before I approach Bob Hewitt with this information, I need to speak to Michael Saxton, find out the name of the other party, and find out everything I can about Tanya Garrison.

Chances are my job will not survive this. Bob has more or less told me so. No doubt, the case will end up with outside legal—shortly. I will be the chump, the reason for the matter becoming too big to stay in-house. The *coup de gr*âce, it will be the crack along which my life changes. I have not created the situation, but it'll destroy me just the same. Caught in the full glare of scandal, I will no doubt become an embarrassment to Brandon. I will be cast aside—no job and no husband. Besides Shannon, they are everything. I could not exist without the entire package.

I stop at Sharon's desk. "Sharon, I'm going now. I'm taking the investigation home with me and you can reach me on my cell phone if you need anything."

"Have fun."

"Thanks."

The phone rings. Sharon retrieves it as I hurry to the elevator.

She races after me. "Heather, it's the investigator. You know which one."

"Oh, right." I allow the packed elevator to go.

"Sorry. I know you're trying to get out of here but she says it's urgent."

"Thanks, Sharon. I'll get it in my office."

Outside my window, the stormy sky darkens. The gloom seeps into my office as I pick up the phone.

"Hi. This is Heather Collings."

The light from my room pierces the blackness on the other side, but it's the darkness I will most remember. My words are mechanical and empty. Words will never again be enough for me. There's no comfort in their edges.

"I have the name of that other executive involved with Tanya Garrison," the investigator tells me. "I should not be telling you this, but I feel like we have a good working relationship and you may need it to figure out how you might want to settle this situation. She's not filing a complaint against him, but she has given me his name for this complaint in case I need to speak to him. She, of course, has no grounds against him, only against her employer, and she made it clear she's in love with him and he with her." The investigator pauses. The light overhead buzzes. I need another aspirin. "It's, um, curious.

He has the same last name as you. Collings. Brandon Collings. Do you know him?"

I've never been able to run from the ugliness of my life. I want to, now, more than ever. But I've never been a runner. I'm more like a drop-and-roll-into-the-fetal-position type.

I gather my files. It's time to pickup Shannon from day care.

The clouds deepen and the dark gray omens a storm. I hope it will hold off until I get across town. I've never gotten used to the violence of spring storms in the East and they're unusually sinister this year.

My head has been pounding since midday. There's nothing that could take the edge off the conversation I had with the investigator. The words still swing around and pound off the walls of my mind, the thoughts moving in quick staccato. The investigator asked me her questions, divulged her own knowledge, and wondered if I understood. How could I understand? She had just torn the shroud from my life. The conversation suffocated me until all I could manage was single-syllable answers. I vowed I would call her back when I looked into it. She let me off easy.

I could still flee. There's still one thing that lets me know I exist. Shannon.

I push the grocery cart with her in the child seat. I need to stock the kitchen before I leave. I open a box of kid's cereal. Shannon reaches into the interior wax bag and cherry-picks her favorite colors.

"Mommy, I wike this cereal. Can we get another box so Daddy and Sir Galahad can have some?"

"Sure, honey." I could lace it with arsenic.

Shannon beams. "I wuv you so much, Mommy. You're always so much fwun."

I could let Sir Galahad slay my dragon. I giggle.

"Mommy, what's so funny?"

"Nothing. Mommy gets some funny ideas."

"I think you have good ideas. Like Sir Galahad. He's the most beautiful dwagon anyone's ever seen. All the other kids want one too."

"You're talking a lot about him today."

"That's because we took them all out and did another play."

"Ah, I see. Well, that might not have been one of Mommy's better ideas. In fact, that could be one of Mommy's really dumb ideas."

"How could Sir Galahad be a dumb idea?"

"Well, sometimes the best ideas are dumb ideas because they're not at the right time or at the right place, sweetie."

Shannon cocks her head. "Mommy, a good idea is always a good idea. Especially when it's Sir Galahad."

"I guess you're right, honey. I'm just silly."

"Mommy, can we go home now? I want to see my toys and Barbie's s'posed to meet Sir Galahad on TV."

Home. I break into a cold sweat. A thought hovers: *Flee before you get the shit kicked out of you.*

"What do you mean?"

"Susan said Barbie and Sir Galahad are going to be on special TV tonight."

"Are you sure it's Barbie?"

"No, but it could be."

"Barbie really gets around."

"That's cuz she's a princess."

"Yeah, well even princesses have to slay the dragon, grow up, and get a job."

Shannon looks horrified. "Mommy! I would never slay Sir Galahad. That's not even nice. Don't you think it's nice having something so pwetty in the world? Honestly, Mommy, I love him." She crosses her arms over her chest, sticks her lower lip out, and turns her head from me.

I've done it this time. Shannon's right. Sir Galahad, after all, is our creation. To slay him would be the same as murdering a dream. Even if such a thing can't exist in my universe, that doesn't give me permission to kill its promise in hers.

"I'm sorry, Shannon. You're right. It's wonderful having Sir Galahad in the world and I don't want him to go away. Tell you what? I'll make sure nothing ever happens to him. I promise."

Shannon smiles.

"Let's go home, my beautiful Guinevere."

Shannon giggles. "Who's Guinevere?"

"She was the wife of King Arthur of the Round Table. Monsters and wild animals and King Arthur get to live forever. Sir Galahad was also part of the story."

"Is Guinevere pwetty?"

"Yes, she was very pretty, but she got herself in trouble when she betrayed Arthur."

"That's not good. What did she do?"

"It's complicated. Maybe we'll discuss it sometime when we don't have to go home, make dinner, and get ready for bed. Mommy has something she has to take care of." And I'm not quite sure Arthur didn't deserve it.

Shannon twists her hands around the handle of the shopping cart. "I wish you weren't leaving soon. I want you to stay here. How can you protect Sir Galahad if you aren't here?"

"Sir Galahad will be very safe while I'm gone. I'm putting a special protection around both of you. Anyway, I'm only going for a short time. You'll have fun with Daddy."

Shannon looks at me. There's no smile in her eyes, just innocence and trust. I kiss her forehead.

We check out and head to the car. The sky is still blistered black and the storm, stubborn, refuses to spend the electricity and humidity in the air. I'm thankful for the steel around us.

The conversation I had with the investigator still threatens to knock me flat. I accelerate and almost miss my next right. The tires squeal into the sharp turn.

I hear the sirens and see the lights.

"Mommy, that was fun."

"Sorry, honey. I almost missed our turn."

The cop lingers before he gets out of his vehicle and saunters over. I long to throw my license and registration at him, but they're always looking for an excuse to torment me.

The bright light from his flashlight hits my eyes and blinds me as I roll down the window. I must look like a frightened doe, because he moves the beam to Shannon and then lowers it enough that I can see.

"License and registration."

I hand him the documents.

"I know I took that corner too quickly, sir. I'm sorry. I had too many things on my mind."

"Maybe you should have the safety of your daughter on your mind instead." He takes a quick look at each document while panning the flashlight. "Wait here."

I watch in the rearview mirror as he swaggers back to his cruiser.

Jerk! He must've been waiting for someone, anyone, and it just had to be me. It always has to be me. The bright lights shoot out from every angle. People pass and slow to peer in at me. A curtain in a nearby house draws slightly aside.

Where were they when I needed someone all those years ago? No one cared what my parents did. Where were the cops then? No one bothered. No one peeped from the windows.

"Okay, you'll have to pay this amount by the date indicated unless you choose to dispute this, in which case, you'll have to do so as indicated by that date. You're free to go. Pay a little more attention to what's going on around you, lady."

Prick! The steering wheel doesn't give way under my banging. I dig my fingernails into the soft underbelly of my hand and find some release in the deepness and memory of the hurt. The air conditioning struggles against the thick, moist heat of the not-yet-dispelled storm. I roll down the window again and shift into gear. My skin screams and I long to break the window and dig a shard of glass into fresh skin.

It's the one word the universe yells in my head over and over. *Flee.*

Thirty precious minutes wasted on my lack of attention and an overzealous cop who has nothing better to do with his life than pull me over. The intensity of my rage is equal to the pulsing air. I drive through a soup of anger. Someone is probably murdering someone somewhere or some child is being beaten and he was there giving me a pointless lecture and ticket. I try to remind myself that the world has become more sensitive to the signs of a beaten child, but I don't really care. Nothing helped me then. I still carry the scars of all that indifference. All I had were my four friends, and their voices were no more believable than mine. We were the undetectable five. Fucking invisible. I pound the steering wheel.

"Do me a favor, Shannon, and don't tell Daddy about this."

"Why? Daddy never puts you in time out."

"No, he never puts you in time out either. He makes me do that."

"Yeah, but I know he does."

"You're a smart cookie. I love you."

"I love you too, Mommy."

Dusk blends with the storm clouds as we pull into the garage. The hairs rise along the surface of my arms and the lowered atmospheric pressure suffocates me. I struggle to breathe; my heart and chest heave with the exertion.

Dusk is my favorite time. It's the dividing line between work and home. It's my frontier between occupied moments. Lights cast a glow against the coming darkness, but today, the lights don't ease my discomfort. There's no divide between my two lives. They bleed into each other.

Crickets bellow from the yard now shrouded in blackness. The garage door closes and we hurry into the house. The faint odor of old smoke suspends itself on the cloying wetness in the air.

The night remains burdened with the storm's promise. The steady hum of the ceiling fan moves hot air from one corner of the room to another as we silently eat our dinner, the utensils sliding across china the only respite from the relentless drone of the fan and the fury of the night insects.

"Did Martha tell you I called this morning?" I wipe perspiration from my forehead.

Brandon's utensils halt midair. Time suspends itself. The heavens could have crashed into chaos and I wouldn't have been deterred from this course. It's not an accident: the day has been moving towards this point.

Brandon looks at me coolly. "Yes, she did. I didn't get a chance to return it. I had something to take care of this morning and I had a lot to catch up on this afternoon."

"Really? What did you have to do?"

Brandon drops his utensils, the noise momentarily dispelling those of the fan and crickets. He wipes his hands on his napkin, the act slow and methodical—dangerous.

Shannon's eyes widen.

He looks at me as he shifts in his seat. He reminds me of a snake. Every ounce of handsomeness I have marveled at for years is gone. Poof. Like magic. "I'm sorry I didn't return your call, Heather, but my business is my business." His voice holds an edge along which his words slice. "And it's none of yours."

"Excuse me? Why wouldn't it be my business? You're my husband. Besides, I was just curious, Brandon, making conversation. You hadn't mentioned you would be out this morning. Normally, we share that information in case day care needs us." I latch onto that bit of truth to cover my lie.

His eyes turn a livid blue. Must be a tropical reptile. His voice cuts through the air. "You haven't been interested in my work or, for that matter, my world for a long time now, Heather." He spits my name like a toxin. "It wouldn't have crossed my mind to tell you my agenda. This thing came up and I had to deal with it. End of story."

"That's not true. I'm always interested in what you're doing. And, anyway, what's all the mystery about?"

"Something that has no bearing on you." He lifts his utensils. "Look, we've both been consumed by our jobs lately. It suits me fine to not discuss it at home."

I should heed and accept his attempt to end the conversation, but I'm not ready to let it go. "I think it's healthy to share."

Shannon looks from her father to me.

His jaw hardens. "I don't think there's anything healthy about the extent to which you are willing to be completely consumed by everything except what really matters. Whether it's a project at day care that you think will win you brownie points or it's your plans to meet your friends for a bitch session. You're selfish. I'm surprised you notice anything else—unless, of course, it affects you."

My cheeks redden. "What do you mean? That's not fair. I couldn't give a damn about day care, and if I'm so very consumed by my job then why do I take care of everything around here, including the plumbing?"

"You don't like day care, Mommy?" Shannon mashes her little fork into her food.

"That's a damn lie and you know it, Heather. You're so hell-bent on your own agenda that you haven't got the time of day for anyone else's. Did you even ask me if I had any plans while you run to Charleston?"

"Charleston was planned a year ago. You knew this. I take a trip at this time every year. This has never been an issue before. I don't know where this is coming from. I only asked you about your meeting this morning and it's turned into a personal attack."

"This isn't about my meeting. You and I both know you have something else on your mind, your agenda. Instead of skirting around the issue, why don't you just ask what you want to ask?"

There it was, the truth of it. Do I really want to know? He's opened the door. Do I dare go in? Can I bear it? I know a form of death hovers somewhere on the other side. Drums pound in my head and the sweat, which has traced a line between my breasts, now bleeds through the weave of my red cotton blouse and pools at my navel, spreading and darkening the fabric to crimson. I want to free myself, but freedom is a very dangerous thing. It can kill you in more ways than the act of dying.

I force the question through my teeth, but it comes out soft and muted. "Where were you this morning?"

He looks straight at me, straight through me. "None of your fucking business."

Shannon's breath hisses, her mouth and eyes widen in shock.

The pounding in my head matches that in my chest. "It is my business. Because we're married. And because I care. I wouldn't be asking if I didn't. You and Shannon are my life. Everything I do, I do with you in mind." A liquid veil obscures my surroundings. Terror squeezes my insides. My eyes plead with his. But it's only partially true. Part of me wants to be free and the other part seeks the lie, needs the comfort of it. It'll become complicated.

He pushes his chair back and stands. "You're full of shit." Through clenched teeth, he continues. "Maybe we should discuss this later."

"When?"

He glares, clenches his fists, turns, and throws his plate into the sink. It shatters against the porcelain. He storms from the room.

Thunder, low and far away, cannot mask that of the fan and crickets whose continued onslaught deafens me. I press the palms of my hands tightly against my ears. Shannon's little mouth trembles.

Why didn't I force him to come clean? Force him to say it?

My chest aches. I clutch at it, and the fabric of my blouse yields and soaks my hand. The questions swirl like tiny blood-sucking insects, devouring all reason.

Why did I take the call?

Do you know him? I was stricken but calm. He had been intimate with someone who I had unwittingly helped fire. I'd been forced to handle the situation, a situation that violated a code. A conflict of interest, and I was totally blind. Betrayed from every side, including my own. A million ways to betray and I had tapped them all.

But could it be someone else? Another Collings? The investigator had more.

Tanya Garrison had been found dead in her apartment. She was sorry. Detectives would be visiting me as they had visited her. The whole affair had become . . . complicated. The death was suspicious, and everyone who'd had anything to do with her would be looked at differently.

Suspicious? How suspicious?

Homicide suspicious.

The words kept replaying: Dead . . . Homicide . . . Same Name. There have to be other Collingses. But is there another Brandon Collings? Another Brandon Collings who works for his company? And who killed Tanya? Is he capable of that? I'm no longer sure. What was the thing he had to do? I don't want to think. I push my fists into my eye sockets until I see stars, but it doesn't stop the questions. Can I sleep next to a man who, at minimum, slept with someone else, and possibly even murdered her? Can I trust the most important person in the world to his care?

And will they figure out I was the one, the one married to her lover, who signed off on her dismissal? The jilted woman.

But there was more. Tanya was pregnant. Did he kill her and his own baby?

Shannon whimpers.

"I'm sorry, baby. Do you forgive Mommy?" Shannon's quiet tears turn into sobs and her body heaves with emotion. Thunder rumbles closer. "Mommy and Daddy sometimes fight over stupid stuff, but it doesn't really mean anything, sweetheart."

Shannon looks up and her blue eyes glisten through her tears as she breathlessly whispers, "Why is Daddy so mad?"

"Daddy's not that mad. It's just we're all so hot. Sometimes the heat gets to people."

"But Mommy, why would the weather make Daddy mad?"

A flash of light pierces the darkness. A thunderclap follows, silencing the crickets. Another flash of light catches the entire landscape. Thunder follows. Shannon jumps from her seat and crouches under the table. The air pulses. Another flash of light outlines the silhouette of the garden. Drops of rain streak the windows. A loud thunderclap immediately follows a streak of lightning.

I jump.

Shannon peers fearfully from under the table. Her tear-streaked face is etched with fear. Tiny tufts of hair lift from her scalp, drawn to the electrostatic charges in the air. I smile and extend my hand.

Torrents of rain thunder along the roofline and in sheets against the panes of the windows and sliding door. The old oak tree in the backyard moans under the weight of the downpour.

A blinding white light fills the space around me as a deafening noise rends the air. Wood splits as if the Earth itself has cleaved in two. A huge blow tightens my chest, and even as I draw away from the light I am filled with tiny needles of pain. Glass shatters around me. A high-pitched wail, frightening and familiar, fills the space around me. Shannon!

* * *

I swim. The sound of water is familiar. My mother turns on both faucet knobs right before she pours the bleach. Thunder and downpours—pain always follows. I can't open my eyes in the bleach-tainted water, but I need to surface to catch a breath. If I accidentally swallow, I will lose. The tightness in my throat asphyxiates me. My lungs will soon burst. I have to open my eyes. I must find the surface.

I am drowning.

The weight crushes my breath.

I open my eyes.

Brandon hovers, his fingers wrapped around my throat. His face contorts as he exerts pressure, a mask of hatred and something far more intimate. I squirm but my limbs are caught. I don't have the strength to equal his. It's like every other time. I'm helpless against the will of others. Others have the power and I have none. Stars dance.

"Why couldn't you let it alone? Why can't everyone leave it alone? I've lost everything. Everything. You are nothing to me. Do you hear me? Your mother was right. You're weak and pathetic. You make me sick. God! You make me want to vomit." Tears stream from his eyes and splatter. "I've lost everything that matters."

The light recedes.

Shannon!

* * *

A scream pierces the darkness.

I wake.

"Mommy! Mommy! Mommy!"

I struggle. Shannon needs me.

The sound of shattering dishes terrifies me. I raise my hand to my throat. A knife of searing pain throbs against my vocal chords. I lift my unwilling head an inch. It is enough to see.

Brandon clears the remainder of the counter with his arm. His sobs are thick. "How could anyone think I did it? I loved her."

I beckon to Shannon. "Shannon." The sound is raspy and weak.

"Mommy!" I watch helplessly as she sobs under the kitchen table now littered with broken dishes and scattered utensils.

I think, but I cannot gather up the threads of my thoughts and stitch them together. Split, they dangle in the elements. I'm dizzy, my breath is shallow; I fight to stay conscious. I can't succumb. Shannon is alone.

"Daddy!" Shannon pleads.

Brandon stoops against the counter. He turns to Shannon. His eyes are full of tears. Seeing them, a part of me breaks too. He would never have cried like that for me.

"Daddy is sorry."

Shannon runs from under the table and hugs him but he pulls away. He looks at me.

"I'm sorry. You and Shannon used to be enough. But everything's changed. Everything's dead." He puts his face in his hands and sobs. "I'm sorry."

Shannon hugs him. He pulls away again, walks to the door, and leaves. The sounds of the garage opening and the car pulling out mingle with that of storm-quenched rain.

"Shannon. Come here."

Shannon crawls next to me, tucks herself into my side, and sucks her thumb, a habit she relinquished a year ago. I don't have the heart or the energy to remind her of this.

We lie and listen to the rain, now a gentle patter that subdues the night. We need to go, but exhaustion enslaves my will. It's not the first time someone's tried to kill me. I stroke Shannon's hair. She grabs my hand and tucks it into her body.

I was alone the first time.

We had hitchhiked to Tallon Park. I was returning home. I focused on each step to quiet the rising panic. I was late. Walking straight through the deep carpet of newly shed needles, I concentrated on the scent of crushed pine. The terrain was steep and slippery, but I didn't have to think about tomorrow. Now there was only the forest, the shifting of the trees in the fading sunlight, and the slipping needles that caused my feet to slide. I only had to keep my footing.

Deep down, I sensed that things were far darker than in that soundless forest. My hair stood on my neck and a chill coursed through my limbs. I felt a set of eyes on my back as I ascended through the trees. I turned. There were only shadows. I watched and listened. Nothing changed. I continued to climb, but the needles shifted under my feet and gave way.

The force of the fall knocked the wind from my lungs and I slipped helplessly to the bottom. I should've stayed there. Let the damp night air take me. I knew it then even as I know it now.

My pants ripped and I was covered in dirt and pine needle sap. I had been so close to home.

* * *

The air was crisp the following morning. A certain resolve hovered in the cloudless sky. My mother had used her fists, and the purple of those bruises mingled with those from my fall. It was an unspoken knowledge that the signs of the beatings were to remain unseen, but I had ducked and one of the punches had caught me on the jaw.

I skipped breakfast. My mother accused me of rebelliousness. Absence was rebellion. Part of me wanted the world to see even if it didn't care. Death would be better. A friend had hung herself from the stair banister with her father's belt.

I understood. That was the moment when the pain stopped forever.

I perched at my window and thought about death. Would my parents cry? Would my father notice? It didn't matter. Their pain was guaranteed. Society questioned young death. It didn't fit into an understanding of a world in which people were required to grow old and die naturally. Society would whisper behind my parents' backs and the words would be unkind. The loss of order demanded judgment. My parents wouldn't be able to hide behind the lies anymore.

I wanted death.

From my window I could see into the expanse of shade-infused gloom punctuated by a lone patch of sun-dappled earth. A rickety fence wedged behind the mature trees separated my yard from Mariah's. Long ago we'd discovered several attached boards we could flip. I perceived the fence at the border of the garden, and whether by actual sight or by knowledge, I traced the contours of Mariah's house and the window from which Mariah gazed out to my side of the hilltop. There was love in her house. Not that they didn't have their own suffering, but they wore it together. I longed to be a part of their world, to be loved simply because I existed. There were times her mother caressed my face and there was never a greater sorrow than leaving her side. But she was Mariah's—not that Mariah wouldn't have shared. It was the Indian way. But my mother would've found me, ripped me away, and moving again, I would've lost everything. There was comfort in knowing my place. And there was comfort in knowing I still had something that could be taken.

My side of the yard was swathed in the shadow of a lone avocado tree that spread its branches towards the light. Mateless, it couldn't bear fruit, but its broad, waxy leaves made intricate and protective shadows that played across my bedroom walls. Deep in the night, when the old stairs creaked with the weight of their history and unidentifiable noises filled me with dread, I could count on the moon to leave its glistening mark through the leaves. Moonbows crossed my quilted bed and illuminated the dark corners of my room. She was my tree. She belonged to me and I to her. I too could grow into barren loveliness. Large and round, the trunk soared toward the sky even as its branches reached toward the world and its roots cleaved the ground—earthbound and sky-bound. No, one did not have to have a mate in order to be strong or captivating. I reached through my screenless window to pluck a leaf. I turned it in my hands and placed it on my dresser, my altar. It was the one special thing I was still allowed to have besides my friends.

No. One did not have to have a mate to die. It was the one thing you did alone.

I gathered my things. I wore my bathing suit underneath my clothing and tucked an old towel into my embroidered Indian purse. Leaving my room, I made sure my door was wide open. A closed door inferred secrets and those weren't allowed.

I learned early to live with hypocrisy.

I crept down the stairs. Mariah's voice mingled with that of my mother's in the kitchen. I perched at the bottom step, catching the last scraps of conversation.

"Where will you be?" My mother's tone was uncharacteristically light.

"We'll be around town. We might go to the swimming pool at the Rec Center and the park. Fiona has some new records so we might go there too."

"I see. That's fine." My mother's voice trailed off as she ran out of questions.

I came off the last step and entered the kitchen. Mariah seemed to have dispelled all misgivings. It was a tricky matter getting out of my house. Today was a good day. It could turn bad quickly.

I reveled in the excitement of adventure and of something more—a trespass. My stomach twittered. We skipped and jumped down the stairs outside the front door and ran all the way to Esperanza's house.

Walking down Main Avenue toward Hillcrest Park, we received a mixture of catcalls and disapproving looks. I tried to make myself inconspicuous between Eve and Esperanza. Someone I knew might call mother.

"Quit acting weird." Fiona clucked.

"Someone might see us and tell." I shrank between my friends.

Eve giggled. "C'mon, Heather. These people are from Sycamore. They don't care what we're doing and they don't know us. It's totally cool."

"Yeah?"

"Yeah."

Mariah, Esperanza, and I caught the first car. An elderly man scolded us on the merits of taking public transportation versus that of catching rides that could end up poorly for us.

I smiled shyly and thanked him.

"Say, where did you get all those bruises?"

"I . . . I . . . I ran into a door."

"Uh-huh. Don't let anyone slap you around, little one. No one has that right. You understand?"

"Yes sir. Thank you."

Mariah was the last one out of the car. She smiled at the man.

Esperanza frowned. "What a square."

Mariah pulled her hair back. "He's an elder, Espy. He didn't mean anything. He cares about us."

"I guess so."

Fiona and Eve got a ride a little later with a recently married couple going for a picnic.

Our day was carefree. The events of earlier in the year eased under the sun-warmed eucalyptus trees. We laughed and sunbathed.

The trip back was uneventful, but Eve felt the weight of her brother's absence as we approached the Grand Hillcrest Theater.

Before her brother left, she'd spent her summers with him. But then he went to Vietnam. Infantry. Her idol was going off to kill or be killed. There was no ambivalence in war. One always had a 50 percent chance of coming home in a body bag. A classmate of his was going to college on the East Coast. Why was one going and the other wasn't? She felt betrayed—betrayed by her country. That same classmate was from Upper Sunny Hollow, his father knew a couple of senators. His life would be college and a career. The operative word was life. Eve's father was a black man from Mississippi via Detroit. It just wasn't fair. Her voice trailed off. We worried for Terrell. He had always been our protector and now no one could protect him.

"Let's hitchhike to Tallon again tomorrow." Fiona bubbled with the success of the day.

"No way. I'm tired."

"Ah, c'mon, Eve. That went so well and we had so much fun. We have to do it again. Besides, we can't go back to the Rose Garden. I think it's pretty obvious we're no longer welcome."

Esperanza found the middle ground. "I agree. Let's wait, though. We can always hang out at someone's house."

"All right. Whatever. We'll wait a day," Fiona said.

Mariah looked at Fiona as she addressed me. "Don't worry, Heather. I'll butter your mother up again. It'll be fine."

"Yeah. I hope so. I'm not sure I want to do this all summer long. I'll run out of excuses. She'll start tracking me down at the Rec Center and she'll flip when she finds out we haven't been there all summer."

Mariah hated the purple that marred my left jaw line and she told me so. It looked dirty. "Don't worry," she said. "We won't make a habit of this."

"I get it. Day after tomorrow it is, then." Fiona swung around toward home, her long golden hair swishing with every step.

We stared after her. No one dared move.

Eve was the first to break the spell. "All right. I guess we're going back day after tomorrow."

"I guess so," Esperanza said.

Mariah watched her. "I know that girl has something up her sleeve. I just don't know what it is."

"I guess we'll find out later." Eve slung her arm over Mariah's shoulder.

"Well, I hope it's not going to get us all in trouble," Esperanza said.

"Yeah, but I'm not actually worried about being found out." Mariah frowned. "I'm worried about her intentions and I'm worried about getting Heather out of her house again."

I tried to smile. I turned and shuffled toward my end of the street. Despite my fear, I took the stairs. I couldn't risk a repeat of climbing the hill. And that's where I saw him.

"Hey beautiful. What are you doing?" Sitting outside the house where the angry guy who'd returned from the war lived, he sat hunched over, his elbows resting on his thighs. His blue jeans were tattered, but he exuded something I didn't understand. His chest was muscular and lean. There was something about him. He was dangerous and vulnerable. He was handsome and terrifying.

"Nothing. I'm going home."

"Why don't you hang out here for a while? You're beautiful." His smile was genuine and sexy.

"I can't. I have to go home."

"Ah, c'mon. You're breaking my heart. You're the most beautiful woman I've ever laid eyes on."

"Th-th-thank you. But I have to go."

I ran.

That night, he was all I could think about.

* * *

It was supposed to be a trip without any hitches—like the previous one. But then, nothing can ever be replicated. The impermanence of experience has its own immutable laws. It was the kind of day you wish had never happened but know, in the cold light, that nothing, absolutely nothing, can change it. There just simply was no taking it back.

Fiona's father had once told us that time slowed in comparison to one's rate of motion. The faster one moved, the more time slowed, and the more one sat on one's butt, the faster it flew. A tweak of velocity was all that was needed to make time one's friend. If we ran like hell, could we make it all go away?

Our childhoods unraveled swiftly then.

For Eve, the change had already started. None of us experienced space and time identically. Suffering no more so. If we lived in motion, one girl following the other, our watches would tick a fraction off from each other. That difference was real. It would require a fusion of wills to meet the world we had just unleashed.

It started with the simple act of sticking out a thumb. But life is that way. Karma doesn't yield even to the most simple of deeds.

I woke that morning with a jolt. My mother hovered . . . waiting . . . patiently, coldly, intent and satisfaction a gruesome smear across her lips, which were pressed into a thin line of determination.

"Mom, what are you doing?"

"Mariah called. You're not going anywhere today. I have things I need you to do today."

"But everyone's expecting me. Everything's already planned."

"Do you really think I care what a bunch of teenage girls think?"

"No, Mom. It's just I promised them." My voice cracked and I cringed against the backboard. There was no shelter against the hardness of it.

"Are you talking back to me?"

"No. B-b-b-b-ut they're expecting me."

The movement was swift. My cheek stung with the force of the blow.

After all those years, I still couldn't anticipate it. Not that knowing would have made it hurt any less, but had it been more predictable, the anticipation might have served to counterfeit the violence. The tears streamed hot down my bruised upon bruised cheeks. I crumpled on the bed, my hand held against my smarting skin, my eyes fixed on my mother.

"What? Have you lost your tongue?"

I shook my head. My mother disappeared into the watery landscape. I didn't have to see her clearly to know she was there. The tears hid nothing.

"Fine. You'll call your little group of friends and let them know you won't be there."

My mother turned, left the room, and slammed the door. I buried my head into my pillow and let the tears loose.

By the time I had dressed and wiped my eyes, the sun sparkled in the California sky. Its beauty was almost sacrilegious, as if all that joy could negate my despair. After all, it was the universe that had given me these circumstances.

Mother sat at the kitchen table with a list of chores. Wordlessly, she handed it to me. It was the longest list I'd ever seen. The tears flowed anew. Mother pursed her lips and pointed her long, lacquered-nailed finger at the phone.

I dialed Mariah. She wouldn't judge and she would know how to handle Fiona.

"Mariah, it's Heather. I can't go out today. I have to stay here."

"I had a feeling. I spoke to your mom earlier. Fiona's here and she wants to talk to you."

"No. I can't."

"She's not taking no for an answer."

Fiona's tone was firm. "You need to get out. You're not getting out of this. Would it be better if we came over and came up with a story for your mother?"

"No, I don't think that would be a good idea."

"Let me talk to her."

"I don't think that'll help. It might make things worse."

"Don't worry. I won't make it worse. Just let me talk to her."

"I think that's a bad idea."

"Just put her on."

"She wants to talk to you, Mom." Sheepishly, I handed the phone to her.

"Yes."

I watched as Mother settled her icy gaze on me. I thought of every room that could be locked and barred. There was no shelter in the house.

"No, she can't. She's needed here." Her lips disappeared. She clutched the phone so tightly the veins popped along the back of her hand.

I inched backwards.

"I told you before, Fiona. She won't be coming out today!" She slammed the phone down on its receiver.

Mother's barely suppressed rage reached deep, her frosty heart turned into an inferno. She walked over to the stove, picked up a frying pan, spun around, and hit me squarely across my torso. The sound of cracking terrified me.

Doubling over in pain, I heard another crack. The ice burned like fast-moving wildfire across my scalp. Within a moment, I found a black hole. I knew nothing of the rest of that beautiful blue-sky day. That nothingness was what little mercy I knew. It was the fog that concealed the ugliness of my life.

* * *

I'm not that defenseless girl anymore. I can't let the fog creep back in. Glass crunches as I raise myself on my elbows.

"Mommy. I don't want to get up."

"We have to get up, honey. It's time to go. We need to pack up a few things. Special things. And then we need to leave here."

"Why?"

"We'll go somewhere fun while someone cleans up the glass."

"I don't want to leave. What about Daddy?"

"I'm sorry, sweetie." I stroke her hair, though I know it won't take away the pain. "We need to leave Daddy alone. He is very angry right now. We need to leave before he gets more angry."

Shannon whimpers.

"I'm sorry, baby. We'll go see Aunt Mariah, Eve, Espy, and Fiona. We'll have so much fun. C'mon, baby. Let's get your best toys." I tug her up and she melts into my arms.

It's time to leave now. I was alone the first time someone tried to kill me. I was amongst strangers the second. This time, the third, I'm with Shannon. Third time is the charm. Third time is the last. I will be my daughter's shelter. She is all I have left.

There is shelter in acting, in being someone else's. That is what my friends have been trying to tell me for years. I just couldn't see it. Letting things happen is the worst sort of action. There is no protection or salvation in hiding. Someone always finds you. It's time to stand up and move.

16 Fiona

Sunday dawns cold and somber. Large gray clouds roll tersely across LA. The air has the distinction of being named after the baby Jesus, *El Niño*. But rain in Southern California is a mixed blessing. There is no gentle terrain to soak up the drops; torrents of water wash through gullies and canyons and fill concrete-encased rivers. Water, cool and benevolent in glistening turquoise swimming pools, lays bare the illusion that constitutes Los Angeles. The city is a brilliantly engineered lie that morphs the arid environment into an oasis from appropriated water.

The image of undulating and morphing glass stares back at me through the mirror-lined wall. I shimmy in the water-like illusion. Or is it my tears? Maybe the wind and rain are causing the mirror to shake, or maybe I have been looking too long and my eyes are betraying me. It's like the beginning of the year that forged our friendship into an unbreakable bond. By the end of that 365-day stretch, the world in which we lived had shifted. 1968. January began with a minor earthquake that warranted a fleeting comment on the radio station—a recalling of the epicenter, those affected, and what it registered on the Richter scale. The announcer stated a few windows were rattled, but barely noticed by anyone, the quake helped get the new year off to a rocking-n-rolling start as The Doors' "Light My Fire" blasted through KFRC's airwaves.

Living along "The Ring of Fire" is consumptive, but fire suits me.

My favorite book when I was a kid, dog-eared and stained, brimmed with images of bubbling viscous lava and incendiary blasts. Fire under my feet. Becoming knowledgeable did little to close the gap between knowing and understanding. But that breach was closed the day I witnessed the wreckage at my feet—my prized antique perfume bottles lying at the base of my dresser, all broken. The world continued as if nothing of note had happened, even as I stood amongst the ruin of my favorite possessions. That was when I understood. It would not be an ordinary year. But by the end of the year, I knew the world could move on even when mine couldn't. Rocks break into fragments. The whole is changed. But the pieces continue on.

Daddy once explained to me that tectonics push the land upward to create steep-walled canyons, but gravity brings it down again. Water can make or break the fantasy. Rock, young, vulnerable, and too weak to support the steep slopes it creates, invariably collapses and brings down the mudslides that dispel any illusion of indestructibility. The sin is in the perception. No matter how many times the mountain comes down, people build new houses to cling to its sides. Optimism on steroids.

I snort into the covers. Sort of like my face.

Last night's party was a disaster, a magnitude ten. I stare at my reflection in the mirrored closet that banks my side of the bedroom—half moons of despair shadow my eyes. Those same mirrors used to mimic the act of love I shared with Gavin. Watching me heightened his desire. That was a long time ago—another universe, really. Now the lines of my life are etched out in every gully of my face—lines my husband, who is trained to see every imperfection, has sworn do not exist. He has become more reluctant to tweak my flaws, less and less interested in me. The knowledge stares back through the looking glass.

Sam shut herself in her room last night and threw things against the wall. The thud of every piece resounded below, where our guests mingled uncomfortably. I ordered another cosmopolitan and then another. I contrived to act as though nothing was wrong, but my demeanor couldn't hide the truth any more than the walls could hide the violence being done to them. Eventually, the party dispersed. I tripped over my gown on the way to say good-bye to our guests.

Gavin gave me a disgusted look, and his parting shot was something to the effect that I could no more control my daughter than I could control myself. Turning, he dismissively closed the door to his den.

Small and alone, I sink into our giant bed. I created this crumbling perfect life. I cannot stop my life from cracking wide open any more than I can stop the earth from shifting. When did everything start to fall apart?

Of course, I know. It overshadows the smallness of everything around me. The guilt of it tingles deep inside and spreads to the outer limits. Tiny red bumps rise along the seams and contours of my body. Hives! God, I haven't had them in years. Tiny little busy bees of torment ripple along the surface, and in a fit of salvation from the sensation, I throw off the covers and claw at my skin. I shout from the top of the staircase, praying Abella will hear me.

"Abella!"

"Yes, Mrs. McDermott."

"I need a box of baking soda."

"*Ay, mija!* What's wrong?"

"I've got the hives, Abella. I don't know where they came from."

"That doesn't look so good, Mrs. McDermott. Has Dr. McDermott seen it?"

"No!"

"Oh! I'm sorry Mrs. McDermott. I'll bring up baking soda right away."

Abella leaves me clinging to the balustrade. I climb these stairs daily, but from this angle they appear unassailable. From the first step to the last, I cannot count my mounting troubles.

I'm mad at Gavin. There's one thing I know. Once the mantle of fury is blown, there's no way to hold back its course. I watched the same volcanic process in my own parents' marriage. With every eruption, every toxic word spat in rage, every moment of irreconcilable hurt, a crack deepened until eventually all that was left was a wide chasm of cooled lava. That my parents are still together, sharing separate lives, is a testament to the resigned capitulation of their generation. They remind me of Sean's wind-up robots who, upon spinning and facing each other, think better of sparring with each other and spin back around to do it with someone else. I ran from that life. I wanted no part of it. In running away, I came home.

Abella reappears at the bottom of the stairway and makes her way to me. Within her deep brown eyes, I see compassion and love. I am not deserving of either. She hands me the box.

"Are you all right, Mrs. McDermott? I could stay here while you rest today. I can go to Mass later. I could take the kids out to breakfast."

"No, that's all right, Abella. Everything is fine. I just need to soak in a cool tub. It's an allergic reaction. That's all. I haven't had one since I was a child."

"Allergic reaction to what?"

"I'm not sure. Maybe it's a sensitivity to something I ate at the party last night." The words are hollow. Maybe it's Gavin, for whom I am the perfect prized wife? Or was the perfect prized wife? Or is it Sam? I knew the day would come when she would disentangle her identity from mine. I imagined I would help give her wings to fly. Idiot. I didn't see this coming. Gavin cannot nip or tuck the untidy pieces of our imperfect marriage or the illusion of our fast-disintegrating perfect world. Everyone has witnessed the myth of it. No! I have fared no better than my own mother. It's morning and I'm too weary to face the day. "I'm sorry, Abella. Don't mind me. You need the rest of your day off. We'll be fine."

"Okay, but I wouldn't mind staying if it would help you."

"Thank you, but you do more than enough to help us. Now it's time to rest."

"But it pleases me to be here, Mrs. McDermott. You're my only family and it makes me *muy* sad to see everyone so sad. Everyone is jumbled against each other." She wrings her hands through her apron and her face twists with anxiety.

Abella. I know some of her story, but I have never completed the picture. It is more comfortable not knowing. Another one of my transgressions. She traveled with her husband from Ecuador on a work visa and they stayed in the US on green cards. Happy and planning a family, they worked hard. But a stray bullet killed that dream. Her husband's murderer was never found and Abella buried him without justice. She contemplated returning to Ecuador but it didn't seem right. Their dream was all she had left. She answered my ad for a family assistant, and when she arrived ten years ago, she somehow fit seamlessly into our busy lives. She has been one of us for so long that she is, I realize, one more person for whom I feel responsible; the guilt of my only just having recognized this spreads thickly through my now itchy iron appendages.

On my way to the bathroom, I grab a large bottle of vodka from my closet. The walls are frosted with mirrors and I close my eyes to their ice. I draw the cool water and pour the contents of the baking soda box into the tub. When the tub is full, I disrobe and gently lower my body into the water. The biting cold of it pricks at my raging skin.

I drink straight from the bottle, a long, sucking gulp that releases an enormous bubble in the bottle. I will the pain of last evening from my mind until a lone image seeps into my consciousness. Hovering waif-like at the center, Heather, mysterious and beautiful in her complexity, appears. I reach for the mirage but it disappears. I am left with the carcass of my disintegrating life and the bones of my calcified guilt.

I slide further into the tub, until the water seeps up my nose and finally over my eyes. My long blond hair floats weightless and free along the surface of the clear water. A mermaid encapsulated in a feather-light world. Everyone thinks the world revolves around me, but it all started with Heather.

Why couldn't I just leave it alone? Mariah warned me. Heather told me. Her mother's tone informed me, but I believed I could move mountains and part seas by the sheer power of my charm and beauty. I was legendary, after all. I, one Fiona Shit-for-Brains, could sway the heart of one Evil-Icy-Hearted-Mother.

I hung up.

"What happened?" Mariah asked. "Is she coming?"

"No. Her mom said no. There's no way she can come and I'm really worried. Her mom sounded really mad, like ice queen mad," I said.

"She is an ice queen." Mariah knew. She lived on the other side of the fence. "You shouldn't have tried to convince her. That might have made it worse. You yourself told us that long ago. Remember?"

"I remember. That's what Heather said. What do you think we should do?"

Eve considered. "I think we should go without her. Let the whole thing blow over. She'll be fine. If we do anything else, it might set Mrs. Lynch off."

Mariah agreed. "We can't do anything now anyway. Let's just go. I'll check on her tonight. I can cut through the fence and climb the tree by her window."

We had a plan. All would be fine and we would hitch a ride more easily with only four. I gathered my things and slung my purse over my shoulder. "Well, I'm ready."

Eve spun on me. "Well, of course you're ready! You're always ready. You try to make things go your way and when they don't, you drop it like a hot potato. You've probably screwed it up for Heather and now *you're ready* to forget about it. Leave it to poor Heather to pick up the pieces. Typical Fiona."

"Jeez, Eve. Why are you being such a bitch? Maybe you should've tried talking to Mrs. Lynch. Maybe *you* could have done a better job."

"I probably could've. I at least know you can't bully Heather's mom into anything. She's a bully herself. She's the queen of bullies. I would've let the whole thing go. But no. You had to insert your sorry ass into the situation."

"Screw you, Eve."

"All right, let's just forget about this and go." Esperanza hated fighting.

Mariah shrugged. "Let's stop fighting and go. What's done is done."

"We have to get to Tallon."

Esperanza and I got the first ride with a cowboy on his way to pick up a couple of horses from a Berkeley Hills stable that was "bustin' at the seams." He hated to see a couple of pretty girls "puttin' themselves in all kinds of danger." I smelled the odor of hay and sun-dappled horse haunches, the same scent that lingered on Mariah when she came home from South Dakota every August before school started.

It took Eve and Mariah longer to hitch a ride. By the time they arrived, the sun was low in the sky. We hung out, but soon we had to find rides home. Our parents would expect us home for dinner. Trust was such a vulnerable thing—one violation and it became a contingency.

"We should get the first ride since we got the last ride coming here." Eve paced.

When a young couple came along, Eve and Mariah fit perfectly into their backseat. Esperanza and I watched the back of their heads as they drove away.

I thrust my finger into the roadway. The first two vehicles passed, but the third slowed and finally came to a stop just past us. It was a love bus. The side door slid open to reveal a hodge-podge of mattresses and dirty blankets, and a young man with greasy hair and spaced-out eyes. I headed toward the bus, but Esperanza recoiled.

"What's wrong?"

"I don't know, but I'm not getting in."

I motioned to her. "C'mon. We have to get home."

"No way, Fiona."

I looked at the guy. "We're not ready to leave yet. We'll catch the next ride."

He smiled, said, "Yeah, later man," slid the door shut, and the bus inched away, its exhaust backfiring as it caught speed.

I watched the vehicle go around the bend before I turned to Esperanza. "What're you doing? That could be the only ride we get in time."

"No way, Fiona. That guy was creepy. I'm not getting into a car with anyone like that."

"Well, you might have to if you want to get home."

"I'd rather walk."

"We might have to. Seriously, my parents will kill me if I'm not back by supper."

"Well, you should've thought of that when you came up with this crazy scheme."

"I didn't hear you complaining or coming up with some other plan."

"I didn't exactly pull out the pom-poms either. Oh wait, that's you, the *gringa* cheerleader."

"You're just jealous, Espy."

"I'm not jealous. I'd rather not be a *gringa* prancing around with a bunch of shredded plastic and chanting while I do the splits. It's embarrassing."

"Quit calling me a *gringa*. You know I hate that."

"That's what you are."

"Yeah, but you don't hear me calling you a spick."

Esperanza eyed me coolly. "Do you really want to go there?"

I held my hands out, palms up. "I'm not calling you that and I never would. But then I'd prefer it if you didn't call me a *gringa*."

Esperanza shrugged. "I'm sorry, Fiona. Besides, *gringa*'s only a bad name if you want it to be bad, if you use it in anger. Otherwise, it's not so bad." Esperanza turned back to the road. It was empty. "Mimi is preparing a special summer meal, diced and sautéed pork and boiled plantains fufu. She got plaintain leaves, too, to cook fish in. I'm hungry. How're we going to get back home?"

A loud, discordant sound entered the space around us first—confusing, hard to place. Seconds later, the bang of a car backfiring and the sound of a door sliding along its hinges warned us.

Esperanza was the first to react. "Run!"

The love bus had returned and three men were moving toward us. I watched, my mind caught in mud. "But they must just want to talk to us. We could catch a ride with them now. Honestly, Espy, we need to get home. I can handle them."

But Esperanza was already running toward the eastern bank of trees. I turned back to the men; they did appear sinister in the gleam of the descending afternoon sun. It took me a moment to figure out the problem: one set of eyes glittered with malevolent excitement.

I was in a dream. I needed to run. My limbs moved in slow motion, in direct opposition to the men's increasing speed.

It took me forever to reach the bank of trees into which Esperanza had disappeared.

I felt hot breath on my neck.

I sprinted as fast into the forest as my lungs would allow.

I ran for my life.

I ran until I no longer could.

There was nowhere to hide. I had no bearings other than that provided by a glimmer of the setting sun.

And Esperanza was nowhere to be found.

I didn't dare call for her. I didn't know how far she had run and I didn't know where our pursuers were. Not knowing gnawed at me.

Footsteps came from all directions. Twigs, leaves, and needles crunched far and nearby, the sound maddening. My terror was heightened in the lightless world.

I had to move forward, a moving target was still safer. I couldn't wait for them to find me.

The sun disappeared and the forest turned strange. The darkness reached for me.

I had to keep moving or it would seize me.

I wandered for hours. Dad used to tell me that black holes squeeze the life from everything, creating dense matter that can fit on a pinhead. I was like that: lifeless matter compressed into a point. A point that bore no relevance to the world that continued around me, I would die and everyone else would go on.

Fleeing was pointless.

Daddy!

I stopped to lean against a tree. Dawn lightened the forest or maybe I was just used to the darkness. The finality of being alone sat heavily in my chest and wrung my innards like a wet and soiled rag. The sweat of my wandering now chilled into a cold dampness that plastered itself against my skin.

Don't lie down.

I looked toward the top of the canopy. The pink of the dawn sky softened the edges of the treetops. I would be able to figure this out in the light of day. Hope floated aloft of the forest. I moved forward, but the darkness followed.

Something smacked me full in the face, and blackness found me.

* * *

The blackness eventually gave way to the light. And I loved the light—but it was rough.

"She's over here."

Noise. It, too, should have been welcome, but it hurt my head.

"Miss, can you understand me?"

Who was he talking to?

"Are you Fiona MacDonald?"

Of course I was. The question was absurd.

"Huh?"

"She's not responding."

"Well, give her a minute. It looks like she took quite a hit from that tree limb."

My face burned.

"We've been searching all night for you."

I struggled to move. Mom would be distraught. Mother's distress was . . . well, distressing. I lived in a gilded birdcage.

"Don't move."

I lay still.

"Have they found the other one?"

"Yes. She's just over that knoll."

Espy was just over the knoll. What knoll? I hadn't seen anything. She had been so close, but in the dark she could have been on the other side of the world. I struggled to look but couldn't; defeated, I slumped to the ground.

"We'll get you to the hospital as soon as possible. Just don't move."

My tears slipped and stung and I stopped fighting.

I drifted in and out of consciousness, a ring of fire consuming me. The hands pushed something into my arm—another assault on my fire-consumed body, but this monster was merciful, because it helped me fall back into the black hole.

* * *

I drifted back into a haze of whiteness. Mom wrung her hands, a cotton handkerchief knotted and twisted into a sharp point between them. I didn't need to see the act to know it—to know the cloth.

"Fiona?"

I couldn't answer.

"Fiona, what on earth could you have been thinking?"

The surrounding shapes remained edgeless. When I lifted my hand, I couldn't tell where my hand began and the air ended. My fingers touched something foreign.

"Mom?"

"Yes, Fiona."

"What happened?"

"Eve and Mariah came home and told us where you'd gone. I can't imagine you doing such a thing. I would've driven you girls to Tallon. Do you know what could've happened?" She sobbed.

In a million years, I couldn't have foreseen this anguish. What had I been thinking? I've caused her enough heartache in her life.

"And your father hasn't been able to go to work. He's been by your side since they found you. I finally told him to go home and take a shower and eat something. Fiona, you have turned our lives upside down. We've been sick with worry."

"I'm so sorry, Mama. I'll never do it again." The tears stung. Somehow, the pain felt right.

"God almighty. You have a concussion, multiple scrapes, and hypothermia. I think it'd be wise if you rested a bit. Esperanza's family agrees."

Espy! "Mom, what happened to Espy? I couldn't find her. I tried so hard, but I couldn't find her!"

"They found her near you. She has hypothermia, but she's doing well. Better than you, in fact."

I heard my own sigh. Pieces of the night came back to me. It had been so dark and cold. Why had it been so cold when the day had been so warm? And Espy, missing, had been close all along. Somehow, the memory felt less ominous. She had been so close, but we couldn't save each other. Still, we had survived together.

"Mariah and Eve are fine. They've been worried about you. Mariah's parents are taking her to South Dakota. Her grandmother wants Mariah with her this summer. One of her uncles was killed in Vietnam. The other is missing."

"She should be there. It's where she belongs."

"Yes, I know." My mother paused. I wanted to see her face. My blindness was frustrating. "Esperanza's father is taking his family to Mexico for a couple of weeks. Away from here. They're waiting for her release from the hospital."

I took it all in, the loneliness and the hurt. I still had Heather and Eve.

Mom leaned forward and grasped my hand, her flesh soft and warm. "Fiona, this is very . . . difficult."

I squeezed her hand. "I know, Mom. I really am sorry."

"That's not what I mean. I am so sorry for what I'm about to tell you, especially in this condition, but we all feel it's best. You'll have questions that can't be answered unless I tell you. That doesn't mean it isn't . . . difficult."

"What?"

The silence was a wall through which I could not see. I struggled against it but it wouldn't give. If only I could remove the pieces of pain from my eyes.

"Mom?"

"Oh, honey, I'm so sorry." Her sobs filled me with dread.

"Mom?"

"Heather's in a coma. She fell down the stairs. She cracked her ribs, punctured her lung, and hit her head. She has a brain injury. Her parents are beside themselves with worry. I don't know how this is going to turn out. This has been the worst night."

I clenched my fists. Liars! All of them! She didn't fall down the stairs! Liars! The pain made the medicine and bandages useless. I lay very still, but my internal emotions ignited into waves of agony, into raging rivers of fury.

I clenched my teeth. "Mom, she didn't fall down the stairs."

"Yes, honey. She did."

"No, she didn't. This isn't the first time her parents have done something to her."

"Honey, you're upset. She fell. They found her at the bottom of the stairs."

"No, she didn't. I'm telling you, her parents beat her or pushed her or something."

"You have a concussion. You don't know what you're saying."

"I know what I'm saying, Mom. I'm telling you, she didn't fall down those damn stairs. Why won't you believe me?"

"Why would her parents do such a thing and then sit by her side in the hospital? It just doesn't make any sense. You kids concoct the wildest stories."

"No, we don't. We know what goes on. I swear to you, she didn't fall down those damn stairs."

"Watch your mouth. It's not just me. The authorities believe she fell down the stairs. Why would they lie? Did you see her being beaten? Because the last time I checked, you were lost in the woods."

"No. But I know."

"You don't know and it doesn't matter anyway. Her parents are well-respected members of the community. The police looked at the situation and it has all the signs of an accident. Kids fall down the stairs every day. They're too busy to pay attention to the steps."

"That's what you tell yourselves because it's easier to believe. Believing she was beaten into a coma by her own parents would be too messy. They're all hypocrites, Mom."

Mom released my hand and I could sense her moving away from me. "You're upset. Please don't talk to me this way. I'm going to forget about this because I know you're in pain right now. But I don't wish to discuss it any further."

I whispered as much to the universe as to my mother, "No, of course we won't. The truth is too ugly to talk about."

"What did you say?"

"Nothing. Absolutely nothing."

"You need to rest. Your father will be here soon." Mom got up from her chair and stroked my hair. "Rest. We'll figure it all out later."

"Yeah. Later." I turned my back to her. Oh my God, Heather. Sweet Heather! I punched the pillow, but was immediately sorry.

I heard my mother open the door and leave. Good. She didn't understand anyway. Mariah's mom would.

The door opened and firmer footsteps moved toward me. I turned. "Fiona."

I waved my hand into the air. "Yes, Daddy."

He took my hand. "Thank God you're all right." His voice cracked.

"I'm so sorry, Daddy."

"What were you thinking?"

"I guess I wasn't. It seemed like a good plan at the time."

"Fiona, you know we don't approve of hitchhiking."

"Yes, I know."

"Then how could it have been a good plan?"

"I guess it wasn't."

"No, it wasn't. It defies logic. You knew we didn't approve. Therefore, you knew the potential consequences. This is most disappointing."

"I'm so sorry, Daddy."

"Your remorse cannot abrogate your actions. There are always consequences. Always, Fiona. You must comprehend this truth."

"I do." I clutched the hospital sheet. Daddy always turned into the theoretical physicist when I most needed him to be somebody else. I would've settled for a chimpanzee at that point.

"I'm not convinced you do. If you did, we would not be here. I have considered all the options, and your mother and I have decided to ground you for the month."

I didn't see that one coming. He delivered it like I was one of his errant research assistants. I deserved something, but a whole month? It was my first punishment—ever. Thirty days was over the top. But then Espy and Mariah would be gone. Heather was in a coma. Eve had been distant since Terrell left. It would be a lonely summer no matter what the punishment. Just me and Rory.

"All right, Daddy. I understand."

"Fiona, I love you, we love you. Your mother and I recognize how bad this could've been. We think it's better you stay close to home."

"Okay."

"All right. The doctor says you can come home tomorrow. The bandages may take longer. Get some rest."

"Yes, Daddy." I hated the way I surrendered. I didn't even put up a fight. Did Mariah fight?

I turned on my side and punched the hospital pillow. The torture around my head nearly made me faint. I lay still until the shards of pain mellowed around the edges. Good. At least I knew I was alive—and I certainly deserved more punishment. Of the pain kind, not the grounding kind.

"Fiona."

I didn't know how long I'd been lying there.

"Fiona."

The whisper was a creature of the fog, the same haze that had been floating around me since I had woken from the night in the woods.

"It's me. Espy. Are you awake?"

I turned towards the voice. "Espy!" I held out my arms.

"Oh, Fiona. I was so worried." She hugged me.

"Espy. I looked for you. I couldn't find you."

"Me too. But hey, *chica*, we're all right. Everything turned out fine."

"I know. Have you heard about Heather?"

"Yes, I went to see her."

"She's here? You saw her?"

"Yes, she looks horrible. There are a lot of tubes. She's black and blue all over." Espy's' voice cracked. "Her face is more puffy than yours is right now."

"Oh my God, Espy. They're lying. You know she didn't fall down the stairs."

"I know, but my parents don't want to know about it. Her parents aren't leaving her side. They watched me the whole time I was there."

"Jeez. Mine didn't believe it either."

Esperanza was quiet for a moment. "Fiona, we have to hope she comes out of this and then we have to get her away. There are no adults who are going to save her. They don't care."

"I know."

"We have to talk to Eve and Mariah. We have to get her out of here."

I nodded.

"Don't cry. We need to get through this. Then we have to protect her."

"I know."

"I have to go back to my room now. Mimi is coming soon to get me."

"You're leaving?" I grabbed for her, but I only caught air.

"Yeah. They're letting me go today. I'm leaving for Mexico tomorrow. I'll be back soon, though. Everything will be fine when we're past this and everyone gets better."

"*If* she gets better." I sobbed. "It's all my fault. I've killed her like I killed my baby brother."

"Stop it. You know this has happened before. Maybe not this bad. But her mom could've woken up on the wrong side of the bed and done the same thing, with or without you. We have to believe she'll come out of this."

Bitter tears let loose. "You're right. Shit! I feel so helpless."

"We'll figure this out. We're a butt-kicking, horse-stomping, kick-ass, bitchin' posse. Remember?"

I smiled. "I remember."

"*Manana.*"

"*Maka Manana.*"

Esperanza kissed me. She left as quietly as she had entered.

The buzz of the hospital light grated on my nerves. I could not think through it. I lay back down and drew lines around the edges of the images that shifted through the haze. It would be a long month. But long months are great for making plans. We would need it to save Heather.

* * *

Of course, the wanting and the doing are never the same. Heather came out of her unconscious sleep. Eve and I tended to her every day. Heather's mother tolerated our presence, either out of remorse or a desire to be seen as the solicitous and loving mother. It didn't matter which. Heather was safe while we were there.

We were like dying roses without Mariah and Espy. Our month of separation became defined by watching Heather heal. Her head injury was not as severe as the doctors had thought. The relief registered more with me and Eve than with Heather's parents, who appeared unfazed and unrepentant. But the front they showed the outer world was different. Who were we? Kids. And our opinion didn't matter. Heather couldn't remember anything of that day; her injuries were a confusing mystery for her. We stayed away from the subject.

The bruises turned their alternating rainbow of colors, but no one took notice. Heather melted into the walls, the bruises were the only color to an otherwise invisible life force. But even her bruises faded.

My injuries followed suit, but I couldn't blend so easily. Everyone noticed me. I grew tired of the questions. Was I so different than Heather? Heather, unlike me, was allowed to blend. My vibrancy served as a counterpoint to Heather's lack of it. Eve took little notice. In fact, she took little notice of anything. She didn't fade though. She simmered. The quiet of anger and forgetting maddened.

I wanted adventure. A month was too long. I wanted to forget it all. I wanted to go back to the way things were.

I take another long gulp of vodka. God, I was so stupid. I am so stupid. Things can never go back. Change is a river. The past is subsumed by the present. Is that not a special forgetting?

But Eve, my precious Eve, stood in my way. "Stop whining, Fiona. I don't feel like going to Sycamore."

"We haven't done anything fun in a while."

"No? I would think recovering from the last fun would be enough for you. Besides, Heather isn't up to it."

Heather looked at her feet.

"We don't have to do anything crazy. I just want to do something, anything."

"No, you want to find Damon and you want us to go with you. You think that will make you forget. How's that fun for us?"

"I don't care about Damon," I said, lying like a common criminal.

"You know you do. He's like a force field, and now you don't have any scars or bruises."

"That's not fair. And no, I don't. I'm just bored." I looked toward our Rose Garden. Its luster had faded. What was Mariah's favorite rose? It didn't matter. All the roses in the world couldn't save us from the world we were now living in. "Oh, let's just go back to my house."

Eve smiled—rare lately. Espy and Mariah would be home soon.

Things had shifted. My friends bored me. Espy and Mariah would turn things around. We would be the same again. I just had to wait. A couple more days and we would be on the way back to "normal." Heather and Eve would have to follow.

But Espy returned with a broken heart. She was in love and she had lost her virginity. I still had mine, and I sensed myself slipping in the one thing at which I was best: sex appeal. I needed to catch up.

Mariah, meanwhile, came back all fiery and radicalized. There was no taming her. It was as if she had breathed in the spirit of the horses she rode under the heat of the South Dakota summer.

"Mariah," I asked her on her first day back, "what are we going to do about Heather?"

"What can we do? Do you think the police will care? They're part of the establishment."

Eve weighed in. "I tried to tell my parents. I don't think they were paying any attention."

Mariah considered. "I'm sorry. They're still upset about your brother. They can't really do anything anyway."

"I know, but they might've been able to give me some ideas."

Mariah scoffed. "What ideas? No one gives a shit. She's just another kid. We don't have any power. It was an accident. Who will people believe? Us?"

I could never stand helplessness. "Someone has to do something to get her out of there."

"What can we do?" Eve said.

"Hide her?" Espy suggested. "We have to figure something out. She's going to die next time."

"I know." The truth of it ran like ice water through my veins. We would have to find a way, even if it meant losing everything.

I take another long sip of vodka. It seemed so easy. How could we have known it would be the hardest thing we had ever done? How could we have known things would take such a disastrous turn?

No one on that hill was ever the same. Karma is like a river. Once you step into it, the consequences, good or bad, are unstoppable. You cannot go back. The current is swift and dangerous. All you can do is swim with the tide like your life depends upon it.

17 Mariah

Running like hell, as fast and as far as my heart and lungs will take me, can't erase the experience. In all the years I've witnessed death, it's always like the first time. I know I should be numb to it, or at least less affected, but I'm not cut from Hollywood cloth. The smell clings to my clothes. I retch into the naked red earth outside the makeshift hospital. There are times when I think I'm diminishing. Fading by the touch of others' deaths. Yet, I hunger for the meaning, even the intimacy, harbored within the folds of dying. Worse than disease, it's the drama of war that magnifies its touch. Yet, plagues and ferocious pathogens feed on war. In the struggle to survive, heroes are bigger, evil is more malignant, foes are the darkest of enemies, and endurance is the sweetest of gifts. In a world in which we fight for control and authority over our lives, helplessness is our greatest fear. The power manifested in remaining alive, even in thriving, often comes at the expense of the other. That is the catch—the conundrum. I have borne witness to others' helplessness, and in so doing become an accessory to the stripping of power to that other. Worse, I've witnessed things I wouldn't wish to be done to me. That's a powerful karma. The trickster mocks me, *Wak'djunk'aga*. The same was done to my own. To my family, to my tribe. But now I've watched it happen. No, I've crawled into the belly of the beast. I'm crawling even now.

It was only yesterday I crossed the bridge over the Rio Grande from Del Sierra in Texas to Ciudad Frontera, but that moment is already light years away. The immediacy of the crossing is gone, and a powerful terror matches my steps.

This morning, my dread traveled with me through the silent mud-sloshed streets of the makeshift neighborhoods surrounding the AAC complex. A few stray dogs with mud-hardened flanks whined and scavenged for food. Knocking on doors, I hoped to catch an occupant willing to answer my questions. I had anticipated their reluctance. They need their jobs. But they weren't avoiding me. The place was a ghost town. A tumbleweed diaspora, untended and colonizing against empty houses, rattled and whistled in the hot wind. Dust devils swirled in the vacant streets and open sewers, drying and caking in the high sun, cracked and formed rifts along the edges of the desolate town. Only newly abandoned, the remains of the town were yielding quickly to the elements.

After fifteen minutes, a member of AAC security stopped me.

"This area is in quarantine. You have to leave."

"Quarantine? Why?"

"That's privileged information. This area is owned by Astride Amalgamated Corporation. Any unauthorized persons are to be escorted to its boundary. I need to see your identification papers."

I produced my District of Columbia driver's license. No way he was getting my passport. Without it, the border became impermeable.

"American?"

I looked into his hard blue eyes. What did he see? "As American as it gets."

He drove me away from the complex and deposited me in the center of town.

"The bridge back to the United States is that way. If you know what's good for you, you'll leave this place. It's not safe here."

The car sped back toward the factory complex.

I stopped someone in the center of the city, far from the makeshift *barrio* on the fringes, and asked about the hospital. Yes. That way.

Médecins Sans Frontières, Doctors Without Borders, had arrived. There was fear in their eyes. But I knew wherever MSF was would be a relatively safe area, and it was even possible I would know someone. Maybe they could tell me where all the people from the *barrio* had gone.

As luck had it, I did find someone I knew.

And now standing in the middle of a hospital gripped by an epidemic brought my co-worker's words flooding back to me.

I grabbed his arm as he walked by. "Enrique, thank God. Do you have a minute?"

Enrique's brow furrowed. "Mariah? What're you doing here? You shouldn't be here. There's a cholera epidemic."

"I thought so. Why are all the neighborhoods vacant? It doesn't look like there are enough people here to account for just one of the neighborhoods I was in."

Enrique pulled off his protective gloves. "I'm just a doctor, Mariah. That question is for someone else." He looked around and motioned his head down the hallway. "There's a patient down there, last cot on the left. His name is Jorge Nunez. He has some crazy story about his wife and children disappearing. It could be his delirium. We're administering fluids, but the company doctors don't seem to be too excited about saving him. We're watching him and they're watching us. Something's not right. Be careful."

"I will."

Enrique gently grabbed my arm. "Mariah. I know you're fearless. We all know you. We'll do our best to make sure you're okay, for old time's sake, but be careful. Something's not right here. We're hearing a lot of stories that I doubt the company wants the world to hear. This isn't our first gig. If they find out a journalist is here, we could all be in trouble."

"Thanks Enrique. I'll be quick." His tone unnerved me. Since when did MSF worry about some corporation on the wrong side of the law?

"He only speaks Spanish." Enrique slipped his mask back over his face and pulled new gloves over his hands.

I pulled up a seat next to Jorge Nunez's cot. "*Con permiso. Lo siento.* I'm a journalist. Can you tell me what happened to you and your family?"

He looked at me—grief and bitterness fused in his eyes. My announcement sank in, but it was clear he hadn't come to terms with his situation. As if the happening was no more than a bee sting. He squeezed his eyes shut and tears traced streaks along his dark brown cheeks. I gently coaxed him—assured him I would tell the world of his plight. I was the hope of justice. If only he'd tell me.

He confirmed my suspicions. His job was to pour the worst of chemicals down a drain. He didn't seem to know many details about where the water drained to, but between what he told me and what I'd already dug up for myself, I could connect the dots. There were no usable containment ponds and no chemical or hazardous waste capabilities. The wastewater treatment facility fed raw sewage and chemically tainted water into the river—a river that eventually sloshed into the Rio Grande Valley to be used as irrigation for grapefruit, cotton, and vegetables. The river and its estuaries also passed through several wildlife refuges.

He rubbed his tears with his swollen and scabbed fingers.

Lo siento. Just a little more and the world will know the truth.

He shook. He knew something was wrong, but he needed his job. It was his fault. He was the reason his wife and children, his family, were dead.

No. What could he have done? It was AAC's fault.

He was silent.

Anger made me reckless and I stayed longer than I should. Toward the end of our conversation, Jorge told me the bodies of his wife and children were gathered up with others in the neighborhood and taken somewhere. He'd overheard someone visiting the cot next to him telling of a mass grave.

"Why would they do that?"

Jorge looked at me with sadness in his eyes and shook his head.

The woman in the cot next to him grabbed my sleeve. "They don't want anyone to know. We are just poor Indians. We are untraceable, *ilocalizable*." She pulled me closer. "Some of the people they put into the grave were still breathing."

The woman, a grandmother, watched and waited, her grip on my sleeve strong for her small frame. Her eyes shone with a vibrancy that mocked her chiseled features.

Sweat dripped into and stung my eyes. What had I walked into? "I'm sorry. I'll make sure you're not forgotten. Does anyone else know about the . . . others, the ones who were still living?"

"*Sí*. But they've all left. They've fled to the desert. Better to be lost in the desert than to be left in the desert. Tell your story, little one, but don't go into the desert. Some stories are best left buried." The old woman smiled and, pointing at Jorge, never took her eyes from me. I shook my head and she relaxed her grip on my sleeve and settled back against the bed.

I turned to Jorge. "All right. Jorge. One more question, *por favor*. Where are you from?"

"San Juan Pinas in Juxtlahuaca, Oaxaca."

"Mixteca?"

"*Sí*. I should've never left. I need to go home to my people." He closed his eyes again and the tears flowed. "I need to take my wife and children home." His voice broke and he rested his forearm over his eyes.

"*Lo siento. Lo siento.*" But there weren't enough apologies. This was always where words withered against the power of sorrow.

Before I left, the grandmother pulled on my sleeve once more. "Do not go into the desert."

"I won't, Grandmother."

Enrique stopped me on my way out. "Follow me. We have to get

you out of here. AAC's goons have been asking questions about you."
He walked me down the hall and through a side door.

I followed him. "But there's still more to find out. You know I've been in worse situations than this before." I was lying. There was something evil here. I needed to uncover it—expose it.

"Not like this, Mariah. You need to get out of here. We need to get this epidemic under control and covering your ass isn't going to help us. You understand?"

"I won't get in your way. Promise."

"That's not the point, Mariah. We'd still know. We have to focus. We don't need any more problems."

"All right. I get it."

Outside, the air was hot and dry. The wind whipped off the land and dirt swirled into a mist of finely ground dust that blanketed everything. There was something about Jorge's eyes that stayed with me. Familiarity stalked me. I've always known there will be a day I'll have to go home. Soon.

A car waited outside the door. The driver deposited me at the bridge with a warning to cross and get lost. Fast.

The crowds crossing the bridge were easy to blend into. Across the bridge, I jumped into my nondescript midsize tan rental car and hit the highway to the airport. Fear and sadness weighed on my chest but I didn't have time to stop.

* * *

I've rebooked my flight to DC, but it doesn't leave for another hour. The minutes tick slowly. Every man wears sunglasses and bears a sinister appearance. The flight-or-fight impulse is making me crazy, and I imagine running through corridors, imagine myself locked on the plane without any way to escape. I need to get home. I need to write this story. I need to get rid of it. What is the point of putting myself in this danger if it is all for nothing? And clearly, not writing the story won't lessen my danger. I'm already knee-deep in it.

Finally, I'm on my way. The first leg ends without incident. But then two men who boarded the plane in Texas transfer with me in Houston and board my plane bound for D.C. Coincidence? No way! I'm being followed. There's no way I'm letting on, though—letting them know I know or letting them see me sweat. It's not like danger's new to me. And I'm not in Chechyna, Rwanda, or Beirut; I'm in the U.S. Though in some ways, that actually doesn't help. I can't defend myself. This isn't a war-torn country where civil society has broken down. The wheels of justice turn differently. I can't go to the police. They can't do anything until I'm actually dead. And chances are, there won't be any evidence to prove homicide. It'll look like an accident. Where can I go?

The Rez?

I keep picking the same answer. One of these days, it'll be the right one. It's just the wrong one now.

I need my dogs and they're still at the kennel. I don't want to think too much. Short-term planning ensures my sanity. Shadow and Luna can't protect me, but they can . . . make me feel protected, make me feel like someone is in this beside me.

* * *

The air is close and humid and the scent of death hovers. I smell my clothes, but they're not the source. The stench walks with me to the kennel. The odor is as strong as it was in the *barrio* in Ciudad Frontera.

"Hi, Ms. Westerman. Shadow and Luna will be so happy to see you. But we thought you weren't coming back until another ten days?"

"Oh, I was always coming back for a couple of days." I search for the story that will make sense to her, but nothing makes sense, even to me. "I wasn't going to get the dogs—I didn't want to upset them—but I decided I want them with me. I have to bring them back in a couple of days, though. I'll be going back out of town. Is that okay?"

"Of course. We have their kennels reserved for them anyway."

Back out on the street, the dogs pull on their leashes. The air is filled with a heady stew of earth, flowers, and excrement. I'm sure it's the latter that pulls the dogs forward. I look around. I'm one breath away from hyperventilation. Loosening my shoulders, I focus on my breathing, but I must look like a . . . what did we use to call it . . . a spaz attack?

The walls of my apartment are as foreign as those used to imprison people. This used to be my sanctuary from my hard travels, but I've never really made it my own, and now it doesn't even feel safe. It is just the place I stop on my way to somewhere else—someplace to lay down my head and my suitcase for a time. There are no pictures or well-loved items to make it my own. There are ragged chairs and a sofa, some old tables, a small and usually empty refrigerator, and an oven that has never felt its own warmth. I call it home, but it's an illusion—or a delusion. Grandmother used to say we're from the stuff of stars and we were created where the two mighty rivers, the Minnesota and Mississippi, meet. Many years ago my parents took me there, to *Bdote*, where Grandmother's people were first created. The noise outside and the silence in here drown my memories of the softly lapping water. But then, the cars and roads of the Twin Cities were no different than other cities, and low-flying airplanes reminded me that the past was dead. The information at Fort Snelling, rising high upon a rock bluff, glorified frontier history. There was no story of Grandmother's people's suffering. It was a great forgetting. Home exists at the frontier of the imagination.

It was Grandmother who told me we must be the water keepers. *Mni*, water, is pure and the source of life. It holds great power and is sacred, *wakan*. By the waters of *Mde Wakan*, the Creator gave us *psin*, the wild rice that grows in the water. Her stories were filled with the beauty and bounty of the maple groves, the plentiful fish, and the wind in forests that stretched for miles—the world before its destruction. And now here I sit, surrounded by four white walls. I'm miles away from home.

I'm also miles away from people who are dying from contaminated water.

The front door looms and beckons to me. What good am I here? The least I can do is tell the story. Be the keeper of the water. Free the truth. The first thing intruding man takes is story. It's time to take it back.

"You will save me, won't you?" Shadow and Luna wag their tails.

It's 4:30 p.m. It'll be a long night.

Heather works for AAC. She must have some insight.

Her secretary answers. "Heather Collings's office. May I help you?"

"This is Mariah Westerman. Is Heather there?"

"No. She's in Charleston. She wouldn't tell me why, but she sounded nervous and it's earlier than she had planned. She has some important stuff happening here that I know she didn't want to leave unfinished. I know you're supposed to meet her there, right?"

"Yes."

Sharon's voice dropped to a whisper. "You need to tell her things are bad here. I don't know what's going on but her boss has been asking about her and he's on a mission to find her. I don't know how much longer I can hold him off. Something bad must've happened for him to be this worked up *and* for Heather to have left so suddenly. She didn't even tell me."

"I'll try to find her. Thanks, Sharon."

"I'm sorry I couldn't be more helpful. Tell her I'm trying to hold down the fort, but I'm not sure I'm doing a very good job. Ask her for me, what is going on?"

"I will."

What's she doing?

She must be at our hotel in Charleston. I dial the number.

"I'm trying to reach Heather Collings. Would you ring me up to her room, please?"

There's a pause. "Certainly, ma'am. I'm ringing her room now."

"Hello."

"Heather? Is that you?"

"Yeah."

"What on earth are you doing there?"

Heather begins to sob. "Brandon tried to kill me."

I freeze. "What?"

"He tried to kill me. He's been having an affair with a woman who was having his baby un . . . un . . . til . . ." Her sobs intensify.

"Until what, Heather?"

"Until she was murdered."

"What? Who murdered her?"

"They don't know. It could've been Brandon, but they don't know. There was a sign someone else was there."

"What sign?"

"They won't say."

"What did Brandon do to you? What happened?"

"I'm not sure. There was a lightning storm and it was getting really close. I guess it got too near and I blacked out. I don't know. When I came to, he was choking me. Oh Mariah, if you could've seen the look on his face."

I've seen the worst of mankind. But this is different. He tried to kill Heather. His own wife. He's a rat, but I didn't see this coming.

"I'm so sorry, Heather. Where's Shannon?"

"She's with me. She was there. She doesn't understand."

"God, Heather. Stay at the hotel. I'll try to come early. Tomorrow might be perfect—if I can make it through tonight."

"What do you mean?"

"Oh, nothing. You have enough to worry about."

"Mariah! What do you mean? I told you, now you tell me. That's not fair. You guys are always trying to hide everything from me like I'm some . . . some weakling. I'm not, you know."

"I know. I'm sorry. Actually, it's about your company." I explain to her everything I witnessed in Mexico—the contaminated manufacturing chemicals dumped down the drain, the rate hikes for access to treated clean water, the dumping of raw sewage and waste in the river, the cholera epidemic, the missing dead, and the threats. I leave out only the worst: the undocumented and unconfirmed live burials.

Heather sucks in her breath. "You should come tonight."

"I can't. I have the dogs and I have to submit this part of the story that I haven't even written yet. I haven't even decided the angle."

"Mariah. You're playing with fire. I think I know who's behind it all."

"Who?"

"I don't know for sure and I'm not sure if anyone else is involved, but Michael Saxton is the current CFO. He's been handpicked to take over the helm. He's evil. I know that sounds sinister, but I've never liked the guy. He got me to do something shady, and everyone is pretty much marching to his drum. And there's more, I think."

"Wait, but how does that implicate him?"

"I don't know. It's a feeling I have. Besides, I overheard my boss discussing some unsavory employment practices in—get this— Mexico. We only have one facility in Mexico. It's in Ciudad Frontera. And I know they've been dodging some malfeasance issues. There've been rumors."

"That still doesn't mean he's behind it."

"No, but I think he had something to do with Brandon's mistress's death, too. The investigator told me the actual claim of discrimination was against him. She told the investigator he was the father of her baby and that's why he fired her. She told Brandon he was the father. I don't know the truth and I don't know what game she was playing, but the affair and baby would definitely have a chilling effect on Saxton's rise to the CEO position. The board at AAC doesn't like any controversy. She obviously didn't know who she was messing with."

"We need to find out what that clue is."

"They're not going to let me know, Mariah. They like to keep information secret that only the killer knows."

"Have you told them about your suspicions?"

"Of course not. I'm here because Brandon tried to kill me. I still need my job, especially if I'm going to be a single mom now. Besides, it's just a theory. A hunch. They won't do anything with that."

"Yeah. You're right."

"But just in case I'm right . . . You should get out of there. I don't trust any of them."

"But not trusting someone and believing they are capable of murder is a stretch. You haven't told me anything to implicate this Saxton guy."

"No. I just know it's him."

"So you really think I could be in danger? From him? I mean the guys at MSF thought I was, but nothing has happened and it could have easily enough. Someone could've picked me off at half a dozen places between Ciudad Frontera and here. I think we're all being paranoid."

"Mariah. You're the one who always has the good instincts. But I'm telling you. My instincts are screaming at me. It's like I can see all of a sudden. Things have been bad ever since Michael Saxton received the royal blessing. He's changed my boss. I don't even know who he is anymore. And I always had a good relationship with him. I'm telling you. The man is awful. Come to Charleston. *Come now.*"

"I'll try, but if all of this is true then someone has to tell the story. I have to at least tell the story of what I've seen in Ciudad Frontera. It's not just what I witnessed—it's a promise I made."

"Mariah. Come quickly or you're going to end up in some hole in the ground with a bullet in your head."

A hole in the ground? Buried alive? There's the rest of the story, but I'm already in over my head. Focus on what you can prove. "Let me get through tonight. I'll focus on getting this story out. I also have to get in touch with the tribunal that Espy and Tomas told me about. It's a water tribunal in Latin America. It will definitely make AAC squirm. I also have to pick up my coworker's flash drive. Then I'll get on the first plane to Charleston tomorrow. Okay?"

"Do I have a choice?"

"No. I'll be there tomorrow. *Manana.*"

"Mariah, be careful. I think there's more to this."

"I will. I promise. I'll be there. *Manana.*"

"*Maka Manana.*"

How does one find language for the meanness of men? Mom once told me that spirits are sometimes good and sometimes bad. It all depends on the circumstances. Just focus on the issue of access to clean water and wastewater treatment plants. If I keep my article limited to what I do know, there will be another day. There's more to uncover, and I intend to get to the bottom of it. Someday. If I live through this.

It's 4:00 a.m. now. Time to let the article go.

"Time to get some shut-eye. Right?"

Shadow and Luna thump their tails.

We retreat to the bedroom and the dogs settle into the folds of the sheet.

Sleep doesn't come. The dogs are quiet, but that doesn't put me at ease. Somewhere, trouble lurks. My journey through AAC's compound trails through my mind. What if Heather is correct?

The whiteness of the ceiling and the perfect circling of the paddle fan are maddening. Whoo-whoo-whoo. It's a perfect backdrop for my waking nightmare and the images of past horrors cycling through my head. The empty streets of Ciudad Frontera's makeshift neighborhoods haunt me. They were like war-torn streets. Powerlessness seeped through the mud and grime. The streets spoke the same language. Frontiers rest at the outer limits of space and time. It's the point at which the unfathomable becomes limitless.

The Russians had a word for "no limits" in Chechen fighting: *bespredel.* I was reporting for Reuters when I came upon a group of soldiers. They had captured a female Chechen sniper. They tied her ankles with steel cables to two armored personnel carriers and slowly tore her apart. She screamed. The soldiers laughed. When they were done, her blood soaked the earth and her screams followed me everywhere. I heard them in my waking hours and in my nightmares. The Russians thought they had found justice, but the Chechens were the ones who had been wronged for centuries. Does power always have to determine the conditions and limits of justice? Does only power maintain the right to the language of justice?

I bore witness to the sniper's suffering, but I couldn't write it. It has remained locked in my brain. I'm a writer, but there are things I cannot express. There are no words in the universe. There is no narrative for understanding. The language of compassion and empathy is mankind's strongest armor, but it's silent at the outer reaches of the frontier. *Bespredel.*

18 Esperanza

My suitcase lives and breathes. It is now home to many animals. For every one I remove, two more gain ground. The contents swell in proportion to the jumble of my fast-moving thoughts. Angelica shoves her favorites deep into the pockets of air, mixing the smells of home with those of my suitcase. I remove the animals again.

"Angelica, I can't take these with me."

Angelica bats her long brown lashes over her large eyes. Her eyes remind me of Gabriel's, but that's impossible. Angelica is Tomas's. "But Mama, you need someone to keep you safe and bring you home."

"Don't worry, I'll be safe and I'll be home before you know it."

Angelica turns as Izzy brings in a picture. They smile at each other conspiratorially. A Pegasus flying over a city of dots with a wide expanse of water in the background swims across a white sheet of paper. A single airplane enters from the left-hand side and, over the entire scene, obliterating the sky, hangs a rainbow unattached to the Earth.

"Izzy, that's beautiful."

"It's for you, Mama. So you don't forget to fly back home."

"Izzy, why would I forget to fly back home?"

"Well, they're your secret best friends and you seem really sad lately. I would stay with them if I were you, but I want—we want—you to remember to come home."

"Silly. How could I forget to fly home? You're my family. I'd swim the seven seas, climb the tallest mountains, and scale the biggest sky-scrapers to get to you. I love you too much to forget."

I open my arms wide to show them the magnitude of my love and the girls fold themselves tightly into my arms. They still need and want me. Such moments are fleeting. My oldest has already bowed and shifted under the pressure of adolescence.

Carlos no longer needs me. Busy on his computer, his social life has taken front seat. Soon, he'll leave his room to ask to meet up with his friends for the evening. Once again, I will have to explain it is late and they should plan their social life for an earlier time. I like my kids safe under my roof when night falls. Tomas concurs. But it'll be me upon whom Carlos will tally another adult transgression, another assault on his yearning for absolute freedom, another wave crashing against the shore.

Those heady days of hormone-induced yearnings are a memory not easily forgotten, though the sense of it diminishes with time—a deep knowing that stretches in front of me like a vast ocean, capable of swallowing whole all that I cherish most. I am afraid for my chil-dren. I cross myself, as I have seen my mother do a million times. The gesture gives me comfort and ties me to my history. *Hail Mary, full of grace* . . . I remember what happens after all that hope and wonder is destroyed. Crushing disillusionment and finally, heartbreak. I couldn't bear to be away from my children when such a storm blew through. I should be here. In an instant, life can change forever. I need to tell them so they will understand.

The sound of Izzy's voice startles me. The suitcase still yawns like it did all those years ago in Mexico. "What are you crying about, Mama?"

"Nothing. I'm just already missing you."

Angelica retrieves one of her favorite animals. "You better take this, Mama, so you don't get so sad. Remember us and you'll be happy." Her smile is wide like the ocean.

I take the fluffy, floppy bunny and hold it to my face. It's soft and smells of home and dust and love. I kiss it hard and it caves into my embrace. "Thank you, honey. I think I will."

The girls smile at me. Together, as if joined at the hip, they skip from the room giggling and, just like that, I am alone. Wisps of clouds.

I peek down the hallway. Carlos's door is plastered with signs warning any and all visitors against entrance. Noise filters from his room, music and television murmurs exhale from the crease of his door.

I knock.

"What?"

The knob won't move. I knock again.

"I said what?"

"Carlos! Please open the door. *Por favor.*"

Finally, he opens the door and light seeps from his room. "Carlos, I'm leaving tomorrow morning. Can't you spend a little time with me? With the family?"

"Why? Dad's not with you."

"That's different. He's working and I'll see him a little later."

"Well, I'll see you a little later, too, Mom. Everyone's on right now."

The screen behind him is filled with tiny boxes, bits of truncated conversations. How can he carry on so many discussions at once?

"All right, but soon, *por favor.*"

"All right, Mom." He smiles. God, but love can crack the world in two. His door clicks shut.

I drift along the hallway before I find the top of the stairs. At the bottom, Snoops, our retriever, raises his head, flops his tail against the bare floor several times, and rests his head upon his paws, never letting his eyes leave me. The sound of the television carries from the den and the hum of the dishwasher mingles with it—sounds of domestic life that evoke strong feelings to stay. *Do not venture back out into that world. It's not always kind.*

Tomas is probably asleep in his favorite chair. He's been busy with next week's lectures, but night creeps up on him. He will wake soon and, sensing the immediacy of deep night, will rise to join me. The men in my life, present yet absent, are like driftwood along the shore, reminders of the forever-changing patterns of Mother Earth.

The women in my life are altogether different. They're beacons across the bay emitting light that sparkles along the water, vibrant in their ability to sustain safe passage. I love the men in my life, but it's the women who sustain the roughest battering, shining brilliantly in spite of adversity. I am leaving the tranquility of home and the strength of my men to plunge back into unsafe waters. If the man of so long ago is still alive, we will need to pool our combined strength. If he merely walks in Heather's fragile mind, we'll have to be strong enough to hold her to a fast-eroding shore.

And then there's Mariah. Full of mystery and always at the threshold of danger, always running from who she is. She asked about LAWT. I need to talk to Tomas about it tonight.

Before I fall asleep and before I leave.

I dread this trip. The sounds of home root me here. Nothing is out of the ordinary. I prefer normal. *Hail Mary . . .* She will have to protect me. I touch the cross at my neck.

Snoops lifts his head to stare at me, turns his head to the den, and, with a deep sigh, returns his head to his paws and closes his eyes. Yes, I love the men in my life. They're calmly and surely here, but they rarely throw themselves at me with the passion of unbridled exuberance. It was that way once, long ago, in the Yucatan. And it nearly broke me. Still, it was the hope of Gabriel that allowed me to survive the terrible aftermath of that night in 1968. Can I lay him to rest without grieving that hope and rescue?

I finish packing. I suppose I'm as ready as I can be.

Carlos enters and hugs me. "I love you, Mom. I'll miss you, you know."

"Yeah?"

"Yeah."

"I love you too. I'll be home soon. You won't forget to look after the girls and feed Snoops, will you? You know your dad gets overwhelmed when I'm away."

"Yes, Mom. I've got it under control. We're cool. Have fun."

"Okay. You're the second-in-command."

We hug and he slips from the room. The moment is like liquid seeping through the cracks of a closed door.

Tomas passes Carlos on his way into the room. Snoops follows, his tail wagging, and drops onto his bed.

"Tomas, did you let Snoops out?"

"No."

"Tomas, please, I need you to let him out and then close up the house for me. *Por favor.*"

He looks at me. But then he turns. "C'mon, Snoops. Time to go out, buddy." He grabs my suitcase on his way down.

"Thank you, Tomas. *Te quiero*, my love." He waves behind his back.

When they return, Snoops once again collapses onto his bed. Tomas begins his nightly routine for bed.

"Tomas, I got a funny call from Mariah. She needed information on LAWT."

"What did she need that for?"

"She's researching a water situation with Heather's company and—"

"Wait. AAC?"

"Yeah. How did you remember that?"

"What is she doing, Esperanza?"

"She's looking into some malfeasance. There's also a cholera epidemic going on."

"Esperanza. Tell her to stay away from that. AAC won't look nicely upon someone asking for LAWT's help. They don't want the bad press. I've heard some things lately."

"Things? Like what things?"

"Never mind. Tell her to stay away. How far in is she?"

"I think pretty far. I gave her what information I knew, and told her I'd ask you about it too. Why are you looking at me like that? What?"

"Don't go to Charleston. I think she could be in danger, and anybody else with her could be too."

"What do you mean? I have to go. We've seen each other through everything. Heather is . . . troubled. I have to go, Tomas. So what are you telling me?"

"I'm telling you Mariah might be in way over her head."

"So what? She's survived worse. If there's been a battle zone, she's seen it. We'll be fine. She'll be fine."

"This is different. You can't see this enemy. They're assassins. She won't know it's coming. Neither will you. Stay here, Esp."

"Assassins? Now you sound like one of those crazy conspiracy theorists. This is America, Tomas. Don't be crazy." I laugh, but I'm not convincing even myself.

Tomas doesn't speak.

"What?"

"I can't stop you, but I'm asking you. Don't go."

"I have to."

He knows I'm scared too. He kisses me. His arms fall gently around my torso and he squeezes. My tears spill over his naked skin before I find his lips.

Afterwards, deep in the night, the stars blink in the heavens and steal through my window. We're all stardust. We're full of grace. And we're always one moment away from our destiny. Please God, let me find my way back home.

19 Eve

Jerome's chest rises and falls. Its rhythm should comfort me, but the old shadows dance and creep along the corners of our room. These ghosts of trouble and sadness bedevil the night. Lights from the sleepless Manhattan streets play along the walls. Chances are, Mariah's up. That girl never sleeps. I raise the covers slowly and sneak from bed. Our apartment is small. I grab a shawl, the key, and my phone before I leave. The air in the hallway is damp and smells of days-old spices and garlic. The balls of my bare feet are grimy by the time I reach the stairwell. I'm ankle-deep in shit. Perched at the top of the landing, I wait for the sound of shuffling feet along concrete to cease, but the top of my neighbor's head clears the stairs below, rounds the corner, and climbs the remaining stairs.

He smiles as he continues the ascent, his feet grinding against the concrete. "Hey Eve. What are you doing out here at this time of night?"

"Can't sleep. What are you doing out this late?"

He doesn't move. "Work." He rubs the back of his neck. "Always work."

"I've never asked you what you do. Funny. That's usually the first thing people find out."

His blue eyes soften and the tightness in his jaw lessens. "That's what I've always liked about you. You don't seem to care about that stuff. Come to think of it, I don't know what you do either."

"I'm an aid worker for an NGO. My ship sails for Darfur shortly."

"Ah. Darfur. Well, you certainly have your work cut out for you. Cholera season is here."

It's rare to find anyone interested enough to know about the diseases of the Displaced Persons Camps. "You know more than most people."

He shrugs. "I'm an attorney with Amnesty International by way of several corporate law offices. I'm trying to cleanse my soul." He laughs derisively.

"Is it working?"

"Ask me in a few years."

"You don't look old enough to have law school and that much working experience under your belt."

"Ha! Law school and a master's in international affairs. My dad's idea. I didn't last long in the corporate world. My stint at a company called Astride Amalgamated Corporation did it for me. The pay was awesome, but you paid for every dollar earned. After a while, the golden handcuffs began to chafe."

"Wait. You worked for AAC?"

"Yeah. You know it?"

"Yeah. My friend works for them and I had a few run-ins with them in the Congo."

"The Congo?"

"I was working at one of the big camps after the Rwandan genocide. At first it was filled with people fleeing the situation, but then the Hutu perps sort of took over and started running things. It made our job difficult. They were financing their military efforts against the Tutsi by mining the minerals for AAC's computer operations. AAC had its own security services. Subcontractors, of course."

Why am I talking about this? I don't feel like going down memory lane.

Eric's jaw tightens again, and he sighs. "Of course. We should get together sometime. Clearly, our paths have probably crossed at one time or another besides this hallway. When do you leave?"

"Morning after tomorrow." The time's bearing down on me.

"Wow. That soon? Maybe when you get back from Darfur."

"It's a date."

"Good luck. If you need anything, I'm at Amnesty. Give me a call."

"Thanks, Eric. Listen. Do you have an extra cigarette?"

"Yeah." He retrieves one from his pocket, along with a lighter, hands me the cigarette and lights the flame. I inhale and exhale.

"Thanks."

"Be careful and be safe. Good night."

"Night."

The stairwell is suddenly empty. Noises echo off the concrete walls below. I dial Mariah's number.

"Hello." Her voice is husky.

"Did I wake you?"

"No. I'm still writing this article. Jeez. It's one o'clock in the morning. Are you okay?"

"Yeah. I'm just feeling sad. Wanted to hear your voice."

"Glad you caught me before I left. I'm heading to Charleston as soon as I can get out of here."

"Earlier than planned?"

"Yes. I'm finishing the article tonight. I got out of Mexico as fast as I could. In fact, I had a little help with that. Heather's already there, she wants me to come as soon as possible. I'll let her tell you why she went early. The big boss at AAC scares her and I might have pissed him off. I think everyone's making me feel paranoid, but I had a scary conversation with my coworker, Daniel; he sounded like he was in trouble and now I can't get a hold of him. I have to pick up a flash drive he sent before I leave. Otherwise I'd leave this morning."

AAC. What are the chances? That much synchronicity has to

account for something. "Funny, I was just talking about AAC with my neighbor. Is that why Heather left early?"

"No, but she needs to tell you herself. She wants to tell everyone when we're together. And what were you talking about AAC for?"

"The trouble I had in the Congo with them. He used to work for them in the legal department, but he works for Amnesty now."

"I don't remember that. What trouble did you have?"

"Mineral extraction for their computer operations. They paid and the Hutu made war with the proceeds." The line is silent. "Mariah? Are you still there?"

"Yeah. I'm thinking. Computers, huh? Go figure. There's a coincidence. The minerals get mixed and sort of lost and sent to Kuala Lumpur, where Daniel was investigating the operations. And now he's missing. I think I heard him being . . . I don't know. I need that flash drive. Worse, there's a cholera epidemic in Ciudad Frontera and there are some serious water issues there."

I stand. The concrete on which I've been sitting has frozen me to the marrow. I wrap my shawl tighter around my shoulders and move back through the hallway. "Mariah? Is that the article you're writing? If it is, you're playing with fire, girl."

"Yes and no. I started writing about the virtual water in computer production and I sort of picked AAC to highlight it, but it's turned into something much bigger. It's not really what I started out to do and it's not what my assignment is . . . technically."

"You mean, like *a minefield* bigger and not really a gig your boss knows about?"

"Yeah. Something like that. I called the Latin American Water Tribunal and—"

"You what?"

"I called the—"

"I heard what you said. Are you crazy? If the company's involved in something dirty, they don't want it smeared all over the place, and that's what the tribunal will do. I've seen AAC's goons in action, Mariah. I've seen them 'dispose' of anyone who gets in their way."

"That was in the Congo, Eve. They wouldn't do that here."

"Mariah? You and I know better. This is me you're talking to. You'll be some random murder statistic or some random 'accident' and your death will become a cold case. End of story. Your story will end up in some storage facility in cockroach-infested cardboard boxes."

"You're being melodramatic."

"Am I? Really? I seem to recall a few stories of Indians off the Rez who couldn't find justice."

"That's different. I'm far away from the Rez and I don't have a tribal card or tribal plates. I'm floating out in the white man's world."

"I didn't mean they wouldn't solve it because you're Indian. I meant you wouldn't be the first person to be denied justice against those who might benefit from a case becoming cold. From becoming a statistic."

"Yeah, well . . . I'm already in. I had to finish this article and that was the unfortunate path I took, and obviously Daniel took it as well. At least I might find justice for those suffering in Ciudad Frontera and maybe a little justice for everyone who's suffering because of AAC—or I should say, this guy Saxton."

"Who's Saxton?"

"He's supposed to become the CEO when the current one steps down. He's also implicated in a sexual harassment and discrimination case where the Claimant has mysteriously been found murdered. Heather was involved in the case."

"What the fuck? Mariah, this isn't funny. Heather too?"

"Yeah. It seems our paths are colliding."

"Be careful, Mariah. I don't trust anyone or anything right now. Too many coincidences. And what does our friend Paul the Stalker have to do with all of this? Why now? Nothing makes sense anymore."

"Yeah, I know."

"Well, I guess we'll find out soon enough. I'll see you day after tomorrow."

"Fatalism? That's unlike you."

"You're right. Are you going to the water conference or sticking with us?"

"Tickets to the conference are too pricy. Can't afford it. You're stuck with me."

"Good. Be careful. *Manana*."

"*Maka Manana*."

Two puffs and my cigarette's done. What does it matter? I don't smoke anymore. At least that's what I tell myself when I'm feeling weak. But shit, it tastes good. Nothing like a transgression to remind you of your past.

The door to the apartment creaks. Jerome will smell the smoke. I spray eau de toilette around myself and walk into the mist.

The mist. It hangs around me as I lie back down. It floats along the ceiling and clouds my vision. The mist and the jungle.

It had been a long day of taking in names and helping people find relatives in the camps that lined the border with Rwanda. Thunderstorms rolled through with bands of heavy rain. Conditions were always right for the worst. Dysentery. Cholera. Malaria. Despair. Uprooted, the displaced sloshed through mud in search of wood and clean water and food and a distant place to relieve themselves. But distance was never far from someone else. The trash and sewage and mud and meanness worked in tandem with disease to kill. I was so tired of keeping track. The jungle of my own despair moved in on me. The Democratic Republic of the Congo killed. There was no getting around it. And yet it was one of the most beautiful places. It was how I pictured it for Terrell. Dying surrounded by beauty. There was some solace in that. Did I have to have his bones to know this truth? Was it not enough to know that he had died doing what was demanded of him? No. I already knew.

And yet I didn't. Not really. I know forensics. I've seen death. The bones tell very little. It's the flesh, or what is left of it, that tells the how. But I don't really want to know the how. Do I? It's maddening. I want answers to things for which I don't want answers. The proverbial Catch-22. It's a big mind fuck.

I sigh and yank the binding sheets from around me. Jerome stirs and throws his arm and leg over me. His skin is clammy. I ease myself out from under him.

David saved me. We took a day to hike into Virunga National Park. Playing tourist, our guide had taken us to see a family of mountain gorillas. Something in my heart melted that day.

I let the tears fall onto my pillow.

The difference between that world and the one below was too much to bear. It's not like the gorillas didn't have their boundaries or even their moods. They just didn't have any meanness in them. That was the moment when my jungle terrors began to fade. There were no gorillas in Vietnam, but somehow that didn't matter. A world of grace was shrouded in the mists.

Gorillas were executed, terrorized, mutilated to prove a point. What kind of a world makes such a point? What kind of world destroys grace? Is this so surprising when children are raped and murdered for a political point? My love for David blossomed in those moments. But how could a love survive such insults? We were doomed from the beginning. If something melted in my heart that day, something is breaking in my heart this night. My sob wakens Jerome. Shit! I can't burden him with this.

"What? What's the matter? What's wrong?"

I lean into him. "I'm sorry. I didn't mean to wake you."

"What's wrong?"

"It's nothing."

"Are you thinking about your brother?"

"Yes. I'm always thinking about my brother."

He leans back and sighs. "I'm sorry, Eve. I know you can't stand not knowing, but you have to face the facts. You may never know. You have to find a way to go on."

"I know. I'm sorry."

"Don't be sorry. It's okay." He turns and pulls me to him. "I love you."

"I love you too."

His kiss is long and tender, and I surrender to it.

Later, when his breathing is calm and rhythmic, my thoughts wind back up. Most people find contentment and sleep after making love. Not me. Not tonight. I slip from the bed and fling myself onto the couch. What does it matter where I lie? It's six of one and a half dozen of the other. Only the couch is less likely to wake Jerome.

There was something in the Congo. A long-forgotten piece of information. What was it? There were so many things I wanted to forget. David wanted to save me. We needed rest and relaxation, he said. I laughed at the time. How does one find relaxation in the middle of war? But he tried. We headed to Goma. Our guide from the Park was genial. From Goma it was an easy climb to the lava lake on Nyiragongo Volcano. We reached the summit in six hours. It was a rare, clear night. The stars littered the sky and the lava lit the world around us. It was the most peaceful sleep I had ever found.

Breakfast consisted of ancient dry granola bars, but somehow the food tasted better up there in the heavens. We descended to the Mikeno Sector of the Park, and that's where we found the gorillas. Those eyes. There were no words for their souls. I cried. My tears fell and I didn't try to hide them. The gorillas remained impassive, but I knew they too knew the great suffering. If they could endure, so could I.

We made our way back to Goma and the Camp and the war and the violence and the death. It's always amazed me. This opposable thumb condition and genocide wrapped up in a territorial imperative.

Resources. Somehow we humans sense a future lack where there may be none. The gorillas didn't defend what they had no fear of losing. There was plenty of greenery to go around. Content in the moment, they only had man to fear. It's a sobering thing to know you're part of the species that simultaneously must control resources and seeks to share it, all rolled into one. The complicated species. I roll over on the couch, but the cushions scratch and peck at my skin.

Goma. I went with two fellow Western aid workers to a bar in town. Our escape was rare and we were dressed up. Betsy, blond, blue-eyed, and Californian, caught the eye of Francois Flambeau, an ex-pat in town for the evening. Men were always underestimating Betsy, but she didn't seem to mind that night. He bought us drinks, and the conversation was light and flirtatious. Until . . .

"So, what are you doing here in Goma, Francois?" Betsy leaned her elbows against the table. Her cleavage winked from her V-neck happy face T-shirt.

Francois smiled and slowly dragged on his cocktail. "I'm working for a company that, you know, is here to save these people from themselves. Give them access to American dollars and Western market economics. Let's face it. They'll kill each other without us."

My normal reticence melted with the ice in my second cocktail. "What do you mean? What company? How are we the great saviors?"

"Fuck me." He swallowed the remains of his cocktail and motioned to the waiter for another. "These people are children. They have to be guided. We need to bring the colonies back. It's the only way they can save themselves. Let's face it, my friends, they're squandering their good fortune in resources. We know how to give them the full benefit of their good fortune."

Betsy leaned in further. "They're hardly children."

Francois raised his eyebrows. "Look at them. They have so many rebel groups who think they stand for something. They spout it to the world. But their real agenda is money and power. Who or what does that money go to? More armaments and more conflict. They're bloody stupid. They need help. They need to be managed." He leaned back and swirled his new drink. "I can pay them and help them obtain more guns and watch them kill each other, but there's a better way."

"What's that?"

"My company is part of the solution. We know what's best for them."

I leaned into the table and took a long swallow from my glass. "What company is that?"

"Astride Amalgamated Corporation. They're the solution for Zaire."

"Yes, but isn't that corporate philosophy what got Zaire into trouble in the first place? While the rest of Africa was being carved into colonies, Old Leopold privatized the Congo and allowed it to be ruled by corporations who pillaged their resources. And who extracted those resources? The Congolese. Millions were killed and mutilated. Give me a break. They've never recovered. They don't need to be managed. Especially not by a corporation. And what about Lumumba? He was executed in the name of mining interests. They don't need your company."

Francois's eyes hardened and glittered in the low light. He raised his glass and pointed at me with his index finger. "Listen, my friend, that's ancient history. This is a new world. They have to be saved from their warring ways and we need to make sure their resources aren't misspent. We can help them reap the benefits of this worldwide economy. It's not our fault they're killing each other. They aren't civilized like us. You should know this. Just look at your little camp."

Betsy laughed. "I'm sorry. It's hardly little."

Francois winked at her. "That's my point, my beauty. Their problems are big."

Who could argue with that? But his solution was hardly the answer.

A siren closes in on my street and I turn on the couch to watch the lights. There's trauma somewhere in the city. I'm exhausted. The clock on the wall clicks to five. I have not had a drink in months, but I feel as hung over as I did the morning after we met Francois. I'm also as unsettled now as I was back then.

And then it hits me. That thing I've been trying to remember. In the middle of the displacement and mayhem of the Camp, the rumors took on an immediacy we couldn't ignore. There was a company willing to pay for child labor and minerals in exchange for weapons. AAC. We started a list of missing children.

20 Michael

Sanctimonious pricks! Who the hell did they think they were?

"Michael. I hope you realize we're not questioning your motives. Just your methods." Lawrence Schmidt, Chairman of the Board, slid his fingertips along the highly polished mahogany tabletop. He regarded his fellow board members from under bushy eyebrows. There was no sparkle in his eyes. Only his flat, tired gaze gave any hint of the trouble he felt in his heart. It wasn't like he cared about the casualties—only the reputation of the company his father had built from scratch. Michael knew he wanted damage control before any was needed. He was a little late for that.

Lawrence had swiftly called the meeting, and his fellow board members had traveled from far and wide to decide behind closed doors the next course of action. Michael had given them great results, and they didn't want to do anything to jeopardize the returns. But any hint of a scandal or unethical behavior would be felt on the stock market. They couldn't afford to lose stockholder confidence now. No. They had agreed, it seemed, that Michael needed to be made aware and brought back into line.

Warren took over from Lawrence. He smiled. "Michael. You're doing a dynamite job. Spectacular. I think everyone here would agree things have never been better. We just need you to tone it down. Just a little. Let things settle down. We don't need anything that will mar our reputation here. Keep the stockholders happy. You know what I mean?"

"Sure. But I have a couple of loose ends I need to tie up."

"How bad would it be if you didn't?"

"Potentially very bad."

"Can you tie the loose ends up without jeopardizing . . . everything we've accomplished?"

"Yes. Of course."

"Well, then. I think it's settled." Warren looked around the table as everyone nodded their assent. "Go to it, Michael. Just keep it quiet. You know what I mean."

"Yes, of course."

Michael retreated and closed the heavy wood doors on the low buzz of male voices. The anger in him wanted to bust down the doors and mow them all down. That would put a real damper on his prospects. He snickered as he walked into the empty elevator. The doors closed and the box swooshed down.

Self-righteous assholes. Why didn't they just say what they wanted to say? Why tiptoe around? Avoiding getting their little souls dirty? Well, they were knee-deep in it as well. If he went down, they went down.

Sniveling idiots. He knew how the game was played. He knew how it was done. He might even know how to do it better than them. Why should he be prohibited from playing the game?

After all, he'd been born and raised on the south side of Muncie, Indiana. Everyone thought they were better. His dad lost his job at Ball Glass when production ceased. His mom went to work as a waitress. Good old Dad mopped out shit in the local school, and Michael was left at home with Mrs. Trowell. He watched. He was just six years old, and the old battle-axe locked him in his closet and denied him food when she felt like it. You got what you paid for. That was how he learned about money and power.

In school, he learned how Muncie got its name. The famous Penn brothers swindled the Lenape out of over a million acres. The Penns got their fastest runner to go as far as he could when the Indians thought it was meant to be a walk. Ethics only work if it's your side. The Lenape had to leave the Walking Purchase lands and ended up in Ohio Country, along the White River in Munsee. Twenty years later, they were forced out again by the federal government to make way for more white people, who changed the name to Muncie. The government said they were protecting the savages. Now *that* was how it was done. Force the weaker to vacate under threat of violence, change the name, and wipe the fucking slate clean. Bam! Did they think it was magic? How was anything he was doing any different? Hypocrites. They couldn't tie his hands. AAC's hands had been dirty way before he started working there.

"You have messages, Michael." Angela Martin, his secretary, watched him. One needed to know his mood at all times if they were going to work for him, and she was particularly good at it. She protected him, and he knew she hoped he'd protect her. She also needed the job and enjoyed the prestige of being the right-hand person to a rising star. He was careful to reward her handsomely for her loyalty.

Michael grabbed the messages and leafed through them. He flung his office door open and turned to Angela, "Hold my calls. I have to make some important phone calls."

"Michael, Heather Collings has been calling."

"What does that—I mean, what does she want?"

"Um, she wants to talk to you about a sexual harassment claim against you." She watched his reaction.

"That's a joke. I'll take care of it." He slammed the door.

He took his briefcase from the closet, unlocked it, and retrieved another cell phone.

"Hello."

"Have you taken care of the mess in Mexico?"

"We're taking care of it now. We've run into a few problems, though."

"Problems. Like what?"

"The survivors are in a hospital set up by Doctors Without Borders. There are rumors World Health is on the way. Could get bigger. Do you want us to enter the hospital and take care of them before it gets out of control? We might have to take care of the doctors, too."

Michael paced. "What? No! Don't be ridiculous. It's too risky. Leave them be." He massaged his chin. The idea was intriguing. "If they ask about the bodies, we can say we did it to protect everyone. The faster they went to the grave, the faster we could clean up the place. As for the cholera, they refused to be hooked up to safe water and they soiled their water source with their own feces. It'll get a little blurb on the eighth page and everyone will forget about it. I'll take care of the damage control on this end. Just take care of the cholera situation. Get it under control."

"Okay, boss."

He had one more call to make.

"Harold. Where are you on that little problem?"

"Tom and Jim are outside her apartment, but her dogs are a problem. She's heading to Charleston. I decided to get ahead of her."

"Since when are dogs a problem? Kill them."

"I think it'll be easier to take her here in Charleston. Besides, she doesn't have the flash drive yet."

"All right. Try not to be seen, but if you have to, take her in broad daylight and get rid of her for good. And get that damned flash drive. I have a mess here I have to clean up. She and that flash drive are my only other loose ends."

"There might be another problem."

"What's that?"

"That woman married to Brandon Collings—"

"Heather Collings?"

"Yeah. She's here too. She's staying in the same hotel."

Michael stared out the window. What were the odds?

"Hey, boss."

"Yeah. I'm thinking."

"You think it's a coincidence?"

"I don't know. She's my other loose end. I thought she was here. Watch them and find out. But Harold, we need that flash drive. Don't take too long."

"Okay, boss."

"Remember the bitch in Connecticut?"

"Of course. I can still get a hard-on thinking of that one."

"Make this one go the same way."

"My pleasure."

Michael sat in his chair and swiveled to his spotlessly clean and ordered desk. Damage control. What could they be doing there at the same time?

"And Harold."

"Yes, boss."

"What's better than killing one bird with one stone?"

"Killing two birds with one stone?"

Michael laughed. "Double the pleasure."

"Got it boss."

"And Harold. Make it look random. Like a serial rapist is on the loose. And nothing to tie you to it. You were never there."

"Sure, boss. In and out. Quiet as a mouse."

Michael put the phone down. He thought of the self-righteous hypocrites up in the board room. If they only knew. He could bring them all down as easy as sugar cream pie.

21 Heather

Shannon's mouth twitches. I stroke her arm. Tomorrow, we'll all be together. We're better together.

Lately, it seems like we're all at a crossroads. Perhaps we've been moving toward this—toward the consequences of that night. Destiny knocks. We should've come forward then. We should've told someone. Sometimes silence is worse than the sin. It's the sin of silence, the sin of neglect, the sin of avoided consequence. But isn't that the way it is? The avoidance creates its own consequence. One can't find invisibility except in death and even then . . .

It was Fiona who wanted to save me. Even then, I knew it was impossible. Poor Fiona. She can't forgive herself, even now. I have to tell my friends that it's time. We can't go on this way. I can't go on this way.

His name was Paul. He followed me to the airport. Waited at the luggage carousel. Flagged a taxi behind mine. Stood outside the hotel. Brandon won't save me. He doesn't even want me. I have to protect my baby girl.

I slide out of the bed and double-check the locks on the hotel room door. We are secure. I spoke to the front desk at check-in and they assured me security would be alerted. I slip back into bed and snuggle the covers around us.

Once it started, we couldn't stop it. Not then, not now. He's come for his reckoning.

So much changed during that summer. It's hard to remember the moment when everything shifted, but I've pinpointed the moment: It was the most peaceful of sunlit days. A soft breeze mellowed the heat of summer and my head felt lighter than it had since the beating. The Rose Garden was empty of people, but it buzzed with activity. Iridescent wings fluttered in the sunshine and the din of life sounded through the coniferous forest surrounding us. The scented air was an intoxicating elixir. Time stood still even as the wind lifted our spirits.

Ancient roses bloomed, unbending to the graceless passage of time. Mariah, shielding her eyes from the August sun, smiled and her happiness softened my fears. This was the portal to nirvana. We would be shielded from the adults' world. Mariah kicked at a fallen pinecone, and its fragrance mixed with that of the roses.

There were many hiding places—the tall trees that ringed the garden were shelter enough from curious eyes—but there was no need for secrecy today. Today was a beautiful day, and all the turmoil of the early summer was a distant memory.

Promise glistened in the air.

We grabbed at each other's hands and skipped in a ring before crashing to the ground, giggling. The green grass growing around the fountain cushioned us as we rolled on its softness. The sky, blue and infinite, held traces of white strings trailing from far-off airplanes. It was a dreaming-time day.

The nearby roses danced on the light breeze. Mariah reached for one, remarking that it was her favorite, the *Félicité Parmentier*. Double-blossomed blooms of fragrant petals, pink in the interior fading to white at the fringes, its fragrance was as alluring as the rose itself. An interior world of pink could not be eclipsed by the white predominance at the edge; its sheer beauty transformed that of the borders.

Mariah plucked the white petals until the soft pink core remained.

The core, disarmingly beautiful, evoked conflicting emotions. There was a fine line between the innocence aroused by the color of pink and the desire to transcend it. Mariah flipped the remnants of the flower into the bushes, where it lay crushed in the dirt. She propped herself on her elbow. I couldn't take my eyes from the dismembered flower.

Mariah broke the silence. "Are we going to lie here all day or are we going to do something? We don't have many days of summer vacation left."

Fiona sat up. "Mariah's right. Summer's almost over, and let's face it, it's been a depressing summer. We've hardly done anything."

Esperanza propped herself on both elbows. "Speak for yourself. I've had plenty of adventure, and it didn't all end that well."

Fiona rolled over and pulled the leaves of grass from her hair. "C'mon, you guys. Who says we have to have adventures that end poorly? Soon we'll go back to school. Everyone else is going to have stories of going to the beach, or Lake Tahoe, or Hawaii, or Disneyland. What'll we say about our summer?"

Eve sat up. "I know. We can say one of us lost our brother, another one lost her heart, and another one had the crap beaten out of her. Two of us got lost in the woods on a stupid trip to the park and spent a lovely vacation in the hospital, and one of us hung out on the reservation minus two uncles who are dead or missing in Vietnam. And three of us feel like characters from a bad episode of *Dark Shadows*. Sounds like a winning fucking time. Oh, and then we came home and had to dream up things to do so we could say we actually did something this summer. Who gives a shit if people think we had a boring summer or not? They think we're ridiculous anyway."

Fiona sat up. "Jeez, Eve. Who got you fired up? And who says we're ridiculous?"

Eve collapsed back on the grass. "Everyone does."

"Speak for yourself."

"I didn't mean it that way, Fiona. You live closer to the big houses in Sunny Hollow and you're blond and . . ."

"And what?"

"And beautiful and white, Fiona. You don't want to admit that gives you a pass, but it does."

"I don't get any passes. I get just as much shit as anyone else."

Mariah sat up. "Give me a break, Fiona. You don't know what real shit is. All you have to do is flip your blond hair at people and you're off the hook."

"You're just angry you're not blonde, Mariah. You know, you're white too. And Heather's white."

Mariah wouldn't let it go. "That's right. I am part white. So why does everyone pay more attention to the part of me that isn't?"

"Maybe you just see it that way."

"Maybe people want me to see it that way."

"Maybe they don't. And maybe they do. And maybe it's because you want them to see it that way. But why should that stop you? The only person who can stop you is yourself. Because you don't see any of us stopping you."

"You've been listening to Reverend Thomas too much." Mariah fell back down on her elbow.

Esperanza giggled.

"No, I haven't. I just think things are changing. Like you say all the time. I think we create our story. I think we make our own tune and our own dance. I think, together, we can dance better than all the people you think are stopping you. And I'm dancing with you. So get up and dance." Fiona tossed her blond hair behind her.

Mariah was silent, as if she was turning Fiona's words over and over like unprocessed stones, the gem buried deep within the ugly rock.

Eve snorted. "That's trippy, Fiona!"

"I mean it."

Eve laughed. "I don't doubt it." She began humming Otis Redding's "Sittin' on the Dock of the Bay." Within seconds, they were all humming.

The sounds from the dark interior of the forest coalesced and harmonized with their voices. Even the insects seemed to dance in rhythm. Their friendship was strong. Some things were too powerful to extinguish.

But life has a funny way of mimicking the natural world. The calm before a storm is often the sweetest of times, the most poignant of moments.

A swift breeze caught the discarded rose petals and lifted them until they merged with the other spent leaves of the garden.

Mariah shivered. "I feel trouble, you guys. My mom says spirits dwell in every object, even immovable rocks. If you pay attention, the living essence of the universe communicates through them. I should've been paying attention. The moment's gone, the message delivered, and I'm not sure what it was. The breeze is an omen. I feel it in my bones." She lay back down. "*Wanagi*. Ghosts and spirits." Quickly, she stood. "I have to move. I agree with Fiona. Let's do something. Anything."

Fiona rose too. "We could go to my house. I have Creedence Clearwater Revival's new album. We could have a sleepover. My parents will be out of the house tonight. We could hang out. What do you think?"

Eve looked at me. "It sounds like fun to me. Do you think your parents will let you, Heather?"

I thought about it. "Maybe. Maybe not."

Fiona was undaunted. "Oh, c'mon. My parents can call them. She can't say no to other adults. They hang together. And my parents still feel bad about everything. They're not going out until later. What do you say?"

I had to think.

"Oh, c'mon. I won't try to convince your mom, Heather. It'll be an invite from my parents. Nothing more."

Mariah picked at a piece of grass. "It might be the perfect chance to get away."

"What do you mean?" Fiona asked. "It's a simple invite to my house."

"But it's also the perfect chance to get Heather somewhere else," Mariah said.

I blanched. "They'll kill me."

"Not if we take you somewhere they don't expect."

Fiona was incredulous. "Where would that be?"

"I have an idea." Mariah smiled.

Eve perked up. "What's your idea? This is the perfect time."

Fiona shook her head. "I can't believe you guys are entertaining such an idea. What about Tallon? We didn't exactly succeed at that. They'll find us. Besides, who said I want to run away? My parents are only just forgetting about it."

Esperanza jumped up. "I don't want to run away. My family is the whole reason I didn't run away on the Yucatan. That was my moment to run."

"Sit down, Espy. No one has to go who doesn't want to."

"Then who's going?"

Mariah raised her hand. "I will."

Eve smiled. "My parents are so sad they won't even notice I'm gone."

I shrank against the thorns of a rose bush. "Wait. This is moving too fast. Where would we go?"

"My cousin lives on a reservation in Montana," Mariah said. "They would never think to look there."

"We'd stick out like sore thumbs. Have you looked at my hair lately?" Fiona lifted a tuft of blond hair.

"It would only be for a little while. The reservation is big. There are lots of places to not be found. I already talked to my cousin."

I shook my head. It was moving too fast. "No. They'll kill me. Forget about it. Things are fine right now. If we do something to make them mad, they'll find me, and things will be worse."

Eve looked at Mariah. "Why don't we think about it? It doesn't have to be now. We can talk more about it tonight. We haven't even planned it. What do you think?"

Mariah nodded. "You don't have to do anything you don't want, Heather. We'll just hang tonight."

Everyone nodded. But I knew they were planning. We had already jumped on the runaway train. And now that night stalks me.

I didn't have Shannon then. Can we now stop what we started then?

I snuggle against her. We have to amend our wrongs. Perhaps this is the year when it all comes full circle. Mariah will be here soon. We need a plan before we're assembled. I feel stronger than I have in a long time. Brandon or no Brandon, it's time to find myself.

The hotel room door lever clicks and slowly returns to the upright position. My heart skips. Shannon stirs and sighs.

Tiptoeing to the door, I look through the peephole, but no one is there.

My hand shakes as I open the door. Now is the time to find some courage. I peek out. The hallway is empty.

A lone rose lies at the crease in the doorway. A double-blossomed bloom of pink and white.

22 Sunny Hollow 1968

They assembled at Fiona's house at five. Fiona's mother supplied them with pizza, popcorn, soda, and brownies. Full, they settled in. Fiona's sisters were spending the night with their friends, and her parents left shortly afterwards for a dinner party across the bay in San Francisco. They wouldn't be back before sunrise. It was a moment of independence; the night spent in the darkness of the forest faded in the light of possibility.

Fiona headed for the fully stocked liquor cabinet.

Heather, grateful to be free of her parental chains, protested. "Fiona! We can't raid your parents' cabinet. They'll notice."

"No they won't, silly. What makes you think they'll know?"

"My parents know. They mark everything every time they drink anything. They know exactly how much is missing."

"Oh my God, Heather. My parents don't do that. They won't notice and they won't care. And guess what else I have?" She proudly pulled out a joint.

"Trippin', Fiona!" Mariah said.

"We can't do that," Heather said. "Where'd you get it, anyway?"

"Oh, don't be so square, Heather. Plus, I have several of them." Fiona pulled two more from her tight jeans pocket. The smashed joints looked harmless.

Eve and Mariah giggled. Excitement tinged the air.

Esperanza shied from the offending cigarette. "I don't know if I want to do that."

"Oh, c'mon, Espy. It can't do any harm. We're here, safe at home, and no one will catch us. It'll be fun. I'm tired of being square. I'm tired of being the good girl."

"Amen to that." Eve wanted danger. Caution had not served her family well.

Fiona handed the first joint to Eve and Mariah, along with a lighter. Eve dragged on the joint. The smoke, sweet and earthy, enveloped Eve's head and she coughed it out. She handed it to Mariah, who did the same. Fiona smiled and removed several bottles of alcohol from her parents' cabinet. A faded picture of a Highland ancestor hung over the decanters, guarding the finest of her father's single malt scotch. Fiona saluted him and took the shortened joint, dragged deeply on it, held it, and coughed.

Eve, Mariah, and Fiona fell into a fit of laughter. Heather and Esperanza stared at them in disbelief.

"Don't you feel funny doing that in front of an ancestor?" Esperanza regarded the stern eyes in the picture.

Fiona giggled. "No way. Highlanders were wild freedom lovers. They were Celts, *chica*. He's probably doing a Fling in his grave. His descendant has Highland gumption."

Esperanza smiled. She was the first of the two remaining to surrender. She, too, coughed up her first drag, but she eased into the next couple of shared joints. Heather remained aloof. Fiona opened her parents' half-consumed vodka and poured several glasses. After filling the glasses with orange juice, she passed the drinks to her friends. She looked at Heather. Heather knew everyone was watching. She couldn't refuse. She took it. Fiona smiled and returned to pour herself a glass.

Heather loved the taste of the orange juice drink. Her insides tingled. She lost her fear and drank it quickly. Freedom oozed at the bottom of her glass. She dabbed at the ice cubes coated with juice. Then she reached for the remnants of the last joint, took a drag, coughed, and took another drag.

Fiona smiled. "Wow, Heather. You're diggin' that joint."

"Do you have another?"

"No, I only got three. But I know where we can get some more."

Eve and Mariah mixed more drinks. The orange juice ran out. Rummaging through the cabinets for a substitute, they returned with a container of Tang and armfuls of snacks.

Mariah wanted more of the forbidden cigarette. "You really know where we can get more?"

Fiona looked mischievously from one girl to the next.

Mariah stamped her foot. "Well . . . where?"

"Juniper Street." Fiona fell on the floor laughing.

"Son of a bitch, Fiona." Mariah wasn't laughing. "You got that from Damon? Are you fuckin' nuts?"

Fiona rolled up on her heels. "What? Why does it have to be Damon?"

Eve planted her fists on her hips. "Well, was it Damon? Tell me it wasn't Damon? Who else lives on Juniper?"

"Well, what if it was?" Fiona asked.

All four moaned.

"Are you crazy?" Eve demanded, echoing Mariah.

"Well, are you interested in getting more or not?" Fiona asked.

"No. I don't have any money anyway, and even if I did, I wouldn't give it to him." Mariah's voice traveled through a tunnel.

"Oh, c'mon. Jazmin doesn't get involved in his drug deals."

"This is crazy, Fiona. I know someone else we could get this from without involving Damon. There's no way I'm seeking that asshole out."

"Ah, you're such a drag, Mariah." Fiona sauntered over to the counter where Mariah and Eve were standing. "You wanna know what I think?" Her forefinger was within an inch of Mariah's nose.

"No. What do you think?"

"I think you secretly have a crush on him. He's a total fox."

"Ewww." Mariah made a face. "He's a rat."

"Jealous." Fiona smirked.

Mariah's face reddened. "No. I'm not. He's a total loser."

"I'm just saying. You seem to have intense feelings about him. Anyhow, I have birthday money and I want to buy some more."

"Not from him," Mariah moaned.

"Oh, c'mon," Fiona whined. "I wanna have some fun."

Heather felt freer than she ever had. She cocked her head. "Let's get some more." She wasn't ready for the sweetness of the night to end. She wanted to be as free and audacious as her friends. She felt honored by their friendship, but she was insignificant in their presence; they eclipsed her. For once, tonight, she felt significant. If she smoked more, could she feel this way forever? She reveled in the sense of her power. Power was an elixir and she now understood why everyone wanted it. But why did they have to take hers to add to theirs?

Mariah and Eve were stunned. Fiona smiled. "That's my girl."

"Are you sure, Heather? Because I'm with Mariah, I'm not sure about this." Eve knew that none of them would be able to deny this to Heather. It was only a short while ago that she had lain, broken, in a hospital bed. The flirt with death had made her life, and theirs, that much sweeter.

"Yeah, of course I'm sure." Heather rocked and swayed in place.

Eve didn't hesitate. "Then let's go."

It seemed like a good plan. Fiona called Damon. Jazmin was with her gang in Sycamore. They could score an ounce of good shit if they came now. Fiona emptied the chamber of her piggy bank, swept a brush through her long mane of blond hair, swiped her lips with gloss, and shoved the money into her back pocket. When she descended the stairs, the girls had cleaned up the kitchen and were ready to go. They would be fine if there were five of them. "Ready?"

"Ready." Heather stumbled backwards and erupted into giggles.

Eve held out a hand to steady her. "Oh boy. This could be fun."

They walked out into the night. The air was clear and warm. Moving down the stairs to the street, they headed toward Sycamore. Quiet enveloped Fiona's street. A half-block walk away, they turned onto a main street that now teemed with late-summer traffic. The lights of the street fused with those of the cars to brighten the night sky into something that resembled the day. Shortly, they were on another quiet street.

Damon sat on the stoop of his house. His blond hair and blue eyes matched those of Fiona. Yet their spirits were so different, Mariah reflected. She was light to his darkness.

"Hey," he said as they walked up. "I was wondering if you were for real."

"Oh, I'm for real." Fiona tucked a strand of hair behind her ear.

He looked her up and down before licking his lips. "Yeah, you're for real all right."

Mariah rolled her eyes. "C'mon Fiona. Let's do this already."

Damon turned to Mariah with equal interest. "Yeah. Why don't you and I do this already? You know, we're a lot alike, baby."

"What are you talking about?" Mariah eyed him coolly.

"I'm talking about you."

"I have no idea what you're talking about, man."

"Don't you?" He rubbed his hand across his naked chest and left it to rest on his breastbone.

"No, I don't!" Sex was as natural as dirt. Her parents were traditional even though they made her go to a Christian church. But that didn't mean you had to lie down for just anyone. Indians respected themselves. And there was no respect in Damon.

"Too bad. We could've gotten it on."

"What? You see what I mean, Fiona?"

Fiona nodded. "C'mon, Damon. I've got the dough, do you have the stuff?"

Damon slowly rose from his perch. He winked at Mariah. Winking blue eyes—a demon with an angel's face.

"What the hell are you winking at her for?" Fiona fumed openly.

"I dig both of you. In fact, I dig all of you. When the cat's away, the mice will play."

Fiona's slender nose flared. "Let's just finish this."

He reached in the right front pocket of his jeans, tattered and slung low on his youthful hips. Fiona grimaced. She was glad her friends were with her. She wasn't sure what she would be capable of alone. He stopped and smiled. "Better yet. Why don't you come get it?"

Fiona's head was light. "Just give it to me."

"I will, but which do you really want?"

Fiona's face flushed. "The pot."

"Are you sure?"

"Yeah." Fiona gulped. "I'm sure."

"Too bad. The other is better."

He grabbed Fiona by the back of her head, and kissed her, long and hard. She kissed him back. Their blond hair fused into an image of one.

The girls shifted nervously and looked up the street.

Fiona pulled herself away and ran down the steps. "C'mon. C'mon. Shhh."

They headed toward the Rose Garden. There were corners of the dark garden in which they could hang out and smoke in peace.

On their way, another group of girls emerged from the garden and moved as one down the street, noisy and self-assured. This was their street. *Jazmin.* Fiona looked for a way to escape.

They headed to the other side of the street, and Jazmin and her friends didn't seem to notice them—until they were parallel to them. Then one of the girls glanced across the way and yelled.

"Hey! Who are you? What are you doing on our street?"

Mariah whispered. "Don't acknowledge them. Maybe they'll move on."

"Hey, bitch! I asked you who you were and what the fuck you're doing on *our* street?"

"No one and nothing."

"Damn fucking right, no one."

Jazmin headed their way.

"Run," Fiona said. "*Now.*"

The girls bolted for the Rose Garden. "You better run, *gringa*. I'll beat the fuckin' shit out of you if I catch you. You better not mess with my man."

They hit the Garden. Old lights bathed the grass and walkways in soft light. It would be easy to slip into the shadows. They scattered.

Heather headed toward the stairs that climbed to her street. Mariah grabbed her. "Not there, Heather." Mariah's heart beat thickly in her chest. Heather couldn't run home. If her mother found out, she might kill her this time. They had to get to Fiona's house. She followed Heather.

Leaving the concrete path and stairs, they headed into the quiet of the forest. Mariah searched below for movement. Jazmin and her friends were obvious, but Fiona, Esperanza, and Eve were, thankfully, well hidden. The fog she had moved through had completely dissipated now, and she realized the trouble they were in.

"Stay here, Heather," she said. "I have to try to find the others. We have to get back to Fiona's house soon."

"I don't want to stay here alone."

"Please," Mariah pleaded. "You'll be safe here. I can find the others more easily alone. Just don't move."

Heather, trembling in the dark, nodded.

Mariah made her way along the periphery of the forest. She knew these woods. She crouched behind the public restroom first and then moved farther toward the end of the building before stepping cautiously into the moonlit walkway. Tiptoeing across the grass, she crouched behind the first bank of rose bushes

All movement was up ahead. There were angry voices and the sound of running. She moved forward more comfortably, as the danger was well ahead of her. She ran along the walkway in the hopes of coming up behind Jazmin's group. If she could surprise them, she might be able to distract them from Fiona. She sprinted in their direction, but the girls seemed to be moving swiftly toward and through the trees above her. Shit! She forgot about the path through the trees. She worried they might surprise and scare Heather if she wasn't hidden well enough. She didn't want a repeat of Tallon Park. She needed to find her friends and herd them back to Fiona's, where it was safe. Where they should've never left. She sprinted back to Heather.

"Heather! Where are you?" Mariah called in a loud whisper.

Screams and scuffles filled the air. Two girls wrestled on the path and Mariah caught the glimmer of silver in the light of a street lamp that bathed the stairs. The blade, held high, came down quickly, but the other figure moved out of its way. Mariah ran toward the fighting. She pulled short at the sound of glass breaking.

Whoosh! A house caught fire. She knew the house—a memory of Halloween, candy, children, and an adult tirade. The blaze grew quickly in intensity. A scream, high-pitched and terror-filled, spilled into the confusion.

Heather! Oh, God!

A flash of silver caught the light again. Fiona! Jazmin would rip her to shreds. There was so much anger and rage in that girl. All she needed was one score, one drop of blood, and she would know the kill was within reach.

Mariah froze. Save Heather or save Fiona, she couldn't do both.

Jazmin moved closer and lunged, plunging the blade, but Fiona moved away. Jazmin paused. She was clearly weighing her options, her intent unrelenting. Fiona smiled and softened her knees into an *en garde* position, ready to parry the next offense. Years of fencing maneuvers served her well for once.

"Fiona! Heather's in that house."

"Go get her!" Fiona yelled, momentarily distracted.

Jazmin made her move. Mariah watched as the silver, glinting and animated with the proximate fire, plummeted toward her friend.

Mariah gasped. "Watch out!"

Fiona screamed and fell to the ground.

Jazmin turned toward Mariah, the fire illuminating the surprise on her face. Mariah knew that look. A beautiful buck had once wandered out into the headlights of her family's car. Her father had braked hard and missed him, but the look Mariah had seen in the deer's eyes still haunted her. It was the same look in her grandmother's eyes when they told her that her son was missing in Vietnam.

"Fiona!"

Fiona moaned and held her shoulder. Jazmin threw the knife into the forest and ran for the top of the stairs. Mariah raced to Fiona's side.

"Mariah. You better go get Heather."

"You need help. Where's everyone else?"

"I don't know. I think she just grazed me. I'm scared, Mariah. Please! You have to get Heather and we have to get out of here. Some of Jazmin's friends went to the house. That man and someone else was yelling and cussing them out. I think Damon's there too. I saw him throw something at the house right before the fire started."

The house was now in flames. A raging fire fed by dry air and sea winds could ignite whole neighborhoods. The fire crackled and spit out sparks, the threat of consumptive destruction. Everyone would be in danger, including her family.

Several figures ran from the house.

Mariah had to find Heather.

She moved without thinking.

She took a neighbor's hose, doused herself with it, and ran into the building. "Heather! Heather!" Her voice was cut off as the air seared her vocal cords and lungs. She dropped to the floor and coughed and heaved at the offensive heat. Black smoke roiled in the cramped space. The noise reminded her of howling monsters and angry spirits. Through the sounds of the disintegrating house, she heard whimpers and moved towards it.

"Heather!" Her voice now nothing but a whisper. She crouched further down out of the black smoke. A back bedroom door was shut and Mariah leaned into it. The door gave way gracelessly and fire followed her. Knocked to the ground, she struggled to find her bearings. She was blasted with the specter of someone tied to the bed, another unconscious and prone on the floor, and a third hovering over the figure tied to the bed, sawing at the bindings. Through the smoke and the terror, cold gripped her heart and she moved. Her grandfather had called it a warrior's *sang-froid*.

"Heather!"

Heather didn't move. She was still, bleeding and naked in the light of the monstrous fire.

The man turned his head to Mariah. Tears washed his face and glistened in the shadow of the inferno.

He cut the final binding.

He turned to look at Mariah. It was the second time that night she had witnessed that look. He rose and ran toward the inside of the burning house, toward her, past her, through the fire. Mariah stepped over the fallen figure on the floor.

He didn't move. His eyes were open and watching, a huge hole opened in his middle, a fountain of blood seeped through his dirty tee shirt. She shook Heather.

"Heather. C'mon. We have to get out of here. Heather! Please! You have to help me get you out of here." Mariah lifted her by her arms. "I can't do this alone."

Heather roused herself enough to allow Mariah to lead her to the open window. They climbed from the almost fully engulfed house. Mariah got Heather as far away as she could. Firemen arrived as the house blew out its remaining windows and became an inferno. She knew it would take everything in their power to contain it before it destroyed everything in lower Sunny Hollow. Neighbors hosed down their houses. In the grip of the calamity, no one noticed two teens emerging from the burning structure.

Mariah searched for their friends, but even Fiona was gone. The blood left by her injury gleamed in the light, though rescue feet destroyed its integrity.

Mariah removed her own T-shirt and pulled it over Heather's head. Her white bra was conspicuous in the gleam of the fire, but Heather's nakedness had been no less so. She didn't want to draw attention to them. She grabbed Heather, who put her arm around her shoulder, and they hurried toward Fiona's house.

Sanctuary, a short distance directly, took them a long time to reach because Mariah avoided the busy street. Dogs barked as they traveled through foreign yards. They stumbled several times under Heather's weight, and Mariah feared discovery. The horror of their situation gripped her. This was far worse than the Tallon fiasco; Heather might not survive this. They should've been planning her escape instead of chasing after a score.

Mariah tapped at Fiona's door and waited. Esperanza opened. Mariah and Heather stepped inside the relief of light. They were all there and Fiona had a bandage around her shoulder. The harsh light threw their wounds into stark relief and each sized up the mountain of troubles they were in.

How would they explain it? Mariah wondered. They should've gone to the hospital. They should've gone to the police. But she knew better. That would only make it worse for Heather, who was already broken beyond repair, beyond despair.

Eve gasped. "Oh my God! Oh my God! What have we done?" She

pulled Heather and Mariah to her and gently hugged them. Mariah whimpered into her shoulder.

Esperanza threw her sweater around Heather's shoulders and turned to Fiona, whose wound continued to bleed.

Esperanza spoke first. "We have to do something to Fiona's shoulder. I don't think the wound is deep, but we have to do something." She looked at Mariah.

Mariah nodded. Her Grandmother had taught her that summer to stitch a wound. "I'll do it, but we need antibiotics, too."

Fiona blanched. "It'll hurt."

Esperanza moved towards Fiona. "I'll hold your hand. You can hold on to me."

Fiona nodded. "There are antibiotics in my Mom's medicine cabinet."

Eve left to find the antibiotics.

When she returned, Mariah had already begun stitching the wound.

Eve turned to Heather. She gently stroked a washcloth across Heather's bruises and the smudges of soot from the fire. She rinsed the cloth and gently wiped the blood streaking down her thighs. Heather, in shock, stared at a distant point.

The silence was unbearable. Outside, the sounds of alarms increased.

Eve moved to the window. Fire glowed across her face. She looked at her friends. A tear slid free. "The hill is on fire."

When Mariah looked into her friends' eyes, she knew the look. It was the same look that had been dogging her all night. But this was the third time, and three was never a good omen.

23　Paul

I was born Paul Ezekiel Marist but I could've been Jim, Bill, Bob, or any other poor fuck. I was gun fodder and my brothers-in-arms were no different. It didn't really matter whether the guns belonged to the Viet Cong or the government of the US of A. We were still the little plastic soldier boys they lined up on their military maps back in Washington, DC. We were grunts, drafted by destiny into a war of someone else's making. That was why we had numbers, numbers inscribed on cheap metal, so that when we got the shit blown out of us they could match our body parts to a name.

Sorry-ass war. Mad as hell, I carried my rage like my duffel bag. But who gives a shit about that, so long as it isn't something you can see, like an arm or a leg. My brothers in Uncle Sam's war weren't so lucky on either account. Most of their tags were collected and bagged for the trip home, their remains shipped in a crappy black bag. Blackness defined the journey, defined the heart of those who waged this misbegotten war.

Mikey made it through boot camp with me but I wore his brain matter two weeks into my tour. All for a fucking hill. Dak To. Kontum Province. We were engaged and then they were gone. Pansies. It was all chaos and gunfire. And then it wasn't. But before they retreated, they blew his head off and I wore his fucking brain the whole way back to Saigon. The smell never left, it was the reminder that a life had once mattered. When they bagged him, there was no brain left. It had crusted itself to me as if clinging to something living could make it whole again, could make Mikey live again. I itched at the fetid remnants, the pieces of pink and red turned to putrid brown. The smell made me retch and the creatures of the jungle feasted on his remains, gnawed at my still-living flesh. But we kept moving.

One year and I said more good-byes than hellos. Before long, I couldn't remember the names of those who were supposed to watch my back. They were all Mikey. The leeches were more constant than the brothers. But that was the way of war. You were always dirty, hungry, tired, and scared. That way you didn't ask what the hell you were doing there.

Things weren't any better when I came home. I was always dirty, hungry, and tired. But I wasn't scared any more. I was just pissed off. I was pissed off and my parents didn't want me hanging around, polluting their safe little piece of heaven. I tried to tell them it was all an illusion. They couldn't believe me. To believe would be an admission of the truth. The truth was dangerous. To protect their younger children, they sacrificed their eldest. Sacrificed twice to the gods of war.

And the protestors didn't make anything any better. They hated the war, but I didn't start it. Fucking peaceniks. I didn't even get to decide where my little plastic soldier body got to stand and try to survive. Someone else did that for me. But it didn't matter. The protestors hated me anyway. And that pissed me off too. I couldn't join them. What did they know about what we had been through? Nothing. The injustice of it was too much to bear.

When I rented a house in Sunny Hollow, I finally found some peace in my waking hours. But then the night was always different. The sound of birds alerted me to another day of survival. They were a reminder that things could be better, should be better.

And then I saw her. She was nothing more than a bird herself. But she was afraid of me. Skittish, broken bird. I wanted to fix her but I couldn't even fix myself. I fixed motorcycles and cars. I wanted to fix birds but my hands were too angry. So I kept fixing bikes. That was how I met Stab. He introduced me to his gang of riders, some of who were back from Nam. People called us Hell's Angels but we didn't wear the badge. They thought they were badass but then they didn't wade through a jungle pocked with land mines and people who smiled at you as they planned to blow your fucking brains out. Death was a game for the Angels but death was reality for us. It's a difference you don't get until you've been in country.

I thought things were never the same after I went away to 'Nam, but they were never the same after that night either. It had started in the morning. The birds were at it again. Stab brought enough hooch for the week. We had enough booze, pot, and smack for a platoon but it was just us and our bender. The cops would've had a field day.

Their neat little uniforms with their neat little book of laws. They didn't get it. Their laws were useless in the jungle. You lived or you died. And the things you had to do to survive weren't in any little pansy-ass rule book. I didn't tether enemy ears and fingers to my gun but I didn't bother with those who did, either. When you've looked down the throat of the Reaper, who could begrudge you a little trophy of survival?

In the end, it was Stab's idea. She was standing outside in the trees. I told Stab she was a bird, a little broken bird. But then he liked broken things. He liked to break things to make him less broken. I tried to stop him but he dragged her into the house and tied her to the bed. She was so small and so helpless. Poor little bird. Some things in life have to be protected from all the meanness. I couldn't fix Stab any more than I could fix her. He wouldn't leave her alone. Her screams strafed through the darkness and I smelled the fear. It smelled like Mikey's rotting brains. I itched at the horror of it but it crawled into the crevices of the room, crawling toward her.

It's a code of honor, a trick of survival, to defend your brother, to have his back. When you beat the bush, you have to know your comrades. Faith is something you don't think about. You try not to think about the things you do or the things you see, it's enough to break your faith. And breaking faith is death. But I had to break faith that day, that night of purgatory.

I broke a chair into pieces and drove a jagged leg deep into Stab's chest. There was madness in the air.

Stab rose and reeled, a deer in headlights.

He looked like Mikey right before the bullet entered his brain and snuffed his life. That moment he knew there was nowhere to run, the moment when time slows down and grants a reprieve to visit all the sweet memories soon to be a history of irrelevance.

Stab lunged but I backed away and he dropped to the floor. The Viet Cong would be there soon. I checked his pulse. It slowed. The jungle rot would get him anyway. If not, the Viet Cong would. Even as I searched for his lingering life, noise of struggle and entry came from the front door. I had to save her.

A Molotov cocktail sailed through the window. You can't turn your back on the enemy. The enemy never sleeps. The flames already licked at the curtains by the time I made it to the front of the house. But I made it in time to see the enemy, blond hair and blue eyes. A wink. The enemy is very crafty.

Fire. Mortar blasts. I ran for the bedroom. I had to save the bird. I had killed a brother for her. I couldn't let her die in her cage. Releasing the bindings was as easy and as sweet as those moments of childhood innocence; floating down the river in inner tubes, swinging out and jumping into clear, cool summer waters, barbecues into late, lightning bug–lit evenings. I remembered all these things. It had been a long time since they'd brought me any joy, any relief from the images that bombarded my head—the noises, the flashes, and the screams that barraged my waking hours, my sleeping hours. There was salvation in cutting those bindings. Does she know I saved her? Does she know she saved me?

I have to let her know. There is only this one last thing. Perhaps all my sins, all my sorrows, have been leading me to this one act. I have to beg her forgiveness. Her father was a coward. Her husband is a coward. I will not be the third.

It took me all day, but my quest has rewarded me. That is a good sign—a sign that I am doing the right thing. I cut the rose and say a prayer for forgiveness.

It is not my rose. The hallway in her hotel is long, but it is quiet. I place the lonely bloom at her doorstep. Will she remember? The girls never knew. They never knew I watched them and watched over them. The Rose Garden was always filled with birds—innocence always blossoms where there is space for the wildness of the world.

24 Mariah

My dreams peel away at reality.

Living in the linear world of fast-paced journalism that requires objective accounting of measurable experience, the idea that I can feel someone watching and tracking my movements should be illogical. But who decides what is logical—or even objective, for that matter? Living requires a certain amount of human judgment. Doesn't it? Are those who determine objectivity merely those who wield the power of social convention? Eve tells me I am sounding more and more like Heather. Heather is losing it. Therefore, she must believe I am as well. Maybe she's right. And maybe she's wrong. Truthfully, there's no room for paranoia in my life. And yet it has taken up residence and torments my waking and sleeping hours. The prevailing culture has no room for it but I can't shake it. My intuition screams at me to pay attention.

Grandmother warns me of attachment to the illusion of order required in the white man's world. There's a part of it that I understand—that makes sense. The observable universe is the part that allows one to hold on to reality, but the rest allows one to infer a world of infinite possibility. Comfortable with at least the concepts of string theory and multiverses, ideas of altered reality don't terrify me. Grandfather, when he was alive, taught me how ghosts infuse the landscape. The memory of events imbues the place, the memory of people transmutes from reality to spirit. Death is just a passage, not an end to that which has no end—it's no more than a jagged bump in the wheel. Grandfather knew energy was everywhere. The observer is the final judge.

The sense of being stalked by something is not foreign or strange. But my dreams play tricks with me—I have no sense of whether I'm asleep or awake.

I did not speak of these things with Grandmother when I called yesterday. I have never kept things from her. Why now? Grandmother would know what to do, she would understand the forces at work, and I don't dare utter these matters and loose their power without some mediation.

The airport bustles. I wait to board, shutting out the jostle and din of other travelers. Finding my assigned seat, I settle in for the short flight. I double-check my purse's side pocket for the flash drive I picked up this morning. It's safe. I need to find a quiet moment to open it, somewhere where there are no prying eyes, but all the possible contents spook me. It is as if the drive taunts me. Daniel would've known I'd reveal the truth to the world no matter the consequence. But that's my problem: I don't care about consequences, because if the world has betrayed me then I can betray it back. It's math. Zero plus zero equals zero. But lately, the numbers aren't adding up. It's an issue of values.

The last moments of my conversation with Daniel remain clear and powerful, to the exclusion of everything said since. Were they his last words on Earth? Does he lie dead or unconscious in some hotel room on the far side of the world? It has to be the flash drive. Someone wants it. Right? Or maybe it was something else; maybe he pissed off some psycho motorist who followed him. Anything is possible. Why do I have to jump to conclusions?

I need to open the flash drive.

"Excuse me."

"Oh, sure. I'm sorry." I retrieve my book from the seat next to me. I smile at my neighbor, then instantly look away like a shy Indian girl. Why? I'm not like my mother or my aunties. And he doesn't look Lakota or Ho-Chunk. Indian Country is large, but even so, it surprises me. What tribe? And what are the odds of sharing a row on the way to Charleston from Washington, D.C.? Meaningful coincidences are rarely anything more than happenstance in the world of news. But my world has lost its edges and chance seems to carry more meaning these days.

My neighbor pulls a large book from his backpack, shoves the pack under the seat in front of him, and opens the tome on water resources engineering to a well-marked page. He's no doubt attending the water conference. Still, the coincidence unsettles me. Perhaps the bad winds in my life are spent. Or maybe they're an impending full gale force storm. My arm tingles where it rests next to his.

I study the world below. We are taking the route that traces the coast of the Eastern United States. It's a beautiful day, even more so at airplane height. The clouds are thin, wispy little things. The brilliance of the sky etches every contour of the shore. The water sparkles and casts diamonds across the window portal.

The events of the past few days catch up with me now that I'm settled and quiet. I finished the last article on virtual water, but I couldn't put together the summary for the series. Unsettling dream images mingled with the sequencing of words. The flash drive had not yet arrived, but its existence unsettled me as it unsettles me now. How does one summarize the importance of one of the most valuable resources now being privatized everywhere? The potential consequences chill me. I trace the deep lines of the seaboard, note where they're broken by the haphazard inlets of marshland.

There is so much to say in the summary. I could begin with highlighting water rights in the U.S., because it's often the benchmark for the U.N. and the world. The department that deals with all resources also deals with American Indians. It's always been about the land and its resources.

I cast a sideways glance at my neighbor, and I catch him doing the same.

I clear my throat. "Um. I noticed your book on water resources. I'm Mariah Westerman. I'm a journalist, and I'm doing a series of articles on water issues and rights."

A geophysicist with a PhD from California Institute of Technology, Dennis is an enrolled member of the Three Affiliated Tribes. He, too, is mixed blood.

The glint of the sun on water brightens our descent into Charleston. Water is one of the last and ongoing matters that shimmies along the surface of human life. One only has to turn on the faucet and the tap water flows. In a world of supply and demand, the exploding world population constitutes an increasing demand without an equal increase in supply. Agriculture alone, the largest consumer of water, will require more in order to feed the world. Once man hits the tipping point of supply, there will be no regeneration of the valuable resource. Desalination is the alternative. Man will be willing to drink the seas dry to survive. But survival has a price.

Dennis describes the issue in cold scientific terms. Mesmerized by his breadth of knowledge, I scratch a few notes.

The first and last issues deal with water rights in the western region of the United States. The Bureau of Reclamation, the doctrine of federally reserved water rights, the states' system of prior appropriation, and the Supreme Court's weigh-ins cast a blueprint for the future allocation of water for the world. Rivers running through tribal lands are technically theirs, provided they use it. But if they don't have the means to harness the rivers, the right passes to those who can. The implied power floats along the surface of water rights. The privatization of water is the first clue that man's relationship to it is changing. Someone is going to die of thirst. And someone else will get rich.

"Our best croplands and tribal capital were inundated when the Garrison Dam flooded the reservation and we were forced to sign away the land," Dennis says. "We were dispersed to the high buttes and the cities. It nearly broke my father. He made sure my brothers and I could speak the language of appropriation. It's the only way to protect our people's rights. And there's oil under what's left in the Bakken formation. The government and its friends in business just don't know how to get it yet."

I hesitate. "But the language of appropriation requires some . . . accommodation." But he has clearly accommodated far less than I have. His hair is long and braided in two tight lines down his chest. He's not afraid to be Indian, whereas I've been blending—poorly— my entire life.

"Yeah," he says. "But it's a necessary risk."

The plane's landing wheels emerge from their tomb. I stare out over the lowlands that ensconce the treasure of South Carolina's coast, Charleston.

"It's beautiful out there. It's hard to imagine so much suffering started here." In some ways, it's where ours started. Grandmother grew up with the memories. I didn't learn that history in school. In college, I did a paper on Lincoln's concept of "hard war." He suspended the writ of habeas corpus. Not that the writ was available to us. He and his generals targeted civilians, the weak, killed livestock and family pets, all before they turned their attention to us. By then, they had perfected the means of extermination. My professor failed me. I even included primary sources.

My words are bitter. "It's impossible to see this place without thinking of the end for us. Lincoln hung thirty-eight Santees to save his precious war. He knew what would happen. He *knew.* My grandmother's grandfather was saved from the scaffold and marched off to Fort McClellan, where he died of starvation and exposure. His wife and most of his children died at Pike Island of starvation. My great-grandmother was all that was left. If consolidating and saving the union justified total war, then the unified principle of progress and manifest destiny justified genocide. And Plymouth became the rock, the story, upon which the country was founded. They certainly wanted no part of our story, now or then."

Dennis chuckles. "I don't know. It sounds like you're telling it anyway."

"Yes, but no one wants to hear it. The lie serves power."

Charleston gleams in the distance. Its irrelevance is not neat. In fact, it looks more pertinent than ever. Political relevance is a fickle mistress. Plymouth has been inching south for years. And tribes have been flexing their muscles with each casino that promises survival and an ability to tap their fundamental water rights. Accommodation and the language of appropriation. I have to smile.

Dennis smiles too.

Neither of us needs more words; the meanings are firmly rooted in the language of our tribes.

Once the seat belt signs turn off, I stand, a sense of excitement and dread comingling. I still have the same teenage butterflies in my stomach. They're caused by more than just the anticipation of seeing my friends.

I swap business cards with Dennis. His smile is easy and I feel flushed. He's disappointed I won't be at the Water Convention. I am too. I watch him travel swiftly ahead of me through the concourse. He makes me feel truly alive—like my quest for truth has meaning. His card is crisp and strong in my hand. It was only a chance meeting. Or was it?

Now I'm alone.

I have to look at the contents of the flash drive tonight. I could upload its contents and send it to my boss. Be rid of it. Finish my summary and head over to the Water Convention tomorrow—just for a few hours, before everyone else arrives. Heather and Eve would understand. It's my job. I clutch Dennis's card to my chest. I could call him tonight. My head swims as I step onto the down escalator and trip over the suitcase trailing behind a passenger two steps lower. He glances back and scowls.

"I'm so sorry."

The man turns away disdainfully.

I watch at his back as I step from the escalator. The light is blinding. I rarely check my luggage, but life is more complicated when I'm with my friends. It requires eveningwear and bathing suits and makeup and more than one pair of shoes and all the other trappings of being a tourist. I detest the role, but I love my friends.

Retrieving my bag, I turn and walk into a man who's been standing behind me.

"Oh, excuse me."

The man doesn't respond. His jaw is hard. His eyes are cold—not that I can see them, glowering from behind dark sunglasses, but I can feel them. Turning, he bumps me hard and moves quickly toward the exit doors.

I fall backwards onto the conveyor belt full of luggage, and my head hits the cold metal as the belt continues to move. Hard luggage pens me in.

I can't breathe.

My head is cotton candy between my ears.

I'm spinning.

A fellow passenger offers me his hand and pulls me up. "Are you okay?"

"Yeah, I think so. Thank you."

Several young onlookers giggle.

The man's concerned face makes me feel weak. "I can't believe that man pushed you like that." He smells of stale cigarettes but he reminds me of someone.

My shaky fingers reach for but can't find my head. "I know. Thank you again."

"You're welcome."

He moves away.

I know that face. I'm sure of it.

But it can't be. I move through a fog. How could he have known to come to Charleston? Did he follow Heather from Connecticut, or me from Washington, DC? What could he want from me?

But I know the other face too. Or do I? The man who bumped me onto the carousel is familiar. Even hiding behind those sunglasses, I know him. Mexico. I know one of those faces from Mexico. Which one is which?

Call Eve.

My hands shake and I misdial several times before I get the number right.

"Hello?"

"Eve! Where are you?"

"I'm at LaGuardia."

"I think I saw him. I'm pretty sure it was him lurking behind me as I waited for my luggage. Then he pushed me onto the carousel. Or maybe it's the guy from Mexico. I'm not sure. But one of them was him. You know? Him who pushed me."

"What are you talking about? What guy from Mexico? And do you mean Heather's guy? You must be mistaken. Why would he be in Charleston? And how did he push you out in public?"

"I'm telling you. One of the guys pushed me. He was weird. Psycho. Both guys."

"I'll be there in a couple of hours. Don't do anything stupid. Go to the hotel and I'll see you there shortly. Find Heather." Eve paused. "Did he hurt you?"

"Yes, but I think I'm fine. My head hurts. But what if he follows me? He'll know where we're staying. He'll know how to find Heather."

"Calm down! It wasn't him and no one will follow you. And who is this guy you're talking about from Mexico?"

"I don't know. I just know one guy pushed me and one guy helped me and I'm no longer sure who is who. But I'm sure both are follow-ing me. They're after my flash drive."

"Don't be ridiculous. Go to the hotel."

Eve's composure annoys me. "I'm telling you, it was him. There's no doubt. The man was next to me. He practically ran. He's in Charleston. There's no mistake."

"Then why weren't you sure a moment ago?"

"I don't know. But I'm sure now. What else could my dreams mean?"

"All right. I can't do anything here. Wait until I get there. Meet me in the hotel bar. He won't be a problem there. I should be there around 10:30. Just wait. Okay?"

"I don't want him to follow me. He's seen me now."

"If it's really him, he knew you were there anyway. Just go to the hotel."

"Hurry."

"You'll be fine. Just wait in your room or find Heather until you're ready to come down. Then go to the bar. You'll be fine there."

"All right. And Eve, keep your eyes open."

"I will. And you need to chill out. If it's him, he's enjoying watch-ing you come unglued. That's precisely what he wants. Since when do you give people what they want?"

"This is different."

"How?"

"He scares the shit out of me. Actually, I think they both do."

Eve doesn't respond.

"Eve?"

"Yeah, I was thinking. He wants to scare you and you're playing right into his plans. Call Clay. He'll remind you how unbelievably ornery you are."

I look around. Several men wearing sunglasses linger. "I can't pull him into this. He doesn't know anything about our problem."

"Maybe he should."

"No. Besides, he'll tell Grandmother." My head throbs.

"You better figure out why you're not telling your grandmother anything."

"Yeah, later, when things make more sense."

"Now is when you need help making sense."

"Just hurry. I don't want to talk about my family while this lunatic is around."

"All right. Hurry to the hotel and wait till I get there."

I flag a taxi. When it drops me at the hotel, I wonder why I listened to Eve. I'm completely exposed here. I can feel his eyes on me as I hurry into the safety of the building.

I close my room door against the quiet lurking in the long, vacant hallway. The foreign walls close in on me as I pace the floor. My mind sees the opulent bedding and artwork, but I can't seem to register it. My perceptions run through a sieve—thoughts come and go like pebbles washing down a waterfall.

I glance at my watch. Five minutes have passed. I lift my suitcase onto the bed and sort my clothing. I recheck my watch, but only two minutes have passed. I clutch at the throbbing in my chest. It can't be a heart attack. Panic. I'm having a panic attack. That's something other people get. Not me.

Summoning courage, I step out and quietly shut the door. Moving helps. The elevator bings loudly when it arrives.

The long and opulent crystal chandeliers cast bright light against the white polished marble and gold-filamented wall mirrors. The bar broods against the brightness of the adjacent lobby. Surrounded by other guests, I settle into a well-cushioned and secluded corner with a glass of white wine to wait for Eve. My hands shake but I know I'm safe here. His clothes and demeanor are contrary to the quiet elegance of the city. To be able to place him will be our only advantage. I'm not sure about the other one. Black. He was wearing black. I can't remember the cut or material, but it was black.

The hours tick by and I finish my second glass of wine, but it does little to soften the edges of my nerves.

Heather's line is busy, which is just as well. There's no point in upsetting her. I pull out Dennis's business card and read it over again. I'm not the only mixed-blood playing the white man's game. We are legion. We just don't know it.

My heart skips a beat. I feel his presence before I see him. Dennis. He's nearby.

I can't make out anyone's features inside the bar; the light from the lobby obscures the darker corners. I cast a glance at the offending light, and see him. He's checking in. My skin remembers the touch of his as we shared adjacent airplane seats. The intensity of my feelings terrifies me. I'm falling, and my arms and legs have become mush. It's the first time I've known what it's like to fall head over heels. It defies logic—but logic has ceased to serve me any purpose these days. I'm terrified of the unchecked free fall and the inevitable hit.

Dennis must feel my presence too, because he looks my way, smiles, and tips his hat. I consider running, returning to my room, where it's safe, but I also hope Eve will take her time. I wait and sip my wine. He approaches, and the light that follows him intensifies his magnetism and increases my unease. My insides turn to butter. He almost chases away my fear.

I have lived a life of adrenaline and danger that is catching up to me. I know this. And I've lived far from home. The debt is up. This sense of increasing terror is the price. But if falling for a man like Dennis is part of the price, I will gladly pay it.

A shadow passes between us. A man in a black collared shirt, black tie, black pants, and black jacket strides easily between us and, turning his head, stares directly into my eyes. His cold gaze cuts a deep channel through my heart. My panic is gone, and in its place is stone-cold dread.

Then he is gone.

25 Fiona

The trip from Los Angeles to Charleston consumed an entire day and deleted three hours in time difference from my life. My heart is heavy with the memory of the war zone I left at home.

It's been a month since the soiree, since Sam's spectacle of a temper tantrum. Her sullen demeanor was predictable, the slamming doors music compared to Gavin's silence. He left early in the morning and returned late to lock himself, brandy in hand, in his den, his impenetrable fortress. It's the same kind of withdrawal my parents exhibited—the difference only in the liquid of choice, brandy instead of scotch. It's different from that of a defiant teenager. Defiance is temporary. Teenagers become adults. A withdrawn husband is another matter. It's the mark of a dying marriage.

The trip East was long and punctuated the danger. Uncomfortable with so much aloneness, I stewed over every moment of the past month. I've spent a lifetime exiling guilt to the shadows, but now it's returned to the light. It is as if, in its exile, it has grown larger and angrier.

By the time I arrive in Charleston, I have consumed numerous airline bottles of vodka. It does little to numb the truth. I collect my luggage and catch a cab to the hotel. The opulently grand staircase in the lobby should excite me, but I am in no mood for reminders of my life in LA. I'm here to forget. Or am I? No. We are here to fix what we long ago tried to forget. Maybe that's the real problem. The thing you try to forget exists anyway. It can't be destroyed until it has been reckoned with. It just hovers and buggers the mind.

I need another drink. The pleasantries of checking in are annoying, and I move toward the clink of glasses in the bar area.

"Fiona. Where are you going?"

The familiar voice propels me forward, but my feet hold in place. Should I laugh or should I cry? I sprawl forward and land at my friends' feet, my skin slapping the dead marble.

I can't hide. I can't hide from what just happened any more than I can conceal the grotesqueness that has rooted itself in my mansion in Beverly Hills.

Eve and Mariah reach for me and pull me from the floor. My clothes twist around me like a swaddling cloth. I embrace my friends, but the awkwardness hems me in. It's a slow strangulation, all this familiarity.

"God, I'm so glad to see you," I say.

"Fiona, you look beautiful as ever. I've missed you so much." Eve's voice is clear and musical.

I glance toward the bar. "Let's go have a cocktail and catch up."

"How many have you had already?" Mariah asks, eyes narrowed.

"It's wonderful to see you too, Mariah."

"You know I'm asking out of concern."

"Well, I would hope so or I've come to the wrong place. Don't worry about me. I'm just fine now that I'm here. I needed to get away from home; everyone's going crazy there."

Eve's shoulder is a handy support. People are watching. Normally I love the attention, but in this moment it doesn't feel flattering.

"I need to sit down. Preferably near the pretty little bar."

"We're worried about you," Mariah says. "And we need to have our wits about us. All of us, Fiona. We think he's here. And actually, there may be more than one problem."

"Who's here? And why are you whispering?"

"You know. Him. And that's why."

"Oh, *he's* here. I get it."

Eve reaches to wrap her arm around my shoulder.

"Ah, I missed you, too, but I need to sit down," I say, inching toward the bar. "Let's get a cocktail and catch up. We can talk about him there."

Eve looks around. "No, let's go to your room and get you unpacked. We can catch up there."

"What are you looking around at? And why? I want to catch up down here. I've been locked in my room at home for weeks. I want to be out. I bet there are some handsome young Southern gentlemen around."

"Well, let's at least get your stuff to your room and let you freshen up. Then we can get something to eat at the restaurant." Eve glances around the lobby again.

"What are you looking at?"

"If he's here, he's enjoying the show," Mariah says. "C'mon. Let's go to your room."

"All right." My hair is unruly and creating little webs of irritating strings around my face. Does everything have to be out of control these days?

Eve picks up my bags and leads me toward the elevator. Mariah follows wheeling my suitcase, the noise grating and conspicuous.

The bright interior of the elevator nauseates me and my reflection in the highly polished walls teases me. Distorted, my appearance melts into something alien and disgusting. The smooth ride ends with a stomach-dropping lurch and I catch myself by leaning against the cold glass, but gentle hands on either side are already rescuing me from another tumble. It's not my fault. The elevator is old and rickety.

Growing up, I always imagined myself to be the strong and beautiful one, the one everyone wanted to be. That was an illusion. My friends were the strong ones—fierce, complex, and compassionate. I paled in comparison. I pale still. I am the beautiful shell and they are the substance that animates it.

"I love you guys." I wipe my tears with my jacket sleeve. "I hate my life. My life hates me. My family hates me. I hate me. Oh my God, *I hate me.*"

Eve tries to console me. "Fiona, stop it. No one hates you."

"Let her express herself," Mariah says.

"You hate me too, Mariah."

"Of course I don't hate you. Why the hell would I be hanging around with you for the last several decades if I hated you? You're a pain in the ass. You just hate yourself so much that you can't tell when someone loves you for yourself and not who you want them to think you are."

"What do you mean?"

Mariah looks at me with that vexing Indian look. That flat look like she's seeing something new but totally gets it. Deadpan and smack-the-fuck on. I want to slap her silly. Like that might animate her face. But I don't. It wouldn't change her anyway.

"We've always loved you. You've just blinded yourself."

Eve looks at Mariah—over my head, like I'm invisible. "This is a fine time to be getting real with her."

They're not going to treat me like I don't exist. "What are the two of you talking about?"

"Nothing, Fiona." Mariah waves her hand in dismissal.

"Well, it must be something."

"Look, Fiona. All your Gucci bags and male conquests can't change how you feel about yourself. Strip all that shit away and just focus on the part of you that we see and know. Trust me, it's not the Gucci bags, the men, or the fucking diamonds. That reminds me. You didn't bring all those ridiculous diamonds, did you?"

"No. I didn't."

"Good. I don't want to be any more conspicuous than we already are."

"You don't like my diamonds? They add to everything you put on. They go with everything, you know."

"No. I don't like your diamonds. You sparkle without them. Quit hiding behind them."

"Well, that's really pissy, Mariah. Do you like my diamonds, Eve?"

"Leave me out of this. What the hell would I need diamonds for?"

The hallway is long. Eve grabs my purse and, after rooting around, pulls out my room key. She swipes it, and the green light on the door illuminates. Cold air blasts my face and clears my head enough to remind me of how long the day has been.

Falling is forgetting. I plunge onto the bed and sink into its crisp cotton covers.

"I'm sorry. I'm so tired. It was a longer trip than I thought."

"Why don't you go to bed? It's been a long day for all of us. We can deal with everything in the morning." Mariah moves to cover me.

I need to know. "Did you mean what you said?"

"Which part?"

"The part where you said I sparkle without the diamonds."

"Yeah, I did."

Eve removes my shoes and coat and pulls the comforter over me. They're breaking my heart.

"But I don't sparkle inside. Do you forgive me?"

"There's nothing to forgive."

"I mean, do you forgive me for our disagreement last year?"

Mariah smiles. She's so beautiful. "That's old history."

"I forgive you. Will you forgive me?"

"Yes, of course. I was never upset with you."

"Then why did you call everyone else more than me? I needed you."

"I'm sorry." Mariah presses a hand to my forehead. "I didn't realize I was doing that."

I drift and my voice floats away from me. "Love dies without forgiveness."

Mariah and Eve flatten the coverlet under my chin.

"I've been dying for a very long time."

The room dims as they retreat from me. The darkness keeps me company and I forget the sadness three thousand miles away.

* * *

Bright sunshine beams through the window of my seventh-floor hotel room and intensifies the headache that reminds me of my vodka-soaked plane ride. What was I thinking? This was not how I wanted to arrive.

Well, I did it again.

The illuminated bedside clock blinks eleven o'clock local time and I'm still in bed. The ringing phone dispels the quiet of the room.

Eve's voice is sparkly and clear. "Good morning. Wake up, sleepy-head. Espy is here. We've ordered a table of coffee and breakfast to be sent to your room. We figured we'd invade your space." She laughs. "We'll be there shortly to share it with you. Breaking our fast together."

"Okay." I rub my eyes, but the air is still hazy.

"Wakie-wakie, sunshine!" Esperanza's voice is equally cheerful. God, I've missed them.

"All right, I'm getting up."

"We'll be there shortly."

The bathroom light is harsh and day-old mascara darkens my eyes. I need a shower. I need coffee. I need aspirin. I need, need, need. I have everything in the world and I still need. What the hell is wrong with me? Dabbing at my eyes and straightening my hair does nothing to fix my reflection.

The breakfast table arrives.

The waiter, attired in a crisp white shirt, apron, and immaculate black pants, greets me with a charming smile. He sets up the table and lifts every silver lid, then moves toward the door.

"Wait," I say. "Don't I need to sign something?"

"No, ma'am. It's been taken care of. Can I do anything else for you?"

Well, that's a loaded question. Eve's voice is in my head: *He's a baby, Fiona.*

"No. I'm fine. Although I'm not used to being called ma'am."

"Welcome to Charleston, ma'am." His smile is dazzling. Maybe it's time to move. Charleston might be a good place to start. I'm already old and forgotten in Beverly Hills.

"Sorry. I didn't realize. Please forgive me."

"There's nothing to forgive. Enjoy your breakfast." Absolved again—twice in the past twelve hours. He turned a rhetorical plea for forgiveness into the real thing. Charming. Perhaps I should accept it as a beginning. He is a disarmingly handsome young man—his mother should be proud. Will my Sean be like that? Or will his heart turn to stone with each passing moment of mine and Gavin's increasingly loveless marriage? Will he become aloof and unavailable like his father?

The coffee, rich and aromatic, slides from the ornate silver pitcher and swirls darkly against the crisp white cup. Steam curls up and floats toward me. I have the power to float along and accept everything that has been given to me in my life. Is that what I want? Because it is the path I have taken for years.

A knock on the door breaks the spell and everyone spills into the room.

Esperanza smoothes back my hair the way my mother used to do. My mom never touched my sisters that way. How that truth must have crushed them every waking day. All these years and I've never thought of the loss in my sisters' lives. Worse, I've never stopped to imagine how they felt losing Rory, witnessing him drowning. And I've never stopped to remember that moment I came out of the house to see him floating face down. The horror. The way everything became a bad dream. I've never gotten over losing him, losing a part of myself. That was the moment I stopped allowing myself to be loved, even by me. Hate rippled out from his death float.

"What's wrong, *chica*?"

I choke back the tears. "Nothing, Espy. I feel so much happier and lighter now that we're together. Heather? God, I've missed you." I don't want to let her go, but Shannon is watching and I crouch to look into her eyes, the same eyes as her mother. "Hi sweetie. And how are you?"

Shannon blushes and hugs her mother's legs. Heather reaches down to smooth her hair. "I've missed you too."

Eve smiles cautiously. "You're feeling better, then? We were worried about you last night."

Mariah nods. "You were depressingly sad last night."

"I'm so sorry. That's not the way I wanted to arrive. I don't know what got into me."

"Vodka. Vodka got into you."

"Yes, Mariah. Thank you. And you're right. It was a long trip."

"Well, you're fine now. Right?"

I nod. If I nod enough, even I will believe.

"Well, let's have some breakfast. Four of us are on Eastern time. You get a pass on sleeping in so late because I'm sure you have jet lag." Mariah pours four more cups of coffee and hands them out.

Eve smiles. "And you missed Mariah's . . . friend."

"Friend?"

"Friend. Flat-out handsome friend." Eve winks. "Who knew? In fact, if Jerome and I weren't already an item, I might have to make it a competition."

Esperanza giggles. "Oh, yeah right, Eve. Tell me more!"

Mariah blushes. "Stop it."

"How did I miss that?" Heather asks.

It's afternoon and another breakfast cart later before Shannon, who has been quietly watching cartoons, yawns and closes her eyes. Heather tucks a flannel blanket around her.

"It's two o'clock, guys." Mariah rises from the bed on which we have been sitting cross-legged. "I feel safe in this room, but somewhere out there is a stalker waiting for us."

"*Wait.* What?" What have I missed? "What are you talking about? Who's waiting for us?"

Mariah tips her head to the side. "Heather's visitor. Remember? We told you about him last night."

"Oh, *him.* Wait. He's here? In Charleston? How?"

"I don't know," Mariah says. "He was behind me, or I *think* he was behind me, while I waited for my luggage at the airport carousel. I bumped into him, but he knocked me onto the carousel and then left the airport. Or maybe it was the other guy. I'm not sure anymore."

"What other guy?" I'm confused. "Eve?"

Eve shrugs. "I haven't seen him or any sign of him."

"I know it was him, or that one of them was him," Mariah says.

Eve shakes her head at me so Mariah can't see. "Mariah. You hit your head really hard. If you're confused about who pushed you then maybe you're confused about whether it was even anyone you recognize."

"Listen, I'm sure if Mariah saw him he's here," Esperanza says.

Tiny pins of heat rise across my cheeks. Please don't let me get the hives again. Not here. "But how would he know to come here?" It's a puzzle. An enigma in our youth, there was something dangerous and mysterious about the man. His disappearance that night and his reappearance now makes him that much more perplexing.

There has to be an answer. "Mariah, are you sure it was him? What have you found out? I mean, from the investigation you were doing before you got here."

Mariah shrugs. "Nothing. He disappeared that night and his existence left with him. It doesn't make any sense. He disappeared from the face of the earth."

"Is there anything else to do to find him?"

"No. We can't go to the police. They would want to know why we think we're being stalked. Then they'd have to call Sunny Hollow, and no one knows we were even at that fire. And then there's the problem of the unsolved murder of the dead man. There's no statute of limitations on murder and, quite frankly, we don't have the answers to any questions they might have for us, which will make us look very suspicious."

Our options are slim. Wait or move. I'm not good at sitting. "We have to go out and hit the streets and hope that he finds us, if that's what he's after. We can't stay here, cooped up in this hotel room. It's pretty, but I'm feeling a little claustrophobic."

Eve looks around the room. "Yeah. I can't think of any other way."

"Well, that sounds like a plan to me." Esperanza slaps the heels of her hands on her legs.

Eve considers. "Should we break up into groups or stay together?"

I don't like the idea of breaking up. It reminds me of a night long ago that didn't end well. This is supposed to be our girls' vacation.

Heather clears her throat. "Um. I'm not sure this is such a good idea. I don't think I want to be found. Besides, Shannon has been through a lot and she's still sleeping. I can't leave her here alone. Besides, we're safe here with the doors locked."

Eve smiles. "You should stay here anyway. I think we have to break into two groups. That way we have a better chance of one of us finding him and making contact."

I shake my head. "But this was supposed to be our vacation together, Eve. I don't like the idea. Breaking up doesn't usually end well for us."

"I know, but I don't see any other way. And besides, breaking up was originally your idea. Remember? Plus, we have a better chance of him approaching us if there are only two of us."

"Yes. Must you remind me?"

Mariah grimaces. "We've been lucky we've had so many wonderful vacations together through the years. But now that night has caught up with us. Together, we have to try to set things right. We can't call the police and we can't pull our families into this. If we don't take care of this now, he'll continue to show up. And we'll never stop running. He'll pick us off, one by one."

"You're right," I say. "Nothing bad has happened yet. Let's take care of this before it becomes something beyond our control." My own resolve empowers and emboldens me.

Eve moves toward the door. "We don't have a lot of options. I say we hit the streets and see the sites. Maybe he'll think we're playing tourist—unaware of things around us. He won't suspect that we're actually trying to find him."

I feel lighter. Maybe all I need is a mission with a little dash of spice mixed in. When I'm done, I'll deal with whatever is going on in my marriage. I need to show my children that they don't have to float.

"I need to get dressed," I say. "Heather, you and Shannon can stay here in my room until we get back. And make sure you keep the door locked and you don't open it for anyone. The rest of you, let's meet in the lobby in thirty minutes. "

"Thirty minutes," Mariah echoes.

Our window of opportunity is small, but that's all we need—a window. And we need him to come through it.

26 Eve

The lobby is strangely quiet. Everyone arrives slowly at our meeting place: the ridiculously grand staircase. It's out of place in my life. For years I have run from my losses by living in the desperate lack of refugee camps—living amongst the displaced. Now my life is turned upside down, and it makes me question every past, present, and future decision. Jerome may or may not wait for me. Heather is in trouble. Someone who may or may not exist, who played a decisive role in our lost childhood, stalks us physically—or, at minimum, in our imaginations—in Charleston, and he seems to have a better sense of our whereabouts than we have of his. I don't want to ponder the meaning of Heather's mental health if he only exists in her mind, or Mariah's. Mariah's dreams seem to be driving her waking hours more than the reverse. And now she has two stalkers. My relief job in Darfur is a far-off world that somehow no longer matters to me. Its immediacy has vanished. Maybe that part of my life was never anything more than a mirage, a dream of a better world.

But then the dream of a better world is never any more real than the people who live in it. My life really ended that summer long ago when my brother disappeared and shattered my family's world— shards of broken glass ripping at our equilibrium. Grief is an abyss; sometimes you crawl out and sometimes you don't. I've spent years trying, and now that I've reentered the land of the living, reality is more elusive than ever.

"Where shall we start?" Espy says.

Fiona pulls out a map she picked up at the travel agency in Los Angeles. "The Market and historic district. He's probably anticipating it. He might already know where he expects to intercept us. Why not play right into it? He's expecting us, but we're expecting him, too."

Mariah shifts uneasily and shrugs. "I can't think of a better idea. Esperanza, why don't you go with Fiona and Eve can come with me."

Fiona cringes. "That reminds me too much of old times." She pauses. "Maybe we can get it better this time, right? What if he doesn't reveal himself today? Where should we meet?"

"I say we meet back here at six o'clock to freshen up and have dinner," Mariah says. "Hopefully, one of us or all of us will see him today, but if not, we'll have to try again tomorrow."

I need resolution. We need to find him. "There is no tomorrow."

"Well, then, let's go!" Fiona says.

The afternoon is sweltering and the damp air clings to my skin. The hotel is a short block from Market Street and we move sluggishly towards it. Southern time is elegant and relaxed, but I have no doubt that has as much to do with the climate as the culture—they reinforce each other.

Arm in arm, Mariah and I navigate the tight streets. If I hang on to her, can I keep her feet in this world?

Gullah, the English-based Creole language, drifts from a shed in the Market in which a beautiful old woman weaves baskets of low country sweet grass.

I stop to admire a bowl. I smile at the old Creole woman. "That's beautiful."

The woman's smile is radiant. Mariah often speaks of the wisdom of the elders. Grandmothers. I would love to have such a woman as my grandmother. She pats my hand and I feel only loneliness in the middle of the packed market.

Mariah steers me away from the table. I don't want to think about loss right now. It just clouds our mission.

But I'm enchanted with the sense of this place. It's the first time somewhere has the feel of home—a home for me. There's something kindred in the history—an oppositional history, a history that survived despite the odds. White plantation owners imported slaves from the "Windward Coast" of Africa, Sierra Leone, and Senegal to cultivate rice, their traditional crop and food staple, a commodity upon which South Carolina ultimately prospered. Of course, it was cotton that sealed the deal and it was the Northern colonies that got rich from the slave trade. Rice and cotton made South Carolina, and Charleston, its port, became one of the most urbane and fashionable cities in the South. The dominance of West African slaves created the rich and cohesive culture that now floats from the shop. But Charleston is more than Southern and more than Gullah, it's now a city of transients. What did Mariah call them? Transplants. Those who have planted themselves over what came before.

I marvel at the ease with which I recognize something kindred, a connection I haven't experienced in a long time.

Mariah nudges me. "What're you thinking about?"

"I was thinking what a beautiful place this is. I was thinking about how easy it would be to call this home."

"Solo or with Jerome?"

"Well, I guess with Jerome, but then maybe alone too. Maybe it's time to stop wandering."

"You've been doing that for a long time."

"Yes, I have. Being with Jerome has brought all of that into question. And then this situation has just magnified it. I think it's time."

"Yeah. It's time for a lot of things. Time to come to terms with that night. Time to bury Terrell?"

"I'm not sure I can do that. Your uncle was MIA. How did your family deal with it? You were close to him."

Mariah shields her eyes from the sun as it filters through the palm trees. Palmettos. Even the name enchants me.

"Yes, I was close to him. I loved him. My love can't be changed by his loss. His spirit is where it always was. It's at home. It imbues the places he loved. Long before the white man, we left no remains of our loved ones. They followed us wherever we went."

I nod. Terrell is where he has always been: in my heart. There are vast changes on the horizon—my world heaves with it. It's not so overwhelming, knowing my friends will be there. They always have been. We backtrack toward Meeting Street and head south.

I can't help wonder if the apparition of Heather's stalker, our stalker, is just that: a ghost of a thought, a spirit of guilt. In front of us looms the awe-inspiring edifice of one of Charleston's many beautiful churches.

I clasp Mariah's hand. "Mariah?"

Mariah is silent.

"What's going on with you? I know your head hurts and you're worried about the two men who were at the airport and your visions, but you seemed to be happier. I mean, you *were* so happy, last night. Now, you're . . . gloomy. Are you afraid of a relationship? Is that it?"

"No. Who says there's even a relationship? I just met him. I don't even know him." She sighs. "No. That's not it."

"Then what is it? You're not the same person I had drinks with last night. And you've definitely changed from the woman who sparkled every time she looked at Dennis." I pinch her side and she giggles, but then she turns serious.

"No. A note was shoved under my door this morning."

"A note?"

"Yeah. It was threatening. Like the one I got several days ago."

"What do you mean?"

We wander through the building and exit into the ancient grave-yard behind the imposing structure. It's a tourist attraction, but it's oddly vacant and silent. Spanish moss hangs from trees and shrouds the ancient gravestones. Quiet, unearthly and sacred, prevails, cool and calming compared to the heat and noise of the street on the other side of the church. My own thoughts scream into the space between us.

"Remember those water rights articles I've been working on?"

"Yes. I know you think you were followed from Mexico because of them."

"Not because of *them*, because of *one*. The one I was doing on virtual water."

"Why would virtual water land you a stalker?"

"It's complicated. I know I was followed here. In fact, it was a weird coincidence that Dennis sat down next to me. Like it was fated. It made me forget the earlier threat. Like everything would be okay because he showed up in my life. But I know better. My coworker and I uncovered some . . . unethical deals made by AAC."

"Yeah. You and I talked about that and I told you to stay away."

"I know, but I didn't think things would get this bad. I've never seen a deal like this. The water entitlement or rights portion was tied to the utility and management portion. It was a complete package."

"In Mexico?"

"Not totally. It's complicated. It's happening around the world."

Images of missing children in the Congo flash into my consciousness.

"It could be happening anywhere, to anyone who is powerless to men like those at AAC. I spoke to Dennis about it. He was very aware of who they are. He warned me that I might be in danger." Mariah looks around. We're alone amongst the headstones. She continues. "The deal was with the IMF. As a condition for a loan, the country in question had to guarantee AAC a 50 percent profit margin. The company moved in and raised prices fourfold. Those who couldn't afford it—those who could least afford any loss—had their water turned off. On the sanitation side of the agreement, the multinational made some . . . changes. There is a cholera epidemic they are trying to hide. Hundreds have died and are still dying. The government couldn't keep the thing under wraps so it said the outbreak is a result of the unusually heavy rains contaminating the water supply and the unsanitary practices of those who were not hooked up to the sanitation system. Yesterday I picked up a flash drive from a colleague in which he lays out the other side of AAC. He was investigating the conflict minerals in the Congo and the computer cycle. I got a call this morning. He was just found dead in his hotel room in Kuala Lumpur. Suicide, supposedly. But I was on the phone with him when he was . . . silenced. "

"Mariah, why didn't you say something earlier? God. I told you AAC was bad news. What did this note say?"

"It said I needn't worry about them finding me—that they know exactly where I am, which I already knew. But I don't know *why* they alerted me, except that maybe they just want me to feel terror before . . ."

"Do they know you've contacted the water tribunal?"

"LAWT? No. I don't think so."

"Well, that ought to really piss them off."

"I guess so."

"And we're out here by ourselves, chasing someone who, for all we know, is on the payroll with a multinational with far-reaching arms, loads of cash, and a hard-on to see you silenced. I thought we were just chasing a ghost from our past. This is different. It's nuts."

"I told you someone else was following me."

"Yes, but I wasn't really sure. Between you and Heather . . ." I hit my forehead with the palm of my hand. "Mariah? How do you know Dennis isn't in on it? He's a water guy. The fact that he's Indian could be clouding your normally good judgment."

"I'm not totally sure of anything anymore. The Sunny Hollow guy might even be the one who helped me. It's all so foggy. I can't even see either one in my head anymore. It's like my memory is gone. But I am sure of Dennis. He would have nothing to do with this. Trust me."

"How do you know? Your instincts are on the fritz right now."

"Hush. There are no Indians in this. I'm sure of it."

I look around us. It's so quiet, but nothing seems right. "Have you seen anything else to make you suspicious?"

"No."

I stare at the headstones, many of which have been rendered illegible by time. Gravity and the forces of weather have pitched the markers into chaotic formations. They are more representative of life than the neat little rows in modern-day graveyards. They remind me of teeth. This is a bad place to be at this moment.

I think of all the grief in my life. Terrell would have been able to cut through this craziness. He had a knack for breaking mysteries down into their simplest components. He would have protected us both.

A headstone. I would prefer the chaos of this ancient cemetery because, in truth, my brother's status has meant nothing but unremitting grief. The day I was informed of his status change from MIA to PFOD, presumptive finding of death, was the day my heart rotted from the inside out, a desecrated core. There should be something to mark the death of hope. A headstone. But there are no true headstones for nothing but the dirt down below. It's just a fucking piece of rock.

I stop. Mariah stops with me. I look her in the eye. "What are you going to do about the flash drive and everything else you've found out?"

Mariah stares at the ground. "It's complicated."

"No, it's not. It's a simple question with a simple answer. Terrell would've said the same thing to both of us."

"You really have started to come to terms with his being gone."

"There's no other choice. Whatever you do, keep it simple, Mariah.

I don't want to bury you too. I don't want to deal with another MIA. You got me?"

"Yeah. I got you."

I stoop to read one of the newer markers. People, related and unrelated, through the ages, come to rest here, a tribe in slumber.

"Is that your answer?"

"I've written the summary, but I haven't submitted it yet. I can use it to expose AAC or to plant the seed for a more in-depth article. There's a lot at stake. I think it's the blueprint for the future. I don't think I can be quiet on this issue." She smiles. "Besides, Terrell would've told me to stand up for what's right."

"Yeah. I know. It would be unlike you to stop."

"There's more. Dennis thinks I need to be careful, too. It's how I know he's not involved. He's from The Three Affiliated Tribes in North Dakota. They've had some of these same types of people sniffing around. There's oil in the ground. Someday, they'll figure out how to extract it."

"I see your point."

"Things are already beyond my control. Doctors Without Borders is involved, and LAWT considers it a serious story."

"Is there any leverage you have against AAC?"

"Just the flash drive. Their water business might be in trouble, but their more lucrative computer business isn't."

"Does anyone know you have it?"

"My colleague had already sent it out when he died. But he was telling me about it when the phone went dead."

"That means someone knows and is probably looking for it."

"I guess so." Mariah kicks a pebble in front of her. The sound of it hitting stone jars my nerves.

"And I guess they might think you have it?"

"Probably so."

"Maybe, if you turned it over . . ."

Mariah gives me a sharp look.

"I guess not."

"I already downloaded it anyway and sent it to my boss, and I have another copy in my safe deposit box. And there's more, Eve. There are people who might have been buried . . . alive."

"*What?*"

"There were people buried alive in Mexico."

"Can you prove that?"

"Probably not to the satisfaction of my boss. He won't risk a lawsuit."

If there is a threat, it's had plenty of time to reveal itself. Right? Surely something would've already happened if it was going to. Maybe Mariah's wrong.

The mood lightens as we continue our walk without trouble. The mind has a funny way of talking itself out of danger.

I look at Mariah. "Do you think we're still looking for Heather's visitor?" I want to ask her if she thinks we're really looking for hers, but I talk myself out of that line of thought.

Mariah shrugs. "I honestly don't know."

We walk further into the ancient cemetery. The light breeze flutters the Spanish moss and the heat dulls my senses. I daydream of crisp white sheets in my cool hotel room. And more than once, I imagine Jerome waiting for me. My eyelids grow heavy.

"Mariah, what time is it? There's a part of me that thinks I could stay here forever."

"Well, if you were dead, you would."

"That's not funny. That's not what I meant."

"I know. It just struck me as funny."

"Very funny. I guess I meant this is where I would like to call home. I mean Charleston."

"You said that. I guess you meant it."

"I do."

"Well, those are the key words. 'I do.' The question is, 'With whom do you do?'"

It feels good to laugh. "I don't think I'm going to Darfur."

"I figured. You shouldn't feel guilty. Let someone else go. You've seen so much horror and hardship already. You're better off taking care of personal business. You have a lot of it right now."

"Yeah. I'm beginning to realize that all these years, my life hasn't been mine. I prided myself on my independence and free-spiritedness, but that was just a lie, a cover-up for the lack of it in my life. I've been a prisoner all along. Freedom is far more complicated than catching a plane and changing your address."

Mariah nods. "I think I'm beginning to see some parallels here."

"Probably. We're kindred spirits. We always have been."

"Yeah. The borders of the Rez are just a line on the map. There's no one who can keep me in or out except myself."

"And there's no one who can keep us in exile without our permission."

The cool air turns cold. Goosebumps cover my body. Mariah disentangles herself from my hold. I search the dark shadows of the trees and the hanging moss. The graveyard is suspended in timeless space. There is no breeze and no flutter of wings—just absolute stillness. The eerie atmosphere chases away all my previous sleepiness.

Mariah moves first. She grabs my hand and pulls me toward the church. We sprint up the steps. I look behind me, but nothing follows. Still, the chill remains.

Mariah whispers. "What do you think that was?"

"I don't know. I didn't actually see anyone. I just felt it."

Mariah leans against the stone wall. "I know. He's here. We're supposed to be finding him. Instead, we're running."

"How do you know it's him and not someone from AAC?"

"I think someone from AAC wouldn't bother hiding. They'd just kill us both, if need be."

That thought is chilling. "Great. We have two people stalking us. Should we go back out and search for him? Or I mean, them?"

"I'm not sure I want to confront anyone in a deserted graveyard. I had envisioned it happening in a more crowded spot."

"Do we have a choice? Assuming it's the Sunny Hollow guy, since the other one would've probably killed us by now. I'm not sure he'll let us call the shots on this one. After all, he thinks he's stalking us, not vice versa."

"True, but I'm not going back out into that graveyard."

"We can't let this continue," I say. "We have to find resolution here, in Charleston—for Heather's sake, for all of our sakes. I want to know if he's real or if we're just chasing some boogeyman."

"You're right," Mariah says. "Just not in a graveyard."

She has a point. "Okay," I say. "Not in a graveyard."

We move toward the door. My muscles turn to jelly. I instinctively reach for Mariah's hand and squeeze it. If I hang on tight enough, nothing and no one can separate us. At this moment, I would promise the remainder of my life to Jerome. I wish he were here now. I will tell him that if we get out of this alive.

Mariah opens the door. Stagnant warmth hits us in the face, and the traffic on the other side of the church is now audible. The terror dissipates. Even the breeze has returned, and the birds chirp from the trees.

Still, I shudder. "We didn't ask permission of the inhabitants before entering the yard. There's bad *juju* here. I don't care how much better it feels."

Mariah looks at me. "*Juju*? Now *you're* freaking me out."

"Sorry. Africa stays with me. We should get in touch with Espy and Fiona. Did you bring your cell phone? I didn't."

"Yeah. Hold on." She pulls her cell phone from her pocket and dials Fiona's number before handing it to me. She drifts toward the shade near a large brick mausoleum. She peeks around the structure.

"Hello."

Fiona's voice is garbled. I move toward the headstones to get a better connection.

"Fiona. We're in the cemetery at some church on Meeting Street. We think we sensed him. We didn't actually see him. If that makes any sense."

"What do you mean, you sensed him?"

"I know it sounds crazy, but he was here. I don't know if he is now, but he was here. I just feel it."

"Do you want us to come there? We haven't seen anyone. We have been enjoying the sights, though."

"How far are you from here? I'm a little spooked in this cemetery. So is Mariah." Speaking of whom . . . I turn to find her, but I am alone.

"Hold on, Fiona. I don't see Mariah."

"What do you mean, you don't see Mariah?"

"Mariah? Mariah? *Mariah!*" I move toward the mausoleum, thinking she must be around the corner, but the only movement I see is the rustling of the trees and the tendrils of Spanish moss. I am utterly alone.

"Eve! Eve!" Fiona's voice is disembodied and far off.

"Oh my God, Fiona. Mariah's not here."

"What do you mean?"

"She was here when I called you. She was right in front of me. She was looking around the mausoleum. When I looked again, she was gone."

"What mausoleum?"

"There's a big brick mausoleum here. No, there's a row of mausoleums. She's gone, Fiona." I begin to sob. "I'm telling you, she's gone. I told you he was here. Now he's got her. Or someone has her."

"Eve. Stop crying."

"Oh my God, Fiona. I let go of her hand. Why did I let go? I never let go, but everyone dies anyway!"

"She's not dead."

I turn around and around. The gravestones mock me. Silent and foreboding, they reveal nothing.

"Hold on. Don't go anywhere. Wait there for us. We're coming."

"Come quick. He's got her. They've got her. I know it. She was right all along. I should've believed her." Tears fill my eyes and the gravestones morph into menacing shapes. Unearthly evil surrounds me. The bad *juju* from the Congo has followed me.

Time is not on our side. I cannot bear to wait. Every minute is a minute he can travel farther away with Mariah. But I cannot bear to move, either. Every step is a potential step away from Fiona and Espy being able to find me. I need them. Three of us are better than one. We are always better together.

In the back of my mind, I pray it is him. The threat of AAC goons is more than any of us can handle. Our man from Sunny Hollow is simpler—he has to be real. There can be no other choice.

I pull at the mausoleum door, but it is sealed against the world. There is no sign that it has been opened in years. Where else could she be?

"Hold on Mariah. We're coming." I whisper the words into the fragrant air. It does not answer me. But I know Mariah can hear. She can hear the wind.

27 Mariah

"We're coming." The words are plaintive.

There are so many of them—so many wraiths. The leader sways and wrings his hands.

I move, but my head doesn't. Leaden and shooting with pain, it is dead weight. My head is attached to the hard ground. Everything shifts in and out of focus. "Who are you?"

"We're coming." The voices, soft, whispered, are tethered together, in unison. The smell of earth, cold and mildewed, mingles with decay and, filling my nostrils, travels deep into my chest and claws at my heart.

"Coming where?"

"Shhhhhhhh." The wraiths bind me.

"Stop it!" I struggle, but the bindings tighten. "Please. Stop!" The sound of shredding cloth fills me with terror. Is it mine? The wraith leader shimmers in tattered white cloth. I struggle more but the bindings refuse to budge. "Please let me go."

"You were warned."

"Yes. Warned." The wraiths sway in unison.

The sound of skin on skin . . . a sharp pain across my mouth . . . the taste of iron . . . spinning vertigo . . . there's no world of edges. Why can't I move my head? A piece of shroud is stuffed in my mouth and the sound of tape terrifies me. I'm being mummified.

Oh Spirit, I'm going to die. I sob, but even that is silenced as I am thrown on my stomach.

"You were warned."

"Mmmmmmm."

A searing pain in my side follows a muffled thud. I struggle, my breath jagged, my lungs flounder against the confines of my flesh.

"Mmmmmmm."

"It'll be over soon."

I sob through the gag and stretch at my restraints. He hits me again, hard. He enters me then. He is hard and angry and uncaring and brutal and inhuman. He turns me over like a piece of meat on the grill. He balls up his fist and cracks it against my face. Blood flows into my mouth and I struggle to swallow, to not drown. He enters again until he is wasted. When he is done, something hard and not human plunges deep inside of me. He is close and he watches me. He laughs as I climb into the blackness.

Cold and wet hits me.

"Wake up. I'm not done."

I must survive. I am Ho-Chunk . . . I am Dakota . . . I am Lakota. Hear me, my relatives. No matter what horrors were unleashed upon us, we survived. We are here. We walk back. We are walking. I walk to survive. Please, Grandfather, tell me how to do it. Tell me how to walk.

A gentle hand caresses me from the darkness.

I do not struggle anymore as pieces of my life are picked from me, bit by bit, until there is nothing left. My innards are pulled and deposited outside of me. I am a watcher. I watch as everything moves outside the prison of my flesh, now flayed and rotting in the must of the sarcophagus. And then the wraith moves to leave. A glint of silver appears at my throat, hesitates, and moves to the tape around my head.

I shake my head, but he laughs.

The wraith pauses and straightens. He slices at the tape until it releases.

"Scream all you want. Only the dead can hear." He laughs. "Your friend died the same way. Like the animal he was. Now you'll know what it is to die of thirst. To die like the animal you are." He laughs again. But am I not already dead? He hits me again and my cheek burns with fire. He hits me again. The pain is too much to bear. I roll over to avoid the next beating.

The sliver of light that has illuminated those around me diminishes slowly until I hear stone scratching on stone. The bone man leaves with them.

Darkness.

And there is a deep cold.

"Help me please. Somebody help me." I spit blood onto the cold floor. The answer comes in whimpers. "Mother, please help me." Not all of the wraiths have left, but they don't move to comfort me. Their chill seeps into my bones.

The darkness creeps, twisting and burrowing, until there is nothingness and I float along its breath.

And still the spirits watch.

Time and space are nothing. I hover along the boundary.

28 Paul

It had been a long exile—too long to go home. But then, home was something that existed in my heart, not my head. Solitude was the grace given by God. Man couldn't give it to me, it had been taken from me by a man-made war, a war that had no reason, no meaning. Fear was the demon that stoked the fires. Fear was the monster that reduced man to something ugly. But it was a girl who set me free.

In reclaiming the freedom of another, I had mended my polluted soul. The choices made that led to that corruption weren't options at all—not, at least, of my making. Destiny is funny that way: it leads you to a path with several possible courses of action, but the reality of it is illusory. Free will is woven into the story of mankind, a product of the human condition, his consciousness, but then so is destiny. When your CO tells you to blow all the VC to hell, it's not really a choice. Did I choose to be there when all my options had been exhausted? Did I choose to dehumanize another human being so I could survive? Surely, the alternative wasn't to die. The choices weren't spontaneously born in a cataclysmic big bang of free will. Destiny blew them into existence. In the end, life is nothing more than a road of choices, destiny rooted in and defined by those choices, the choices spawned by destiny. It's a fucking Catch-22. And maybe the possibilities are a great big mind fuck and we're just puppets reacting to all the randomness in the universe.

I used to believe that being in country was purgatory. The leeches, banana grass, and mosquitoes were the devil's brood, napalm its elixir. But being in country is much more: it's the prison of flesh and bone. The Freedom Bird was deliverance but that was never more than leaving one hell for another. Home was an illusion, an oxymoron for the guileless. You could never truly get to home from being in country. But I had to find my home of four safe walls, the shelter of something more than remorse. It eluded me until that fateful night. I found shelter in that single act of humanity. Redemption. Redemption is home, forgiveness its hearth. It took me so long to find it, to find myself. But in the end, it found me. It was a little bird that sang me home.

I had to run that night. Freedom demanded it. I never stopped. I had to keep one step in front of the Viet Cong, with an eye out for the *punji stakes*. There were enough booby traps and land mines to fill a continent.

My brothers were gone but *Papaver somniferum* kept pace with me. She followed me into the darkest corridors of night; she wandered with me through the longing of days. Always by my side, spawned from the loveliest of flowers. I chased the Asian opium poppy. Gossamer petals dressed the blackness of her heart. The years dimmed her loveliness, but she chased away my fears and my binding pain. Ever present, I was Heros, and she was heroin.

But she betrayed me in the end. My lungs consumed, I sank into a coma and she left me for dead. I woke to a stranger.

"Mr. Marist? Are you awake?"

"Huh?"

"You're in the hospital. Someone found you in a park. You overdosed."

"Overdosed?"

"Yes. You'll feel better soon. We're here to take your vitals now."

They pushed and pulled on me. I prayed for my mistress's return, but there was no going back. She was gone.

The doctor came and sat with me several days later.

"Mr. Marist. This is difficult. The overdose should've killed you, but you were saved."

"Thank you."

He held his hand up. There was more. "No need for thanks, Mr. Marist."

"Paul."

"Paul." He shifted uneasily in his seat and looked me squarely in the eyes. "We believe you have lung cancer. We'll know more once we run some tests. We can't define what type or stage it is until then."

I didn't respond. What was there to say? I had been dying my whole life.

I thanked him. I dressed and left before anyone saw me, before anyone could stop me. It was a trick I picked up in 'Nam. The Viet Cong moved and disappeared at will. They were crafty pests, but I learned their ways. They had cut me before. I couldn't let them cut me again. A jungle rat belongs in the jungle—that's its home. But I preferred the birds. They were mine.

I had to find my bird.

She had sung me home.

She had to know that before the Freedom Bird came again to take me in country. The nesting period over, it's time to fly.

29 Mariah

Stone scraping on stone and a blinding light shreds the blackness. I cannot welcome it. My voice, committed to the darkness, has withered in its depths. My mouth is sealed with dry blood. The taste of stale iron makes me heave, but my stomach convulses in pain and nothing comes up. I can't even cry. There are no tears. It feels better to pull myself up into a little ball.

I lift my disembodied hand, marveling at its animation. "Help." Deadweight, my hand drops.

Has he come back to mock me? The bone man sits in the corner and laughs silently, his body shaking.

The man comes toward me. I don't have the energy to struggle. He will finish me off without a fight.

"No. No."

"Shhhhhh, little bird. I won't hurt you."

He lifts my head and lets me sip at water. "Spit it out."

I should be afraid, but he covers me with his jacket.

"Why are you here?"

"I'm here to save you. You're one of my little birds. My two birds who shivered outside the fire."

"But how did you get here?"

"Shhhh. Rest now. I have to take care of the other."

"No." I shake my head. Black pins of pain shoot around corners and I close my eyes against the horror. "He's dangerous."

He smiles. "I know how to take care of his kind. Don't worry, little bird. You're lucky he wanted you to suffer. He killed all the others."

"What others?"

"Shhh. He doesn't matter anymore. Help will be here soon."

He stands in the sun, but I can only see his shadow.

"Don't leave me. The bone man will take me."

He stares into the corner. "He can't hurt you anymore."

And then he is gone and the light fills the interior of the chamber. I close my eyes against it and find darkness again.

* * *

I open my eyes to light and noise. There is no kindness in the commotion. I should be thankful to be found, but the sleep was far more merciful.

Men in uniforms scramble around me. My head is rooted to the ground and every movement is an agony.

"How did she get in here? She couldn't have gotten in here herself."

"She didn't. Better get the police in here." His companion's head turns as he yells for a stretcher. I cannot make out their uniforms, but the fresh air mingled with the stale reminds me I'm still in between worlds.

The light assaults me still. I'm beginning to welcome the reprieve from the darkness that was so final—the terror of it! I have always been a witness to others' terror. It's the reptilian snake that slithers into man's consciousness and makes him an animal. I felt that animal—and its monstrous child, fear—inside me. I could have been the perpetrator of those same acts if it had only stayed the growing void, the gnawing nothingness of starvation and death. And now I know what it is to be more than the witness—to be the experienced.

I turn my head to the light and let it bathe my skin.

"Who are you?"

"Don't worry, ma'am. We'll have you out of here shortly. Don't move." A look of concern crosses his face. "Where do you hurt?"

I lift my fingers to my head.

"I thought so."

His companion reaches to maneuver the stretcher. "That would explain how she got into this mausoleum."

"Sweet Jesus."

It would have been a slow and terrible death. Invisible to the world, I would have diminished until there was nothing left but the agony of my last dying breath. Alone. Is that how it felt for Great-Grandmother?

"They were coming." The tears, unbidden, overwhelm me and scald my face.

"Who was coming?"

"The bone man."

The men look at me. "Let's get you to the hospital."

They lift me onto a stretcher and cover me with blankets, but I shiver against the memory of my ordeal.

As we emerge from the mausoleum, Fiona and Esperanza appear.

"Oh my God, Mariah," Fiona cries.

"Oh, thank God." Esperanza crosses herself. "What the hell happened?"

But I do not have any words.

"Eve!" She is speaking animatedly to a man in uniform who writes in a notebook.

Esperanza grabs my hand. "What is it, sweetheart?"

"Why are we here? Weren't we searching for something?"

Esperanza's voice soothes me as she strokes my throbbing head. "Mariah, you have to go the hospital. I'm going with you. I won't leave you."

"The bone man took my clothes. He took everything. He wanted my soul. He wanted me to die with the ghosts."

"I know. It's going to be all right. We're going to the hospital now." Esperanza gently strokes my bruised flesh. I float through the anguish and feel myself being lifted, rolled, and buoyed until I'm no longer aware of the light, just the unspeakable torment.

Noise and movement linger, but they are a reminder I still belong in the world. I cling to that truth. I am still here. Gentle hands lift and tug at my head. I don't mind; I cling to what is real. It is my salvation. The alternative terrifies me and it is equally as real as the pain. It is far better than to be dead, spirited away by the creatures that bound me.

There are so many hands and so many voices as I drift along the fringes of consciousness. Something jagged pierces my flesh, and my awareness fades.

* * *

"Mariah?"

My head won't move. "Eve. Where's Espy?"

"She went to get a drink. You have a nasty concussion and . . . other injuries. Do you remember what happened?"

"No. I remember being with you. We were looking for something, and then the spirits came for me. They wanted to keep me. They hurt me."

"We were in the graveyard at the church. You disappeared, and then we found you in a mausoleum. We were looking for him. He must have found you and taken you away while I was on the phone. Listen, honey, the police have discounted the idea of a multinational like AAC. They think it's far-fetched. Besides, people have seen a scruffy man who fits our guy's description lurking around the hotel. They have an APB out for him. No one has seen anyone else suspicious."

"No. It wasn't him. I know it wasn't. It was the bone man and his wraiths."

"What bone man? What I don't get is, if it's not the AAC guy, then . . . why you?"

Why is Eve not listening? "I don't know, but it wasn't him."

"It had to be. But why you? Or is he toying with us, one by one? He showed himself to Heather, and now you."

"What are you saying, Eve?"

"I'm trying to figure out why you? We've been so worried about Heather, but it seems he's after you as well, or maybe all of us. It's clear he meant you great harm."

"It wasn't him."

"It had to be. Anyone else would've left you dead."

"I'm telling you, it was the bone man."

"Who's this bone man? You're not making any sense."

"Yes, I am. It was the bone man." I close my eyes and he is as clear as the light on the other side of my eyelids. He smirks. "He's still here."

Fiona quietly opens the hospital door and Esperanza follows.

"What?" Esperanza's voice trembles.

Eve looks at her quizzically. "What do you mean, 'what'?"

"You were looking at the door like you had seen a ghost."

Eve blanches. "I thought I might. Mariah says her attacker is in here now."

Esperanza's eyes widen. "What?"

Eve shrugs. "He really messed her up."

"I'm telling you. It wasn't him, and the bone man's still here."

Esperanza leans against my bed and caresses the bandages around my head. The action makes me want to cry. "What happened? I don't understand. We were supposed to stay together. Why did you leave?"

"I don't know. I don't remember anything. I don't remember leaving. I swear I don't remember moving."

Eve lifts my hand, holds it, and caresses it. "Maybe she didn't leave. Maybe he hit her while I wasn't looking. We can't really rule out anything here. He was always very strong and totally fearless."

Esperanza shakes her head. "Fearless, yes, stupid, no."

"We need to talk to the police again. This could be much bigger than anything we can handle. Mariah has already been assaulted and left for dead. I can't bear to think of what happened to her in there. Next time, there may be no one to save us. One or all of us could end up dead. Just like we thought he did that night. Just like the other. And we need to protect Heather. Shannon could be in danger, too. Our little Shannon."

"Yes, but Eve, that was all caused by Jazmin, not us," Fiona says.

"How can you say that? We were there and we were the reason his house burned down. Do you think any of that would've happened if we hadn't been there? And what about the guy he killed? We know he's capable of that, even if we can't tell the police that."

Fiona was incredulous. "We were there because he had Heather."

"He had Heather because we were someplace we were not supposed to be, *Fiona!*" Eve said. "Do you think Jazmin or Damon would've gone to his house if they hadn't been chasing us? Chasing you? Think about it. We may not have wanted it to happen, but we're the reason it happened. And then we ran away. Pretended it never happened. Well, a house burned down and someone died because of us. Worse, the whole damn neighborhood caught fire."

"*Ay, Dios.* Stop it, both of you," Espy says. "We can't turn back the hands of time. We need to stay in the present."

"How can we stay in the present when the past is tormenting us?" Fiona moves closer to Eve. Her voice quivers. "I never meant anything to happen. I was as much a victim as anyone else. Do you think I would have wished any of this on us? Do you think I would've wanted Mariah to be assaulted? To die like that?"

Eve sighs. "No, Fiona. I'm sorry. We were all equally responsible."

"Responsible for what happened to us?" Fiona shakes her head.

"We were just unlucky. We were at the wrong place at the wrong time."

"Well, we need a plan now," Eve says.

Fiona's cell phone rings.

"Hello." Pause. "What do you mean?" Pause. "You're kidding me. This is disastrous!" Pause. "Well, have you called the police?" Pause. "Yes. We'll be there in a minute. Thank you." Fiona clasps her hand to her chest.

It has to be Heather. He couldn't have been here and there at the same time. Nothing makes sense.

"All right. Thank you for calling. We'll be there as soon as possible."

"Fiona, what's happened?" Eve's voice wavers.

"I asked the front desk to send someone up to my room to tell Heather we're at the hospital with Mariah. I told them to check mine and hers, in case she took Shannon back there after she woke up from her nap."

"And?"

"And no one is in either room. And someone thinks she was the woman who ran out yelling call 9-1-1."

Esperanza's voice is heavy with emotion. "Wait. Maybe they're mistaken and it was someone else."

Fiona shakes her head. "No one was in the room when they called up, and she wouldn't have left voluntarily. We need to go find her and Shannon."

"We can't leave Mariah," Espy says. "What if he didn't do this to Mariah after all and someone else is out there? What if the police are wrong and this AAC guy was the one who abducted her? Then he's still out there. He's still a threat to Mariah. Besides, Heather would've called one of us. She wouldn't just leave. Nothing's making sense. And what did the police say when they arrived?"

"They took down the information, but no one saw anything so they're not sure there's anything wrong," Fiona says. "They said she should've stuck around to tell them what her emergency was. Without that, they have nothing to go on. Our rooms looked normal."

Eve shrugs. "Espy's right. And the real danger could be here, for Mariah. Even if the police don't believe it. Mariah believes AAC is serious about stopping her from exposing them."

I have to shake my head. The pain medication is wearing off. "No, it's the bone man."

Ignoring me, Fiona says, "And what if he's searching for Heather now or he has Shannon and that's why Heather ran out?"

"I don't know," Eve says. "And I'm still worried about AAC. I know the police don't believe it, but they've already killed a friend of hers."

"Oh my God." Fiona holds her palm to her forehead. "This is way over our heads. Let the police deal with that. It's doubtful we can even handle a lone man from our past—forget about an assassin. I'll talk to the police. Maybe they can put some extra security at her door."

Eve considers. "We know there's danger here. I'm worried."

The bone man winks at me. He knows I will soon be alone. My friends have discussed it in front of him. Security will be outside the door, not inside with the bone man and me.

"It's a chance we have to take," Fiona says. "Heather is in trouble, whether it's from him or someone else, and no one can give us any answers. We have to find them out for ourselves."

"What about me?" I ask. They cannot leave me here. The bone man will tell the others. They'll come for me!

Espy lays a hand on my leg. "*Chica*, you're not strong enough to come. It's a miracle you're alive. Fiona's right. We need to find Heather and Shannon. We need to leave you here. It's safer here. There's security outside your door. We'll be back before they discharge you from the hospital. We'll make sure of that."

"How can you be sure? What if you don't make it in time?"

Eve squeezes my IV-festooned arm. "We will. I promise. I'm

telling the police what you told me in the cemetery. I'll make sure you have a guard the whole time."

I grab her arm but she's slipping away.

"They're coming," I say. "I know they are. He's coming and he's bringing them."

Fiona frowns. "Mariah, no one's coming. You're safe here. There's security everywhere. Right now you're safe here, but Heather and Shannon may be in trouble."

"There's nothing in the dark, nothing but the cold. Nothing but the bone man." A lone tear slides down my raw face.

In the corner of the hospital room, the bone man smiles and licks his lips.

30　Esperanza

It's been six hours since we left the hospital. Six hours since we left Mariah by herself. Six hours since we received the desperate call from Heather. Come. Brandon has Shannon. Heather in the rental car, racing up Highway I-95 like a bat out of hell. Following Brandon. We are going. Heather has the rental car we would have all been using for the vacation. Our vacation, which has turned into . . . what? Revenge? Punishment? Reckoning? What did we ever do but be normal teenagers? God is merciful. He protects innocence—and we were so damned innocent. No! We were one up from that . . . we were naïve.

I take Angelica's floppy bunny from my suitcase and lay it next to Izzy's Pegasus drawing. My precious relics will take the last place in my suitcase, on top. It was only yesterday that I first packed them. I thought the next packing would take me home. Life has a funny way of changing plans midstream. Running home is not an option. To be surrounded by my husband, children, and the comfort of everyday domestic rituals—what a stark contrast to the unknown danger ahead. I retrieve my rosary from the bedside table and tuck it into the side pocket of my purse.

A knock on the door startles me. Fiona and Eve are distorted by the curvature of the peephole.

Fiona practically falls through the door when I open it. "You're shut up in here like it's Fort Knox," she slurs. Her gestures are extravagant.

"How many?"

"How many what, Espy?"

"How many drinks have you had?"

"What does it matter? I've only had a couple. I need them to make this ridiculous trip."

"Why do you need them, Fiona?"

"Because I won't be of any use to you in Connecticut, but Eve's still making me go." Fiona plunges onto the hotel bed.

"We're all going or we're not going at all," Eve says. "How many times do I have to tell you this, Fiona?"

"Yup. You've already told me, my fine, serious friend."

Eve moves to the window. Folding the curtain back, she peers down at the courtyard. The light illuminates her worry lines. "We need to go now. Our ride will be here soon. We have to get on that plane."

"Aren't you a little worried about Mariah?"

"Of course I'm worried, Espy. I don't know whether we should move forward or stay. But look, Mariah is safe in the hospital. The police have put a guard at her door and detectives are going to ask her some questions."

Fiona, giggling, kicks off her shoes and belches into the comforter.

"Fiona, get up!"

Fiona rolls over and swipes blond tendrils from her face. "I guess this means Mariah's better off in the hospital than Heather is out of the hospital." She laughs hysterically before rolling off the bed.

"She's got a point, Eve," I say. "We're leaving Mariah alone to deal with this awful assault. It's not right. We're better together. Remember? I just don't feel good about this."

"I understand, but what do you want to do? Forget about Heather? She asked us to come. We don't even know what's happened to her. It's a long way between here and Connecticut. Who's going to let us know? Moving makes more sense than sitting here waiting for the next thing. We're like sitting ducks. And we can't really go to the police without telling them everything that happened that night and revealing the part we played in it. A man died and we don't even know who he was. So how are we going to defend ourselves in his death? And the guy who probably did kill him doesn't even exist anymore, except in our minds." Eve pauses. "And there's more."

She tells us about Mariah's threatening letters from the multinational water company. That her coworker was found dead in his hotel room.

"Fiona's right," she concludes. "Let the police deal with it. This is bigger than we can handle. We're in way over our heads. Heather we might be able to handle. It's Brandon. He's a snake, but he's just an ole rat snake."

"But I can't bear to think of her lying there alone," I protest. "She's so lost and terrified. It breaks my heart."

Fiona lifts herself from the floor and clings to the edge of the bed. Her eyes, half closed, peer at us. "Mariah needs us. Actually, I think my family needs me. It feels so good to be needed." Sobbing, she blows her nose into the hotel comforter.

Eve puts her back to the wall. "God, Fiona. All of our families need us. This is not how this is supposed to go. I left my boyfriend to come here. We have to focus on Mariah and Heather, not on running away. We have to fix this."

"Yes, but—"

"But what?"

Fiona sobs. "Yes, but he's leaving me."

"Who's leaving you?" I ask.

"Gavin." Fiona cries. "Gavin is."

"Did he tell you that? Why didn't you say something earlier?" Eve asks.

"I didn't want to think about it. And no, he didn't say anything. He didn't have to."

"I'm sorry, Fiona," Eve says. "I truly am."

Fiona wipes her tears. "I'm scared."

I kneel next to her, as much to comfort myself as to comfort her. "*Chica*, I am so sorry, so very sorry."

"I'm not just scared for my marriage. What if none of us returns home to our loved ones? What if . . . ?"

Eve sits on the corner of the bed. Her shoulders slump wearily as her resolve melts into the cushions. "Don't say that. I'm scared too." She straightens her shoulders. "But we have to do something. We can't sit here. There are only three of us left. Right now, we don't have any answers." She sighs. "Fiona, Gavin may leave you and Jerome may leave me. Heather and Mariah may not survive. But I can't see any alternative but to move toward this problem. We've always been moving toward it, even as we ran as fast and as hard as we could to elude it. We have to go. There's nothing else to do." She rises from the bed and waits for us.

There are no more choices. We will go.

* * *

The airport is choked with travelers. I face the wave of humanity that threatens to swallow or break me. The feeling of abandonment I experienced those long years ago on the Yucatan haunt me. It was the same then as it is now, loneliness and destitution in the midst of many and plenty. The incongruity of it makes me cry. And now I'm abandoning Mariah. Mariah, who has been everyone's rock.

"We have to keep it together, Espy," Eve says.

"We shouldn't leave Mariah alone."

"We already talked about this. We don't have a choice."

"One of us could stay."

"Who?"

"Me."

"Well, we don't know if we can even get out of here. There may not be a flight for a while."

We watch Fiona as she moves slowly through the reservations line.

Eve hooks her arm in mine. "It's not too late. You can still stay. Fiona and I will be fine. We'll find Heather. I think Mariah is safe in the hospital, and you would be too if you decided to stay."

Yes. If I stay, I will be alone watching Mariah, with her perpetrator still out there. Fiona and Eve will have one less person with them to deal with whatever is happening or soon to happen in Connecticut. I don't like either option. Whether I stay or go, I will be as bereft as that moment I made the same decision in Yucatan. The wave carried me then. But then waves are like that. They smash against the coast and leave with a piece of it. Nothing is ever the same afterwards. Bit by bit, the action whittles away the land. There is no defense great enough to prevent it. The sea always has the final say. Gentle and enigmatic in calm, she is fierce and unwavering in her retribution during storms. She is the final say of life and death, both at sea and on shore. Man is nothing more than a gnat, an ego-driven gnat, on the ass of life. I snicker.

Eve glances at me.

I could still run. Like I should've run on the Yucatan. I should have found Gabriel and run with him, for him. I should have been stronger. But I always come back to the same thing I've always known: I could never run from my family. Without them I would be storm-tossed, bereft of the roots that bind me to my life. No love can sustain such a loss of moorings. Without our native land, family is all we have to define ourselves, our culture. Without native land and without family, we are nothing. No love can withstand such a stripping of the soul. I chose to relinquish love. The wave broke me.

But then a greater love washed ashore. If I had run, Tomas, my children, my life would've been but a dream. No. I made the right choice. Now I need to make the right choice again, even if it means the wave will break over me.

Eve continues to look at me. "I'm glad you're finding some humor in this."

"Humor and sadness, *chica*. It's a funny thing."

Eve puts her arm around my shoulders. We have always been there for each other, been there for Heather. The world is a safer and saner place with my friends breathing the same air. Somewhere in the world, our breath mingles as it crosses the globe. Our stories are different but we share something that transcends that: humanity, sisterhood, and the knowledge of a deeply shared secret. Nothing can diminish us. Our differences are trivial in the face of our commonality. But that is the thing about quantum states of interactions: no one can be fully described, fully articulated, without considering the other. Our lives are entangled at the most basic level.

Fiona sneaks up and hugs us from behind. For a moment, the wave of people parts and moves around us. Fiona lets go and holds up three tickets. We know where we're going. It is better to move toward it of our own volition. We have always allowed events to wash over us, but it has never had the desired effect, surety and safety. It is time to seek.

Fiona smiles. "Do you remember the story of Moirai?"

"The Fates in Greek mythology. Yes, I do." Eve smiles.

"It's time to meet the bitches." Fiona laughs hysterically.

Now is the time to let them know. I cannot go with them. "My fate is here."

Eve hugs me. "It's right. She needs one of us."

Fiona's smile disappears. "What do you mean? Aren't you going with us?"

I hug her. "Someone needs to be here with Mariah. No one should be left alone. You need to be strong for Heather and Eve. I'm counting on you." I kiss her cheek. "I love you both. We'll all be together soon. I know this in my heart."

I turn and head toward the door. No matter what, none of us will be alone.

31 Paul

I do not fear death; death is something to be feared in the land of the living.

When I was little, I was afraid of the monsters that lived in my closet. No one told me monsters lived outside in the world. They walk amongst us. They smell our fear.

They can no longer smell me.

Long ago, I learned to tame the beasts. It is an edge when you have to track one.

All those years ago, Stab lured and caged a beautiful bird, and now the monster I track caged the other. The world has been better off without Stab and the world will be better off without Harold.

Harold. He does not know I know him. I have been tracking him. Watching him. Waiting.

Soon, it will be over.

I follow him as he finds a quiet corner in the airport. Just around the bend, I can hear him. Charleston is loud and open, but there are still corners in the world. Everything must have an edge. Things are clearer without my Asian mistress, but there are moments when I miss her cloak. I stand, exposed, on the other side of the wall.

"Yes. I have it. Where do you want me to meet you?" He is silent. "No. She's dead." Silence. "They weren't together and she slipped away while I was preoccupied with the journalist. But she's headed your way. I can take her out when I give you the drive. I can spend a little time with her."

I can almost hear and see the man on the other line. The best trench coat cannot hide his hideousness. I can still smell his cologne and the overpowering stench of his piss.

Harold's phone clicks shut and I leave my listening post. The security line is ahead and I walk toward it—ten steps ahead of him.

We board the same plane.

I exit ten people behind him.

I watch as a black car picks him up at the arrivals gate.

I flag the first taxi. "Follow that car."

"Mister, where's the car going?"

"I don't know yet, but follow it."

The man looks at me in the rearview mirror. It no longer matters. I no longer dread being caught. Death is already upon me. There is nothing else that can be done for me or to me. There is no greater danger than a man who no longer fears his own death. And the most dangerous of all is the man who has no fear.

We cross the line into Connecticut. Ah. He seeks home. He seeks his territory. But I, too, know these hunting grounds. He believes he hunts without being hunted. I have spent years in the jungle. No one knows it better than I.

The black car pulls up in front of a nondescript ranch house in Stamford. It pulls away as Harold puts the strap of his bag over his shoulder and mounts the stairs. I assume the flash drive is in the black car. That will have to wait for another time. This is my mission now.

The lights go on in the house. I pay the taxi driver.

It is easy work to break into the garage, and the van seat will be the most comfortable bed I have had in weeks.

Harold opens the door from the house into the garage and packs a black satchel in the back of the van. It does not take me long to remove the clip from his gun and return the weapon to the satchel.

I take my time looking around his house while he sleeps.

Rest well. It will be your last. The monster is in your closet.

The man has no imagination. Inside a dehumidified closet, I count twenty-four large locks of hair tied expertly into bundles and attached to key rings. Each one is labeled in code. Moron. His kill trophies are barely hidden in a locked basement room.

Were they all birds?

Cold blood pumps through my veins. Ice veins.

Soon, little ones.

Soon.

I will fly you home.

I lock the door. The police will find it anyway.

I am back in the van by daylight.

Harold follows soon after.

I think I know whom he is hunting. And he will know me soon enough.

In my hiding place, I lift my shirt and touch my MK-II. She is a steady blade.

I hunker down for the remainder of the trip.

Soon, it will all be over.

32 Mariah

They come in the darkness. I have been dozing in and out of consciousness. My limbs, battered and heavy, throb through the pain medicine. There are two of them. They flash gold badges. Detectives. So many questions. Veiled words. Pauses and attenuated sentences. Tired. I am so tired. So alone. The ice still flows through my veins. Can they not see? I answer their questions. Or is it a dream? Everything moves through a tunnel. I cannot make any of it real. My memories are cloaked in shadows, and as hard as I might, I cannot make out any details. I am claimed by a world of wraiths.

The dead are laughing. I will die here. I will die with them. Keep company with them. Such horror. Grandmother. No! I cannot become a shade, an invisible aspect of myself. Grandmother would tell me that. Grandmother would have saved me before I needed saving. I scream but there is no one to hear me. Not even I can hear my scream.

I do not know when they left me. Did I answer their questions? I am not sure. I cannot even be sure they ever visited. I am aware of a bright light and quiet figure taking my vitals and checking my IV tube, but then the figure recedes and the light goes with her. I reach for the path of energy that trails the figure but it dissipates, evaporates, with the touch of my hand. Maybe that never happened either. Or maybe the wraiths have come to check, waiting patiently for me to give up, to join them.

All the while, smiling, the bone man watches me. Esperanza sits at my bedside. But she is with Fiona and Eve. It is her shadow-self that keeps the bone man in his corner. Esperanza is like that. She can stay the heaviest heart.

I am not ready for the bone man. "Make him stay away, Espy."

She holds my hand. I drift.

Time curves in front of me like a scythe. The horizon bends into the future but I cannot see past it. The sun, sharp and unyielding, crosses the boundary of my vision. I wait for something. A high-pitched howl reverberates off the canyon walls, balls of energy ping-pong from one canyon wall to another.

He is coming.

I am slipping.

I cannot bend.

I move forward. He knows I will fight. He snarls, saliva dripping in long rivulets. Instinctively, I draw back. Yield and I will lose myself, run and I will become nothing.

"You are mine," he snarls.

"No." My scream rises to the heavens. The sky splits in two and he is gone.

"Ms. Westerman? Are you awake?"

"Huh?"

"Are you awake?"

"Uh-huh."

"The doctor can't see you tonight. He'll be in first thing in the morning. I won't be here, but the new shift is coming in. If you need anything, press the button."

"Thank you."

"You're welcome." But she is looking at Esperanza's shadow-self.

Esperanza's spirit thanks the nurse. The bone man watches her leave before he turns his gaze back. He smiles and winks.

I drift back out into the light of the canyon. It is warm there.

The canyon rips in two. I am on one side; he has to be on the other. I turn toward its end. I search the tunnel created by the high canyon walls, but there is no movement. I walk until I approach the opening, where Clay and Chase motion me to them. Where is Grandmother? They do not smile. Lightning streaks the sky. The prairie grass shimmers in the storm-charged sun, the Badlands rises ominously from the blackness of the beyond—death on top of death, layer upon layer of dead animals, fauna, and insects entombed in the land.

I must move. The barn is far away and my brothers run toward it and the community, my tribe, sequestered inside. The faster I move, the farther the barn is. I yell to them but they can't hear me. Each pulls the double barn doors closed and the light diminishes to a red laser point. I clutch my chest. The sound of beating drums pounds in my head. Blue ribbons course along the surface of my skin. And then I stumble.

I try to stand but the ground gives way. As far as I can see, the Badlands stand stark naked against the stormy sky. Nothing lives within its boundaries. I am utterly alone. I try to balance. The land continues to crumble, crumble like grains of sand drying in the sun. I will be trapped on a spire of death.

Beneath my feet, fossils, animated in a sarcophagus of ancient earth, seethe, but I am not afraid. Life is precarious, no more so for me than for those who swim in their death soup. I cry for them. They are the children of the eons, and they were born, suffered, and died together. We are all born to suffer together. I reach for them as the land disintegrates. In the distance, a great dire wolf, a most ancient of wolves, shakes free from his earthly tomb. He quivers and, turning, winks. I am no longer alone. I wave. He raises his nose, sniffs the air, and, in an instant, bolts for the border. He is gone as quickly as he arrived. My loneliness will kill me.

Why did my beloved brothers close the doors?

The distant sound of a ring wakes me and I open my eyes to a semi-dark hospital room. The phone rings again. Esperanza answers it.

"Hello? . . . No, she's been sleeping fitfully . . . Yeah, Fiona told me. I'm glad she's okay. I'm glad they're okay. That's horrible . . . She must be horribly upset . . . I know . . . All right. We'll be here." Esperanza smiles at me and puts the phone down. "Do you need anything?"

"Espy?"

"I'm here."

"How long have you been here?"

"All night. Do you want me to get you anything?"

The clock on the wall says it is midnight. "Have you been able to sleep?"

"No, I'm fine."

"What happened to Heather?"

"Mariah. Rest. We can talk about it when you're stronger."

The bone man finds me.

I struggle to breathe but he tightens his grip around my neck and the lights from the home fires twinkle brilliantly before they are snuffed. He has me this time, and I am completely alone.

The phone jars me awake. Where is Espy? The phone rings again and I reach for it, but the line is dead.

I hang up. If I fall asleep again, my dream will swallow me. I pray Espy returns soon.

The noise of the bustling hospital drifts through the crack of the partially open door. People come and go, passing through the corridors outside my room. I am in a cave, solitary and dispossessed. Maybe I am the living dead and they are keeping my ghost, afraid to release me into an unsuspecting world when I am at my most dangerous. I am *wanagi*—a confused spirit that should not be allowed back into the world. My eyes are heavy and I look for Espy.

The bone man wraps his fingers around my neck and secures the gnarly, dirty rope.

"Dance, my Midnight Dancer. Dance?"

"I can't and I won't."

He laughs and spits bones at me. "You won't? How does your will have anything to do with it? It's your destiny little one. Now, dance!"

I begin to dance and the earth is made firm again. I hop and spin and twirl until the drums compel me faster. I am a whirling dervish. From the perimeter, he hisses, but he can no longer stop me. He cannot stop what he has started. I am alive with motion and he is dying to me. His bones, spinning, disintegrate, but still I dance and then the home fires, once confined to the caves, dance with me in the midnight air, fragrant with prairie sage. I dance and collide with life, and there is no reason to define time or space, and I know. There is a place where terra firma and terra infirma, a moment when solitude and community, and a point at which stasis and evolution meet and blend. Where they converge is the point at which the truth peels back upon itself, and love, eternal and unattached to human convention and language, springs forth without restraint or condition.

"Ms. Westerman?"

I still dance. Spinning is like breathing.

"Ms. Westerman?"

I am falling.

"She's still sleeping. She's been dreaming all night." Esperanza's voice is silk.

"We can come back later."

No. It's important that I wake up. But why? "I-I-I'm here."

"Ms. Westerman. How are you feeling?"

My body is broken, but I am more alive than I've been in years. I am more whole than I have ever been. I vanquished the bone man.

"I'm fine."

He clears his throat. "The detectives processed your rape kit. There's no reason for you to stay here. You'd probably feel better at home. Do you have any concerns?"

Esperanza smiles at me. She's reading my mind. She looks at the doctor. "We'll be fine. Thank you."

I watch him leave. "Espy. I remember everything. We have to get to Heather."

"Yes. We'll go soon as you're stronger."

"No. Now, Espy. My attacker was looking for my coworker's flash drive. He knew all about it. He took it. He works for AAC. The stalker, Paul—he saved me from dying in that . . . tomb. He saved me. He's going after the AAC guy and the AAC guy is going to Connecticut. He has to get the flash drive to Michael Saxton, who also wants Heather gone. She's the one who told me she believes Brandon's mistress was murdered by this guy. And Heather's walking right into it."

"Mariah, are you sure?"

"I've never been more sure. He believes I'm dead, and Heather is the last and only thing standing in the way of Saxton's' plans. She's the only thing that could blow the roof off his plans and she doesn't even know it."

I want to go home. It's time. It's time to collect my dogs and head inland. A tear slides past my swollen eyes. But first we have to finish this.

Esperanza releases my hand. "Are you up to flying? We could drive. I think there's some unfinished business in Connecticut."

"Yeah, it's time to finish it."

Esperanza leans over and hugs me. "You're unstoppable. Most women would find a room to hide in. You're my rock, *chica*."

"Love is a rock, Espy."

33 Heather

"You have no right. You lured Shannon from my hotel room right under my nose? How dare you." The tightness in my back from the ten-hour race up the coast sits in my chest.

Brandon runs his hands through his hair, now unkempt. Deep circles crescent his eyes and midnight shadow darkens his complexion. He is a reflection of my unease. It was only a short time ago that we were the image of the perfect couple. Now everything is out of place, including his askew buttons. This is the same man who tried to kill me, but I want to reach out and caress his haggard face. He stares at me, his eyes haunted and watery. "I'm sorry, Heather."

"Sorry for what?"

"For trying to . . . hurt you."

"Oh, is that what it was? Because I had the distinct impression you wanted to kill me."

He rubs his face. "No. I wanted to hurt you. You were hitting me with your questions when I had just found out that someone important to me was dead."

"You mean Tanya Garrison."

"Yes, I mean Tanya."

"But no one knew she was dead yet. How could you have known unless—"

"No. I had nothing to do with it. I loved her. I had gone back to tell her that. To tell her that I would . . . I would leave you."

"That you would leave me. That wouldn't be enough hurt? You had to wrap your fingers around my throat to prove your point?"

"Quit skewing my words, Heather. I never meant to hurt you that way."

"No. The other way was less . . . hurtful?"

"Look. We haven't been a couple for a long time. I was deeply in love with her. I had been in love with her for several years, I just didn't act on it until a year ago . . . but she was seeing Saxton too."

"Well, that must've been a chummy trio."

"I didn't know it until later."

"So whose child was it? Or did she do the old eeny, meeny, miny, mo thing?"

I don't see his hand coming. My head spins. Blood trickles from the side of my mouth where he's split my lip. Tears always come. Damn! I never see it coming. I could never see my mother's coming either.

"Get out! Get out, you son of a bitch!"

"No." He takes a step back. "You provoked me. I didn't want to do that any more than I wanted to hurt you before. You provoked it. We need to talk this through."

All the old images ooze up like vomit. The taste of bile is foul in my mouth. I provoked it? What the hell does that mean, anyway? I have provoked everything in my life? Even when I was a baby, I was provoking the shit out of people? I can finally see it. They think they can transfer their weakness onto someone else. I won't accept it anymore. It's time to grow up and kick all the shit to the curb. Starting with Brandon.

"We're not talking anything through. Our lawyers can talk. Get out or I'll call the police or I'll call—"

"What? You'll call one of your loser friends?"

"Well, if they're losers, I'd hate to think of what you are. You're a coward. So, fuck you, Brandon."

He moves toward me, aggression taut in his expression. "You think you can hurt me with your words. You hurt me every day I had to look at you. Every day I couldn't wake to Tanya's face and I had to wake to yours instead. I had to wonder if I had ever loved you. You were never anything but an empty shell, a piece of shit people could kick around. I felt shame when I looked at you."

I ball my fist into a punch and let it rip, but he catches it before it lands. His lips curve into a snarl. "Look at you! Little miss toughy. You can't even fight back. You're so damn pathetic. Who could ever love someone like you?"

He disappears behind my watery vision. Anger defiles my senses.

"There are more people who love me than love you. You lusted after a woman who slept with two married men. There's no honor in your love. There's nothing decent or good about your lust. You're just a bunch of fornicators caught in a predictable situation. You couldn't begin to have the authority to utter the word *love*. Now get out."

"This is my house. I'll get out when I damn well please." He balls his fists and moves towards me.

"Daddy. What're you doing?"

Shannon. I don't know when she crawled out of bed or how much of this she has witnessed.

"Go to your room, honey. You'll be safe in there."

"I don't wanna. I want you to stop yelling." She sobs and rubs her eyes.

Brandon bends to her. "Please, honey. Your mommy and I have something to talk about. Okay?"

"Okay." I watch her run. She has already witnessed too much for her years. I was broken when I was a little girl. Fists and belts were the means of breaking me. But Shannon is breaking, too. Words and images are the method this time. I have to protect her. And I have to show her how to transcend those words. To stand tall and sparkle because of, not in spite of, what the world has to give. There is immensity in the universe and in the human heart, but there is parallel darkness too. It is important to break open the closed soul and render it to the open air. The darkness will have its play, but there is no need to be its prisoner.

I lift the phone from the receiver and dial 9-1-1.

I muster my most terrified voice. It comes easily. I know the rawness of my anguish and I use it and marvel at it—my actions are no longer under its spell. "Yes, my husband is here. He tried to kill me earlier." I sob and whisper, as if in hiding. "He hit me. He's trying to kill me now. I'm afraid. Please hurry."

Brandon frowns. Confusion mars his face.

"Now's a good time to run."

But there is no sound. The phone is dead. He cut the line.

"What did you do?"

"I didn't do anything. Is the line dead?"

"Yeah. You have to have done something."

"No. I didn't do anything."

"What the . . ." My words sink. There's movement downstairs.

Brandon turns to the stairs. I follow. It's a force stronger than reason. He picks up his baseball bat. My cell phone is in my purse downstairs. "Do you have your cell phone?"

Brandon turns and puts his finger to his lips. "No. It's in the car. I didn't think to bring it to our little rendezvous."

"Well, that might've been helpful."

"Now's a shitty time to get some balls, Heather."

"Shhh."

We descend quietly, but the stairs creak. I'm not sure it matters. Something tells me our presence is already known. There's something inevitable about this moment. I know it's time to face whatever this thing is that has popped up in our lives. I try to sprint past Brandon but he catches my collar.

"What the hell are doing?"

"It's time to face the music."

"What are you talking about?"

"Something happened in our lives. Something that we've lived with, and now it's time to face it."

"Who the fuck is *we*? It's not time to face anything. Stay back."

"Oh, sure. Now you want to be my hero."

"What the hell has gotten into you?"

"You and the world have gotten into me and I'm tired of being the punching bag. Move over, Superman." I tear free of his grasp and start running down the stairs.

"Heather!" he calls. "Get back here."

But I'm already gone.

And I walk right into it—right into the barrel of a gun.

"Well, Mrs. Collings. I've been looking forward to this little meeting. You and your husband are hard to find lately."

I recoil. "Who are you?"

"I'm good friends with Michael Saxton, and he's not very fond of you right now."

Brandon is behind me and pulls me back. All these years and he decides to be a hero when all is lost. But he moves toward the gunman. "I recognize you."

"I'm sure you do. I knew your little whore Tanya, too."

Brandon swings at him but the man parries and, raising the gun, pulls the trigger.

Oh, God! No!

But nothing happens. Dust swirls. All the rest . . . suspends.

A voice, low and chilling, laughs from the doorway. The gunman spins around. But I already know who it is. I would recognize his face anywhere. He has walked in my dreams ever since that night in Sunny Hollow. I gasp and his smile turns forlorn. "I'm sorry, little bird. I swore I would never let anyone hurt you again. But I've been lost for so many years."

Brandon tackles the gunman, but the gunman lands a fist on Brandon's jaw. Brandon crashes to the ground.

"Daddy." Shannon runs down the stairs.

Please. Not her. "Shannon. Go to your room now."

But it's too late.

The gunman and I lunge for her.

My nails scrape skin free from his face. He fights through my claws; he's too strong. The sound of my head hitting the floor stuns me. But it's just enough time for Shannon to run.

It is a funny thing how the sequence of events becomes mixed up when all is in peril. When every truth you've believed in is shredded into a million pieces and you can't piece the why back together. When all that matters is on the line, your mind squirrels away the nuggets for the winter. Later I will remember Brandon lying still, Shannon running, the sound of scuffling, a gasp, being pulled around. But all those things collapse into one: the look on the gunman's face as he clasps his neck, the flow of blood from the gaping slash in his neck.

And then he crumples to the ground and his eyes become vacant.

I will always remember those eyes—those eyes as they moved from surprise to knowledge to nothingness.

34 Heather

Surrounded by my friends, I shift in my now-uncomfortable bed. My body is healing but my soul is cleaving in two, disunited by years of abuse. I've been standing at a precipice my whole life, dancing around its perimeter. Some people never move away. They become victims *in perpetuam*. All the strength I felt in my career was a farce. Has my job ever been anything more than a shield to the truth? I want to scream, but it won't change anything. Maybe I was born that way.

Esperanza is driving Mariah. They'll be here soon. But how can I welcome them to my house when it no longer feels safe? It feels like an extension of someone else's life. Paul appears when I least expect him and disappears just as quickly.

He has cleaned up everything from last night. He moved the gunman to the man's house. Or at least, that is what he told me. I should care. I just do not.

He shared the truth of that night long ago in Sunny Hollow. We stayed up and watched the sun rise.

I move as if in a dream, but Fiona and Eve are moved differently by the melting of their memories. They had woven stories that now have to be unwound. They create new ones as I lie in bed, in Brandon's and mine. It is a bed of betrayal. I cannot move beyond that truth. I am stuck sinking into the too-soft mattress. I am in quicksand. I smile, but I cannot share their new vision of that night. That story is still too far away. It will not unwind as quickly without killing that part of me that keeps myself together.

Brandon's face, full of rage, keeps shifting in and out of my mind. People who were supposed to love me and people who were not—they're mixed up in my head. Strangers protect me and family destroys me, nothing makes any sense in a world turned topsy-turvy. My world makes no sense. It never has.

I was so in love with him. Or was I?

Maybe I deserved to be betrayed.

The sound of Esperanza's voice climbs from the stairway—"We're here!" Mariah will be behind her.

As Espy hugs everyone, Mariah limps into the room. My heart stops. Some of the pieces fall together. Bad things happen to those you love and believe are strong. But then, love is not love until it is allowed to flex and spread in spite of the bad things.

It is impossible to hold back all the tears that have been dammed up for years. Eve puts her arm over my shoulder. It feels good to be like this.

Mariah looks questioningly at us, and I catch Eve shaking her head. No more secrets. No more hiding.

"Why are you looking at each other that way?"

Eve squeezes my shoulder. "We're not. You're under a lot of strain and the doctor wants you to rest."

"I've been resting."

Fiona looks at me. "Everything will be fine. Just like it always is."

Mariah gasps. "Nothing is fine. What are you talking about? You're always in some rose-colored la-la land, Fiona."

"I didn't mean it that way. You're always taking me the wrong way."

Mariah takes a wobbly step forward before Esperanza pulls a chair over to her. She sits down gingerly. "How should I take it? Because if that's not what you mean, why don't you say what you mean?"

"I know you think I'm superficial, but sometimes you have to imagine the glass half full for it to be half full. Anything else has to be a disappointment."

Esperanza smiles. "That's actually so true."

Mariah shrugs. "You think my glass is half empty?"

Fiona looks down. "I think you perceive it as being gone or misplaced."

I want to know. "How 'bout my glass, Fiona?"

She considers. "I think yours is broken. Every time you try to fill it back up, it leaks."

Esperanza giggles. "Our philosopher."

The sound of movement downstairs interrupts our reunion. Mariah springs from the chair.

Eve rescues her. "It's Paul, Mariah. You're safe. He won't let anything happen to any of us. I promise. We never understood him. You were right. He was freeing her that night. He saved her last night, too."

Mariah shakes her head. "I told you. He saved me from the tomb." She looks at me. "Are you okay?"

"You're too much. I have a few bumps and bruises. You've been to hell and back and you want to know if *I'm* okay." I reach for her but she winces. "I'm sorry, Mariah."

Mariah smiles wanly. "You had nothing to do with any of this. The man who abducted me wanted my flash drive and wanted to silence me."

"I know. He was here last night."

"He was here last night? I thought it was just you, Brandon, and Paul."

"No. He was here too. Paul intervened—he killed him. Then he took his body and put it in his house. I assume the police or FBI will do their magic and link his DNA where it needs to be linked, which will probably exonerate Brandon."

"Are you okay with that?"

"Yeah. I don't want him to suffer. He's already suffered. He's Shannon's father. I would prefer it if we could find a way to make things easier on her. Besides, I think it's time to bury my old life. It might be time to see a psychotherapist."

"To deal with some things you've never dealt with before," Eve says, turning to Mariah. "To deal with post-traumatic stress. Might be good for someone else, too."

"To deal with everything." I dig my nails into my palm. The pain gives me a measure of relief.

"Stop hurting yourself," Eve says, gently slapping my hand down.

"I know." Old habits die hard.

Esperanza startles. "Where's Shannon?"

"She's with Paul," Fiona says. "He's probably making her an ice cream sundae topped with fruit loops, chocolate milk with a straw-berry Twizzler straw, and brownies with hot chocolate syrup. That would be my guess."

I laugh through my tears. "He's incredible with her."

"Yes, he is." Eve's smile is like a caress.

My friends are my strength. We will carry each other. I may have been born into hell, but I am not condemned to it. "I thought it was Paul. The other man had told me I was beautiful. I would've believed anyone who said something kind. But it was just a way to get to me. He's the one who raped me. All this time, I didn't remember. I just kept seeing Paul's face because he was there, watching, like my mom. He didn't stop it. I was sure he was the one who did it. He's lived eternally in my mind. The mind does funny things. It makes you sure when nothing is sure. Sometimes, I even thought he was in cahoots with my Mom."

I thought he had died in the fire, but only one body was ever accounted for. Now I'm not sure . . . of anything. Nothing has ever been the same, and yet nothing has ever changed. Life is like that. I simply changed one form of suppression for another, switched one abuser for another. Mariah taught me that changelings are the great tricksters of life. They are meant to make you laugh at yourself, see yourself. I was born and raised by them, I was married to another, but I do not intend to die in the graceless presence of one. This cannot be my story, my legacy. Shannon deserves something better. I am done. It is finished. Here.

I have always fought the idea of psychotherapy, but now I know it is the only way to gain back everything that has been taken from me, all that has never been allowed to blossom. Paul and my friends have given me the gift of seeing clearly. Shannon is the reason to fight for it.

Mariah sits down again. "Has Paul told you who the guy was? I mean, it's not like finding out is going to get us into any more trouble than we've already been in. Besides, there are no parents to ground us now."

Fiona smirks. "Speak for yourself. My mom is itching for a reason."

This, at least, this I know. He told me last night. "He was one of his friends. He killed him for me."

"And why was Paul in your office that day?" Mariah asks.

"He wasn't," I say, shaking my head. "I don't know why I thought I saw him that day. Maybe my mind was playing tricks on me. Maybe I had a premonition of him. I can't explain it. Maybe, it's just part of my . . . my craziness." My voice cracks.

"You're not crazy, *chica*," Espy says. "You're just . . . prescient."

"But why is he here?" Fiona asks. "Why would you have a premonition at all?"

There's been so much sorrow lately. I'm not sure I can bear this one. "He's dying. He has cancer. I guess he wanted to find some peace."

Eve smiles. "Peace. Maybe none of us will have it until we find home. And we can't go home until we understand the price of exile."

* * *

I return to work within a week. There's no reason to delay. The police found Harold but it's hard to link him to Saxton. We're all being watched. Esperanza and Fiona went home. Mariah will stay with me to recover. Her summary on water will be published. The piece on virtual water contained in the computer cycle was brief—the flash drive hasn't been recovered. But she is undaunted. The rest of her assignments are on hold. And she always has her backup disk, the one she sent to her boss, when she is ready again to find her fire.

Eve has gone to fetch Mariah's dogs and will be returning with them tonight. Then she will go home to New York and Jerome. Paul takes Shannon to and from day care and tends to me and Mariah in between. Brandon has disappeared.

My house does not feel like home anymore, but it's evolving into something more organic and reflective of the complexity in my life—a place full of love.

I've only been settled in my office for thirty minutes when Sharon buzzes me.

"It's good to have you back. Bob Hewitt's looking for you."

"Thanks, Sharon."

Bob Hewitt. I assume he will inquire after my welfare and catch me up to date on affairs. The Dallas audit went well, but Michael Saxton must still answer for the sexual discrimination complaint, and the police consider him a person of interest in Tanya's death. The future company savior is squirming. I smile.

Bob's secretary watches me over her eyeglasses as I pace in the small waiting area. Finally, the door swings open and Bob motions to me. He offers me a seat.

"I see you're back."

I smooth my skirt. "Yes, and happy to be here."

"Well, things have certainly gotten complicated."

"Yes. I'm sure Michael Saxton's situation has the company nervous."

Bob looks at me. "Nervous?"

"Well, I mean, the situation can't be good for the reputation of the company. I mean . . ."

"How would his personal life affect the reputation of the company?"

"Well, she was an employee, he was an officer, and it went on under . . ." I force myself to stop talking. This is not going the way I anticipated. Something is wrong.

Bob frowns. I wait for the jingle of coins, but he is unnervingly quiet in his crisply tailored suit. I catch myself digging my nails into my hands. I promised Mariah. I rub my hands together, smoothing the newly indented skin.

"Yes," he says. "But I'm sure you know we've already put some damage control into place."

"I see. That's smart. Get some distance."

"Yes. Distance." Bob moves to the other side of his desk. I can see more clearly from this vantage point. His normally congenial manner is absent. Any trace of the old friendly working relationship is gone. The man who stands in front of me is a stranger. "A lot has been going on since you left two weeks ago. Things have been coming to a head."

"What do you mean?"

"Heather. This is difficult, but we have to let you go." He clears his throat. "You need to leave now. You may return to your office to retrieve your things, but security will escort you to the door and take your employee ID badge."

I must have heard wrong. What could have happened in the two weeks I was gone to lead to this? There's only one explanation. What did my psychotherapist call it? Dissociation. I laugh.

Bob scowls. "I'm surprised you find this funny."

"I think I heard you wrong."

"You didn't. You're being let go, Heather."

I sober. "For what reason?"

Bob lowers his voice. "Failing to perform your duties in an acceptable manner, and insubordination."

And there it is—the catchall excuse, the ultimate betrayal. It is the same cause for termination as Tanya. So, that is it and that is all. I was never more than a function.

I struggle for breath. I put my head between my legs.

"I'll let you regain your composure, but then you'll be escorted off premises. I'm sorry, Heather. I really am."

He thinks he's sorry. "And Saxton?"

Bob clears his throat. A frog of deceit? "He'll be fine. The CEO has decided to stay on for a little while."

"Just until things blow over. Right?"

Bob looks at me. Actually, he stares through me. "I don't know why you're putting a spin on this. There's nothing going on. Michael is the best man for the CFO position and the CEO has chosen to stay. It's simple."

"You said the word. I didn't. Well, I have to hand it to you. You're more simple than I thought. Good-bye, Bob."

I leave and disassemble my office until there's nothing left to mark my passage. It's as if I've never occupied the space. I take one last look in the rearview mirror at the building in which I have spent so much of my life. Did it ever mean anything? I watch it disappear. It was part of who I was. It was what made me visible for so many years.

* * *

At home, I close the curtains and curl up in bed. There are no more tears.

An eternity slips from my life. I watch it go by and I do not mourn it.

Mariah tiptoes into my room and lies down. Our eyes lock until we hear a little girl's giggle downstairs. A deeper voice follows.

I have been dreaming. None of it can be real.

"Mariah?"

"Yeah?"

"I think I've been sleepwalking for a very long time."

Mariah smiles. "Nah, you've been awake. I know because you've affected so many people. You can't do that while you're asleep." She reaches her hand out to me.

Shannon jumps on the bed. "Mommy!"

"Hey you. How was your day?"

Shannon giggles. "Good. Paul's getting me lotsa treats."

"Where?"

"He went to the grocery store."

Mariah laughs. "Well, aren't you a lucky girl."

"Yeah. He said I could have anything I want."

Anything one wants.

But nothing is ever that simple, and nothing ever stays the same.

35 Eve

It feels good to stretch. The sun filters through the blinds of my Manhattan apartment. I am alone. The noise on the street is chaotic—cars honk, pedestrians speak in loud voices, and distant emergency vehicles wail, reminding me of the calamity that can so easily transform life. But I am safe here now. Africa fades in the light of the teeming metropolis I now call home. Home. It is a strange word. But the seed of the thought took root and I spoke it into life. I willed it. Or did I? Perhaps it was destined.

Predetermination is an abhorrent idea. Was my beloved brother, Terrell, destined from birth to die alone in Vietnam? Had it always been decided that he would perish without a trace, die ignominiously in some foreign land amongst foreign people, discarded in the jungle of a country we had no business fighting? No, I cannot abide a world in which loved ones are discarded like garbage. He was so much more than that. And yet life has given me plenty of cause to believe that fate holds some sway in the world of mortals. I, however, have never held sway in the fate of the world. It suffers despite my earnest efforts to rescue it. In the end, I can only rescue myself.

But we rescued each other, my circle of friends. I have never been certain that I actually chose them as friends. They just sort of happened to me. I know I did not choose them as sisters. We are as different as peanut butter is to jelly. And yet that truth cannot kill the heart of it: we are sisters. Which begs the question, which part of them is destiny and which part is choice? I suppose I do not care. They are the thread that binds the cloth together. As a sisterhood, we are stronger. But that is what makes man strong. It is what makes animals strong. The pack is always more apt to survive than the lone wolf. Prairie dogs stand vigil to warn their community of predators. The lone calf is defenseless against the lion, but it has a chance when adults stand in a circle to protect their weak. And man has congregated around the fire since time immemorial, his safety found in numbers. Evolution is nothing more than the story of community and its language, of culture and its defining gift of relevance. Man claims his significance, his purpose, through the language of culture.

I turned from that safety long ago. And I was alone. Community is where humanity finds the best and the worst of itself. I want the dirty business of togetherness. Disagreements and strife may be inherent to the human condition, but I am willing to accept that condition.

I stretch and yawn. It is as if I never left.

* * *

The day I returned, I caught Jerome by surprise.

I had finished unpacking by the time Jerome returned from work. The sound of his keys dropping on the front table stirred up butterflies in my stomach. I could almost see him leafing through the day's mail. And then I heard his footsteps. Hiding in the closet, I was a little girl again. All the monsters were gone, and Terrell was smiling in my heart. I could feel him.

From the slit in the closet door, I watched Jerome shed his suit coat and tie. He looked at the rumpled bedspread, his brows knitted. I placed my hand over my mouth. Then his brows unfurled and I watched his confusion turn into a smile. He found me out.

I lunged from the closet, laughing. There was no way to contain my joy.

He caught me and wrapped me around him. His kiss was long and deep and tasted like strawberries. I kissed him back.

"Are you back for real?"

"I'm home for real. There's nowhere else I want to be."

* * *

I stretch again and roll over in bed, treasuring the softness of the mattress, sheets, and pillow. It is all so different from the refugee camp beds. The smell of laundry detergent is a welcome reminder of that which others do not have. Always in the back of my mind is the remembrance of the hardships of others, those with whom I shared so much of my journey. At the forefront, though, is the memory of their joyful hearts, their pirouette of life. In the darkest of times, they found the light and made it twirl with them. That was their gift, their destiny. I always had community with them, the women of Africa. No matter where I call home, they will be with me. They are the light dancers and I am their humble apprentice. My pillow is soft under my embrace. I have so much to be grateful for. Am I worthy? I will try to be.

"What are you doing?"

Jerome. He is home. He is my home.

I turn and smile at him. The mirror behind him shoots my image back at me. My hair is tousled and wild. It is as wild as my heart is at this moment. This most precious of moments.

"I am light dancing, my love."

36 Fiona

I pack again. Charleston is a distant memory now, but so much has transpired since that trip a year ago that things are just a relief against the backdrop of that canvas. I survived. We survived. But my marriage did not. I had been lost for so many years that it could not survive that much desolation.

I was the toast of the town of beautiful people, Beverly Hills—elegant, rich, admired—and yet I could not really look at myself in the mirror. My parents loved me, but I was never allowed to flourish, to be authentic, to be loved for who I was and not the dream of me. It was so easy to be cherished that I never really aspired to anything else. Mariah, Eve, Heather, and Esperanza were so brilliant that I only needed to bask in their brilliance. Because I was popular in school, a goddess, they congratulated themselves on being in my entourage in the beginning. But I always knew they would trump me.

They would never let me believe that. Even when I believed the worst of myself, when the shadows talked and the bottle could not quiet them, they loved me. There is grace in being loved. And sometimes that's all it takes. The wreckage of life can never be total in the wake of love. Even when my sisters knew the truth of me and my self-hatred filled me with anger and bitterness, the love of my friends stayed.

Gavin never understood. They were not the type of people with whom he rubbed elbows. They were not in his social class. I accepted his class distinctions in the beginning. I tried to be the good wife—and I succeeded, if only for a while. I was his trophy. It never occurred to me that a throne can diminish, a crown can tarnish, and the illusion of trust and love can crumble like the sausage Abella stirs into the kids' morning eggs.

My kids, they are everything. There was never any illusion there; I just didn't trust or love myself enough to believe they could either. But they did. They believed in me, even if they did not understand my desire to divorce their Dad.

I could not burst their bubble. The lie of omission would have to do for now.

* * *

I had just come home from three months of rehab when Gavin opened the door to our master bedroom, walked inside, and sat on the edge of our bed.

"I'm glad you're back from rehab."

"I'm glad to be back too," I said. "I feel pretty good."

"Good. I'm glad." His tone was formal. I watched him run his hand through his hair. He was trying to gather his thoughts. Between Charleston, Connecticut, and rehab, I had not seen him in several months, but it felt like a century. The gulf between us was immense and I wanted to bridge it. Soon.

"Gavin. We should all go away together. Maybe a short family vacation. Rediscover each other. Or maybe just the two of us. Like old times."

But he did not look at me. He looked at the mirrors. "I stopped loving you a long time ago. I'm not sure I ever really loved you. I loved the idea of you. We were never compatible. You must understand that?"

"No, I don't. What are you saying? Of course we loved each other. Love each other."

He shook his head. "No. Look, I've been your faithful servant for the sake of the children and social convention. I've done everything that was expected of me. But I'm tired of the charade. My career has benefited from our alliance, our marriage, but I can't pretend anymore." He paced as if to gather his thoughts. "I've been seeing someone else for the past year. I can't endure this lie, this marriage, any longer."

I crumpled. "No . . ."

He did not pause. "Since I've benefited from our union, you're entitled to a certain . . . remuneration, but I want a divorce. I've already filed for it."

"*Remuneration*?" I knew the gist of the word, but I was half tempted to get out the dictionary and throw it at him.

"Yes, Fiona. Compensation."

I stared at him in disbelief. So this is what it came down to: remuneration! That was a word for the decade.

"Really, Gavin? Well, you're damn straight about one thing. This is California! I'll get my fucking remuner-whatever." I picked up a vase of flowers and pitched it at the bedroom mirrors. The sound of breaking glass was music. I left him staring at me as I slammed the door.

He is just like my father. Intellectual love is straight-up cold. *I will enumerate your remuneration and up you one, sweetheart,* I thought as I stomped down the stairs.

* * *

But the kids don't need to know this. Not now. Getting divorced is painful enough. Later, when things are settled. It is the journey that matters.

"Mama, how long will you be gone?" Sam has not called me Mama in years.

"Not long," I say. "There is nowhere else I want to be."

"You promise?"

"I promise, cross my heart, and swear to die."

She looks at me sternly. "Don't ever promise to die, Mama. It's not good luck."

"I'm sorry. I didn't mean to bring any bad luck to this trip."

She hugs me. "Will we be allowed to go someday?"

I love the idea. "Yes. I think that might be a great idea."

Molly and Sean join us. I have the best part of Gavin; the worst is no longer in my life. I do not feel that loss, not anymore. My pride was wounded, but that was my ego, and I have been putting that baby to rest for the past year. It feels good to be free of it, to be unattached to that part of me that lives at the command and instruction of others, that element of me that acts a part. I am now rewriting my role. Perhaps it is nothing more than a fulfillment of my destiny.

"Ah, my darlings, it is time to eat, no?" Abella stands at the threshold of the room.

I wink at her. "No, Abella, it's time to move. Come along. You're part of this family. We can't do this without you. Time to shake your groove thing."

Sean laughs. "Groove thing? You're twisted."

I twist my hips. "Peaches & Herb, baby boy."

Sean and Molly laugh.

Sam watches us, smiles, and holds out her arms. "We love you, Abella. Dance with us."

Abella clasps her hands to her chest. "Ah, *mija*. I love you too." She moves into our outstretched arms.

I think Eve is right. We create our own fire.

37 Esperanza

"Mommy, take my rabbit. She protected you last year."

My suitcase is overflowing again. Angelica watches me. "I wouldn't dream of going away without bunny." I take bunny and place it on top of the pile of clothing. Whatever else flows out will be left.

Izzy pops in the doorway. "I made you a picture, Mom." Déjà vu. We went through these motions a year ago.

"What did you make, Izzy?"

She hands me the picture. Gone are the rainbows and Pegasus, but what has replaced them is more sophisticated. My daughter is growing up and growing into her own as an artist. A group of people, dressed in a rainbow of colors, dance underneath the heavens, the stars illuminating their clothing. A large moon hovers and lights the inky sky. "It's a midnight dance, Mom. Their souls are whirling."

I have never seen anything so wondrous. My eyes water up despite myself.

She rolls her eyes. "Oh Mom, you're always crying."

"I'm happy crying, Izzy. It's so beautiful. I love it and I'll treasure it."

"Don't forget to dance home, Mom."

"Never."

And then I remember all the stargazing I have done in my life. Daddy used to call it daydreaming, but Mom knew better. The stars are the windows into the universe. Explosive, they blow and spend themselves, to be born and die and be reborn. Equal parts creation and destruction, they tell us the tale of life. They taught me how to salsa. They are teaching even now. And Izzy has been paying attention. My little dreamer has been awake the whole time.

"What are you laughing at, Mom?"

"Nothing, Izzy. I guess I was just thinking how much your picture reminds me of the universe—colliding stars, colliding galaxies, colliding matter. We do the same thing, don't we?"

"Yep. Our love collides all the time, and then it's made better than before because two people colliding is superlative."

"Superlative? Where did you learn that word?"

"Oh, I have my sources."

I reach out to tickle her but she scampers away, calling behind her, "We already collided tonight, Mom."

I turn and walk straight into Angelica's embrace. "I wanna collide too, Mommy. Can I collide with you?"

I have to laugh. They are surprising me tonight. "I'll collide with you any time." I plant kisses everywhere. Angelica giggles and shakes her head free. "Okay, Mommy. Let me down now." She runs after her beloved older sister, her object of worship.

Carlos stands in the doorway. "Mom."

"Yes, Carlos." I wait for the moment he reveals his motive. No doubt social plans have been made.

He smiles. "I'll miss you."

I wait.

"Mom?"

"That's it?"

He shrugs. "That's all."

"I'll miss you too, *mijo.*"

He embraces me. He is awkward, which makes it more real. It is a precious gift, this love without motive, without qualification. It is pure and clear, like the cenotes of my long ago dreaming. The memory of that love no longer aches; it is the deep source of so much more. It is this love, more real and immediate, that sustains me.

A soft muzzle pushes my hand. Snoops wants in on the action. He is a joy hound. I scratch his ears. When I look up, Tomas is standing in the door.

"And you too?"

"And me too."

I move toward him for a hug, but he reaches for my mouth.

"Oh, get a room." Carlos moves to squeeze past us.

Tomas laughs. "You don't think every teenager in America hasn't said the same thing?"

"Yeah, Dad, and they all mean it."

Tomas hugs me and kisses me again. "Don't forget to come back to us. You're our center."

I watch him walk back down to his den. Sometimes it is the simple things in life that remind me who I am, and why.

38 Mariah

I have been riding Storm Chaser for hours. He is wild and strong; we understand each other.

The Charleston police and the Connecticut State Police matched the DNA on one Harold Skule, suspect *numero uno*. He was my attacker and the serial rapist that had been terrorizing the I-95 corridor. It was a wrap.

Of course, I know he was AAC's chump. Their tool. Walking evil, they had him employed and justified before he knew his mission: keep AAC clean. Now AAC's out of the water business, but divesting themselves simply caused their stock prices to rise. They smell like a billion. And it's rumored Michael Saxton will take the reins in the fall.

Justice is not forthcoming, but, like my tribes, I've learned to live without it. In a land that prides itself for its truth and justice, the lie of it requires silence. After all, we stare out at the stolen Black Hills every day, a constant reminder of so many broken promises.

I put the bone man to rest. There are always more articles to write. Someday I will find justice for Daniel. My copy from my boss of the flash drive is on the Rez. Let them come get it.

I've made peace with my life. I have the blood quantum levels to be Lakota, Ho-Chunk, and Dakota, but I do not need it. I know who I am. I am neither separate from humanity nor am I disambiguated by homogenization, an assimilated person. I told myself I don't belong for so long I believed the thought had come from somewhere else, but the voice was always mine. I silenced it when I vanquished the bone man. It's my destiny, straight up. I'm not a wannabe, a "nosebleed Indian." Even 50 percent blood loss constitutes a trauma. It will still get you a trip to the ER. Blood quantum be damned. I will never again be a fraction.

And anyway, blood quantum has never been a reality for any other than those from whom the land was taken, inevitable or not. It's just a tool to sanction its allotment. It's a way to avoid the apology. As if the land could ever be taken. It is no one's to own. The provenance of the universe, it belongs to everyone. You can break a horse, but a horse without spirit is not a horse. Just as a land without spirit is not home.

In that mausoleum, inside the hollow darkness of my terror, I called on the spirits of my ancestors and they answered. They delivered me. It is time to honor them—time to sit with Grandmother. Time to learn the old ways.

Storm Chaser stamps his feet. In the distance, the barn is open and the sun, low on the horizon, shines through from the other side. The barn is alive. Storm Chaser neighs and paws at the earth.

Chase rounds up the horses. He waves. I wave back. He will not close the doors until Storm Chaser and I are home.

Out on the prairie, buffalo graze and switch their tails. The scene is peaceful. Peace for the moment. But the moment is all one ever has.

A familiar pickup truck kicks up dust as it pulls up to the barn. The dogs approach joyfully as Dennis emerges, his long braids gleaming in the sunset.

A noise behind me reminds me of past dream states, but I know who it is. Clay rides up behind me.

"*Weeko*! You are strong on that horse."

"And you as well, my brother."

"Yeah, it's our blood."

"Yes, it is."

A hawk circles above. Its cry, fierce and brave, reminds me that our kinship with other creatures is older than that of those who took the land. Standing on the open prairie, I do not fear the bone man. There is nothing but space, horizon to horizon. I kick Storm Chaser into a gallop and my brother follows. His spirit is fierce like the hawk. We are fierce like Grandfather and Grandmother, fierce like our tribe. I am headed home.

38 Heather

Death waits.

Shrill sirens herald tragedy. It has not always been that way. There was a time when it meant mystery and adventure. As children, we chased it. We never considered the destination or the people for whom the siren signaled comfort. But all of that changed the moment it became an omen, a warning that fate had once again delivered a surprise. The unexpected demanded choices, a maneuver across destiny. I was never comfortable with decisions. They often ended poorly.

And now they are taking him. For so many years, he was no more than a ghost of my darkest moments. A brooding force, he had borne witness to my greatest degradation—that moment when the very last shreds of my innocence were stripped away. His face was hidden in the blur of chaos, but the moment of loss was not so easily forgotten. Now, I know him best. It took as many years to unveil that knowledge, to unveil his intent—to discover that all the choices, good and bad, were necessary. But I could never be prepared for this, not now. Not when I am learning to wear a new sense of strength, not as my old self, tiny and afraid, is becoming a relic of some distant past.

I follow the ambulance to the hospital and wait. The doctor approaches, his shrouded shoes mute testimony to their task, but he cannot hide what I already know.

"He can't be saved. I'm sorry."

We have already saved each other.

* * *

Drawing aside the curtains, I search the streets, unsure of what I seek, only that I have to find something. Bathed in the yellow warmth of the early summer afternoon, the street is empty. The houses, neatly laid out, are part of a planned neighborhood. Green lawns and white picket fences delineate the lives of the occupants, who are busy doing what I would normally do. They put on their suits in the morning and return to their domestic lives, their roles, at dusk. I do not do that anymore. And now I know what I have been seeking: The street is a reflection of my life. I performed admirably. The knowledge of it makes me sick.

I need to put distance between that life and myself. My belongings are packed in a moving van that waits in the driveway, and my car is filled with everything we will need for a road trip. There is no reason to ever return.

I spent hours with Shannon deciding on places to visit and places to live. We cut a hundred maps into pieces, dissected them into grids of possibilities, morsels of dreams. In the end, the middle of the country found a place in the center of our hearts. Shannon clapped. "Mariah! Mariah!" It's a good place to start.

I shimmy into my car seat for the ride to the cemetery. I have been procrastinating. It's the one good-bye for which I am not prepared. It splits my heart straight down the middle. I throw the car into gear and face the inevitable.

* * *

I gaze at the casket, perched on the solid earth, still. Soon it will be lifted over its grave, an unfathomable darkness, as dark as the center of our galaxy. I do not want to acknowledge his tomb. I want more of a life with Paul. I want to give him the shelter he never had in his life—the same shelter he tried to give so many others.

Fiona reaches for my hand. My four friends are gathered here to pay respect to the stranger who shared our journey and who bound us in ways that no other earthly force could have. Born of fire, our unity is described as much by one as by all. And he was our fire keeper.

We each move forward to place a rose upon his casket. I save mine for last. I have been raising Mariah's beloved *Félicité Parmentier*, and this, its first, fledgling offspring, graces his last home. He told me I saved him. But did he know he had also saved me?

A duo of fawns leaves their mother lingering at the fringes of the cemetery's ring of forest and sprints into the open to dance amongst the graves. The choice has always been mine. Life is where free will and destiny meet and fuse, one defined as much by itself as by the other. It has been a hard truth, one with which I am still learning to exist.

Shannon drops her flowers and runs towards the fawns. I follow her as she twirls in the fading afternoon sun. Removing her shoes, Mariah skips towards her. The others follow. I kick mine away. The grass gives way and holds my footprints as I run toward my loved ones. We have the moment, and maybe grace is nothing more than an abiding conjunction with impermanence. Life is here, in this moment, and it is as easy as dancing under a midnight moon.

Acknowledgments

It takes a village to raise a writer.

My village is large, and it has an immediacy and presence that sustains and nurtures me. Filled with love and inspiration, I am forever grateful for its occupants.

To my dad, who still reminds me that when I walk on, I will be, as always, the stuff of stardust. I miss him every day. To my mom, who has taught me that no one ever promised a rose garden, but you can pick the roses just the same—minding the thorns along the way. Thank you for believing in me. To my brother, Mark, who inherited the same insatiable thirst for intellectual wandering. Who doesn't love a good rabbit hole? Aline and Ruby, you gave me the love of storytelling. Kath and Deb? I love you to the moon. Jay, Tommy, Catherine, Bruce, Elizabeth: you remind me that life is an adventure.

To the family into which I married: Paups, you taught me about courage and integrity. I miss you. Nanny, you continue to define unconditional love. Scott, Kyle, and Susan, thank you for your endless love.

Margaret "Mags" Doner, Karen Kaufman Orloff, Angela Hooks, Druzelle Cederquist, Elaine Andersen, and Jeanne-Marie Fleming—you were the first, and you inspired me beyond words.

Thank you to Heather Webb, Jessica Vealitzek, and my steadfast and growing tribe on Facebook for making the craft so real.

To Barbara Elmore, Tracee Beebe, and Cecily Watson Kelln, thank you for reminding me that tribe is everywhere.

To Mary Anne Dorward and Lisa Anne Gaston, childhood classmates and fellow survivors, who send me unsolicited morsels of encouragement when I am most in need.

For Laura Furber, Catalina Siller Villarreal, Gretchen Sidlo, Susan Ellsworth, and Dixie Hodson, y'all make me laugh every day and make the sometimes unbearable light.

For Lizbeth "Lizzie" delaCruz, my BFF and soul sister, the world is big and full of love and Cuban spice. Te quiero.

And to Brooke Warner, Lauren Wise, Krissa Lagos, Chris Dumas, and everyone else at She Writes Press, for all that you have done and all that you do—you are the fire in this thing called publishing.

But most of all, to my beloved, Phil, who makes me fight for all the reasons why and then makes the magic happen. For Megan, who makes life poetry and inspires it in me—you are lightness and joy. And for Patrick, who makes me smile, asks all the same questions, and follows me down the rabbit hole.

And to Yellow Thunder, who reminds me to walk back through the truth and tell it. Man has and will always seek truth in story. The craft is in the telling.

About the Author:

Elizabeth Campbell Frey has worked in Fortune 500 companies in positions dealing with systems analysis/project management, human resources, employee relations, and affirmative action. After surviving cancer, she switched gears and, during her studies for a master's in history and non-Western cultures, she focused on water rights and resources and completed a thesis on the Doctrine of Discovery and land issues in Indian country. Born in the Philippines to chronic expat parents, she has lived in too many places to name and now lives in Texas Hill Country with her husband, two gypsy-hearted kids, dogs, cows, chickens, a horse, and a swarm of transient, kamikaze hummingbirds. Learn more at www.elizabethcampbellfrey.com.

SELECTED TITLES FROM SHE WRITES PRESS

She Writes Press is an independent publishing company
founded to serve women writers everywhere.
Visit us at www.shewritespress.com.

Last Seen by J. L. Doucette
$16.95, 978-1-63152-202-4
When a traumatized reporter goes missing in the Wyoming wilderness,
the therapist who knows her secrets is drawn into the investigation—
and she comes face-to-face with terrifying answers regarding her own
difficult past.

The Tolling of Mercedes Bell by Jennifer Dwight
$18.95, 978-1-63152-070-9
When she meets a magnetic lawyer at her work, recently widowed
Mercedes Bell unwittingly drinks a noxious cocktail of grief, legal
intrigue, desire, and deception—but when she realizes that her life and
her daughter's safety hang in the balance, she is jolted into action.

Water On the Moon by Jean P. Moore
$16.95, 978-1-938314-61-2
When her home is destroyed in a freak accident, Lidia Raven, a divorced
mother of two, is plunged into a mystery that involves her entire family.

Watchdogs by Patricia Watts
$16.95, 978-1-938314-34-6
When journalist Julia Wilkes returns to the town where her career got
its start, she is forced to face some old ghosts—and some new enemies.

Murder Under The Bridge: A Palestine Mystery by Kate Raphael
$16.95, 978-1-63152-960-3
Rania, a Palestinian police detective with a young son, meets cheeky
Jewish-American feminist Chloe at an Israeli checkpoint—and soon
becomes embroiled in a murder case that implicates the highest ech-
elons of the Israeli military.

Again and Again by Ellen Bravo
$16.95, 978-1-63152-939-9
When the man who raped her roommate in college becomes a Senate
candidate, women's rights leader Deborah Borenstein must make a
choice—one that could determine control of the Senate, the course of a
friendship, and the fate of a marriage.